RAPHAEL

RAPHAEL

Power of the Amulet

GABI TAMMAN

Rev. date: 11/06/2018

To order additional copies of this book, contact:
Xlibris
800-056-3182
www.Xlibrispublishing.co.uk
Orders@Xlibrispublishing.co.uk
780977

CONTENTS

CHAPTER 1

THE HUNT

2017

"Come in, guys! Welcome! It's so great to see you."

The speaker was Richard. He was young—late twenties—and handsome, with dark hair, dark eyes, and a slender body clad in fashionable jeans with a casual, loose cotton top. Richard had just bought a new apartment in a trendy area of London, and tonight he had invited his siblings over for a takeout and a few bottles of wine to celebrate and admire the new place. Ambient music set the scene for a pleasant evening as a family.

Coats were collected and hung up, pleasantries were exchanged, and the new apartment was duly admired. The small group made its way into the generously proportioned living/dining room. Wine was opened and poured. Laughter filled the air. It was easy to see the camaraderie that marked this group of young people. They had grown up together, sharing holidays and feast days, and they often gathered in their grandparents' home on family occasions.

There was some banter about who had been doing what and with whom, and then Richard interrupted the chatter.

"You know," he began, "I've been spending a lot of time with Grandad lately. I've been thinking how he's not getting any younger. I know that it seems he'll always be with us. He's got that incredible energy and outlasts everyone at a party. But one day, he'll be gone. You know the way he is like a social magnet at any event. Everybody wants to talk to him. But for some reason, I got the feeling that I wanted to hear all his stories again so that I can remember them." He paused and looked at his siblings. "And maybe write them down one day."

"The stories he used to tell us when we were kids?" asked David. "I used to *love* those stories! Remember how we all crowded around? The little ones would fight about who got to sit on his knee, and the big ones would sit on the floor. Those were good times. I remember the stories being exciting, but I don't really recall that much of what they were actually about. It's been an awfully long time since I had the opportunity to just sit with him and listen."

"Well, yes," said Richard. "He's still telling the same old tales. Though now that we're all adults, the stories he tells are—how can I put this?—a *little* different."

"How so?" asked Rebecca. "I can't believe he's started to forget the details. That man has the memory of an elephant! He never lets anything slip by him!"

"Well," said Richard, who had a twinkle in his eyes that reminded everyone of Grandad's, "let's just say that we didn't get the *X-rated* version when we were kids. He left out most of the sex and violence back then, for obvious reasons! I don't think that our parents would have been super happy if Grandad had left it all in—not to mention Granny! He'd have been in trouble if we had heard those stories and tried to live up to his example!"

"Sex and violence? What are you talking about?" asked David. "Surely we are not talking about the same man?"

"Grandad? Do you mean the man who has been married to Granny for like a hundred years?" asked Jonathan incredulously.

"He did have a life before he married her, you know!"

"I don't *believe* it. Not Grandad," insisted Rebecca. "If anyone is a one-woman man, it's him. They have the perfect marriage."

"Sure, but she's younger than he is. It's only natural that he lived a little before he settled down. Anyway, there's no time like the present. Want to hear some of them now?"

"Yes!" his siblings shouted.

"All right then," Richard said. "But I warn you, you're going to be shocked!"

More wine was poured, and the siblings all made themselves comfortable. Richard opened his top button and relaxed against the cushions of his new sofa. And then he began.

"At just 19, in 1950, Raphael was very young to be running his own business in the depths of Nigeria, but he was confident—some would say arrogant—to a fault. He believed that the amulet he had been given as a baby conferred special powers on him, so he never doubted himself or his abilities. He had an overwhelming hunger for money and for power and was invariably sure that he had the capacity to achieve both. As a result, he generally did."

"Remind me about the amulet," Rebecca begged. "I know I've heard it all before, but I would like to hear it again. I might have forgotten some of the details. How did he get it?"

"I'll get on to that in a bit," Richard assured her. "Right now, I am telling the story of the crocodile hunt at Fort Lamy."

1954

Raphael had driven several hours from his compound in Nigeria to Fort Lamy in Chad. Fort Lamy was a beautiful colonial town: a little piece of France in Africa and a welcome change from Maiduguri, which was a British town and therefore more austere and less luxurious. The British just didn't know how to live the way the French did. Raphael was going to relax, visit some friends, enjoy some really good European food, and stock up on delicacies like foie gras and Camembert for his legendary dinner parties. He had been looking forward to the trip for weeks.

The buildings of Fort Lamy were all whitewashed against the heat, with vibrant dashes of colour in the form of the bougainvillea and other flowering plants that filled the gardens. The buildings were low and stately, with none over two storeys in height. While the architectural style was distinctively European, the dazzling whiteness of the walls and the lush vegetation in the gardens spoke very clearly of the town's African location—as did, of course, the dark skin and colourful costumes of the natives. The generally amiable relations between the European colonials and the native Africans did not hint at the political undercurrents that would lead to the region's independence not so very long after Raphael's time there.

Raphael booked himself into a hotel, reserving one room for himself and one for his guard, a former French legionnaire called Levalier, who was in his early forties and who kept Raphael and his compound safe. It had been important for security reasons for Raphael to bring Levalier on the trip, but now that they had arrived safely, the older man could take some well-deserved time off. The two men had a friendly but distant relationship. Raphael had no idea what Levalier did in his free time; he knew that it was none of his business, so he never asked. For his part, Levalier knew a great deal about Raphael's personal and romantic escapades and never said anything about them to anyone. It wasn't his place to interfere or even have an opinion on the matter.

"I'll leave you to rest, Levalier," Raphael said. "I'm going to wash off this dust and look for some fun. I deserve it after the long trip."

"Very good, sir." Levalier nodded politely and closed the door.

Alone in his room, Raphael stripped off his clothes and left them in a corner for the maid to collect and wash when she came to do the room service later. He looked at himself in the gilt mirror that hung on the wall. His young body was firm and muscular, thanks to his intensely active lifestyle, and he was deeply tanned, thanks to the many hours he spent working out of doors under the African sun. His hair was usually carefully coiffed and held in place with Brylcreem, but now it was tousled and dusty from the long journey. At just 19, he still looked very young, but nobody would have mistaken him for a boy. He had an air of authority that made it very clear that this was a man; he had worn it since he had taken over the family business in Cairo at the age of just 14.

A shower is what I need, Raphael affirmed to himself. *Once I'm looking presentable, I can go out and introduce myself to some of the local ladies and see if my friends remember me.*

He put on the bathrobe and slippers supplied by the hotel and padded downstairs to the sun-filled courtyard that housed the showers. Europeans sometimes found it odd that most of the hotels in Fort Lamy didn't have private bathrooms for guests. But they soon got used to showering out of doors under the blue skies, with the scent of flowers in the air. The showers were surrounded by the hotel's lush tropical garden, and an occasional tropical butterfly swooped lazily by. Showering in those conditions was a peaceful, relaxing experience. One was tempted to linger under the water, making it last as long as possible.

After the shower, Raphael returned to his bedroom to dress. Back at the compound, the servants had carefully packed his clothes so that they would not crease, and the hotel staff had taken them out and hung them up in his wardrobe while he was downstairs. The British expatriates near his compound insisted on wearing English-style clothes, which were invariably hot and uncomfortable by the end of the evening in Africa. But Raphael chose instead to wear comfortable cotton trousers and a loose shirt that he brightened with a cummerbund in a vibrant red. He liked to look good but didn't care for the stiff style favoured by the British. With attention to detail, he combed his hair and set it in a fashionable style with Brylcreem. He looked at himself in the mirror again with some satisfaction.

He was ready to go out.

From his previous trips to Fort Lamy, Raphael already had a group of friends in the town: young single women who had jobs in education or in the colonial administration and were enjoying a level of freedom that they could never have experienced at home. They had all come to Africa for an exotic adventure before finding a man, getting married, and settling down, but the reality was that they often found themselves without a great deal to do out of work hours.

Raphael knew that his friends would be pleased to see him and have some fun, and he had just had a great idea for an exciting day out. He was going to introduce them to crocodile hunting. They all knew that he made his living selling crocodile skins harvested in Africa for the fashion industry in France, but they had never seen him in action before. Well, now they were going to get their chance. His hunters sourced most of the crocodiles in the area near the compound, but the river at Fort Lamy was also full of crocodiles—and there were many pretty young ladies to impress with his derring-do.

A big, deep river flowed through Fort Lamy. Its brown, lazy waters provided a pleasant backdrop to the town and a way for more distant farmers to bring their produce to market. The Africans used long wooden canoes for transportation and carried all sorts of fruit, vegetables, and meat from the countryside to the town. The canoes were of very simple construction. A group of men would fell a tall tree, hollow out the inside, and shape the outside to make the canoe pass more easily through the water. Then, with considerable skill, they could travel quite quickly by paddling, or even more quickly with the addition of a petrol-fuelled outboard motor. In this way, even quite distant communities could bring their produce to market and participate in the local economy. Return trips from Fort Lamy saw the same canoes laden down with manufactured goods that the farmers and their families could not purchase in their local areas.

At the riverbank, Raphael arranged to rent a large motorised canoe along with the services of the man who owned the vessel, and then he went to his friends' residence to see if any of the girls he knew— Simone, Annette, and Natasha—would like to go on a crocodile hunt for the first time. The three young women greeted him at their front door with smiles, hugs, and giggles, and all three said that they would like to join him.

"It's been so boring around here since your last visit," Simone pouted. "Just work, work, and more work, and the men in this town think that women exist just to entertain them. They don't even realise that we have minds of our own. They just get drunk and show off unbearably, completely unaware of the fact that they are acting like fools. The married ones are the worst. They are bored of their wives and think that single girls like us should have affairs with them, just to keep them entertained and make them think that they are young again. As if we didn't have anything better to do! You should come here more often; *you* know that women aren't just for decoration. A crocodile hunt is exactly what we need. Maybe we'll catch one each and show those stupid men that women can make fantastic hunters!"

"I can't take you all, I'm afraid," said Raphael apologetically, "much as I would like to. What with me, the chap in charge of the canoe, and his assistant, there will only be room for one more. Between the three of you, you're going to have to decide who gets to go. But if it goes well, I can definitely take someone else next time! So, who's it going to be?"

The girls glanced at each other and then started to compete over who was going to go with Raphael on what promised to be a very exciting trip. Each girl argued that *she* should be the one to go as the most suitable companion for Raphael on what sounded like an experience that they could use to thrill their friends back home.

"I'm absolutely *terrified* of those hideous brutes," said Simone, "but I know I'll be safe with you, Raphael." She fluttered her eyelashes at him seductively. "You wouldn't let a crocodile eat up little old me, would you? If one of them tried to attack me, you would be my knight in shining armour. You would dash to my rescue and make sure that I got home in one piece."

Simone had clearly decided that the best ploy was to present herself as a potential maiden in distress and appeal in that way to Raphael's protective instincts. Simone was very pretty indeed, a classic French beauty with delicate features and large brown eyes, and he did have to admit that the thought of protecting her from a dangerous crocodile while she simpered gratefully held some charm for him. At the same time, the other two girls also put forward some rather convincing arguments.

"Take *me*, Raphael!" insisted Annette, a petite blonde whose pretty hair was cropped short around her shapely head. "I'm not like Simone; I'm not terrified at all! I won't distract you by needing to be looked after. I might even be able to help you. I've never killed a crocodile, that's true, but I know how to manage a boat as well as any man, and I often went hunting with my dad when I was a girl in France. I've killed my own wild boar before, and I am not afraid to get my hands dirty."

"I have to admit," Raphael said, "it might be useful to bring along someone who already knows something about boats. I didn't know you were so tough, Annette. I'd never have guessed ..."

"Forget about those two," purred the voluptuous Natasha, interrupting him. "Annette is lying about knowing how to row a boat and hunt animals. She grew up in downtown Paris, and the only things she knows how to hunt are taxis and men. I won't be able to help at all, but unlike Simone, I won't be scared. I can also promise to make it worth your while afterwards."

Natasha's sultry smile and provocative body language left nobody in any doubt about what she meant.

"I think that settles it," said Raphael with a naughty grin. "Natasha has made by far the most convincing argument of the three of you! I'll pick you up at half past eleven tonight, Natasha, and we'll go on a crocodile hunt. Don't wear high heels; I might have to drop you off quickly somewhere and tell you to run!"

Raphael said goodbye to his friends and headed off to make the arrangements for the expedition, congratulating himself for having come up with such a good plan. All going well, he will have caught both a crocodile *and* a woman by the end of the evening!

At midnight, with the peaceful music of a million crickets providing a percussive backdrop, Raphael and Natasha climbed into the canoe that he had rented. The boatman, a handsome man in his thirties with an air of quiet competence, promised that he knew this part of the river like the back of his hand. He had rigged up a powerful lamp with a large bulb and a car battery with plenty of power so that they would be able to see the crocodiles in the water. His young assistant—a lad of just 14 or so—was able to turn the light on and off simply by putting two wires together. As they moved slowly away from the town, the boy lit the lamp and shone it low over the water so that they would see crocodiles, or any other wildlife, as they moved. Raphael had brought a gun, and the two Africans were armed with spears, so he felt confident that they were more than adequately prepared for any eventuality.

Natasha had been very excited about taking the trip with Raphael, but she was quiet now as they moved through the water, the outboard engine making a steady purr as they went. The light shone out low over the water, occasionally disturbing a sleeping water bird at the verge, which would ruffle its feathers and shriek out its irritation.

"Why is the light so low?" Natasha asked. "It's only showing up the water immediately in front of the boat. We can't really see very far at all. I thought that we'd be able to look around at the town and the landscape from the water."

"That's how we'll find the crocodiles," Raphael explained. "You must have seen them before. They swim along with their heads just barely above the water. Without the light, at night it would be easy to mistake a crocodile for a log, or not to see it at all. But if we had a brighter light, or one that we hung higher up, we would run the risk of waking up all sorts of creatures we'd really rather leave alone. The thing with crocodiles is that we have to be smarter than they are … and the thing with the African wildlife in general is that you have to respect it, because there are plenty of animals that wouldn't think twice before having us for dinner!"

"Oh Raphael," said Natasha. "You know exactly what to say to make this trip absolutely thrilling! I feel as though I am in a film or some sort of adventure novel, and nothing's even happened yet!"

At this, all four sank into a thoughtful silence as they pressed on, watching and waiting. It was oddly peaceful on the river in the dark, despite the flying insects, the *tuk tuk tuk* of the outboard motor, the lapping of the water, and the knowledge that there were crocodiles in it. The boy continued to hold the lamp out over the water, and its steady beam illuminated the still surface, interrupted now and again by a small eddy indicative of an undercurrent or, perhaps, of a large animal moving somewhere just below the surface. After a few minutes, they encountered a small herd of hippopotamuses resting in the water. The creatures observed the canoe move by without much reaction but shifted their enormous heads to splash some water in its general direction—a gentle warning that they were prepared to overlook the intrusion so long as the two-legged creatures in the boat continued to demonstrate that they meant the enormous animals no harm.

"Steer clear," Raphael ordered the boatman. "Leave them their space."

"Don't worry about them, boss," the boatman said. "They're lazy, and they prefer not to move too much. They won't do us any harm."

"Steer a wide berth around them anyway," Raphael instructed. "Better safe than sorry."

Raphael respected the boatman's expertise and local knowledge, but he also knew that the huge animals could be very aggressive when they were disturbed, or when they thought that someone was trying to hurt their young. He had no intention of taking unnecessary risks, especially with Natasha in the boat. Sure, she was enjoying the excitement of being out on the river in the dark, but he didn't think she would enjoy being *too* excited.

"I'm turning the engine off now," the boatman said suddenly. "I can't see any crocodiles yet, but I can definitely sense them in the area. They are close; I know it. The noise of the engine might be keeping them away if we are very near. I think that if we just stay quiet and wait, it won't be long at all until we see them, and then we can take our chances."

All four sat poised for action as the boat moved slowly through the dark waters and then came to rest. Raphael's senses were alert to every sound and change in the environment. He could hear the gentle lap of the small river waves against the muddy banks, the occasional stir and rustle of a bird in the reeds, and even the accelerated breath of Natasha, sitting near him.

Suddenly, as if from nowhere, not one but two crocodiles emerged from the darkness, clearly very angry about being disturbed from their rest. Raphael trained his gun on the closest one, planning to shoot it through the head and dispatch it quickly in this way. While his attention was thus diverted, the other huge beast swam underneath the canoe, whether by accident or design.

"Stay calm!" Raphael shouted as the roughly hewn boat rocked violently from side to side. He was saying this for the benefit of himself as much as anyone else. Nobody had expected the crocodile to swim under the boat, and this was one eventuality for which he did not have a plan. What would happen next was anybody's guess. Would the animal panic and overturn the boat or just swim quietly away into the darkness?

The boatman's assistant was clearly very frightened. He was trying to hold the lamp steady on the water so that Raphael and the boatman could see what was going on, but his hands were shaking so badly that the light moved up and down with rapid, jerky, irregular movements. This agitated the crocodiles further, as they did not understand what it was and were inclined to attack first and wonder about it in their dim reptilian minds later. The water began to churn with their movements as both the boy and Natasha started to whimper aloud, terrified for their lives.

"Boss," said the young boy, "I want to be home. This is not a good place. I don't want to be eaten by a hungry crocodile."

"Raphael," Natasha said, "we're safe, right? I wouldn't have come with you if I hadn't felt sure that nothing bad would happen. I know we were joking about it being dangerous, but … it's not *really* dangerous, is it? You don't think that the crocodile is actually going to … kill us?"

"Don't worry," Raphael said, trying to keep his balance as the canoe rocked violently from side to side. "Everything is perfectly fine. I've got it all absolutely under control."

But Natasha was so frightened that she could not take in Raphael's words. She peered over the side of the canoe, and when she saw the enormous head of the crocodile in the water, its teeth clearly visible as it opened and closed its jaws, tasting the water around it in an attempt to understand what was going on, she started to scream uncontrollably. In response, the crocodile started to display more agitated movements.

"Natasha," Raphael said through gritted teeth, willing himself to stay as calm as possible. "I beg you not to scream. You are making things worse for us all. You're going to wake up every river animal for miles around. The hippopotamuses will think that we are being aggressive and threatening their young, and they'll come over and attack us. You think things are bad now, but you'll feel a whole lot worse when we also have to deal with an entire herd of angry hippos. Crocodiles are dangerous, but hippos can be even more so when they think that they are being threatened. Trust me; this is not the moment to lose your nerve. I need you to be the brave woman I know you are."

Natasha stopped screaming, but she continued to whimper. She stared at Raphael as though he was the only thing standing between her and oblivion.

"Good girl," Raphael said. "You just keep your eyes focused on me. Don't worry. I have a gun, and we are all going to be all right. OK? I wouldn't have brought you with me unless I was sure about that."

Natasha nodded, her blue eyes filling with tears.

Then the huge crocodile under the canoe started to roll. They all clung to the sides and tried to keep their balance as best they could, but when the animal's immense, heavy, muscular tail swung up and hit them all, the canoe tipped all four into the water, despite the best efforts of both Raphael and the boatman. Thankfully, they were not too far from the water's edge, and the enormous splash the boat had made seemed to shock the crocodiles into inertia—at least for a moment. Still clutching his spear, the boatman's assistant scrambled towards and onto the muddy verge. He turned and looked at the three in the water with huge, scared eyes, and then he ran, disappearing into the darkness. Perhaps he was intending to run for help, or maybe he was in such a state of shock that he was beyond thinking. Either way, at least now there were only three people to save, not four.

"Take her and get out of here," said Raphael, pushing Natasha towards the boatman. "Give me your spear. My gun is wet and useless. Get out as quickly as you can."

The boatman shoved his spear into Raphael's hand and helped Natasha to scramble to the water's edge, where they climbed onto the bank and to safety.

"Come with us, boss!" the boatman called. "Leave the canoe. We can come for it tomorrow, when the crocodiles have gone and we can see what we are doing. Don't worry about my boat. I'd rather you were safe than it!"

"No way," said Raphael. "I'm not letting any bloody crocodile tell me who's in charge! I'm going to get it."

The boatman had misunderstood Raphael's intentions. He was beyond caring what happened to the boat and the outboard motor by now. He had come out this evening to get a crocodile, and that was precisely what he intended to do.

The first crocodile to approach them had swum away, and Raphael had realised that the second one had become trapped beneath the upturned canoe. A trapped crocodile was an angry crocodile, and Raphael should have been terrified, but he had adrenaline pumping through his body, and all he could think about was getting the prize and returning triumphant. He could feel his precious amulet, his charm, under his shirt against his skin, and he reminded himself that it was keeping him safe. Since childhood, he had never doubted its power to keep him from harm.

Sliding the spear under the lapping river water, Raphael cautiously approached the upturned canoe. He could see the crocodile's tail sticking out at one end and used this to estimate where the soft underbelly of the animal must be. With all his strength, he plunged the spear into the core of the animal and slit it open with all the violence he could muster. There was a moment of resistance as the blade encountered the skin, and then it pierced the animal's body and eased into its flesh with an almost sensual grace that prompted Raphael to groan aloud.

The huge reptile struggled briefly against the inevitable, but Raphael had calculated the right location to impale it correctly, and it did not last for long. Raphael could feel the tension ease as life left the huge animal's body and it slumped into the water and further onto the spear.

Elated but suddenly exhausted, Raphael struggled onto the shore, where he collapsed onto the ground beside the boatman and Natasha, both of whom were staring at him in awe.

"You did it, boss," the boatman said. "I thought that the crocodile was going to eat you, sure as anything. I had already started to say prayers for your immortal soul. I've seen a man being eaten by a crocodile before, and believe me, it is not a pretty sight. I don't know if you are crazy or brave, but I am glad you're still alive."

"Raphael," said Natasha, "this has been the worst night of my life. I never thought that going crocodile hunting with you was going to be so terrifying, and I am *never* going to forgive you."

"I did promise you some excitement," Raphael teased her with his last morsel of energy. "And it's definitely been very exciting."

"Well then," said Natasha, as her courage returned. "I suppose I'll have to fulfil my promise and make it worth your while ... though I need to get out of these muddy clothes and into a shower first!"

Raphael could see that Natasha was already beginning to move on from her fear and imagine how she would tell the story of her terrifying ordeal to her friends the following morning. He had no doubt that she would make it seem even more thrilling that it really had been.

Raphael slept long and deep that night, after dropping Natasha off at her home and spending some very pleasant moments in her room with her before returning to his hotel. He was astonished when he awoke to find that a crowd had gathered outside the hotel to see him—and that they all seemed to know his name.

"Raphael! Raphael!" the people called to him. "Tell us all about it—is it true that you pierced the crocodile right through the jaws? Were you scared? Have you killed many crocodiles this way before?"

"I wasn't scared at all!" Raphael laughed. "I have something here that keeps me safe." He patted his amulet where it lay against his chest.

The news of his kill had spread quickly through the town, and everyone wanted to see the young man who had destroyed the crocodile underwater, with just a spear. Some local men had gone down to the river and dragged the enormous beast out of the water and onto the ground where it lay inert, its intestines spilling from the huge rent in its belly and attracting flies. A little group of small African boys, many of them naked and barefoot, gingerly used sticks to poke the crocodile from a safe distance, wary of it even though it was so very clearly dead, because they had been warned by their parents on countless occasions to stay well away from the awful beasts.

The excited crowd hustled Raphael down to the riverbank, where he posed for photo after photo. It was hard to tell who was more excited—the white residents, who would take their images home to show their friends and family how brave they were to live in such a dangerous place (when the reality was that the greatest danger most of them faced was falling off a veranda after one gin and tonic too many) or the local Africans, many of whom actually knew people who had been killed or maimed by crocodiles, and for whom the death of one of these dreadful creatures resonated very deeply.

From that day on, every time Raphael went to Fort Lamy, he was referred to as "the Crocodile Killer." When he went into restaurants, people would nudge each other and point him out, recounting whatever version of the kill had reached their ears. The story grew, and Raphael did nothing to stop it, relishing each new twist that it acquired with the retelling. He enjoyed the sense of charisma that it lent him—and, of course, the fact that women were invariably attracted to a man who was able to kill a crocodile with nothing but a spear.

2017

"That's quite a story, definitely," said Rebecca, biting down on a tortilla chip. "I bet that poor girl never wanted to go out in a canoe with Grandad again! She must have had the fright of her life. She didn't know what she was letting herself in for, that's for sure."

"I don't know," said Richard. "The way Grandad told it, the whole episode really turned her on, *if* you know what I mean. She was crazy for him after seeing what he was able to do to a crocodile. The other girls all begged to be taken out in a canoe too, despite what Natasha had been through, but he didn't want to risk it again and left the girls at home after that."

"Grandad the playboy!" David laughed. "Do you think Granny knows what he was like when he was young?"

"Oh, I am sure there are no secrets between them," Richard said. "She wouldn't let him get away with that. But you have to remember that this all happened a long time before they got married. She was just a little girl back in Sudan at the time, ten years younger than him and not even formally engaged or anything yet. Grandad was young, and he was making a lot of money at the time. He was right to have his fun while he could. What harm did it do?"

"Tell us about the amulet again," Rebecca said. "I know he's had it since he was a child, and of course he's taken it out of the safe to show us all on lots of occasions, but I don't remember the details of how he got it, and I've never understood why he says he owes everything he has to it. Do you know the story, Richard?"

"Of course I do!"

Taking a sip from his glass, Richard began to talk ...

CHAPTER 2

BACK TO THE
BEGINNING

2017

"Well, we all know how Grandad is absolutely convinced that he owes all his success to the amulet," said Richard. "He's said a thousand times that if it hadn't been for the amulet, he might be a shopkeeper in Cairo or Israel right now, eking out a modest living or retired on a small pension, instead of a successful businessman—and then all our lives would be very different than they are today. We grandchildren might not even exist!"

"Sure, who doesn't remember those stories?" Rebecca laughed. "And how excited we all were whenever he opened his safe to show it to us—the amulet that made his fortune and that keeps him and his family safe through the vicissitudes of life. It was like being shown something magical from another world. I was always surprised by how very small it is in reality."

"Remember how we used to argue over who would get to inherit it?" asked David. "We all wanted to be the one to get it when we were all grown up and he was gone. We all thought that if we could get our hands on the amulet, we would learn the secret to Grandad's success and be just like him."

"He always said, 'Not so fast, kids, I'm going to need it for years yet to come'!" said Rebecca. "And then we'd feel horribly guilty for even imagining a time when he's not with us anymore. Even now, I have to confess that I think of him as sort of immortal. I know he's getting older, but he doesn't seem to be like other older men, does he? He's got more energy than any of us. Maybe the amulet really *does* give him strength, just like he says."

"I've never been able to figure out how serious he is about it all," said Richard. "Does he really, literally believe that the amulet made him rich and successful …"

"…and lucky in love," interjected Rebecca.

"…*and* lucky in love, or is it just one of his old stories, something that we are supposed to enjoying hearing about without necessarily taking too literally? Come to think of it, how many of the stories are really true and how much are they exaggerated? We only have his word for most of them, don't we?"

"I think he absolutely believes in the amulet," said Rebecca. "Why else would he keep it in a safe like that? You would think it was the most precious thing in the universe. And as for exaggerations? I don't think so. We've all seen the photos, and every so often, when we were kids, one of his old friends would come for a visit, and another of Grandad's stories would be corroborated. I know that some of them seem a little bit improbable on the face of things … but I really believe that they are all completely true! If a Jewish kid from the streets of Cairo can grow up to be such a successful businessman, then why shouldn't the rest of it be true, too?"

"Do you remember how he originally got the amulet?" asked David. "Where did it come from? I'm sure I knew the story at some point, but I honestly can't recall a thing."

"Yes," said Richard. "He told me everything about it just last week. I had only half-remembered the story until then, but it is all fresh in my mind now. I know all the details!"

"Oh, *do* tell us," begged Rebecca. "I think I remember it all, but I would just love to hear it again."

Refreshing everyone's glasses, Richard started to talk.

"Back in the 1930s, when Grandad's mum—her name was Flora— was pregnant with him, things were already really difficult for the Jews in Egypt, where they were living at the time—and getting increasingly difficult in Sudan, where she and her husband Joseph came from originally. There had been a fairly big Jewish community in Cairo for as long as anyone knew, but anti-Jewish sentiment was growing rapidly throughout the region. It was increasingly apparent that war was brewing in Egypt, and there was huge uncertainty about what the future held. It was a stressful environment to be raising a family in.

"On top of that, I think it was a very difficult time for Flora personally. She already had a number of kids, her husband's business wasn't going so well, and now she was pregnant again in Cairo and desperately missed her sisters and cousins, who were all in Sudan. She was scared about what the future would hold for the whole family and for this new baby ... and in those days, women had many fewer choices than men. It wasn't like today in that respect. Scared as she was, she was expected to fall into line with what the men in the family decided for her. She must have felt very vulnerable and alone at times."

1931

Flora flopped into a white-painted deck chair on the veranda of her home in Heliopolis, a suburb of Cairo, and fanned herself with the back of her hand. Her dark hair was damp with sweat, her cheeks were flushed pink, and the dark semicircles beneath her eyes revealed that she was not getting enough sleep. It was hard to rest with the heat and the extra weight she was carrying because of the baby, and when she did manage to get to sleep despite it all, the baby would wake up and make his presence felt by means of a series of swift kicks to her ribs.

She knew that she should get a comb and tidy up her hair, but she just didn't have the energy. She looked down at herself. Her blue-and-white flowered dress was stretched tightly across her swollen abdomen. It was a maternity dress, but at just seven months, she was already getting too big for it. She felt swollen all over, and she hadn't slept properly for weeks. Even her ankles seemed to be threatening to spill over the edges of the comfortable, flat shoes that were all she could manage to wear at the moment.

"What *are* you doing to me, little one?" she murmured. She had been through five pregnancies before, with Avi, Leon, Elie, Isaac, and Renée, but this was the most difficult by far, and she felt as though she was already at the limits of her endurance. "Are you trying to turn me old before my time? You don't understand how much I love you, because if you did, you would be much gentler with your poor mum."

As if he could hear her, the foetus in her belly chose this moment to twist and turn restlessly, making her wince in discomfort and cradle her belly with her hands.

"Sometimes I think you don't even *want* to be born!" she said aloud. "You're not even in the world yet. What are you so angry about? Or is that you don't want to be in there and can't wait to get out? What is in your head, little one?"

Before getting pregnant, Flora had been quite sure that she didn't want to have any more children, or at least not for a few years. She already had five children to care for, and with the political situation the way it was and her husband Joseph's business floundering, she hadn't planned to have another. Maybe if they were in Sudan, where she could have counted on the help of her family—but here, she only knew a few people, and none of them were close family members. She was only 24, so there was still plenty of time to add to the family later on, when things settled down in Egypt or they returned to their extended family in Sudan.

Flora's first child, Avi, had been born when she was just 15, and as much as she loved and enjoyed motherhood, it prevented her from doing anything other than caring, cooking, and cleaning, and it left her little time to use the fine brain that God had given her for anything else. And yet, as soon as she realised that she was expecting a baby, she had been filled with joy and the knowledge that she would do anything to bring her child safely into the world to fulfil his individual destiny. She felt that God meant for the baby to be born, and she was the vessel that would carry him safely until it was time for him to join the world. He would make her complete.

That afternoon, Flora had attended an appointment with Dr Cohen. She liked Dr Cohen because he treated her with respect. So many doctors (all of whom were men) simply dismissed women's fears, especially when they were pregnant, or told them that they were imagining things when they were really in terrible pain and discomfort and needed help. Fortunately, Dr Cohen was different. He was a middle-aged man with a lean, kindly face and—important for a doctor—soft, warm hands that he used gently when he had to touch and probe a tender, aching body. Most of all, he really listened to what his patients were saying about their concerns and did his best to reassure them.

"Let me help you onto my examining table," he said kindly to Flora, "and let's see how the baby is getting on. You're seven months along now, so we should be able to get a good idea of what's happening in there … and then we can see how to take care of you."

With difficulty, and with the doctor's help, Flora managed to manoeuvre herself onto the table. She lay back and loosened her dress so that Dr Cohen could place his hands on her distended abdomen. She felt like a beetle that has been turned onto its back and fears that it will remain stuck there.

Dr Cohen felt the contours of the baby's body carefully through Flora's skin, which was already stretched so tight that he could see the shape and colour of her veins just below the surface. He took out his stethoscope and listened to her heartbeat and the sound of her breathing. He checked her blood pressure, and then he asked her to sit up so that he could peer inside her mouth with his little torch. When he finally sat back, he had a very concerned expression on his face.

"Mrs Romano," he said, "I am not going to lie to you. I have some very serious concerns about this pregnancy. It's true that you have already given birth to several children quite easily, and that in general you are a healthy young woman, but this situation is very different. It's clear that the child is very large; much bigger than it should be at this gestational stage. This means that we're going to have to be very careful with you and—if you don't mind me being blunt—that you are likely to have a difficult and extremely painful labour and delivery … with the risk of something going wrong, possibly seriously."

"I'm not afraid of pain," Flora said bravely. "You know that I've been through it before with the other children and that I can cope. We women are made for it; we're tough. But, doctor, I need to stay alive to take care of my family, especially in such difficult times. Please tell me the truth. Is my life likely to be in danger? Is it possible that I might not survive the birth? Or that the baby might not make it?"

Dr Cohen said nothing, but the grave expression on his face told Flora everything she needed to know.

"I see," Flora said. She sat up, buttoned her dress, and prepared to leave, her mind and emotions in turmoil. She had already decided not to tell anyone at home that she was in danger. What was the point of upsetting them unnecessarily? It wouldn't make any difference anyway.

"I will take care of you to the best of my ability," Dr Cohen comforted her. "But you should talk to your husband about these additional risks so that you will both be prepared for the future ... whatever happens. If it comes to having to make a choice between you and the baby, I will need to know what you both want."

As she slowly made her way home, Flora thought about what to do next. She couldn't—*wouldn't*—accept the possibility that she might die and leave her children motherless, and she was also determined to keep this new baby safe. Despite the fact that she was enduring such a difficult pregnancy, she already loved him (she was quite sure that it was going to be a boy, although the doctor had smiled and said that nobody could tell until it was born) and felt confident that he had something special to bring to the world. If it came down to a choice between her and the baby, she knew what she wanted. She'd already had her chance at life. She would sacrifice herself to let him have his and know that she was doing the right thing. But the thought of leaving the children she already had and the new baby without a mother was horrifying too.

"I will go and see Esther," Flora decided. "She might be able to tell me what to do. Sometimes she can see and knows things that the doctors don't understand. She has special gifts that they might laugh at, but she has a reputation for getting things right. Perhaps she will be able to give me some advice—or at least ease my mind and help me get a good night's sleep for a change."

Esther was an old woman who lived a few streets away from Flora and her family. She was renowned in the area for her wisdom, knowledge, and devotion to God and the local Jewish community. Some people said that she had second sight and could tell what was in people's futures, while others muttered that she was some sort of a witch, despite her piety and devotion, and that she was just as likely to cast a spell on someone she didn't like as to provide help to someone she did. The doctors didn't like her because she gave people traditional cures that they did not agree with (and took business away from them in the process). Most of the men in the area dismissed her teachings as a lot of superstition—women's nonsense, they called it, just a lot of silly gossip that was best laughed at or ignored.

They also distrusted Esther because she had never married. Theirs was a conservative community, in which most women married quite young and devoted themselves tirelessly to their husbands and children. Esther was different. She said that she had never wanted to get married, because then she would have had to do what her husband told her, and she had never been one to take orders. As a young woman, she'd had her admirers, but she had rejected them all because she wanted to be her own boss.

Flora was confident that Esther really did have access to secrets that most people didn't and that she would be able to help where the doctor could not.

"Come in, darling," said Esther solicitously when she opened the door and saw Flora. "I have been wondering how you are. I haven't seen you much lately. Usually I see you going to the market to get food for your lovely children, but you must have been staying at home these days. In fact, you crossed my mind just this morning. I'm so glad you've come by."

"I'm just so big," Flora said. "And it's so hot. I'm finding it harder and harder to get anything done. It took me half an hour to reach you from Dr Cohen's clinic!"

"Well, I hope you didn't tell him you were coming here," Esther said with a twinkle in her eye. "I know he gets cross when I give people advice about their health and things. He says it isn't my place to give advice, because I am not a doctor and didn't go to university like him. I tell him that I was giving advice to people before he was even born, and that one of those people was his very own mother, and I tell him that not all wisdom comes from books. He just scoffs at me, but I know that he knows it, on some level."

Esther beckoned Flora inside.

"Sit down, dear," she said. "Make yourself comfortable—well, as comfortable as you can be under the circumstances! I will go and get you a glass of cold water."

Gratefully, Flora sank her unwieldly body into a battered rattan chair, hoping that the chair would be strong enough to support her with the extra weight that she was carrying. She looked around Esther's home. It was inexpensively furnished with simple tables and chairs, and the walls were plain and whitewashed. Here and there were symbols of Esther's deep and abiding religious faith: icons of saints from long-ago times; an old and tarnished but still beautiful Shabbat menorah candelabra; and a battered copy of the Torah on a wooden wall-mounted shelf. There was a very old photograph on the wall of Esther's own parents on their wedding day. Given that Esther was at least eighty, Flora tried to figure out when the photograph must have been taken.

"Water?" Esther was leaning solicitously over her younger visitor. "It's nice and cool. It will do you good."

Flora accepted the glass and took a sip. She looked at the older woman. Esther's face was brown and sun-spotted from spending her life under the glare of the bright Egyptian sun. Her long grey hair was tied back in a bun, with a few strands escaping around her face. Her deep brown eyes were surrounded by wrinkles. Some of the people in the area were afraid of Esther and said that she liked to cast hexes on people, or that she had the evil eye and cursed anyone she looked at in a particular way, or that her black cat was really her familiar and she sent it around the neighbourhood to spy on people and report back to her. But Flora had always known her to be kind and believed her to be wise.

"No, dear," said Esther. "You don't need to tell me why you are here. You're scared for the little one"—she indicated Flora's huge belly—"and for yourself. Well, you are right to be scared. There is a tremendous energy coming from this baby. He is hungry for life, and he wants to be born as soon as he can, even if that means tearing his way out of your body! But it's not *his* fault, you know. He doesn't know anything, and he doesn't mean you any harm. It's just that he is eager to start experiencing life for himself. In fact, I can tell you that if this baby survives, and if you do, he will grow up to love you even more than the rest of your children do. The problem is that this unruly energy of his threatens to destroy you both before he has even begun to live."

"What can I do?" asked Flora despairingly. "I love the baby, even if I haven't seen his little face yet, but I need to take care of myself too. I have other children, and I am still young. I can't die now! That's why I need your help. Can you tell me what to do to make sure that we are both all right?"

"Fortunately, I know exactly what you need to do. Doctors are wonderful men, but they don't know everything, and sometimes a little advice from someone like me is just what you need. Sometimes a little female wisdom is better than a hundred men and all their book-learning, no matter what they say."

"So, what should I do?"

"Have you heard of Rambam?"

"Of course!"

All the Jews in Egypt—there had been a Jewish community in the country for thousands of years—had heard of Rambam. Rambam, also known as Maimonides, was a rabbi and philosopher from the twelfth century, as well as an astronomer, a physician, and a very saintly man whose name continued to inspire awe every time it was mentioned. His full name was Rabbi Moshe ben Maimon, but he was often remembered by his acronym. Rambam had been well-known during his lifetime and considered the foremost scholar of the Torah, and his scholarly and philosophical work had influenced intellectual life not just in Jewish circles but all over the Middle East, north Africa, and southern Europe. In Cairo, he was remembered not just with respect but with devotion. Rambam died in 1204, and his tomb could be found in the courtyard of the synagogue in Fustat.

Fustat was a city that had been founded in the seventh century, and now all that remained of it were traces that had been subsumed by the vast metropolis of Cairo. The Jews of Cairo maintained that Rambam's body still rested there, although an alternative theory held that his remains had been moved to Tiberius on the shores of the Sea of Galilee, and the location where he was said to be buried there was also held in great esteem. For the Cairene Jews, the mausoleum in Fustat was an important sacred space, and many of them had been to it to pray and ask for his help.

"Well," said Esther, "if you have heard of Rambam, then you know what a great and important person he was. People like him ... well, they are special, and they have powers that can last beyond the grave in ways that ordinary mortals are not capable of understanding. All we can do is see and accept. What you need to do is spend a whole night in his mausoleum, and then you can be sure that Rambam will keep both you and the baby safe—not just during the birth, but for the rest of your lives."

"A whole night in a mausoleum!" Flora exclaimed. "I will be petrified!" She shivered. Not only did she hate the thought of spending the night in a tomb, she was also quite sure that her husband, Joseph—who was seven years older than her and very much the boss in their home—would never allow her to do such an outlandish thing.

"You'll be perfectly fine," Esther assured her. "Just remember that it is a holy place; that the dead can't hurt you, because they are in another place; and that it is for the good of the child, who needs you to be strong for him. I know that it sounds strange, but I don't think you will be frightened. God will be with you all night long, and your faith in Him will keep you safe."

Flora rushed home as quickly as her ungainly pregnant body would allow her and told her husband of the advice she had received from Esther.

As Flora had anticipated, Joseph was immediately sceptical. "I don't see the value of taking the advice of a strange old lady," he said. "It's not as though she has any medical training. Regardless of the importance of Rambam, I fail to see how spending the night in a tomb can be considered a useful thing to do. Wouldn't it make more sense to take proper medical advice from a doctor? We're sensible people; we shouldn't listen to such silly superstitions."

"I saw Dr Cohen too, and he said that I am in danger, and so is the baby, and that there is nothing he can do," Flora pointed out. "The worst that can happen to me at the mausoleum is absolutely nothing! And at least I might feel less frightened and worried about the birth if I have tried to do something to make things easier. I couldn't be more frightened than I am now, so any improvement would be a change for the better."

"I suppose … when you put it like that …"

With considerable reluctance, Joseph gave Flora permission to travel to Rambam's tomb and spend the night there. Her request to stay the night was unusual, but Jewish women often visited the tomb when they were pregnant to pray for help from one of Judaism's great holy men. Joseph reasoned that if it eased her mind and made her less concerned, at least that would be something. He hated the thought of her feeling so unhappy and scared. The reality that he might lose her when the baby was born was something that he simply felt unable to confront, and so he pushed that thought to the back of his mind.

Joseph loved Flora, but he often didn't know how to express his feelings for her. He was challenged by her sometimes, as despite her lack of formal education, on some level he knew that she had a better mind than he. Despite, or perhaps even because of, the fact that she had only had a few years of schooling, Flora had an astonishing memory and the capacity to retain and understand facts. Often, she was able to correct her husband when he had misunderstood something or remembered a detail incorrectly. While this was useful to Joseph—who often asked her if she could recall names, addresses, or other scraps of information that escaped his memory—he also resented it, because it made him feel small.

He tried to show her his feelings and assert his authority over her by being strong and a leader, but often it came out wrong, and she felt that he was bullying her and brushing over her concerns. On this occasion, at least, he hoped that by agreeing to what she had asked, he would show that he did truly love her in his own way.

On obtaining permission from the groundskeeper of the synagogue where Rambam was buried to spend the night in the mausoleum, Flora rolled out her blanket, took out a cushion, and tried to make herself comfortable for the night. She had said goodbye to Joseph and insisted that he leave her alone until the morning, when he could come back to collect her. Esther had told her that this was something she had to do on her own.

The space was damp, cobweb-festooned, and creepy—and to judge by the smell, it was also home to a colony of bats, or maybe even rats. But for some reason, she felt comfortable and safe, and sure that she was doing the right thing. Since arriving at the synagogue, the baby's movements inside her had become less frantic and urgent, as though he found the location calming and felt more at ease and willing to accept what fate wanted for him rather than fighting it every inch of the way.

As the light faded completely from the room, Flora said her prayers and lay down to sleep, putting her faith in the God and saints that she loved and admired so much to keep her safe. She had been sure that she would not sleep a wink, but she fell into a dreamless unconsciousness the moment she closed her eyes.

In the morning, Flora was awakened by the sound of people walking around outside. She yawned, stretched her arms, and sat up. She had slept all night on the hard, cold floor! She could not believe it! Then she noticed something glittering in her hand. What could it be? Raising her hand, she saw that she was holding a small golden amulet threaded on a leather thong. Wondering, she turned it over and held it close to her eyes to examine it. On one side, there was a portrait of Rambam wearing a turban, and on the other, an angel with eagle wings. Was this the miracle she had been waiting for? Flora pressed the charm against her belly. As if in response, the baby inside moved towards it.

"My darling boy," Flora said, her voice thick with emotion. "Now I know that we are both going to be all right, and that this amulet is for you. When you need it, I will give it to you, and it will keep you safe and bring you good fortune for the rest of your life." She rose, rolled up her bedding, and made her way to the gate of the synagogue, where Joseph was waiting for her anxiously.

"Are you all right, darling?" Joseph asked. "Did spending the night here bring you any relief?"

"I feel ever so much better. Don't ask me how I know this," Flora replied, "but after spending the night here, I can promise you that the baby and I are going to be fine. You don't need to worry about me anymore."

Two months later, a baby boy was born to Flora and Joseph when they were at Alexandria, away from the suffocating heat of Cairo. He was the sixth of their children, the fifth of their sons, and the biggest child that Flora had borne yet. While the birth was long and painful, both mother and child were unharmed, and Flora beamed as the baby, wrapped in a cloth, was placed in her waiting arms by a very relieved Dr Cohen, who had dreaded the thought of having to bring Joseph bad news.

"Here he is at last," she said. "My little prince."

"What will we call him?" Joseph asked.

"Well," she said, "he is my little angel, and we were both watched over by an angel the night I spent at the mausoleum, a *real* one, so I am going to call him 'Raphael'." She placed a fond kiss on the tiny forehead. "Can someone send word to Esther that the baby is here? I am so grateful to her for the advice she gave me. I'm sure that I would have died without it! You know, a true miracle happened the night I slept in Rambam's tomb, and from the moment I woke up, I was quite sure that everything was going to be just fine."

Over her head, Joseph and Dr Cohen exchanged a look imbued with meaning. Dr Cohen had been unimpressed to learn that Joseph had allowed his heavily pregnant wife to spend the night in a dirty old mausoleum on Esther's advice, but he had to admit that it had brought her a sense of relief, and perhaps that simple emotion had made it easier for her to relax and give birth. He would go and have a word with Esther later, and ask her to stop giving vulnerable women uneducated advice—but for now, he was prepared to let this one go.

Little Raphael stared up at his mother with huge, dark eyes. Although he had been restless during the pregnancy, moving constantly and keeping her awake all night, now that he was in the world he was perfectly still except for the tiny fingers that he clenched and unclenched, as though trying to grasp at the world. He seemed to be alert and curious, as though he understood that he was here to learn as much as he could. Flora unclasped the chain that held the amulet around her neck and pressed the gold medallion into the baby's hand.

"This is for you," she said. "Let it always keep you safe. So long as you have it, nothing truly bad can happen to you."

Raphael's little fingers closed tightly around the amulet as he continued to regard his exhausted mother with his steady gaze. Caressing his dark hair, Flora brought him to her breast to feed on mother's milk.

2017

"Wow," said Rebecca. "That is really a crazy story. I can't actually believe that Grandad's mum spent the whole night in a mausoleum, especially when she was heavily pregnant. I mean, can you imagine?"

She shuddered. "A creepy, dusty, cold old tomb, for goodness' sake! You wouldn't catch *me* doing that, especially during what was obviously a difficult pregnancy. And good grief—can you imagine giving birth in those days, without an epidural? She probably didn't have any pain relief at all. Rather her than me."

"Well," said Richard, "I suppose if you really believe that a place is sacred, then the creepiness won't bother you, because you know that it's a holy place and that you're safe there. It's obvious that Flora trusted Esther and her advice—otherwise she wouldn't have gone near the tomb!"

"Anyway," said David, "that explains how Grandad got the amulet in the first place—but I don't understand why he has always had so much faith in it, as he's not generally either religious or superstitious. Is it because his mother had such a deep faith, and he loved his mother so much? He still misses her, you know, even all these years after her death. Or did anything actually happen that made him feel that it was protecting him? To tell you the truth, I can't quite get my head around the idea that Grandad believes this stuff. Can you?"

"Well," said Rebecca, feeling a little defensive on her grandfather's behalf, "he's right in a way, isn't he? I mean, he's always been super successful. Even if that isn't because of the amulet, maybe his belief that the amulet was giving him good luck gave him the confidence he needed!"

"Maybe so," said Richard. "And maybe that belief helped him as a kid growing up. His childhood certainly took place in interesting times ..."

CHAPTER 3

GROWING UP IN KHARTOUM AND CAIRO

2017

"It must have been pretty wild growing up in Egypt in those days," said David. "I imagine it was very different from how we live today."

"Well," said Richard, "the family actually had a fairly complicated arrangement. They had a lot of family in Sudan, and then Grandad's father, Joseph, was trying to establish a business in Cairo, so they actually sort of divided their time between two countries, and the kids spent periods of time in school in each. I know that Flora always felt much more tied to Sudan than Egypt. And if you think that Cairo was different in those days from the way we live now, Sudan was off the Richter scale. Seriously, you would hardly believe some of the stories Grandad's told me. It's hard to imagine that some of it took place in the twentieth century. Talk about the land that time forgot!"

"Wow, Sudan and Egypt," mused Rebecca. "Wouldn't it have been very tough being Jewish in those countries at that time? They must have been a very small minority."

Richard smiled, a little wryly. "The funny thing is," he said, "Egypt and Sudan were actually great countries for their Jewish minorities for a long time. People were raising happy families, running businesses, and getting along well with all their neighbours. For the longest time, nobody cared what religion anybody was, and they even attended each other's festivals and celebrated together. It was only later on that things got difficult … and Grandad was there for the start of that terrible period, which began around the time he was born and got worse after that. And he was there for the beginning of a new chapter for Jews everywhere."

1935–42

It was funny, Raphael thought, the way they had two homes. Sometimes they went to Sudan, where Granny and Grandad and all their family were, and sometimes they stayed in Egypt, where they didn't have so many relatives, and kept themselves to themselves much more. He often asked himself which he liked better, Khartoum or Cairo, but the answer could vary from day to day, depending on the mood he was in at a particular moment in time.

In some ways, it didn't make much difference where they were on a day-to-day level. He invariably shared a bedroom with his older brothers, Avi, Leon, Elie, and Isaac; tried to escape the bossiness of his older sister, Renée; took care of his little sister, Leila (a sweet child towards whom he felt very protective because she was the youngest and bore the brunt of a lot of teasing); and did his best to please his mum Flora, whom he loved dearly. In each country, although more so in Sudan, their lives were deeply intertwined with those of the rest of the Jewish community, although the circumstances of those communities were quite different.

Raphael's family had history in Sudan. The story of their family's arrival all those years ago was often told whenever all the uncles and aunts got together. He had often heard the old stories about how his ancestor had arrived in Sudan many years before, when Napoleon arrived at the tail end of the eighteenth century, and he had been among the soldiers. The first of the family to arrive had been of Italian origin, and they still spoke a little Italian at home even now.

By 1899, the British had seized control of Sudan—much of which had been under Egyptian control. Raphael's grandfather, Eli, had fought with the Anglo-Egyptian armies at the time. When they won,

Sudan became part of the vast British empire. This opened up huge business opportunities for a thriving international community that benefitted from proximity to the Suez Canal, and now from access to the enormous market that was the empire. Raphael's great-grandfather, Gideon, had become very successful under the British regime, so he had arranged for Eli, his son and Raphael's grandfather, to join him in business. Soon, father and son were running a successful import-export business in the growing, modern capital of Khartoum. In the fullness of time, Eli opened a shop of his own and did even better than his father. His department store was known to stock everything that anyone might want, from agricultural equipment to cosmetics, and the family name was soon well known all over the country.

The British administration enjoyed a very positive relationship with the very small Jewish population in Sudan, predicated on social and economic exchange, which made things easier than they might have been after the conquest. The British knew that the best way to secure a peaceful future for Sudan was to help the local economy to develop, and they could see that the Jews were investing heavily in the area, providing funds to pay for infrastructure and development that would benefit all of the local inhabitants. They encouraged the Jewish community to continue with their work and also created a business and social environment that made Sudan more attractive to other Jews who might like to move there and take advantage of the growing business opportunities.

All of this was very welcome to the Jews. While many of them were relative newcomers, there were collective memories of a period under Muhammad Ahmed, known as Mahdi, who had ruled Sudan before the arrival of the British. During that time, both Jews and Armenians, who were Orthodox Christians, had been subjected to forced conversion to Islam and forced marriage to black people from a very different cultural background; they were castrated if they did not consent to this. Some of them managed to escape with their lives by pretending to convert and keeping up their Jewish prayer in secret.

The majority population, largely composed of Nubians, was Arabic speaking, and at that time on good terms with both the minority populations and the British administration. Slavery—the slaves had been black Africans, mostly from West Sudan—had been outlawed in Sudan only with the arrival of the British in 1898. Raphael's grandfather, Eli, had recounted stories of how he'd had black slaves but had given them all their freedom of his own accord, as he did not approve of the idea of one man being allowed to own another. Most of his former slaves had gone on to work for him for a wage. There had been some resentment towards the abolishment of slavery at first on the part of many of the former slaveowners, but most of them had adjusted to the new situation relatively quickly.

Khartoum, then a relatively new city compared to the old capital of Omdurman, was located directly opposite the older metropolis, on the other side of the Nile, just where the white and blue Nile waters met—a fascinating and beautiful natural phenomenon that drew many tourists to the area. The two cities were connected by a wide bridge, which had also been constructed by the British, and which allowed for a huge amount of commercial traffic to cross from one side to the other on a daily basis. The city was linked with its hinterland by the to-ing and fro-ing of those who lived outside the city and brought their goods to market. On market days, they used their camels to bring their produce in, showing how porous the barriers between city and hinterland actually were.

While there were quite a few fine buildings in Khartoum, the city still did not have a modern infrastructure, and visitors often found it very old-fashioned. Even in the 1930s and 40s, there was no sewerage system to carry waste away from homes and businesses. Instead, all the homes had lavatories with cavities containing buckets that opened onto the street, and there were professional waste-disposal workers whose job it was to come late at night and replace the used bucket with a new one. Newcomers from better-developed countries were always startled and rather revolted by this particular detail of daily life in Sudan, although they grew used to it quickly.

Khartoum had been established by the British so that they could administer the territory, and many of the buildings displayed their influence. The British, a small community numbering not more than four or five thousand inhabitants, were almost exclusively involved in administration jobs in Khartoum and around the territory, with a smaller number employed in education and other sectors that supported the British regime. The relatively small British administration largely kept to itself and did not mix much with the Jews, the other minorities, or the majority population. The governor general lived in a fine porticoed palace with a graceful double staircase and formal gardens with tall, manicured palm trees, quite cut off from the rest of society, and viewed with a considerable degree of awe by anyone passing by.

Many of the civil servants employed in the middle to higher levels of the state apparatus were imported directly from India (including both ethnic British workers and ethnic Indians). Britain had a long and successful history as a colonising force in India, and many of the Indians who settled in Sudan went on to become very successful merchants. In cultural terms, the Indian influence could be clearly seen in both the clothes the British imported and the architectural style of the buildings they created.

The police force of Sudan had recruited local officers, and at the grassroots level, much of the everyday running of the country was handled by the locals. The British influence was relatively discreet compared to the setup in other colonies in Africa. The Sudanese were proud of the fact that their home was what was known as a "cold colony" in reference to the fact that, while the British were officially in charge and clustered in the highest positions in the state infrastructure, the ordinary people of Sudan were considered reliable enough to handle much of the business of the state on their own.

Eli quickly outstripped his father in business and built a reputation in Sudan as someone who could make money easily. He was well respected and liked in the community. However, he also had the reputation of someone who kept his own money close to his chest and did not like to share it. Eli's wife, Betty, supported her husband in all things, but once in a while she did go behind his back to give a little handout to one or another of her children who seemed to need it and had pleased her recently.

Betty did not get along particularly well with Joseph, Raphael's father, and knowing that he was the less-well-loved son had always been difficult for him, although he was loath to admit it. He often accused her of being self-centred and resented the fact that she seemed not to give him enough respect for the fact that he had a higher level of education than his brothers. The reality was that they were actually very alike, in both good ways and bad, and where they clashed, it was often because of all that they had in common. Joseph was very different from his father in terms of business acumen, but one thing he did share with Eli was his pride. Although there were many occasions when Joseph struggled to make ends meet, he was determined to make his own way, and he never asked for help.

*　　*　　*

The Jews of Cairo were mostly descended from people who had come from Syria, Turkey, and North Africa many years before. In some cases, Jewish families had been in Egypt for so long that nobody even knew when they had arrived; perhaps they had been there since the time of the pharaohs and were descended from the Egyptian Jews of old—the ones mentioned in the Torah. Many of the Egyptian Jews spoke French, but there were also a few like Raphael's family, who spoke Italian.

Napoleon had brought the French culture and language with him when he conquered Egypt. Even in the twentieth century, many of the Jews looked to France for cultural reference, while a lot of the schools that served the wealthier elements of the Jewish community were based on the French model of education and taught the children through French. Nonetheless, all of the Egyptian Jews spoke Arabic, often at home as well as on the street and at business. After all, it was the national language, and most of them identified closely in many ways with the mainstream of Egyptian society.

Most of the Egyptian Jews were in Alexandria and Cairo. Everywhere they went, they opened schools, hospitals, and public amenities, such as swimming pools, that served the wider community. For this reason, they were generally well respected, and their investment in the area was appreciated by all of the people and contributed to a positive relationship between the Jewish minority and the majority Muslim population, as well as with the various other minorities that contributed to Egyptian society. The Jewish community also helped to establish the first stock exchange in Egypt in 1883—shortly after the Suez Canal was opened in 1869—helping it to take its place among the developed countries of the world just as the canal introduced a new level of economic prosperity.

The Jewish community, which reached 80,000 at its peak, was economically and socially diverse. In the Jewish Quarter of Cairo, located in the packed city centre, could be found the poorest and also the most religiously observant of the Jews, who wanted to live together in a tightly knit community, as they did not have the economic means to buy or rent homes elsewhere. They liked to live together because of the sense of security it gave them. Here, Jews had large families and lived in small apartments, often just one or two rooms in dimension. Children were put to sleep wherever a little space could be found, and mothers were good at making improvised cots and playpens out of tea-boxes and drawers. The busy streets around the Jewish Quarter, stuffed with small shops of every kind, were so full that it could be difficult to walk on them without bumping into other people—housewives, barefoot children playing in the street, and men on their way to the café for a cup of coffee and a cigarette.

While the shops within the Jewish Quarter itself were Jewish-owned, the streets immediately outside contained similar shops run by Muslim Cairenes. All the shopkeepers got along and helped one another out. There were lots of beggars on the street in this area; in the more upper-class areas, beggars were quickly moved on so that they would not disturb the wealthy housewives and their well-dressed children going out for a walk. The number of beggars swelled on Friday, the day of prayer for the Muslims, when people were more likely to be charitably inclined—charitable giving is a tenet of Islam, and giving alms on a Friday was considered particularly pious.

Daher, by contrast, was a comfortable middle-class area that was home to observant Jews who built a range of synagogues for their religious needs. It was quite unusual for middle-class Jews to have very big families, like Joseph and Flora's; usually, they confined themselves to two or three children and invested heavily in the children's education and futures. Many of them could afford to hire Egyptian nannies to do a lot of the childcare, as well as Nubian maids to handle cooking and cleaning, so the women were free to devote themselves to beauty treatments, shopping, and drinking coffee with their friends. The husbands worked in their offices all day, and in the evenings, they often collected their wives—now dressed for the evening, coiffed, and perfectly made-up—and brought them to the country club, where they could socialise with their peers, playing tennis and gossiping among their friends.

The wealthiest Jews mostly lived in the luxurious neighbourhood of Zamalek. Some of them were very rich and could afford beautiful homes, with servants who lived in special servant quarters, cooks who prepared delicious meals, and a full set of staff to take care of the children and collect them from school. Here, one could find the families who had founded and ran Cairo's best-known department stores. A lot of Jews worked in retail, and some of them had been very successful. Cicurel's, for example, which had been founded at the turn of the century by Moreno Cicurel, who had immigrated from Turkey, was very well known for its luxury goods. David Addis sold textiles and clothing in a store aimed at the middle classes, while Orozidack was a huge shop with many floors, unusual at the time, which also sold a wide range of goods, including clothes and textiles of high quality. In fact, the whole department store industry was dominated by Jews.

For many years, the successful Jewish families of Egypt did not attract any jealousy from the other populations because they were very friendly with the locals; although each community had its own specific niche in society, they mingled quite freely together. There was a particular sense of brotherhood among the minorities—the Greeks, Italians, and Armenians—who largely worked in groceries and controlled that trade, with small local grocery stores all over Egypt selling goods including salted fish, cheese, high-quality olives and sardines, and other Mediterranean products.

The Armenians had settled in Egypt in the first instance because of the persecution they had faced at the hands of Turkey. The early-19th-century Armenians of Turkey had been categorised as subhuman and targeted for extermination by a hostile state. The Turkish government had slaughtered a million people in their attempt to destroy the Armenians completely. Some of the survivors had managed to make it to Egypt as refugees and set themselves up as shopkeepers there. Of course, some of the Jews were also Greek or Italian, and like other Greeks and Italians, came to Egypt because of the business opportunities it offered them.

Cairo was very different from Khartoum. For one thing, Cairo was about twenty times bigger and home to a much more diverse community, with many long-established minorities who played an active role in the life of the city. For another, whereas Khartoum was a modern colonial city, Cairo was extremely old. Both Cairene society and the physical reality of Cairo reflected the uncountable strata that had been formed by many centuries of a civilised society living and conducting business in the same place. In Cairo, the ancient and the modern jostled cheek to cheek.

While both Khartoum and Cairo were located along the banks of the Nile, in the upmarket neighbourhoods of Cairo the river had been developed as a resource—with walkways, gardens, and cafés—where members of the public could walk and enjoy their free time in the company of friends or family members. While there was little to do in Khartoum beyond socialising within one's own extended family and ethnic group, Cairo could offer an extensive array of theatres, cabarets, and nightclubs that catered to every taste imaginable. Overall, the Jews in Cairo were a well-known and well-accepted element of society, to the extent that their important holidays and festivals were well known to the broader public.

In both Egypt and Sudan, because each community had its own economic speciality and cultural and economic niche, there was no competition between them and no tension. Even though most of them did not socialise much with one another (although the elite in every cultural group in Cairo did socialise in luxurious settings, such as Shepheard's Hotel), and certainly did not intermarry—nobody thought that would be a good idea—they were happy to live and work alongside one another in a spirit of friendship, respecting one another's separate cultures and traditions—which were different right down to the clothes they wore and the food they ate.

Muslim Egyptian women typically wore a loose wrap over their inner garments, big enough to draw over their faces if the need arose, although they were not usually veiled. Younger women were very good at drawing the fabric across their faces in a way that drew attention to how pretty they were rather than detracting from it, and they wore heavy eye make-up that gave their eyes an exotic, dramatic look. Egyptian women had a freer life than Westerners might imagine. They were free to walk in the street, socialise with their women friends, and even talk to men.

In the south of Egypt, there was a substantial Coptic Christian population, and there the women never covered their faces at all. The Copts claimed direct descent from the ancient pharaohs of Egypt, whose kingdoms had originally sprung up in the area of Luxor, only spreading to Cairo later on. They took great pride in this story, considering themselves to be the "real Egyptians" and the Muslim majority to be interlopers.

The Greeks and Armenians, like the Jews, generally dressed in a Western style. The women wore knee-length skirts and dresses, while the men had adopted the fez and wore twill trousers and poplin shirts. By then, the fez was considered the characteristic Egyptian headgear, but it had actually been introduced under the reign of the Turkish sultan of Egypt, Muhammad Ali, whose son and grandson had gone on to form the monarchy of Egypt.

Even though the same ingredients were available to everyone, the recipes made by families from different ethnic backgrounds were quite distinctive, giving insight into each culture. When observant Jewish mothers cooked for Friday night, they had to prepare meals that could be consumed without being heated. In general, they ate much more rice than the other groups and tended not to use the same herbs and spices. They also cooked their meat in a different way— grilling it rather than frying it in oil, and eating it simply rather than with the rich sauces favoured by the Arabs. Depending on the cultural background of the cook, Jewish cuisine also displayed different gastronomic influences. Raphael's family's Italian heritage showed in the fact that Joseph liked it when Flora cooked pasta, which she often served with a simple tomato sauce. Of course, there were special Jewish butchers who prepared kosher meat, but (especially after the war started) most families relied on starches, lentils, chickpeas, and vegetables, and ate meat only rarely.

In both Egypt and Sudan, for the Jews, Friday night was the fulcrum around which the rest of the week revolved. Most of the shops were closed, because both Egypt and Sudan were majority-Muslim countries, and the Muslims were at worship in their mosques. For the Jews, Friday night was the beginning of the Sabbath, their holy day.

On Friday nights, the women (or in the case of the wealthier families, the cooks) prepared a lavish meal, and the whole family gathered around the table to eat together. The father of the family read the traditional blessings, and they ate the Sabbath meal, which consisted of roast chicken, stuffed chicken skin, courgettes or aubergines, and vegetables in season. Lentils, which were a signifier of poverty, were never eaten on this special day. Eating lentils for the Sabbath meal was supposed to bring bad luck.

Saturday was a day of worship when no work could be carried out, so lunch on Saturday often consisted of white beans with finely chopped meat or lamb knuckles, left cooking on a low fire since the night before, as no cooking could be carried out on the Sabbath day. Because Raphael's family was perennially short of money, Flora was forced to economise. She served the white beans without lamb knuckles and sometimes used lamb bones to make a stock to give the beans more flavour. As their family was not religious, Joseph usually eschewed the reading of the blessings and simply told the children to tuck in and enjoy their food.

Raphael could never figure out if he was supposed to be a Sudanese or an Egyptian boy, although he never doubted his Jewishness, despite the fact that he only went to the synagogue on special occasions. But, like all children, he was used to doing what he was told, and most of the time he adapted quickly to the current circumstances and fitted in with the other children. The best part about being in Sudan, when they were there, was having lots of cousins to talk to and play with—and seeing how his mum, Flora, flourished and opened up when she was surrounded by people who cared for her. She loved being with her sisters, and she liked the fact that Joseph got along well with her family; in fact, he had an easier relationship with them than with his own.

There was always some item of news and something to gossip about. Someone was getting married, or another person had finished school with high honours, or there was a baby on the way, or a marriage or a bar mitzvah was being arranged and everyone would be invited to the party in the Jewish Club and have the opportunity to put on their best clothes and dance the night away. Flora had more time to relax in Sudan, too, because home help was less expensive there than in Egypt, and Joseph could afford to pay the salaries of several servants who could help Flora take care of the children and run the household. She had the help of a black woman, a former slave who had been freed when the British arrived and abolished slavery, and an Arab nanny who cared for the children and did the cooking. In Egypt, Joseph could only afford to pay someone to come in for a few hours a day, and Flora was run off her feet with the challenge of keeping the household ticking over and feeding her large family. For his part, Joseph seemed to find the atmosphere in Sudan suffocating at times, and he yearned to forge his own way in the bigger, more cosmopolitan atmosphere of Cairo.

It was only when he was 8 years old and war broke out that Raphael truly realised that he was different from most of the children he saw, that his family was part of a minority, and that there were some people who did not like the Jews. At first, the Jews of Egypt and Sudan did not realise how big the war was going to grow, or that it had anything to do with them, or indeed with Jews elsewhere. Gradually, however, the war got closer. News from Europe started to spread, and they learned that their brothers and sisters in faith were being exterminated, just because of who they were. Apparently, many people actually believed the crazy stories about the Jews that were propagated by the Nazis, and newspapers published them as the truth. When the war came, everybody seemed to retreat deeper into what seemed like the safety of their own family circles, and the differences between the various ethnic groups appeared to become more entrenched.

At that time, Joseph was working as the managing director of an Italian company in Sudan. It was a good job, and finally Joseph felt that he might really begin to do well, to make some serious money, and to finally show his family what he was made of. He had always had some anxiety around the fact that the sort of success his father enjoyed seemed to elude him. It upset him that some of his brothers-in-law were more well-to-do than he was, and that his own dad seemed to favour them more as a result.

He started to take a greater interest in local politics and to move in political circles, hoping to better understand how the country was run and to get to know people of influence who might help him to get ahead. He did get to know the governor general and was received at the palace a few times, where he was deeply impressed by the small army of bodyguards and servants hired to keep the governor general safe and take care of his every need. This was a great achievement, as the governor general was viewed almost as though he was a king, and it was very difficult to get an audience with him.

Joseph wanted Raphael and the rest of the children to know English, which was widely spoken in Sudan, especially among the more educated elements of the population. He had a favourable view of the British administration and often invited British army officers and civil servants to his and Flora's home for drinks or dinner to display a sense of solidarity and help them to feel at home among people who were more culturally similar to them than were the native Sudanese. Joseph also wanted his children to know that he was a Jew and that, even though the family was not a religious one and rarely attended the synagogue for religious observance—they did drop in once or twice a week to meet friends and chat—their identity as Jews was important to them.

It was, therefore, quite ironic that the first problem that the war brought to the family was not related to their Jewishness at all but to the family's now relatively remote Italian origins. As Italy had gone into the war on the side of Germany, suddenly Italians were officially enemy agents. They were no longer welcome in British Sudan, and Joseph was hastily fired from his position as managing director—and even confined in a concentration camp for a short period before he was released and allowed to move his family to Egypt. This was a deeply traumatic time for him. He had enjoyed his work—in fact, he would never do so well in any other position he ever held—and he felt that he had been unfairly singled out simply because of his ancestry, over which he had absolutely no control. How could they treat him this way, he wondered, when he had shown in word and deed that he was completely supportive of the British establishment in the country? He was embarrassed and ashamed of how he had been treated, even though it was no fault of his own.

In some ways, Joseph never fully recovered from the injustice of losing his job. For this reason, he was never quite able to commit to developing a business in Egypt, and at the same time he was both drawn to and repelled by life in Sudan. Flora was often frustrated by the fact that she and Joseph didn't have the lifestyle she aspired to. Of course, it wasn't his fault that he had been targeted because of his Italian background, but the fact remained that things hadn't picked up as much as they should have after the war.

"Between you and me," Flora confided in Raphael when he was still very small, "my biggest regret is that I didn't get an education before I got married. Just think, if I had finished school, I would be able to help your father run a business. I know I'd be just as good at it as he is, too. But women aren't supposed to do that sort of thing, and my father didn't want to invest in educating a girl who was just going to get married and raise children, so I have to keep my nose out of it. It's just very difficult having to sit back and say nothing when I can see that he's making mistakes or letting that business about the camp upset him! But I'm telling you, I'm not going to make the same mistake with your sisters. They'll be wives and mothers all right, but they can have an education too! That way, they'll be able to help their husbands out and stop them from being foolish!"

When business didn't do well in Egypt, Joseph moved the family back to Sudan. They would do the journey in each direction several times.

Raphael's first experience of education was among Irish and Italian Catholic missionaries who ran a preparatory school, Comboni Missionary School, in an area near his home in Sudan. For relatively modest school fees, the missionaries provided a decent basic education to the little boys in their class, and also hoped that at least some of their students would convert to Christianity—which of course, as missionaries, they considered to be the one true faith and a prerequisite to entering the kingdom of heaven. As well as the lessons, prayer took up an enormous part of every day, and there were "holy statues" everywhere.

A large plaster Virgin Mary loomed over the entrance hall, spreading her azure blue robes and treading daintily on the head of a writhing serpent. The children were told that this represented the fact that she had given birth to Jesus, whom the Christians were taught had been born to save the world and who conquered the devil, represented by the snake. The children liked the statue's sweet, motherly face, which seemed to smile benignly at them all, but they were a little frightened of the writhing snake.

A large crucifix hung on the whitewashed wall behind the desk in every classroom. Raphael hated looking at the twisted, tormented body of Jesus hanging on the cross. He knew that the symbol was important to Christians, but to him it was just horrid, and he never understood why the children had to study beneath the image of a man being tortured in such a terrible way. He also understood from the religious education class provided by the priests that the Jews were sometimes blamed for what the Christians believed to be the murder of the true Son of God. Like all the other children, he had overheard his parents having worried conversations about what was happening in Europe, and he had picked up that this story was sometimes used as a justification for it. While he was too young to really understand, the whole thing led to a certain amount of anxiety.

"Daddy," a slightly worried Raphael asked. "What should I do when the other children pray? I'm a Jew, not a Christian. Should I tell the teacher to let me stay outside the room so that I don't have to hear what they are saying?"

"Look, son," Joseph replied. "Unless you are worried that saying mere words will make you less Jewish, there's no reason to stop praying. I don't see why you should feel different from the other boys. Culture and faith are important, certainly, but underneath all that, we are much the same. Just stand up respectfully and understand that God will know what is in your heart, regardless of the words you use to talk to Him. And be nice to the others. Just because we don't believe in the Christians' story about Jesus doesn't mean you have to worry about trying to change anyone else's mind. You respect them, and let them respect you. And remember: if anyone is rude to you because of who you are, there is absolutely no need for you to be embarrassed and upset, because that sort of behaviour reflects badly on *them*, not on you."

After that, Raphael was happy to recite Our Fathers and Hail Marys, even though the prayers themselves were irrelevant to the Jewish faith and utterly meaningless to him. And, of course, nothing bad happened to him as a result. He made friends with the other children and they played the usual children's games of football and run-and-catch, with no thought of differences in background or creed.

Raphael and his friends got together at the weekends and went to great lengths to get into the cinema without paying. One child would buy a ticket from the vendor and then quickly pass it to his friend while he slipped in. One by one they would do this until there was a row of ten little boys happily ensconced on the back row of the cinema, swinging their legs and watching the latest film from Egypt or America. Getting in for free made even the Pathé film reels seem worth the effort, but of course it was much more exciting when they got to see something like *The Wizard of Oz* or *The Hunchback of Notre Dame*. Sometimes they got together with their bicycles and cycled up and down the streets pretending that they were the cowboys that they knew only from the American "westerns" that often showed in the cinema.

For Raphael, the idea of himself as a Jew was quite abstract until, at age 10, he came across some Irish boys in school, sons of military people, who jeered at him and referred to him as a "dirty Jew".

"You'd better watch yourself," sneered Eamonn, one of the boys, "because they're burning the Jews in great big ovens, and you could be next! You know when we Catholics put ashes on our head on Good Friday? Well, if you get burned up, we could use *you*. How would you like it if I used your ashes to make the sign of the cross on my head? Pretty funny, eh?"

At school, Raphael tried to confront the other boys with courage, but the children's words struck home, and he started to have nightmares and to experience self-doubt. He thought that the boys were referring to literal dirtiness when they called him a dirty Jew, and he became concerned that he was unclean, so he started to wash his face and hands until they were red and sore. It didn't matter how much he washed, because they continued to refer to him as a dirty Jew, and sometimes the kicked and pushed him around the classroom. Some of the teachers seemed to overlook the bullying, perhaps because they agreed that the Jews were, somehow, less than human. Both the teachers and the Christian children had been brought up with the idea that the Jews were responsible for the death of Jesus and that somehow all of them had been tainted as a result and deserved whatever collective punishment came their way.

"Mum," Raphael said, "is it true that we are dirty? I've been washing and washing, and I don't think that I am any dirtier than the other boys. Look, I've washed my hands so hard they've even started to hurt. I don't think that I can get much cleaner than this."

Raphael held out his hands to show his mother. In the creases of his knuckles, the skin had become cracked and had started to bleed from the excessive washing.

Joseph and Flora exchanged concerned glances.

"Of course you're not dirty, you silly thing," said Flora. "You wash every day, don't you? And I keep your clothes nice and clean. You're probably the cleanest boy in the whole school."

"It's just that some of the other boys said ..."

"*Forget* about the other boys, son," Joseph said firmly. "People who say things like that don't deserve to be paid any attention. All they are doing is displaying their own ignorance, and their parents should be ashamed of them."

From then on, Raphael decided that he was not going to put up with being bullied any longer. He gathered together all of his cousins and all the Jewish children who attended the Catholic school, and they organised themselves into a gang for their own protection. Because there were quite a few of them, including some big boys who were almost ready to leave school, and who seemed very large and strong to the bullies, from then on he was left alone.

* * *

Flora had a cousin, Paulina, whom she loved very much. Paulina was one of the reasons why Flora was always happier in Sudan than in Egypt. In Sudan, she had cousins to talk to—they were her best friends—and Paulina was her confidant, someone she would have trusted with her life. Whenever they could get away from their duties at home, they met to have a coffee, talk, laugh, and forget for a little while the various troubles in their lives.

Paulina's daughter, Lola, was a beautiful girl, and despite the age difference between them—Lola was five years older—Raphael and she had often played together. Lola had enjoyed taking a maternal role and teaching him how to do things like play croquet. Raphael's affection for Lola had been pure and childish. She was so pretty! Lots of girls were really annoying, but Lola was special. At 15, now Lola was a married woman, and she was expecting a baby of her own—her first. Raphael could hardly believe it sometimes, although he knew that she was happy. All Lola had ever wanted was a husband and a home of her own.

One day, while he was playing marbles in the courtyard of their home, Flora approached Raphael with a special, secret smile.

"What's going on, Mum?" he said.

"Something wonderful has happened!" she replied. "Your cousin Lola has had her baby, a little girl, and she's fine. I hear that the baby is beautiful, just like her mum."

"Oh, all right …"

Raphael was not even slightly interested in babies and was a little annoyed about Lola growing up, becoming a woman, and no longer having any time to play. He turned his head back to his marbles so that he could return to his game, but Flora had not finished speaking.

"Look, darling," she said. "I've got a bit of a cold, and I don't want to give it to either Lola or the baby, so I'm not going to visit them until I'm better. I'm sending you over to their place to bring love and kisses from us all, all right?"

"Oh, Mum, do I *have* to go?"

"Of course! I thought you loved Lola!"

"I do, but I don't really want to see the baby. I'm not interested in babies. They're boring and smelly."

"Don't be silly. She'll be so happy to see you and hear our congratulations from you. Go on; this is Lola's first baby, and she needs to know that everyone is there for her."

Grumbling, Raphael went to the bathroom and washed his face and hands as his mother told him so that he would "look nice for the baby". Raphael thought this was stupid. He didn't know much about babies, but he was pretty sure they didn't notice if someone had a dirty face.

Duly polished and tidy, Raphael took the gift his mother had bought for Lola and trudged over to Lola's house, where the baby had been born with the help of a local midwife. When he got there, he knocked on the door, and Lola's grandmother opened it. Granny's hair was a bit of a mess, but she was beaming with excitement.

"Come in, darling, come in," she said. "Isn't it exciting? A new baby in the house! Can you believe that Lola is a mother now?"

"Mum said she couldn't come because she has a cold and doesn't want to give it to anyone," said Raphael, "so she sent me to say congratulations and see Lola and the baby."

"That's lovely, dear, and you look very nice. I see that you've combed your hair and everything. So, you're all ready to meet your promised one?"

"What promised one?"

"Didn't your mummy tell you? She and Lola already agreed that if the baby turned out to be a girl, you'll marry her when you grow up. Well, she's a beautiful little girl, so you are about to meet your future bride for the very first time! Yes, this is a very special day indeed."

"What?"

Granny was already bustling ahead, leading the way to Lola's room.

Fine, thought Raphael. *I'll marry her if she turns out to be as pretty as her mother. Otherwise, no way!*

"Darling, little Raphael is here to see you. He says that Flora has a cold and can't come for now, so he's here instead. Isn't that nice?"

A little shyly, Raphael entered the big bedroom where Lola was lying in bed, her new infant held in the crook of her arm against the warmth of her body.

"Hi, Lola," he said.

Lola's cheeks were flushed and she looked tired, but her eyes were sparkling with happiness.

"Raphael, thanks for coming," she said. "Isn't it exciting? I'm a mummy now."

"Yes, congratulations."

"Don't you want to see the baby? Didn't Granny tell you? You're going to marry her when she grows up!"

"Yes, I heard that Mum said so."

"Well, what do you think about that?"

"I'm sure she'll be very nice," Raphael said politely, trying to hide his lack of interest. "Eh, can I see her?"

"Of course!"

Lola pulled the sheet back from around the baby's face and proudly turned the little scrap around so that Raphael could see her.

"Isn't she the most *beautiful* thing you have ever seen in your entire life?" she said, beaming with maternal pride. "I've decided to call her 'Angel'."

Raphael had to restrain himself from leaping back from the bed in horror. What was Lola talking about? The baby was hideous. She was tiny, wizened, and pink, and her skin appeared to be covered in some sort of waxy substance. Her eyes were slits, all scrunched up, and when she opened her mouth to yawn, it was cavernous, toothless hole.

"Ah, she's very ... cute," he said.

"I *know*," said Lola, oblivious to his reaction. "I think she's the best baby anyone ever made. Didn't Abraham and I do a good job?"

"I brought you this," Raphael said, shoving the gift his mother had sent—a box of chocolates—towards Lola.

"Oh, how lovely. That will make the milk nice and sweet! So it's a present for the baby, too."

Raphael didn't want to think about Lola feeding the baby with her own breasts. He blushed and felt awkward as she started to fumble with the ribbons that held her nightdress closed.

"I'd better go now," he said. "I'll see you soon, Lola."

Raphael left the room, shaking his head sadly. *Lola must be crazy,* he thought. *How can she think that her baby is beautiful? It's a little monster! Well, I'm not going to marry that baby unless she turns out to be a lot prettier than she is now!*

Back at home, Flora was eagerly waiting for news.

"Well," she said, "how was Lola? And the baby?"

"Lola was fine," said Raphael. "But Mum, the baby was horrible. It looked like a grub, or something that might have crawled out from under a rock. I think there was something wrong with it."

"Oh, darling," Flora laughed. "I'm sure the baby was fine. That's what newborn babies are supposed to look like. What do you think *you* looked like, silly? I'm sure she'll grow up to be a beauty. Did Lola tell you that she's going to marry you when she's all grown up?"

"Well, I'm not going to marry her if she goes on looking like that!"

"Of course not, darling," said Flora, amused. "But don't worry. She's going to be gorgeous, just like her mum."

Raphael already knew that his mother had strong feelings about marriage. She believed firmly that people found true happiness when they married within their own cultural and religious community and that it was best to marry as young as possible—especially for girls—so that the couple can grow in their understanding of one another before either of them is too set in their ways. Although he often rebelled against his parents, this motherly wisdom was something that he accepted as simple fact.

In Sudan, marriages were usually arranged privately, between families—but in Egypt, where the Jewish community was bigger, parents often waited until their children came of age and then hired the services of a professional matchmaker, who would do some research and come back with a few suggestions, based largely on cultural, social, and economic considerations as well as the habits of each family. Most of these marriages, freely entered into by the young people, were successful, because they were carefully made on the basis of the couple and their families having common ground. The matchmakers, who were usually women who had learned their skill from their own mothers and grandmothers, took their profession very seriously and did extensive research into both families before suggesting a match. The fact that there were so few divorces testified to the success of this traditional approach to love and marriage.

Shortly after Raphael's introduction to his future bride, Joseph announced that they were all going back to Cairo, without delay. For two years, Joseph had tried very hard to establish a successful business manufacturing and selling thread, but it had not gone very well. In theory, thread should have been a great business in Sudan, because most families made their own clothes and needed plenty of it. The Sudanese people wore simple garments made of voile. The poorer women invariably dressed in wraps made of cheap, rather shiny material that was bought in great quantities to keep the price down, with very simple dresses underneath. Anyone who could afford it embroidered the material with a bright orange thread (sold as "gold") that provided an interesting contrast of colour against the rather sombre blue. Joseph's shop was filled with orange threads of all different widths, but very few people came in to buy anything, and he decided that, war or no war, the family had a better future in Cairo. Late at night, when he was supposed to be asleep, Raphael could hear his parents arguing about the move.

"I can't *believe* you're doing this to me," Flora said. "Not when we're getting settled here, with Raphael in school, and me with my sisters and cousins to talk to me and help me. We've just got properly set up, and I've even sewn curtains for the windows. Now you want to uproot the family and bring us all back to Cairo? What for—just because you're sulking?"

"It's for the best," said Joseph shortly. "I can't get any business going here. We're not making enough money. There are loads more opportunities in Cairo for someone who's prepared to work hard, like me."

"But this is where our families are! I don't want to go back to Cairo. I'm sure your father will help you to set up something if you want."

"What I *want* is to have a happy family life. It's much harder to achieve that when I don't even know how long we can stay in one place. And I *don't* want to go running to Dad for handouts like some little kid. I'm the head of this family, and you need to understand that."

Flora, as a wife and mother, had no choice but to do what her husband decided for the family, and in the end, she accepted his decision and accompanied him back to Egypt with no further recriminations. Realistically, her choices were limited. Certainly, even if she had wanted to, leaving him was never an option. Girls of Flora's background grew up assuming that they would be wives and mothers and nothing else. They were given a very basic education and then taken out of school to focus on learning how to cook, sew, and take care of children and a home. Flora had learned how to read and write but not much more than that, and now she had a large family of her own, to which she was utterly devoted. Her children would go wherever Joseph did, and so would she.

Even at an early age, Raphael could see how his mother was often frustrated by the fact that her natural intelligence had never been allowed to blossom. Even without having attended school for more than two or three years, she had an excellent instinct for business and an incredible memory. Flora's lack of training, and her large family, stood in her way of her ever doing more than housework and childcare. The huge energy that she might, in other circumstances, have put into running a business, she instead devoted to her children and to building their confidence as much as she could. She felt strongly that they should all have the opportunities that were denied her.

"I have a feeling that this time, I'm really going to get my business off the ground," said Joseph happily as the train pulled out. "Cairo is where it's all happening. I don't know what I have been thinking, staying in Sudan for so long."

Flora didn't say anything. She had heard it all before.

In Cairo, Joseph opened a shop and put his older sons to work for him. Raphael was sent to an Islamic school in the city centre, as he was not yet old enough to work in the shop. He was going to the Islamic school in part because there was no space available in their first choice of school, but also due Joseph's insistence, again, that the children should know how people lived beyond the tiny Jewish community of Cairo. After all, when they grew up, they would have to work and do business with people from all sorts of backgrounds. They wouldn't get very far if they only felt comfortable dealing with people from the tiny world of Cairene Jews.

"I don't know about this, Joseph," said Flora, upon hearing the plan. "Have you heard some of the things the Muslims say about Jews? I've never read their holy book, but I've been told that it has nothing good to say about us. Are you sure that this is a good idea? I'd hate for Raphael to be bullied again after what he went through at the Catholic school. He's still very young. If necessary, can't we have him taught at home?"

"Scripture is scripture and people are people," Joseph retorted. "The reality is that we are living in a majority Muslim country, and most of the Muslims are fine, honest people. It won't do him any harm, any more than studying with the Christians did. It'll do the boy good to understand people from backgrounds different to his own, and I won't have him taught at home. You dote on him so much, he would mostly learn how to take advantage of you! He'll be better off running around with children of his own age."

Raphael had been nervous about attending the madrasa. He had heard his mother's reservations, and he was also scared about standing out and feeling different from the other boys.

"Look at it this way, son," Joseph reasoned. "You'll learn all about the Muslim religion. That's not a bad thing, is it? At least then you'll know all about it, and you'll be in a much better situation to get along with the people you meet. I'm sure that it has plenty of wonderful qualities. After all, aren't most of our friends and neighbours here in Cairo Muslims? You like Ali and Jasmine from downstairs, don't you? Anyway, you'll see. The boys in the new school will be just like the ones in the old school in Sudan: football mad."

For a full year, Raphael's childhood studies were mostly predicated around the Qur'an. All of the boys were expected to learn vast tracts of the holy book by heart and to recite them aloud in front of the imam, a tall, imposing man who wore a white galabiyya, a long Egyptian robe, and a white hat. He looked down his nose at each nervous child reciting the surahs of the Qur'an and gently but firmly chastised the students when they got it wrong. They were expected to study their books every night and to absorb all of the lessons of the Qur'an completely and uncritically.

Raphael was the only Jew in the school. However, apart from a little mild curiosity at the beginning, the other children did not single him out for special treatment and rather respected him for coming from a group that they considered to belong to the elite. His schooldays in the Qur'anic school left him with respect for his teachers. Although much of the text in the Qur'an could have been interpreted in a negative way, his teachers focused on the teachings that mentioned love, brotherhood, and respect.

"Boys," said the teacher, "you will come across parts of the Qur'an that suggest that people should be converted to Islam at the point of a sword. What I want you to remember is that those words were written down a very long time ago and that we don't need to follow them today, because we are living in very different times. Mohammed said that all men are created equal, and that is the most important lesson from the Qur'an that you will ever learn."

Although none of the other children bullied him here, the teacher pre-empted any negative behaviour there might be by telling the class that Raphael was descended directly from one of the ancient Biblical tribes and therefore he should be respected.

By the time Raphael had left the madrasa, he had committed most of the Qur'an to memory, and in playing with other children had understood that Muslim boys have fun in just the same way as Jewish children, and as the Christian children in the school he had gone to before. His dad had been right. They were football mad.

*　　*　　*

Joseph and Flora had been in Egypt for a few years when General Rommel, leader of the German Army, was expected to take Alamein at any moment. Thousands of Jews had already fled Cairo, and those who were left were terrified about what might happen next. If the Germans succeeded in conquering the city, perhaps the Jews would be rounded up and sent to concentration camps like their counterparts in Europe. There were different rumours about what happened to the Jews in the camps, but most people suspected that they were killed there and would never be seen again. Joseph decided that it was just too dangerous in Egypt for the moment, and he brought the family to Sudan, intending to return to Cairo at the first opportunity.

Raphael was enrolled in a Catholic school for girls and boys run by nuns. Studying alongside girls was a novel experience for him and something he enjoyed very much. The Italian nuns taught all the children how to sing "Ave Maria", which he enjoyed greatly, despite the fact that the story of Jesus was not something that was relevant to him in any way. The song was in Latin, which nobody could understand anyway. The words just sounded like random sounds, but the tune was pretty.

After a period with the nuns, with the war still threatening Cairo and an immediate return not on the cards, Raphael was taken out and put into an all-boys Catholic school. The principal was a man called Father Barroni, an Italian, who assured them all that they could achieve anything they wanted to if only they put their minds to it and worked hard. He was a kind and open-minded man who arranged for an imam to provide religious education to his Muslim students and a rabbi for the Jews. Deeply religious himself, he did not seek to impose his own religious views on anyone and understood that a path to wisdom could be found in many faiths and good people could be found in every ethnic group. Unfortunately, this was an unusual position to take at the time, when Muslim teachers often informed their students that Jews and Christians were dirty and bad, and Christian teachers often taught the same about the Muslims and Jews. All the boys loved Father Barroni dearly.

When the Germans were in retreat and Cairo seemed safe once more, Joseph, Flora, and the children returned again. It was a routine that was increasingly familiar to them all.

The children were expected to play most of all with their siblings and cousins, so because they had more family in Sudan, they had a bigger array of potential playmates. In Cairo, they had to rely much more on one another. Avi, Leon, Elie, Isaac, Renée, Raphael, and Leila got along as well as could be expected—friends most of the time, only occasionally breaking out into squabbles. Raphael was very protective of his little sister Leila, who was treated as a pet by the whole family and spoiled. With her dark eyes, long lashes, and perfect skin, she looked like a little doll.

The older boys competed a little over who would attract the most attention from the maid, Fatima, a pretty Arab girl in her teens. At night, when the kids were supposed to be going to sleep, Raphael listened to his older brothers talking about Fatima in whispers and sometimes claiming that she had kissed them or had let one of them touch her breast through her clothes. The girls slept in a pull-out bed in the dining room in Cairo, as the apartment had just two bedrooms.

A place had come up at another Catholic school in Cairo, and Joseph sent Raphael to be taught again by Irish priests. He was bigger now and needed an education that went beyond religion. Of course, there was still plenty of religion being taught in the Catholic school, but they also focused on the fundamentals of mathematics, physics, grammar, and so on. Most of the priests were jovial and kind, wiping their red Irish faces when the heat was too much for them.

There was just one priest who was less than kind, and Raphael soon realised that this was because Father Heaney did not really want to be a priest at all but had fallen in love with one of the woman teachers at the school. He came into her classroom whenever he could and held her hand. The two of them would gaze into each other's eyes with longing, and all thought of teaching left their minds. When he wasn't with his beloved, Father Heaney took out his frustrations on the students, taking out a large ruler and beating them across the back in response to the slightest provocation. Raphael quickly learned that the best way to deal with Father Heaney was to sit at the back of the classroom and remain as quiet as possible, hoping to be forgotten.

The funny thing, Raphael thought later, was that although the madrasa had offered only a very rigid, inflexible sort of education, and although the Qur'an was full of violent images and messages, the imam who led the school had told the children that God was love and that they should recognise all men as equals and act accordingly. As a result, despite the violent words the children memorised, they were all taught to treat others with respect, even when they disagreed with them. Conversely, the Catholic religion talked a great deal about love and fellowship, and the words of Jesus on matters such as peace and charity were frequently quoted—but the Irish priests were strict and unbending and sometimes even cruel.

Raphael's own holy book, the Torah, contained many accounts of terrible violence, but the Jewish people—like the imam who taught Raphael—had learned over the centuries to become more tolerant and to focus on the more positive lessons of their holy book, while largely disregarding the rest. Ultimately, Raphael learned that religion does not make the man. Good men find inspiration to do good in their holy book, whichever one they happen to follow, and bad men find the excuses they need to commit evil acts; it was as simple as that. He wondered if the world would be a better place if there was no religion at all. He pondered how to reconcile this thought with the strong sense of community and belonging he experienced among the Jews of Cairo and Sudan and decided privately that he could enjoy a strong Jewish sense of identity without believing in all the theology.

While the family was increasingly settled in Egypt, they continued to go to Sudan once a year to visit their family. The trip took four days and was great fun; the holiday atmosphere started when they boarded the train and left their daily frustrations behind. Moreover, whereas Raphael's family was anonymous in Cairo, his father just one of thousands of Jewish men from the middle classes trying to scratch out a living, in Sudan his grandfather, Eli Romano, was well known and respected as a successful businessman all over the country. Even if his immediate family was not well-to-do, this association with success and the business elite in Sudan helped to give Raphael a sense of confidence in his own abilities. He could not wait to go into business on his own and dreamt of the day when he would no longer have to answer to his father for everything.

2017

"You're right," said Rebecca. "It does all sound like another world. It's strange to think that, back in those days, Britain still owned something like half the countries in the world, and to think of how the people lived—many of them with no sanitation or modern services."

"I was never one to study history," said Richard, "but hearing someone talk about it, about his own personal experiences, as Grandad did with me ... well, it brings it all to life. It was an interesting time to grow up, to say the least."

"So, what happened next?" asked David impatiently. "How long did they stay in Cairo? Do you know?"

"Oh, I know all right."

"Well, what are you waiting for?" Rebecca demanded. "Go on with the story!"

CHAPTER 4

BECOMING A MAN

2017

"Kids grew up quicker in those days," said Richard. "Most of them finished school earlier, started work earlier, and got married earlier. A girl or boy of 13 or 14 wasn't considered an adult, of course, but nor were they thought of as a little child, the way they are today. It's important to bear that in mind when talking about some of Grandad's memories."

"I expect that growing up with the war going on all over the world made them mature quickly too," said Rebecca. "Even for people who were lucky enough not to be directly affected, the fear that it could all start happening to them at any moment must have been with them all the time. It's mad to think that Grandad was already contributing to supporting his family during the war, when he was just 12. I can't imagine any of us having the gumption to do something of the sort at that age. I was still playing with my dolls then, and I think that you lot found it hard to think of anything other than your Xboxes."

"He told me that his girlfriends loved hearing stories like this, about when he was young," said David. "There was one in particular, Nadine ... she always told him that she wanted to know everything about him, to understand him better than anybody else, and for some reason he found it impossible not to do whatever she asked. So even though he has always been quite a private person in a lot of ways, he ended up telling her all about his childhood and the difficult times during the war. I'll tell you all about her in a little while."

"She sounds like hard work," said David. "I'm sure she was gorgeous and all, but with all the women he had around him … and knowing that he was going to get married to Granny one day before too long … why did he let her get under his skin like that? Why didn't he just cut her loose and find someone else?"

"He'd had a soft spot for beautiful women with an air of authority since the very beginning," Richard said. "He was very young when he had his first love affair, and maybe that sort of gave him a liking for a particular sort …"

"What? What do you mean, 'his first love affair'? He was just a kid!"

"Exactly, he was …"

"Well, you can hardly refer to a schoolboy's first romance as a 'love affair'."

"Sure, but then again, we're talking about Grandad, so his first romance was not exactly like most people's. It was not exactly a question of having a crush on some little girl with her hair in pigtails."

1942–4

In Cairo, things were rapidly going from bad to worse as the war progressed. There were even fewer supplies left in the city. The war was not going well for the Allied forces, and the Egyptian monarchy and government were trying to plan for any eventuality, including making suggestions to the Germans that they would be welcomed if they came. King Farouk, a spoiled playboy who had never had to work for anything and who had become king at age 17 when his father died, only cared about his own comfort, and he was prepared to curry favour with whichever power came out on top; he really didn't care which one or what he might have to do to keep the money rolling into his court.

King Farouk had never had to work or achieve anything, and he was like a child, prepared to do whatever it took to get his own way. He would have been more than happy to sacrifice the Jews if he thought that it would make things easier for him or gain him a few more toys for the palace. The monarchy in Egypt had been established during the days of the Ottoman Empire, and even though they and the rest of the aristocrats were now considered to be true Egyptians, the reality was that they were only interested in feathering their own nests at everyone else's expense. They had no interest in what happened to ordinary Egyptians, and even less in the Jews, who many considered to be de facto foreign citizens. They focused only on their own pleasure and indulged their every whim.

Fouad, father of Farouk, had been told by a fortune teller that his lucky letter was "F", so all of his children had names beginning with the letter. Whereas Farouk gained weight and lost his looks in adulthood, his sisters Fawzia, Faiza, Faika, and Fathia were beautiful women whose faces were often seen gracing the covers of magazines that published gossip about the royals and other celebrities. Their dignity and grace only made their brother seem even more ridiculous.

By the time Raphael was old enough to understand much more of what was going on in the adult world around him, the shops of Cairo were largely empty of basic commodities like wheat, oil, and sugar. Housewives queued for hours to purchase any spare groceries that became available. British forces had flocked into Egypt to guard the strategically crucial Suez Canal, until blue eyes and ruddy complexions could be seen on every street. There was very little trade in and out of the country, and chaos reigned in Cairo, where most of the population was now going to bed hungry at night.

Joseph and Flora, with their large family, were very worried about what was going to happen next. Inevitably, this had started to impact on their relationship. Late at night, when the children were supposed to be sleeping, they talked endlessly about what was going to become of the family. Should they stay? Should they go? If they went, where should they go? Was Sudan far enough, or might the troubles in Egypt spread there too? If not Sudan, where?

The atmosphere all over the city was extremely tense. Jews found that their Muslim and Armenian neighbours, who had previously been friendly and accommodating to them, who had considered them friends and invited them to take mint tea on their verandas, had started to turn on them, as though the Germans were already in charge and giving orders that could not be disobeyed on pain of death.

King Farouk was known to have sympathies for the German cause, and everyone knew that he wouldn't hesitate to hand the Jews over if that's what it took to curry favour with the Germans.

There was talk of a Jewish state being created across the border in Israel, but it seemed like nothing but a dream—a fairy tale that people were telling themselves in order to feel better about how difficult things were now. Joseph had built a life and a business in Cairo, even if it was only a modest one, and he didn't want to go anywhere. As ever, Flora's only concern was for her children.

"I want to be sure that they will grow up and build lives of their own," she insisted. "How can we be sure that they will be able to do that here, with all that is going on?" She got impatient with Joseph when he was indecisive about the future. "It's your job to provide for them," she reminded him. "They are growing up, and they need to start planning for their future. How can they do that when nobody knows what is going to happen next?"

But the uncertainty seemed to paralyse Joseph. His leather workshop had never brought home more than a modest income, but now he had almost lost interest in it. Because nobody knew what was going to happen next, he stopped looking for new customers and only just managed to fill the orders he actually had.

"What's the point?" he was heard remarking to Flora. "What's the point in killing myself at work when someone could just come in and take it all away anyway?"

"In the meantime," Flora said, "there's nothing to eat. The shops are empty, and the few goods that are available are more expensive every day. You'd better think of something, or we'll all starve. Thankfully, Raphael has a knack for figuring out how to get to the top of the queue for bread, and he has a gift for talking the shopkeepers into selling him more than they planned to, but he's still just a child. He has to go to school; he can't spend his days queuing for food—and I shouldn't have to feel obliged to send him because nobody else can be bothered. Can't you even begin to imagine how worrying it is for me to know that my little boy is out on the streets, hustling for food like some kind of urchin? Every time he comes home, I kiss him and thank God for delivering him to me, safe and sound."

"He's good at dealing with people," Joseph admitted. "I sent him out yesterday with a few coins to get some fabric and he managed to find enough to make shirts for me and all the boys, even though nobody else seems to be able to find anything and people are having to resort to using old flour bags to make shirts and dresses. I honestly didn't think he'd be able to do it. He appears to have an instinct that tells him where to find the things we need. But even Raphael isn't a miracle worker. Someday, his luck will run out, and he'll be like the rest of us."

Raphael didn't say anything or let his parents know that he had overheard their conversation. He was sorry that his mother was worried and upset, but the reality was that he felt perfectly at home and safe on the streets. He liked the hustle and bustle and enjoyed competing with others for the few resources that were available. Every time he managed to get his hands on food for the family, he felt a thrill of excitement, almost as though he had been on a real hunt, capturing and killing animals for the table. Strangely, the hardest substance of all to obtain was toothpaste, and finding toothpaste and bringing it home had become one of his major preoccupations in life. The only paste available came in the form of a hard cake, with a special brush that could be used to remove some of the dry material and mix it with water to make a paste. Whenever a shop had some in stock, news spread like wildfire, and everyone rushed to get a package until it had sold out in minutes.

As he spent hours every day walking from one shop to another, trying to find the things his mother needed, Raphael's cheap shoes had worn out until there were holes in the soles, which he had tried to patch with some old scraps of rubber. He had blisters on the sides of his feet where the skin was rubbing against the worn lining. While he put up with these shoes, as there was no choice, Raphael was embarrassed by them. Of course, many children in Cairo had similar shoes or wore cheap slippers, and some had no shoes at all, so it was not as though he was uniquely deprived. On the other hand, he was the grandson of a very successful Sudanese businessman, and he couldn't understand how his father had let things get this bad.

When I'm grown up, I'll make sure that I never have to go without anything, Raphael decided, *nor will anyone else in my family!*

Thankfully for the whole family, Raphael was very friendly with a boy called Neil Marsten, the son of a British serviceman, who attended his school. While Egypt had been independent since 1936, the British retained control of the Suez Canal and surrounding areas (they could see how important it was for the purpose of transporting petrol to both Europe and their colonial territories in Africa, which had no petrol of their own, and they were determined to remain in charge) and maintained a substantial army presence there. While the army was British, most of the soldiers were from elsewhere. Many of them were Maltese, with others from Australia, New Zealand, and elsewhere in the Commonwealth. There was even a Jewish regiment, mostly composed of local Jews, and a women's Jewish regiment, who had joined the British army because of their sense that they had a common enemy in Germany and not because of any particular sense of attachment to Britain. These Jewish volunteers were trained and worked separately from the other soldiers because of their particular dietary needs. One of these soldiers, David, was a relative of Raphael's, and he was also courting Raphael's older sister Renée. Every now and again, he came to eat with the family and told them stories about the war.

Neil was a lively lad just entering adolescence, with gangly arms and legs that looked too long and awkward and a big, toothy smile that seemed to split his face in two. Although he had spent most of his life overseas, he still felt intensely British, and the other boys found it amusing when he insisted that cricket was the best sport ever invented or that roast beef and Yorkshire pudding represented the height of sophisticated cuisine. The Egyptians believed that they had mastered the art of fine dining and looked askance at British claims to the contrary. Mind you, nobody in Egypt was eating very much, fine or otherwise, at the time, and the children found it hard to even imagine what it felt like to go to bed with a belly so full that there was no room for more. Thanks to the British army, the Marstens had all the chocolate, bread, crackers, and corned beef they could eat and more. Neil smuggled packages of supplies into school for Raphael to bring home, sneaking the bundles into his satchel when none of the other children were looking.

At first, Joseph and Flora were grateful for the packages but dubious about this unexpected bounty, as they were unused to eating foreign food and had never before encountered corned beef, which seemed very exotic and unappetising to them.

"What is it?" Joseph asked suspiciously the first time Flora presented the family with a plate of corned beef. "It smells like something you might give a dog. Is it kosher? It doesn't look very nice." He poked it around his plate with a fork, and it left a trail of grease as it moved.

"Who *cares* if it's kosher?" Flora snapped. "At a time like this, God will forgive us for not following all the rules. Clearly, God has arranged for this English boy to send food to our family to keep us all alive during the bad time, so it ill behoves us to be fussy. What is it they say? When God closes a door, he opens a window. Well, he's closed the door to the grocery shop, but he's opened a window in the form of Raphael's friend. It's either this, or everyone goes hungry. Do you understand? And besides, since when did you bother following the rules? I don't think you've seen the inside of a synagogue for over a year!"

Nobody complained about the corned beef from then on, or at least not when they were within earshot of Flora. They didn't dare. Compared to the delicious meals she had been able to prepare before the war, the corned beef, which was pink in colour and gelatinous in texture, was quite revolting—but the family soon grew used to it and even to enjoy it. After all, as Flora had pointed out, they had no choice.

Although Raphael's family had always gotten along with everyone—Jewish, Muslim Egyptian, Armenian—in the diverse neighbourhood in which they lived, new tensions had started to enter their daily lives. On the one hand, there had always been a degree of anti-Jewish sentiment in Egypt, even if this was rarely expressed, and on the other, his family was also of Italian origins, and Italy had gone into the war on the side of Germany. This meant that they could be viewed as enemy agents and were liable to be the targets of suspicion, as had happened in Sudan earlier in the war. Thankfully, Neil Marsten and his family did not hold his Italian background against Raphael.

One day, Neil passed Raphael a note during maths class. "Don't go straight home after school," the note read. "I have to talk to you about something very important!"

Raphael was uninterested at first. It was a hot, stuffy day, and he had been planning to go swimming. He mimed swimming gestures in Neil's direction so as to communicate his plans to him. If whatever Neil wanted to talk about was really that important, it could always wait—or perhaps they could swim together instead. Raphael had become more interested in swimming just recently with the realisation that it was really very pleasant to be around girls who were wearing nothing but a swimming costume. The girls their age were beginning to develop breasts and hips, but the girls Raphael really liked looking at were older and fully formed, like women.

"Forget about the bloody swimming," Neil hissed to Raphael's objections. "Seriously, when you hear what I have in mind, you'll definitely lose all interest in swimming!"

"OK," Raphael whispered back. "You've got my attention. I won't go swimming. So, what's it all about?"

The boys looked back at their books when the teacher looked at them sharply. As soon as he had turned away, Neil hurriedly scribbled another note: "Meet me at Kitty's Café near the Roxy Cinema after school. I'm leaving class early and going home to get my dad and bring him there. He's going to buy us both a drink and explain his idea to us. You won't regret it, I promise you!"

After school, Raphael made his way to Kitty's Café, where he found Neil and Mr Marsten already seated, waiting for him at one of the tables on the pavement. They looked at home among the expatriate community the café attracted. Mr Marsten appeared very English, with his reddish complexion, sandy hair, and big hands, and Raphael could easily see what Neil was going to look like when he grew up.

"Nice to meet you, lad," Mr Marsten said, extending one of those huge hands for a handshake. "I hear that you and Neil have become great pals. He's always coming home from school to tell me about the scrapes that the two of you have been getting into."

"That's right," said Raphael cautiously. He was wondering what the big Englishman wanted with him. Was this just a social thing? If that was the case, why had they come to Kitty's Café? He could have just gone to Neil's house after school to spend time together, and he could easily have done it after swimming. So, what was going on?

Mr Marsten ordered cold sherbets for the boys and a cup of tea for himself. He gave the waiter a big tip and waited for the man to leave before he started to talk. Then, gesturing to the boys to lean in, he started to speak in an intense, lowered voice, glancing here and there to make sure that nobody was listening to him. Nobody was; the busy Cairo street was filled with the usual hustle and bustle of housewives and merchants going about their business, children playing, and small flocks of scruffy pigeons pecking around in the dust for whatever titbits they could find.

"Boys," he said, "I want you to think of this as a business meeting. Maybe it's your first one? You're both 13 now, so you aren't kids anymore but young men, right? Raphael, Neil tells me you know your way around the streets of Cairo and that you have a head for business, so that's what gave me the idea. You know I'm with the army. The thing is that the English soldiers have more food and supplies than they need but not as much money as they want to go out in the evenings and have a little fun. How are they supposed to fight a war if they don't get to let their hair down, that's what I want to know? It's hard enough picking up girls in Cairo without having to do it without a few coins to buy drinks with. Anyway, what we are looking for is a way to sell what the soldiers have but don't need, so that they can get a little extra cash to spend at night."

Mr Marsten paused. "Perhaps you can see what I am getting at," he said discreetly.

Raphael thought for a minute. He had no idea what Mr Marsten was trying to suggest.

"Not really, sir," he said politely. "It's a pity about the soldiers not getting to go out, but I don't see how I can help. I don't have any money, and if I did, I would give it to my mother, not to the British soldiers, because she's always worrying about where the next meal is going to come from."

"Don't you see?" said Mr Marsten. "A lad like you, Egyptian, who knows the streets of Cairo like the back of his hand and speaks the local lingo, is just what I am looking for. I can't use an adult as my go-between, and I can't use Neil here, because he sticks out like a sore thumb with his blue eyes, freckles, and light hair—but you would be perfect. You're old enough to understand and be trusted but young enough to pass unremarked. You dress the same way as the other local kids, and you have the same dark hair and eyes. Look at you: you're even wearing the slippers all the lads wear around here. Basically, I want you to get the goods from me—Spam and sugar and the like— and sell them to your contacts in Cairo. I have a contact in the army canteen, and I know that they've much more food than they need. It's no skin off their nose to order the stuff and sell it to me. All I have to do is find a way to get it out. The soldiers will get a bit of money, the Egyptians will have the opportunity to buy some scarce food, and I'll give you a generous cut. I won't take advantage of you just because you're young, and I bet your parents would be pleased if you started being able to bring them home some money and other supplies— much more than we're giving you now. I know that I could do with a little top-up on the bloody miserable wages I get from the army. So what do you say?"

"I'll do it!" said Raphael with a grin. Sure, he was nervous about the responsibility and maybe getting caught, but come on—this was an opportunity to make some money and show the world what he could do.

"I knew you would!" said Neil triumphantly. "I told Dad that you would be exactly the right person for the job. He wasn't sure, you know, because of your age, but I persuaded him to give you a chance."

"I'm counting on you, Raphael," said Mr Marsten, suddenly very serious. "If we get caught, we'll both be in trouble, so your job here is a very important one."

"I understand," said Raphael. "Don't worry; I'll be very careful. You won't have to worry about a thing!"

Shortly after the meeting, Raphael started his illicit work for Mr Marsten. With his small stature, innocent expression, and typical Cairene looks, nobody even cast him a second glance when he went around to the British army barracks to collect the goods. After all, he was just a child, and if anyone stopped him, all he had to say was that he was going to play with his friend. Nor did anyone cast him even a passing glance when he returned from the Marstens' house with his schoolbag stuffed with contraband meat, oil, and sugar, pilfered by Mr

Marsten from the stocks of the British Army. He knew the streets like the back of his hand and attracted no attention at all as he made his way home via the alleys and backyards of Cairo.

Raphael found the perfect outlet for the goods in a neighbourhood store run by Isaac, a distant relation of the family. Isaac ran a general goods store, selling groceries and household supplies to local housewives, but since the war had started, it had got more and more difficult for him to find goods to sell. Nothing was being imported into Egypt, and as it was hard for the country people to bring goods to market, a lot of them had reverted to subsistence agriculture and stopped selling things to the city at all. It didn't matter how much money someone had if there was nothing to spend it on.

Increasingly, Isaac had to dole out the few groceries he had in small quantities so that all the customers had at least a little bit. In this way, he hoped to keep all his customers happy, but in reality, he only succeeded in frustrating them, as nobody went home with enough food to prepare a satisfying dinner. He had taken to closing the shop completely in the afternoons and going home to sleep on the veranda of his house, saying that there was nothing to sell anyway and that he used up less energy and needed less to eat if he didn't have to stand behind a counter all afternoon.

When Raphael first went to Isaac with his idea, the older man was very dubious about it. "You're offering to help me find things to sell, a little whippersnapper like you?" he inquired sceptically. "And where do you propose to get all of this stuff? Do you have a little garden that nobody knows about, or perhaps a direct line to heaven, and God is going to give it to you Himself? If nobody can get their hands on some food around here, why am I supposed to think that you'll be any different?"

"I wouldn't be getting it on my own," Raphael said defensively. "I've gone into business with a British army officer, and he has access to all the chocolate and things you can imagine through his job. The army gets in loads of stuff for their soldiers, and they don't even count the boxes! He's getting it for me and giving me a cut for selling it on to whoever wants it. I came to you first because you're a relative, and my mum always says that family comes first, but if you're not interested,

I'm sure I can find someone else. I know that Mr Ahmed across the road wouldn't hesitate. *He* wouldn't care what age I am!"

Defiantly, Raphael stuck out his chin and looked Isaac straight in the eye. He meant what he said; if Isaac didn't want a share in the bounty, he'd march straight to one of his competitors, and then he'd be sorry!

Isaac was amused by this display of self-confidence from a kid he had seen growing up in the neighbourhood on and off for years. He was a little impressed by Raphael's feisty attitude, and if there was really a chance of getting some stock for the shop, he didn't want to miss out on the opportunity.

"I didn't say I wasn't interested," he added hastily. "So don't go anywhere else. I'll take the goods. Where did you get this sort of business drive from? I like Joseph as well as the next man—there's nobody more fine and honourable than he is—but nobody would accuse him of being the businessman his father is; he prefers to run someone else's business than go out on his own. So what's your secret? Maybe your mother, God bless her, would have been more of a business woman if she hadn't got married young and had all those children. They say that one day, women will run their own companies, but I say that I'll believe it when I see it …"

"Are you interested or not?" Raphael asked, almost snappily. "'Cause if you're not, I'm going right across the street to see if Mr Ahmed might like to have the opportunity instead."

"Hang on, hang on," said Isaac, seeing the prospect of making some money beginning to disappear before his eyes. "Did I say I wasn't interested? Not at all! I'm just impressed, you know, that you are getting into this sort of thing before you're even wearing long trousers or shaving that cute face of yours. Let's do it and see how it goes. Just make sure that nobody sees you with the merchandise, because if they do, we'll both be in for it!"

The very next day, Raphael arrived with the first consignment from Mr Marsten: chocolate, corned beef, the nylon stockings that all the women wanted to get their hands on, and other supplies. Discreetly, word got around the neighbourhood that Isaac was selling things that nobody else had, and soon he was the only shopkeeper in the whole area making any money. All the other shopkeepers on the street begged Isaac to tell them where he was getting his supplies, but he kept his mouth shut. He relied on Raphael to bring the goods, and Raphael was diligent in obtaining them from the barracks and smuggling them, little by little, in his schoolbag under the books he brought home from school.

With the food and the extra money Raphael was bringing home, soon Flora was able to feed her large family the way she wanted, and nobody was going to bed hungry anymore. He was able to buy cloth to make shirts for his father and the boys, and he even found pretty flowered material that Flora used to make dresses for herself and the girls. He was delighted by the praise he got from his parents and siblings and basked in the glow of his mother's gratitude. There were few things he enjoyed as much as being admired and told that he was doing a good job. It just felt good to know that everything was all right at home because of him and his efforts, and he had found his purpose in life: the acquisition of money. It all seemed to come so easily to him, and he wondered why it was that he managed to slip through Cairo without getting noticed and to support the whole family through his efforts.

Avi, Leon, Elie, and Isaac grumbled a bit about the fact that Raphael was getting all the attention.

"It's not my fault I'm not as lucky as him," Avi said. "He's just small and cute, that's why things are easier for him. I'm a man now, and I'd never get away with it."

"Easy to say," Flora retorted, "but I don't see you complaining when his work puts food on the table. No; you eat it all up and ask for more, don't you?"

Now that he was supporting the family though his black-market work, Raphael felt like a man; a real man, like his dad and his uncles, all grown up and ready to go out into the world. The only trouble was, he was the only one who had realised how much he had grown up. Adults looked at him and all they saw was a little boy who might as well be playing marbles or catch on the street. He was still short, and his face was still as smooth as an egg. Although he had begged his parents to let him start wearing long trousers like an adult, half the time he was still in shorts.

"You'll have the rest of your life to be a man," Flora said firmly. "For now, you are still my little boy, and I want you to look like one."

Raphael felt frustrated when he looked in the mirror and, rather than the young man he now imagined himself to be, he saw a child looking back at him. He couldn't wait for his body to start to change so that his appearance would finally reflect his self-image.

"You have no idea how grateful we are for the money and food, sweetie," said Flora, "but remember that you're still a boy; you still need to focus on your studies. God knows how long we're going to be able to stay here. If the Germans come, the Jews are going to have to leave in a big rush. I want you to concentrate on your education for as long as you can, because your future is important."

Another issue was perturbing Raphael at this point. He was thirteen now, and all the other boys his age were doing their bar mitzvah, the Jewish ceremony when boys are presented before the synagogue, given the sacred scroll to hold, and thus inducted into the world of men. The ceremony was deeply important in the Jewish faith, and as well as the religious aspect, families typically marked the occasion with a big party with food and music, in which the boy in question was the centre of attention and received gifts and praise. That's how it had been for each of Raphael's older brothers. Raphael had been looking forward to his bar mitzvah for years, and when he turned 13 and his mum told him that it was not going to happen because the war was on and there was no money for a party, he was desperately upset.

"I'm really sorry, sweetheart," Flora said. "We just don't have the money, especially after paying for your sister's wedding a few months ago."

Renée had just got married to her cousin, David. It had been considered a good match, and they had been pleased to see her settle down with someone they thought highly of and had known since he was a child. In all the excitement of preparing for the wedding, they had forgotten to set aside a little money for their youngest son. Joseph didn't want to talk about it; it was embarrassing for him to admit that he didn't have the means to hold the bar mitzvah. But Raphael couldn't let it go.

A year later, when he was 14, Raphael had some slightly younger friends who were doing the ceremony. Without saying anything to his parents, he arranged to attend the preparation classes so that he too could take part in the ceremony at the synagogue.

If Dad won't organise it for me, I'll just do it myself, he thought. He was deeply offended and hurt by what he saw as his father's lack of interest. As part of the preparations for the bar mitzvah, Raphael studied Hebrew at the synagogue under a local teacher and became friendly with his pretty, fair-haired daughter, Leah, giving him another reason to drop in from time to time. As the daughter of such a religious man, Leah was never allowed to go out on her own, but her dad liked Raphael and invited him to make himself at home. Raphael interpreted this as an invitation to call by whenever he liked and extended it to encompass the understanding that he could share a kiss with Leah—further evidence, he considered, of the fact that he was now essentially a man.

The week of the bar mitzvah, Raphael went to his parents and told them to attend the ceremony at the synagogue on Saturday.

"But we haven't organised anything!" Flora said. "How can you have the bar mitzvah when nothing has been done? What will people think?"

"*I'm* the one who has organised it, and *I* am the one who is inviting *you*," Raphael said. From his pocket, he removed a watch that he had bought earlier that day in Mousky, near the Jewish Quarter, with money he had earned from the sale of contraband. "This is my bar mitzvah present from you to me, so can you please take it, wrap it, and give it to me to open up later on?"

With tears in her eyes, Flora accepted the proffered watch.

On Saturday, Raphael proudly stood up in the synagogue alongside eight of his younger friends and read from the Torah while his parents watched. While he knew that they were still a little embarrassed about not being able to throw him a party, he felt good about being in a position to have organised all of this by himself. Surely, he reasoned, this meant that he was indeed a man.

1945

Raphael was still attending a Catholic school, St Austin's. Most of the priests who taught there were all right, and a few of them were excellent teachers, but some of them liked to brutalise the boys, and they all seemed to suffer in the hot climate of Egypt with their very pale complexions. The hotter it got, the worse their tempers grew, until they snapped and lashed out.

Raphael didn't mind school, really, but now that he had realised that it was quite easy to make money, he had started to disrespect book learning. What was the point of studying things like literature and history when they didn't make any money? And what was the point of going to an all-boys school when the world was so full of girls and women? The only women at the school were the cleaning staff and one or two teachers. The cleaning staff were of no interest to him, and the teachers seemed unapproachable. It was frustrating not to be considered a man by his family, but it was even worse to be seen as a child by girls and women.

Suddenly, everywhere Raphael looked, there seemed to be breasts, legs, and soft voices. He would be walking down the street when a waft of sweet perfume turned his head, or going home from school with the boys when an elegantly dressed lady sashayed by, completely oblivious to the magnetic effect she was having on the young lad she'd just brushed past. Of course, he knew that one day he would grow up and get married, but that seemed like a long time to wait, and he didn't feel able to ignore his feelings until then. Alone in his bed at night, Raphael thought feverishly about the pretty girls and women he had seen that day and wondered when he was going to be allowed to touch one, to run his hands up and down her body at last, and to have her gaze into his eyes while he told her he loved her. Would any woman ever let him do such a thing? It was so hard to imagine!

Raphael's French teacher was a young woman from Malta in her early twenties. Perhaps so that the priests and the schoolboys would not see how pretty she was and get distracted, she hid her face behind a thick pair of tortoiseshell glasses that obscured her big blue eyes, and she tended to wear a rather severe expression that disguised the sweet lines of her mouth. It was harder for her to hide the outline of her luscious young body, which was as ripe and sweet as a plum in springtime. She had a slender waist and plump thighs and breasts that pushed against her clothing when she moved around the room or turned to write on the blackboard to the sound of an entire classroom of boys collectively drawing their breath and crossing their legs in the effort to hide their inconvenient erections.

For some reason, all the boys were very keen on studying French, and even the slowest of them did his best to impress her. Miss Mackzumi wore no wedding ring, and many of the boys had fantasised feverishly about getting to be the one to walk her up the aisle and spend that precious wedding night alone with her. Needless to say, she never gave any of them the slightest reason to hope that they had even a remote chance of winning her heart.

One day, French class had passed without incident, and the boys were putting away their books ahead of going home when Miss Mackzumi called out to Raphael: "Raphael, can you please stay behind for a few minutes after class? I want to go over some of your homework with you."

"Yes, Miss," Raphael stammered, beginning to blush as one or two of the braver boys emitted soft wolf whistles to indicate their jealousy and to try to embarrass their classmate.

"That's enough!" Miss Mackzumi said sharply. "That's quite enough of that! Behave yourselves, or there'll be extra homework for the lot of you!"

The last of the students left the room, and Miss Mackzumi went to the door and turned the heavy key behind them. She returned to her desk and started to shuffle through some of her paperwork.

"Can you come up here, please, Raphael?" she said.

Raphael did as she requested.

"What is it, Miss Mackzumi?" he asked. "Is there something wrong with my homework?"

"No, dear," she said. "I wanted to talk to you about something else."

She put down her papers and came around from behind the desk to stand next to her pupil.

"Something is going on with you, Raphael," she said. "You've changed in the past few months. You're not one of the tallest boys in the class by a long shot, but all of a sudden you don't look like a kid anymore. Is everything OK at home? I know that things are difficult for a lot of families at the moment, and I hope that is not the case for yours. It's not an easy time to be Jewish, is it? We've all been reading the newspapers, and I have to say that I am quite worried about you and your family."

Raphael's heart swelled with pride. Finally, someone had noticed that he was a man; he should have guessed that it would be her, his secret beloved! He could not, of course, tell Miss Mackzumi about his illegal business, so he just muttered something about being busy. He was painfully aware of Miss Mackzumi's bosom rising and falling under the thin cotton blouse she was wearing, and he could smell her perfume and a slight scent of coffee on her breath.

To his absolute horror, he realised that he was getting an erection. This was happening to him more and more often lately, and frequently at the most inconvenient moments. He clamped his legs together and held his French textbook in front of his crotch in the fervent hope that Miss Mackzumi would not notice his unruly body's reaction to her proximity and comment on it.

"Pull up a chair and sit down beside me," Miss Mackzumi's honeyed voice suggested. "Let's get to the bottom of this. I really want to know what has happened to make you look so different lately. After all, I am your teacher, and it is my job to know what is going on in my students' lives."

Awkwardly, Raphael did as she asked, sliding sideways into the chair while still keeping the book in his lap.

"Is everything OK, Miss Mackzumi?" he asked. Perhaps she had heard about his access to nylon stockings and chocolate and wanted to order some. Well, that would be all right. As it was her, he might even give them to her for free! His heart began to race and his face turned red at the thought of holding in his hands the very nylon stockings that Miss Mackzumi would unfurl onto her pretty legs later.

"Everything is just fine, dear," she said. "But I've been worrying about you. You know that the news is very bad for the Jews in Europe, and now the Germans are on their way here. I would hate for something to happen to you, you know. Even though I am just your teacher, I have grown fond of you, and I wanted you to know that I have been thinking about you and praying for you."

To his horror, Raphael realised that hot tears had come into his eyes. What was she playing at? Of course he was worried about himself and his family; they were all worried. Things were bad, and they were getting worse. Nobody knew when or if the troubles facing the Jews in Europe would arrive in Egypt. Why was she tormenting him in this way? Was she being cruel on purpose?

"Oh darling," Miss Mackzumi said. "You're upset. I'm so sorry. I wanted to cheer you up, not make you cry. Look, come here, sit close to me."

Raphael shifted his chair nearer to hers. He could feel the warm firmness of her thigh pushing against his, and the heady smell of her perfume was even stronger now than before.

"Let me wipe away those tears," Miss Mackzumi said. "I don't want any boys crying in my classroom—if they are going to cry, it should be because they are ashamed of their terrible French grammar and not because I care about them and want them to be all right!"

She took a clean, folded handkerchief out of her sleeve and wiped his eyes and cheeks. As she leaned over, her right breast brushed against his arm.

"You still seem upset," she murmured, mistaking Raphael's rapid breath for impending sobs. "You poor little darling."

Impulsively, Miss Mackzumi got off her chair and knelt in front of Raphael's. She held her arms open wide and took him into her embrace. Beneath her silk blouse, he could feel her nipples harden against his chest as she squeezed him tightly. He could hardly believe what was happening to him; Miss Mackzumi was hugging him! Finally, he caught his breath and pulled back.

"Miss Mackzumi," he said. "The fact is that I am in love with you, and it's driving me crazy because I know that it is wrong and that I am only torturing myself with thoughts of you. If you think that I look worried or stressed in class, it's just because it's so hard for me to be around you, feeling the way I do. I think about you all the time. I know that you are a teacher and I am only a boy, but still … I mean … I never thought that I could feel like this about someone older than me … but there it is. I love you, and I think that when I grow up I will come and find you and perhaps we can get married. You're not so very much older than me, after all. In a few years' time, it won't make any difference."

"Oh, my dear boy," Miss Mackzumi sighed. "I've known this all along, you know. I could see you looking at me from your desk. You weren't able to hide your feelings from me at all. Your eyes have been eating me up all year! I should have done something to stop it. Don't feel bad, Raphael; I am the one who should have taken responsibility in this situation."

Suddenly, Miss Mackzumi stood up. As her hands were clasping Raphael's, he did too. His head nearly reached her shoulder, and as he looked up at her, he felt quite sure that he would never love another woman. Finally, he thought, he was a man. He stood on his toes to reach her mouth and covered it with his inexpert but enthusiastic kisses. She did nothing to resist, and on the third kiss, he could feel her starting to respond to his attentions. Her soft hands left her sides and ran up and down his body while she whispered sweet words in his ears.

"You know, Raphael," she whispered, "the fact is, I didn't want to stop you from looking at me … in *that* way … because I feel exactly the same as you do! I love you too, darling, and I wish that we could be together, but it is not to be. Sweetheart, I am your teacher, and you will not always be my student. It's time for you to go out into the world and make your way in it. You'll meet lots of other girls, I promise you, and you'll forget all about your teacher and the silly little crush you had on her when you were no more than a lad."

Raphael burst into tears. "I don't *want* to meet other girls," he sobbed. "*You* are the only one I want."

"Come now," she soothed him, running her hands up and down his chest. "You'll forget about me soon enough. You have a wonderful and very exciting, life ahead of you."

"Please don't make me go!"

Miss Mackzumi relented. "Well," she said. "Perhaps not straight away. I suppose we can have a nice time for a little while first, so long as you understand that you must never tell anyone about it. If you did, I would have to tell them that you are lying, and who do you think they'd believe, you or me?"

For the next hour, the two of them remained alone in the empty classroom, disturbed only by the occasional sound of a priest's heavy tread in the corridor outside. Nobody tried to open the door as Raphael was induced into the world of love.

When it was already dark outside, Miss Mackzumi straightened her clothes.

"I think it is finally time for you to go home, my dear," she said. "Your parents will be getting worried about you."

Reluctantly, Raphael went home. His mind was racing. What had just happened? It had been wonderful but a little frightening. Was this what adult life was all about? He knew that he could never tell his parents or any of his friends, because if he did, Miss Mackzumi would get into trouble. Of course, he wished that he could tell Neil, but he knew that his friend would never believe him.

From that night on, Raphael no longer wondered what a woman's body felt, smelled, and tasted like, because now he knew. And from that night on, he added a new obsession to his apparently endless thirst for money: the desire to make love to beautiful women as often as he could.

2017

"Ha, ha, ha!" said David. "Good for Grandad! No wonder he turned into such a lady's man. I wonder how Granny managed to tame him and transform him into the devoted husband we know today. What a great start to the world of sex. I wish there'd been a teacher like her in my school. I'd have been all over her!"

"Are you kidding around?" said Rebecca, horrified. "That's a story about child abuse, for God's sake! He was 14 years old. Do you think you'd be reacting the same way if it was the story of a 14-year-old girl with her male teacher? I don't think so! She should have been thrown in jail. Maybe he felt that he was a man and old enough to be with a woman, but he wasn't. He was just a little boy."

"You're right," said David, chastened. "I hadn't really thought of it that way."

"No wonder he became obsessed with sex," Rebecca continued. "I suppose he was trying to recreate those early feelings …"

"But it's perfectly clear that he loved sleeping with women," Richard interjected. "I mean, his relationships with women are some of his fondest memories … and in some ways, I think he remembers Miss Mackzumi fondly too."

"Well," said David, "you've also got to put it in the context of the time. Remember his mum's cousin, Lola? She became a mother at 15, so she can't have been that much older when she got married."

"Even still," Rebecca objected. "The teacher was in a position of authority over him. It's not exactly the same."

"Well," said Richard, "if Grandad doesn't consider himself a victim, who are we to judge? After all, it's *his* story, and he has a right to tell it any way he wants."

CHAPTER 5

ALONE IN A
TROUBLED WORLD

2017

"Like I was saying," Richard began, "kids grew up a hell of a lot faster back when Grandad was a boy compared to today. Most of them left school early and started to work for the family business, and they often got married very early, too. They were expected to do what their parents told them, but they also took on the sort of responsibilities that would freak out modern kids. By the time Grandad was 14, he felt that he was ready to go out on his own."

"But he wasn't, right?" said Rebecca. "I mean, he was just a kid. A boy. Don't tell me that his parents let him go off without them."

"Those were different times, and the war was on," said Richard. "Sometimes decisions made in extreme situations are the right ones for them, even if they aren't the decisions people would make under ordinary circumstances."

"And it sounds as though Grandad really was pretty good at standing on his own two feet," added David. "So what happened next?"

"Well, it won't come as any surprise to you to learn that, after his adventures in the black market, Grandad felt more than ready to go into business on his own, and that his parents let him run Joseph's business for them when they fled to safety in Sudan. At just 14 years of old, he had to learn how to stand completely on his own two feet, almost overnight …"

1945

Raphael's business in the black market ended suddenly when Mr Marsten was posted to southern Italy, and Neil was sent back to England to go to boarding school and complete his education. The family was intending for him to go into the army as an officer straight after secondary school, just like his father and his father's father before him. Neil's future life plans had already been written for him since long before he was born. Raphael and Neil said goodbye to one another, hoping that one day they would meet again, although they both knew that it was unlikely. They shook hands stiffly—despite his time in Egypt, Neil remained an English boy through and through—and wished each other luck.

Without the steady supply of food that Joseph and Flora had obtained from Raphael so long as Mr Marsten was running his illegal business, they had no way to feed the family. Joseph's leather workshop hadn't brought in any money for months. Thus far, very few of the Jews had left Cairo despite the hostilities of war and the growing resentment towards them, but now some of them started to go.

Of course, it was far easier for families who were wealthy, well connected, or both to pack up and leave. Without money or relations in a position to help overseas, the poor Jews had nobody to turn to, and travel got harder as the Germans increasingly controlled all the coastlines in the area and could keep an eye on who was trying to leave. By now, it was extremely difficult to travel to Europe. While Raphael's father was certainly not rich, the family in Sudan had means, and their relatives were prepared to welcome them back and provide them with employment for as long as necessary.

"Son," Joseph said one day, "pack your things. We're going back to Sudan."

Joseph's father—the boys' grandfather, Eli—was still working and running a successful business in Sudan, despite the war, and the whole extended family was waiting for them to return. Joseph and Flora planned to pack as many possessions as they could and to leave their apartment in Cairo for the meantime, hoping it would still be there when the war eventually ended and they were able to go back. Joseph hadn't told anyone that he was leaving, not even the four men who had worked for him at the leather workshop for years and who had accepted lower wages recently because they were loyal to him—and because other jobs were hard to come by in these troubled times. They would find out that they had all lost their jobs when they turned up the next morning and realised he wasn't there.

Joseph had many fine qualities, but he was not a courageous man. However, there are times in a man's life when courage is not the most useful quality to have, and now seemed to be one of those times. Joseph had no interest in experiencing the terror that was growing among the Jews of Cairo, nor did he wish to subject his wife and children to it. Raphael, however, felt differently.

"I'm staying here, Dad," Raphael said. "I'm not going anywhere. I'll take care of the apartment and the business so that when the war is over, you'll have something to come back to. I don't want to go to Sudan anyway. I like it better here. There's nothing to do in Khartoum."

"What? Don't be silly. You're just a kid. Your brothers are older than you are, and they're doing what they're told and coming. You can't stay. You just do as I say, like a good boy. And what do you mean, 'There's nothing to do?' Aren't all your relatives there?"

"I'll be fine," Raphael insisted. "I feel like this is the right place for me to be. And I'm not a kid anymore. I'm 14 now, practically a man!"

Joseph and Flora roared and wept, but Raphael was unmoveable, and eventually they agreed to leave him behind in Egypt when he promised to join them in Sudan if things got too dangerous.

"I'll be fine, Mum," Raphael reassured his mother. "You know that nothing bad is going to happen to me. I'll be perfectly safe. Don't worry."

"I knew you'd say something like that," Flora sniffed. "Well, in that case, there's something I want you to have."

Flora reached into her pocket and withdrew a small package, which she carefully unwrapped.

"What's that, Mum?" Raphael asked.

"It's the amulet I was given for you before you were born," she said. "You remember the story. Somehow, Rambam put it in my hand while I slept. I've been keeping it for you, waiting for the day when you would need it, and that day has come. I want you to put it on and keep it with you always, because it is your special charm, and it will keep you safe."

Raphael bent down at her gesture and allowed her to fasten the amulet on its gold chain around his neck.

"I mean it, sweetheart," Flora said. "Never take it off, and it will keep you from harm."

Raphael's hand closed around the golden charm. Although he had just put it on, it seemed warm to the touch, as though alive.

"Thank you, Mum," he said. "I'll always wear it. Don't worry about me, because I know that I am going to be just fine."

The family left early in the morning so as not to attract too much attention from the neighbours. They didn't want to have to deal with dramatic goodbye scenes and hoped that they might be able to come back soon and resume their ordinary lives as though nothing had happened. Raphael hugged and kissed his father and siblings dutifully and then, for a long minute, his beloved mother. He stood in the door of the apartment building and watched as they all went down the street and around the corner in the taxi that Joseph had summoned to bring them to the station. As they went out of view, he suddenly felt very small and very alone.

From now on, somehow, he was going to have to find the rent for the apartment on his own. How was he supposed to manage that? The rent was low, but it was still more than he could afford. For a moment, he contemplated rushing after his family and calling out that he had changed his mind, that he wanted to go with them after all, but then he reminded himself of his brave words and was determined to stay and be a man.

"You all right, son?"

Raphael turned. It was Ali, their landlord. Ali was also the mechanic who had a workshop on the ground floor, and he lived in the apartment next door to Joseph and Flora's. He was good at his job and made a decent living repairing cars and lorries. The courtyard of the apartment building was usually filled with an array of vehicles awaiting repairs and was cleared only when Ali had managed to rent it out for a wedding or another formal occasion, when he transformed it into a banquet room for the festivities. Ali owned the building and collected the rent, and he had already asked Raphael to call him "Uncle" because he had grown quite fond of him. Ali felt that Raphael was often overlooked in favour of his older brothers.

"I'm fine," said Raphael, though he didn't really feel fine. The truth was, he was afraid that he might start crying if anyone asked him too many questions.

"Gone and left you on your own, did they?"

"I don't mind," Raphael said defiantly. "I'm ready for it. I've kind of been working for years now anyway."

"I'm sure you are," Uncle Ali said kindly. He looked at the boy and could not help feeling sorry for him. Raphael was still very young. What were his parents thinking?

"Look," Uncle Ali said impulsively, "as it's just you in the apartment now, I'll drop the rent. And if you find that there are months when you can't make it, come and let me know and we'll work something out, all right? I don't want to think of you going hungry or anything because you can't get it together. Just pay when you can … and pop in if you run low on groceries. I'm sure that Jasmine"—this was Uncle Ali's pretty, blue-eyed Turkish wife— "can lay an extra place for you for dinner. One more mouth to feed won't make any difference."

"Thanks, Uncle Ali."

Raphael wanted to give Uncle Ali a hug, but he restrained himself. After all, he had said that he was a man now; he couldn't afford to look like a little kid.

Now that his parents had gone, Raphael could make all of his decisions for himself. The first decision he took was not to go to school anymore. What was the point of school when the whole world was changing? Who cared about things like history and geography when death was a constant possibility? And anyway, with Mum and Dad in Sudan, there was nobody to pay the fees. He could always worry about books later on, when he had time for luxuries like that.

Raphael realised that the men at Joseph's leather workshop, and by extension their entire families, were now depending on him. Joseph hadn't even told them that he was leaving, and badly off as Raphael's family was, these men were far poorer. They lived from hand to mouth and didn't have wealthy families to support them if things got really rough. Raphael made his way to the workshop to break the news and tell them that, from now on, they were going to have to take their orders from a teenager. He hoped they'd take it well.

Standing at the top of the room, Raphael cleared his throat and spoke in as deep a voice as he could muster.

"My father has had to go to Sudan to attend to some family business," he said, "but he has left me in charge, and I know that we can keep things going without him until he gets back. I just need to know that you are all on board and that I can count on your support."

The men looked at one another uncertainly. *Who* was going to be in charge, if Joseph was gone? This little whippersnapper? Could they really take direction from this kid? They could still remember him in short trousers! Raphael could read their minds, and for a moment he faltered. These were men in their thirties. Any of them was old enough to be his father.

Fareed, the foreman, was the first to speak up.

"All right, Raphael," he said. "You're in charge while your father is away. We'll all work as hard as we can, and we'll keep the operation going. Nobody has anything better lined up, anyway, so what choice do we have? We'll continue to do a good job, and hopefully it'll all work out and your dad will come back before too long. We'll help in any way we can."

The men were all highly skilled and had served their apprenticeships as youngsters in the leatherworkers' area, a part of the city that was dedicated to leatherworking, a craft that Cairo was noted for. They had all started there as children in the tannery, where leather was cured using technology that was many thousands of years old. In Egypt in the 1940s, leatherworkers still used the same techniques that had been around in the days of the pharaohs. Animal faeces were rubbed into the skins, and in particular the droppings of birds, which were so acidic that they could be used to remove hair from the animal skins—mostly cow, goat, and sheep. Next, there was a particular type of bean, high in tannins, that was used to tan the skins and get them ready to be worked. The modern technique of using chromium was not yet widespread.

The process of making leather was very smelly, and nobody who could afford to live elsewhere had a home near the leatherworkers' area—but the leatherworkers themselves quickly became accustomed to the smell and even wore it as a badge of honour, because it showed that they were honest working men. Egypt was considered one of the leading nations in the leather industry. Nonetheless, the war was on, and even the very skilled men who now worked for Raphael would not find it easy to locate work elsewhere, as demand was down.

At home, Raphael allowed some self-doubt to enter his mind. How the hell was he supposed to manage a leather workshop? Of course, he had accompanied Dad to work sometimes and had seen how he did things, but it was not as though he knew how to run a business on his own. Then he banished the doubt. He didn't have any choice, did he? He would have to come up with some plan to start selling goods soon, because he had seen the books and he knew that his father had many creditors.

Then he remembered Lilian Cohen. Lately, Raphael had got to know some of the people who frequented the court of King Farouk, and Lilian was one of them. Raphael was friendly with a photographer, Elia, who lived near the palace and knew all about who went in and who came out. Elia had been hired by the king before to take photographs; despite the pomp and circumstance attached to the monarchy, the palace perimeter was surprisingly porous, and people found it quite easy to go in and out. Moreover, King Farouk couldn't survive without adulation and loved to have ordinary people around him to bask in his magnificence, as he saw it.

Elia was very fond of Raphael. He knew that the boy had been left behind to take care of the business, and he took to giving Raphael information about the goings-on of the courtiers, in case some of the information might be useful in terms of getting work. Elia had introduced Raphael to Lilian some time ago, thinking that she might be a useful contact for him. Lilian was a Jewish girl whom everyone knew to be the mistress of the king, because Farouk didn't hide any of his affairs—rather, he flaunted them. His wife, knowing her place, put up with it.

King Farouk was obsessed with the idea of European glamour and spent a fortune on lavish furniture and house decorations made in the French and Italian style. Farouk had no idea how ordinary people lived, and he didn't care. His whole lifetime had been spent in a gilded palace, being given whatever he wanted by people who were paid to pretend to love and revere him. Well, right at the moment, Raphael didn't have time to worry about matters of social justice. If he could persuade King Farouk to buy some of his products, he just might be able to save the business.

Raphael knew that Lilian would understand what he needed. She was a clever, cynical young woman who knew that the king had other mistresses than her—quite apart from his wife—but that her romantic connection could serve her well and, by extension, help anyone she wished to share her good fortune with. Hoping that Lilian could be useful to him, Raphael called over to see her and decided to turn on the charm, with the idea that she would put in a word with the courtiers on his behalf and maybe even arrange for him to meet the king. Maybe he was being a little cocky, but he was sure that if only he could meet Farouk in person, he would be able to persuade the king to make the workshop the palace's number-one supplier of leather goods. With the constant coming and going of ladies from high society, the palace was already one of the biggest customers of top-end handbags.

"You know, Lilian," he said, "my dad had to go on a business trip to Sudan, and he's left me in charge of the leather workshop until he comes back, which could be months or even years from now. I don't go to school now, because I'm busy at work."

"Really?" said Lilian, impressed. "So you're the boss now? No lessons? Nobody to boss you around and tell you when to go to bed? Not bad for a nipper like you!"

"Well," said Raphael, standing tall and sticking out his chest, "I am the boss until Dad comes back, at least. And then, eh"—here he was extemporising—"I am planning to go into business on my own when a good opportunity comes up."

"That's very exciting," Lilian said, a touch of amusement lightening her tone. "Don't you wish you had someone around to give you advice, though? No offence, but you're still pretty young, and that's a lot to take on when you're only just out of short trousers."

"Well, I know what I'm doing," Raphael lied. "But the thing is ... Dad had to leave in a rush because of some family business, and I've got a bit of a cash flow problem at the moment. I really don't want to bother him, so I am trying to sort it out on my own if I can. I'm trying to think of a way of selling as many handbags as possible as quickly as I can. I was wondering if maybe you could help. Is there some way you could convince the king to buy some of my things? One big order right now would make all the difference."

Lilian furrowed her brow in thought. Then her face brightened.

"I know!" she said. "The Royal Ball is coming up soon. That might be a great opportunity for you."

The Royal Ball was an annual event when all the richest and most influential people gathered at the king's palace for a grand banquet and dance.

"I can always get Farouk to do what I tell him," Lilian boasted. "You know what I am going to do? I am going to tell him that when the queen in England has a ball, all the women have to have matching handbags with the royal insignia on them. I'm sure it's not true, but if he believes it, that's what he will want—he always wants to keep up with the European royals—and that's where you'll come in. Would you be able to make a few hundred matching handbags very quickly?"

"Of course!" said Raphael, though he was not entirely certain of it. "That's no problem at all."

Lilian's plan worked, and the next day, when Raphael came to her house for news, he was handed an order for four hundred identical bags that would be given as gifts to the beautiful young ladies at the ball.

Fareed and the rest of the men worked harder than ever before to meet the deadline, and somehow, they managed it. The bags—dyed, stamped, and embossed with the king's insignia—were delivered on time. With the money they made, Raphael was able to clear all debts with the creditors and give the men a bonus for their hard work.

Well, Raphael thought. *That was easier than I expected!*

That evening, Raphael sat down and wrote a letter to his mother, explaining how he had saved the business. Proudly, he was able to enclose a little money for the family in Sudan, to help them with their living expenses. He knew that it must be really stressful for his mother having to rely on the charity of relatives. In their last letter to him, his parents had explained that Joseph was still looking for work but that nothing had turned up as yet.

"Don't worry about a thing. When it comes to Egypt," Raphael wrote grandly, "I've got everything under control."

Privately, Raphael wondered what his dad had been so worried about and why he was struggling so badly now. Clearly, running a business was not as complicated as he had been led to believe. Then again, Joseph had never had the same talent for business as his father, Eli.

Raphael went around to the palace area in the hope of finding Lilian. Having tracked her down, he invited her for a drink to thank her for the help she had given him.

"I'm just glad it all worked out," said Lilian. "It's good to be able to give a hand."

"I hope you don't mind me asking," said Raphael, "but what's it like, being the mistress of the king?"

"Oh, it's not so bad," she said. "I think of it as a job, in a way. I'm certainly not in it for the passion. I mean, look at him. He's still a young man, but he's really going to seed."

Lilian took another sip of her drink. She was obviously in the mood for talking.

"The king is a *terrible* lover," she confided to Raphael. "You wouldn't believe it—his penis is tiny, smaller than my thumb, and he doesn't have a clue what to do with it. I honestly don't know how he managed to get his wife knocked up. Maybe she's seeing someone behind his back and he's not even the father. He's so lazy he prefers to stay in one spot and make the woman do all the work. He used to be good-looking, back when he was younger, before he got married, but lately he's been eating so much, he's getting really fat. So fat he actually has to lift his belly up with his own hand to see his own private parts. Can you imagine? Guess what he has for breakfast? Caviar and champagne! And he drinks about thirty fizzy drinks a day. Did you ever hear the like?"

"Why do you keep seeing him then?"

For a moment, Lilian looked weary. "I can't stop now," she replied. "Not until he gets tired of me. He's got a morbid fascination with everything Jewish. Although he doesn't understand a word, he makes me sing to him in Yiddish. He'd make things a nightmare for the whole family if I left him, because if there's one thing he can't stand, it's the feeling that he's not in control of the situation. But it's OK; he's already getting bored with me. One of these days he'll pay me off, and I'll be able to buy myself a house, become a respectable lady again, and put it all behind me. Maybe I'll even get married and have a family of my own."

Raphael appreciated the fact that Lilian was prepared to speak to him openly about sex, especially because he was so young. He wondered if she assumed that he was already experienced, or if she didn't realise how young he was. He wished he could tell her, or indeed anyone, that he had already been introduced into the world of sex; he had made love with Miss Mackzumi. He was determined that he wouldn't be like Farouk—a bad lover whose women couldn't wait for the relationship to end.

That night, Raphael went once again to sleep in his family's empty apartment, his head full of thoughts of Miss Mackzumi and what he would do with her if he had the opportunity to see her again. Perhaps now that he was a young gent with his own business, she would see him as a real man?

Raphael couldn't stop thinking about sex. If only he was older, he would be able to take a mistress. The king had Lilian and several other mistresses too, so why not him? Most of the businessmen in Cairo had a mistress, whether they were married or not. They often kept a special room in the office for entertaining them, took them to nightclubs to smoke hashish, or, if they could afford it, rented them an apartment where they could stay and receive visits. Of course, many of the mistresses were themselves the wives of other men. Nobody would have guessed, to see them in their modest clothing on the street, that they had such rich sex lives out of the view of their husbands. This situation was an open secret; everyone knew about it, but nobody ever discussed it, or at least not in public.

Of course, at just 14, Raphael was not yet in a position to take a mistress, married or single. However, he knew that there were women who would go to bed with him in exchange for money, and he reasoned that as he was now making money of his own, it was up to him to decide what to do with it.

One day, on his way to buy supplies for the warehouse, Raphael was walking through the red-light district when he noticed a provocatively dressed woman looking at him invitingly. As his eyes passed over her generous curves, he felt that familiar tingle in his groin.

Why not? he thought to himself. *I might as well. I'm a man now. I know what it's all about. Why should I deprive myself? Anyway, there's a war on. We could all die anytime, and then I'd be sorry!*

He walked a little further until he reached a brothel that he had heard men talking about, saying that it was the best in the business and that the women who worked there were clean and polite and didn't pick their customers' pockets when they were distracted, as so many of the prostitutes did. The ordinary British soldiers couldn't afford to go there on their time off, but the officers did. He knew what the fee was and that he had enough money in his pocket to cover it.

A little nervously, he pushed open the door and walked in. The reception area was clean and tidy and looked reassuringly like the lobby of a hotel. A pretty blonde woman came forward and shook his hand, introducing herself as "Maddy".

"Well," Maddy said, a teasing note in her French-accented voice, "and how can I help you? I don't believe we've met before."

"Umm ..."

"Don't worry, I'm only joking with you. I know why you're here, and it's nothing to be embarrassed about. I've seen it all before, as you can imagine! Come on in."

Maddy led Raphael to an attractively decorated room with a large bed.

"Would you like to sit down?" she asked. "Make yourself at home. You're so handsome, you know. I bet all the girls tell you what beautiful eyes you have. And your hair looks like a movie star's!"

"Thanks ..."

Raphael did as she suggested and perched on the edge of the bed. He could not help feeling flattered by Maddy's remarks about his appearance, even though he knew that she was a professional and probably had sweet words for all of her customers. It was nice to hear her say that he was attractive, and she sounded like she meant it.

He wondered what he was supposed to do next. Should he take off his clothes straight away? Would she want to be paid now, or only after he had done what he came for? Was he supposed to woo her with pretty words, or would she be business-like and take the initiative?

"Is this your first time?" she asked. "You're very young."

Raphael thought about that day with Miss Mackzumi. Did that count? It would be easier to just say it was his first time instead of telling the whole story.

"It's my first time," he said. "I'm sorry."

"Sweetie, there's nothing to be sorry for. Everyone has a first time. Well, let's make sure it's a *lovely* time then. Aren't I lucky, getting to be with you for such a special occasion?"

Very tenderly, almost as though she was his mother, Maddy took off Raphael's clothes until he was naked.

"You're a very handsome boy," she said, looking him up and down. "You look much more like a man with your clothes off than you do with them on. I can see very well that you are all grown up."

"What about you?" Raphael asked. "Aren't you going to take your clothes off too?"

Raphael had never seen a naked woman in real life before—Miss Mackzumi had simply removed her underwear and raised her dress to grant him access to her luscious body—and now that he was here, he could hardly wait.

"Don't be impatient!" she chided him gently. "It's more fun if there's a little suspense. Now that you're naked, maybe you can help me to take off my things. Don't rush now, you've got all the time in the world. I'm not going to make a boy who's here for the first time hurry up."

With eager fingers, he fumbled with her buttons and removed her shirt and skirt. Underneath, she was not wearing anything. Maddy was about 30 years old, and her body was that of a perfect, mature woman. Her heavy breasts were still shapely, and her waist was trim; she was very attractive. Nervous as he was, he was relieved to have an erection.

"Now we're ready for business," Maddy said. She held him in her arms and pressed her body against his for a long moment. Then she let go of him and lay down on the bed, smiling up at him. Raphael stood and looked at her naked body, which appeared to have been made of porcelain. Her skin shone white against the dark red counterpane. Her large breasts hung slightly to the sides of her ribcage, and she had a patch of hair, darker than the light hair on her head, where her legs met.

"Don't leave me on my own down here," she said. "I'm waiting for you. I want to feel your beautiful body pressing down on mine, the way God intended. Are you coming to me?"

Slowly and steadily, Raphael lowered himself onto the bed and lay his body out over Maddy's. He could feel her breasts pressing against his chest and her legs start to part as his thighs pushed against them.

"*That's* more like it," she said. She took his face in her hands and kissed it tenderly. "What a lovely boy you are." Her legs opened fully beneath him, and she tilted her pelvis upward to receive him.

Enflamed with passion, Raphael entered Maddy's body and, moments later, reached a glorious climax that was like nothing he had ever felt before. With a groan, he collapsed onto her body and buried his face against her shoulder, breathing in the scent of her French perfume.

"That was amazing," he said, with genuine gratitude. "I'm sorry it was so quick."

"For a beginner," Maddy said, "you did very well."

"Really?"

"Absolutely, but there's still a lot I can teach you, if you feel like coming back again. I can teach you to be a wonderful lover. That'd be a really good investment in your future. Women really appreciate a man who wants them to have as good a time as him. So many men just want to rush and don't care about the woman. If you can learn how to please women, they can experience orgasms far more intense than anything a man feels. The trick is learning how to control your own orgasm. The more you can delay it, the more pleasure the woman will experience, and the more she'll want to have sex with you again, and again, and again. Believe me, if you can master the art of lovemaking now, the women in your life will appreciate it later on."

"I'd *love* to come back! I'll be back next week, I promise."

Raphael fumbled with the money he had brought for Maddy. He didn't want to insult her by handing it over too abruptly, but he didn't want her to think that he was hesitant about paying, either. Seeing his indecision, she smiled.

"Just leave the money on the dresser, sweetie," she said. "I'm sure I don't need to count it."

Raphael walked home after his time with Maddy with his head in the clouds. He was so distracted, he didn't see Uncle Ali when he arrived at the apartment building. Uncle Ali had to tap him on the shoulder.

"What's going on, young man?" Uncle Ali laughed. "You're lost in thought!"

Raphael just smiled. "Not much," he said. "I just had a nice evening."

"When I saw you walking towards the building," Uncle Ali said, "I hardly recognised you at first. You've changed lately, turned from a boy into a man. I wonder if your mother would even know who you were if she passed you on the street!"

Over the next few months, Maddy taught Raphael all she knew. He took her lessons to heart, especially the one she repeated most often: "Always love your partner in bed as though she is the only woman whom God has ever created. Every woman is special, and they all need to know that they are cherished. It doesn't matter whether the woman is your wife or if it's a one-night thing and you'll never see her again. However long you have together, she should know that you care for her. Women have to put up with so much in their lives. They need to hear that they are special."

Apart from the sex, which he enjoyed enormously, Raphael had grown fond of Maddy and come to regard her as a friend. Increasingly, they shared their stories and hopes for their future. Maddy was from a rural part of northern France. She had gone to Paris as a young woman and worked in an upmarket patisserie, serving clients their fancy pastries on dainty china plates. As a young and very beautiful girl, she had been swept off her feet by an Egyptian man, in Paris for business, who had persuaded her to leave France and come to Egypt, telling her that they would get married and she would have a wonderful life there. He had shown her photographs of a lavish home, which he assured her was his, and promised that she would live there and raise a family with him. Her family had been aghast when she had written to tell them the plan.

Before going to Paris, Maddy had grown up in a small house with her parents, her younger brother, and her sister. Her father and mother were a simple but respectable couple. Her father was a Jewish man from Poland who had been in France as a soldier during the First World War. There he had met her mother, fallen for her, and settled down with her in the small town where she had grown up. He worked as a painter and decorator, she took care of the house and children, and they were known locally as a hardworking pair. Her younger brother worked with his father and was engaged to be married to a local farmer's daughter, which meant that he would inherit the land and take a step up the social ladder. They all wrote to Maddy, warning her not to take at face value any of the plans and promises the man made. How could she be so foolish as to believe that a wealthy Egyptian man would want to marry a waitress from a humble background?

"If he really loves you," her mother wrote, "why has he not asked you to bring him here, to meet your family? Trust me, darling, and leave him at once. He will break your heart."

Maddy had been so angry with her parents for refusing to be happy for her that she had written back straight away, accusing them of trying to destroy her chance at married bliss and telling them not to write again. She was perfectly sure that her lover was Mr Right and that he would give her a wonderful life in Egypt.

However, once he got her back to his own country, he abandoned her and returned to his wife and children. Ashamed, heartbroken, and without funds, Maddy had stayed on, and the only way she had been able to make a living was as a prostitute. Initially, she rejected the idea of working as a prostitute out of hand. She had been brought up in a respectable family and knew that her parents would have been shocked and horrified to hear of her doing this sort of work. If word had got out to their friends and neighbours that their pretty daughter was working as a prostitute, they would have been mortified. But what else was there?

Hearing a French accent in a bar in downtown Cairo, Maddy introduced herself to the barman, who was from Paris, and he gave her a cup of coffee on the house. As she sipped, she asked him what sort of work a girl like her might be able to find in Cairo, adding that she was prepared to do almost anything and wasn't at all afraid of hard work. She was down to her last few pounds and couldn't even afford a hotel room for the night. He had laughed.

"A girl like you? Do you have any training, any education?" he asked.

Maddy shook her head. She was a good basic cook and an experienced waitress, but she had left school early with no qualifications.

"Honestly," the barman said, "if you want to stay in Egypt and make your own living, you're going to have to swallow your pride and start turning tricks. A pretty white girl like you is literally sitting on a goldmine, as the saying goes. Put in a few years in a brothel and you'll be able to save enough money to set yourself up in a little business of your own—or you might get lucky and persuade one of your wealthy clients to take you on as his mistress, or even marry you. It's not easy for women to find other types of work in Egypt, especially foreign women. Unless you've a way to get back to Paris, that's your best chance of making some real money. Look; I know someone in the business. She's a decent sort, and she doesn't rip her girls off. If you like, you can go and talk to her and see if she has a position for you. It's the best brothel in town. They'll take care of you there and make sure that you get a fair share of the money you earn."

The barman gave her a sympathetic smile and turned to a customer with an order. Maddy sipped her coffee and thought. She realised that he was right. And there was no reason for her to be so proud, either. After all, she'd given up a job in Paris to go to Egypt, thinking that she was going to become the wife of a rich man. Was working as a prostitute really so very different to marrying for money?

Maddy finished her coffee and made her way to the address in the red-light district that the barman had given her. She was desperate and knew that this was her last chance. She carried the few belongings she had in a small overnight case, and she had just a handful of coins left. If she wasn't taken on at the brothel, she didn't know what she was going to do.

As it turned out, the French barman was right. The manager of the brothel only had to look Maddy over once to see that she would be a big draw, with her pale skin and picture-perfect appearance. They hired her on the spot and even gave her a small advance so that she could buy some pretty clothes and find a small apartment to live in.

Within weeks, Maddy was seeing a few regular clients and earning a decent living. She had overcome her initial revulsion at the thought of renting out her body for sex and accepted that it was a financial transaction like any other. At the same time, she was too embarrassed to write to her family and tell them that all of their predictions had, in fact, come true. One day, she told herself, she would open her own patisserie back home in France, and then she would get back in touch with her parents and her brother and put things right between them. She was putting a little money aside every week in the hope of making her dreams come true, and she had worked hard to learn good Arabic, so that when she left the brothel she would be able to get a good job somewhere else and strive until she had enough money to make a triumphant return to her homeland. Maddy told Raphael her story, and he shared with her his dreams for the future.

"By the time my dreams come true," he said, "you won't be working here anymore. You're too good for this kind of thing."

"Oh honey, I hope you're right," Maddy sighed. "Believe me, doing this kind of work was never how I saw my life working out when I was younger. I always thought I'd open up my own patisserie one day, and I'm even saving a little money every week … but to be honest, that dream seems as far away as ever."

When Raphael was fifteen and a half, Maddy pronounced him fully trained and told him that she wouldn't see him anymore, because she had taught him all he needed to know to satisfy the women he went to bed with.

Raphael was crestfallen. "Why are you telling me not to come anymore?" he asked. "Our time together is my favourite part of every week, and not just because of the sex. You're the only person I know who I can really talk to."

"Oh, you can still come for a chat now and again," she said. "But I think it's time you started to experience other women. I know two lovely girls, Aziza and Hamida. I've told them to expect you, and

I'm sure you're going to like them a lot. You know, as we've become friends, I've started thinking of you as if you were a younger brother. That's another reason why it's time for you to move on; it doesn't feel right, making love with someone who seems like a brother to me!"

Maddy handed Raphael a business card with the girls' address on it.

"They really know what they are doing," she said, "and they're perfectly clean, reliable, and honest. You don't need to worry about a thing with these two."

"Well," said Raphael rather forlornly. "Thanks for everything."

"You're welcome, darling. Can I just ask you one question before you go?"

"Anything."

"What's that strange necklace you have on all the time?"

"Oh, it was a gift from my mum. She got it for me when I was a baby, and she told me to wear it all the time now that she and Dad have gone. It's supposed to keep me safe. I promised her I'd never take it off. At first, I wasn't sure what to think, but now I really believe that it's helping me."

"Well, do what she says then. Something tells me that it's important—and God knows that these are terrible times, and a kid on his own like you needs all the help he can get."

Maddy was right when she said that Raphael was ready to expand his sexual horizons. Aziza and Hamida—two very pretty girls with lovely, young, lithe bodies—were charming. After the master classes he had received from Maddy, Raphael was no longer even slightly nervous about sex, and he enjoyed their sessions together immensely. He recalled what Maddy had told him about remembering that every woman was special and was always courteous and kind to the two girls. They appreciated it, especially because prostitutes were typically considered to be the lowest of the low in Cairene society. With appalling hypocrisy, a large percentage of the men in Egypt frequented prostitutes but also despised them and bad-mouthed them in public. Raphael found this impossible to understand. He recognised the special gift these women had given him, and he would always appreciate it.

One day, walking back from the brothel, Raphael passed by Elia's photography shop near the palace. Elia came rushing out.

"You'll never guess what happened," he said.

"What?"

"Well, it's really terrible, actually. Remember Lilian? Lilian Cohen, the king's mistress? She was flying back to Egypt from somewhere or other and her plane crashed. She's dead. Smashed to smithereens! And just last week, she was telling me that she was sure she was going to be let go by the king really soon and that she was looking forward to getting on with the rest of her life and forgetting about him at last. I saw her in passing just yesterday—she waved at me from the other side of the street. I can't believe she's gone; it's such a shame."

Raphael hadn't known Lilian extremely well, but the news struck him more than he would have expected. It was shocking to think of someone's life just being snuffed out like that. He wondered for a moment if the crash had been Farouk's way of getting rid of her, but then he dismissed that thought. No; all he had to do was just dump her, like he had dumped so many others. She wouldn't have made a fuss or tried to embarrass him, because she couldn't wait to be released from the relationship. Lilian had been unlucky, that was all. It was just too bad she hadn't lived long enough to make all the tedious hours she had spent with a man she clearly despised worth her while.

Well, Raphael would always remember Lilian with gratitude, as her help had saved the workshop and made it possible for him to stay on in Cairo on his own, without having to worry about where the money was going to come from.

2017

"I'm still kind of shocked that Grandad's parents would leave him alone in Cairo at that age," said Rebecca. "I mean, he was still a kid. Anything could have happened. The war was still on, after all. He was very vulnerable. If I had kids, I would *never* leave one of them alone at that age, no matter how confident they seemed to be."

"Sure," said Richard, "but he didn't see it that way. He got to live in his own apartment and make his own money—and do you think he'd have had a sex life like that, at that age, if his parents had been around to cramp his style? Definitely not."

"Well, maybe he shouldn't have," Rebecca countered. "A boy of that age should be inviting his first girlfriend out to go to the cinema and have an ice cream, not frequenting a brothel. It's not right."

"Good for him, is what I say," interjected David. "He saw what he wanted and he went out and got it. Life was different then. Girls from his own social class were very protected, I bet. Going to a pro was probably the best thing he could have done at the time."

"Look," said Richard. "These were different times. For me, the most interesting part of this story is not the fact that he was going to the brothel at 14 but that the woman he met there became one of the most important and influential friends he ever had."

"Something tells me you'll be telling us more about her," said Rebecca. "She sounds like quite the character."

"Wait and see!" said Richard.

"I wonder what Flora would have thought if she had known about his close friendship with Maddy," Rebecca wondered. "In some ways, it seems that Maddy played a maternal role in his life."

"My guess is that she would have been horrified at first," said David, "but when she realised how much the two really meant to each other, she would have been grateful that someone was there for him, even if that someone worked as a prostitute."

CHAPTER 6

SUCCESS AND TROUBLE

2017

"Grandad was writing regularly to his family in Sudan," Richard explained, "so even though he didn't see them for a long time, they knew that he was just fine. He told them how well the leather workshop was doing, and he sent money sometimes, but of course his mum still worried about him. Sure, she'd given him the amulet, and she had faith in its ability to keep him safe, but he was still very young and very far from his family …"

1947

After the war, all across Europe and North Africa, the surviving troops headed home. The full story of what had happened to the Jews of Europe began to emerge in all its dreadful detail over the course of the next few years. Some people still refused to accept that what they were hearing about the concentration camps and the mass slaughter was true, but it became progressively harder to reject the awful truth, especially when newspapers started to publish images of thousands of bodies, naked and emaciated, piled into mass graves, and of the huge ovens the Nazis had used for burning masses of corpses.

On November 29, 1947, one of the first actions of the United Nations had been to make a resolution in favour of the partition of Palestine, with the aim of creating a Jewish state. In the Jewish cities of Palestine, there had been celebrations in the streets. For the Jews remaining in other Middle Eastern countries, it was clear that their time there was numbered. In Egypt, the newspapers became ever more virulent in their anti-Jewish rhetoric, despite the fact that the sitting government was moderate, did not favour violent actions against what was an increasingly vulnerable minority, and even imprisoned Muslim radicals. The Egyptian press wrote article after article, harping back to the Balfour Declaration of 1917, calling it illegitimate and shameful, and inflaming the sentiments of an already volatile population.

The leather workshop was doing better than ever following the end of the war, and increasingly, fashionable Cairene women came to buy handbags and other leather products, while some of the international pilots flying into Cairo had taken to purchasing bags in bulk to sell in their own countries. Some of the Egyptian movie stars had been introduced to the shop by a movie producer who happened to be a distant relative of Raphael's, and every time one of them was seen—or better yet, photographed—carrying one of the workshop's bags, everyone wanted to buy one for themselves. The Egyptian film industry was big, and very influential, not just in Egypt but right across the Arab world, where it was known for the high quality of its spoken Arabic and the wonderful Egyptian sense of humour.

Raphael loved it when film stars came to the shop, as they were all beautiful women who dressed in gorgeous, provocative, Western-style clothing, with their décolleté very much on display; he deliberately put his most appealing handbags on the lowest shelf in the shop so that the women would have to bend down to see them, showing a generous portion of their busts in the process. Raphael had taken on more workers to cope with the additional demand and was producing a larger number of products than he was able to sell on his own. He had asked a Nubian man working as a doorman in his area if he could recommend anyone who might be able to do some publicity for the workshop, and the man had suggested his own son, who went by the nickname "Sambo".

Sambo—a lively, pretty lad of about twelve, with chubby cheeks and a huge smile—was happy to dress in a bright red coat, white trousers, and a hat, and to stand outside the shop on the weekends. As Sambo made such an eye-catching spectacle, all the passers-by noticed him and looked over. At which point, he would gesture for them to come inside and see the products for sale. Business grew bigger than ever.

Raphael had heard of a Sudanese businessman, a Mr Ibrahim Ali, who was interested in his wares, and he set out one day to meet the man, with a view to convincing Mr Ali to sell some of the products produced at the workshop.

The main street of Cairo, Fouad Street, was lined with department stores—many of them owned by Jewish businessmen—selling high-end products of every description. A large park filled with shady trees and flower beds lay behind it. The street was famous for its luxury shopping, and especially for Cicurel's department store, to which all the wealthy women flocked for their elegant clothing and French perfume. Beyond the park again was the madrasa school that Raphael had studied at as a child, a few years before. As he traversed the park on the way to his meeting, he looked at the low white building. How small it looked now, compared to how it had seemed to him as a child! He remembered when it had seemed enormous.

Raphael wondered how the imam was, remembering how much the kind, gentle man had taught him. He thought of going in to say hello, but business seemed more pressing at the moment. He continued through the park, which was filled with throngs of children and their young mothers, and with ice cream vendors and street musicians. As one of the few green spaces in the city, it was always very popular, even now that the ordinary people of Cairo were struggling so badly to keep their families fed and clothed. Looking around, he enjoyed the sense of peace and the joyful cries of the little children. They were too young to know how stressed and upset their parents were; all they knew about was play. He had been like them, just a few years ago. How long ago that seemed!

He passed by Gategno, a store owned by a prominent local Jewish family that sold silverware, tableware, and beautiful items for the home. How much longer would it still be there? Jewish businesses were closing all over the city. He banished the thought. He had to believe that everything was going to be fine, because what was the alternative?

Reaching the street where he had an appointment, Raphael approached Mr Ibrahim's shop. Entering, he shook hands with the proprietor and laid out some sample handbags for him to inspect. As Mr Ibrahim looked at the leather goods, examining them inside and out, a tall, well-built young man with blond hair and blue eyes walked in.

"Oh," said Mr Ibrahim. "Allow me to present you. Raphael, this is my friend Hans Schwartzkopf. We met in Sudan on one of my recent trips. Hans works in the petrol industry and a few other areas, and he's quite the entrepreneur. Hans, this is my good friend Raphael Romano. Please consider yourselves introduced."

Hans reached out a friendly hand and Raphael shook it.

"It's nice to meet you," Hans said. He had a big, friendly smile.

"Likewise," responded Raphael. He liked the look of Hans. Obviously, Hans could see that Raphael was a great deal younger than himself, but he clearly didn't care. He didn't treat Raphael any differently because of it.

When Mr Ibrahim and Raphael had concluded their business, Hans invited Raphael to go to a tearoom with him for a drink. The two men hit it off, and Hans—who was about ten years older than Raphael, and who had been living in Cairo for some time—promised to stay in touch if any interesting business opportunities arose. From then on, the two young men saw each other socially from time to time. Hans was an open-minded, curious individual who liked living in Egypt and learning about Egyptian culture. Raphael, for his part, enjoyed this new friendship with a European whose outlook on life was quite different from what Raphael was used to. Hans was prepared to make a deal with anyone who could help him to achieve his goals.

*   *   *

Like so many others, Raphael was devastated by how things were changing for the Jews in Cairo. How could the Jews of Egypt go back to enjoying friendly relationships with their neighbours when they had seen how mercurial these friendships actually were—and how little it took for their friends to renounce them? How could King Farouk care so very little for his people that he seemed prepared to give them up just because they did not belong to the majority religious faith?

After the Allies' victory, the collective consensus seemed to be to pretend that the king had never curried favour with the Germans—but the Jews of Cairo had had a wake-up call, and they increasingly realised that as much as they loved their city, it did not love them. They would have to find new homes elsewhere or endure whatever treatment the Egyptian government of the day meted out.

For the remaining Jews, the atmosphere in Cairo had changed dramatically. The main reason was the fact that more and more Jews were moving to Palestine, where they hoped to found a Jewish state before long, pinning their hopes on the Balfour Declaration of 1917—the first time in modern history that a definitive plan for a Jewish Israel had been put forward—and the collective salving of a guilty European conscience, as the full truth of what happened to the Jews of Europe gradually emerged. Israel was their Promised Land, and they were determined to see it happen. The Egyptian government, however, was equally determined to stand in the way of the foundation of a Jewish state, and the press and the mosques were full of anti-Jewish rhetoric.

At the forefront of the movement of hatred was the Muslim Brotherhood, which had been founded in 1928 with the intention of establishing Sharia law worldwide as the basis of law and statehood. It was driven by highly educated men and sought to expel foreign influence from already established Islamic states. At one point, the political party supporting the king had come down hard on the Muslim Brotherhood, which was steadily becoming more radical and more anti-Jewish. But that was no longer the case. The people were told that the Jews had come to Egypt with nothing; they had been given everything they needed to eat and drink and had been allowed to set up homes and businesses and they had now revealed themselves as traitors to the land that had given them so much and wanted to take over Egypt and steal its territory.

Muslim shopkeepers who had once been friendly now barked at Jewish customers to keep their dirty hands off the fruits and vegetables, or even refused to serve them altogether. It really hurt when the shopkeepers and stallholders in question were ones who, until just recently, had always had a friendly smile and had addressed their Jewish customers by name. It was as though some evil force had taken over their bodies and transformed them from friends into enemies.

For Raphael, as for so many others, one of the final straws was the case of the beauty queen and the king. Claire was a schoolgirl, age 15, who had been presented as a debutante and had been crowned Miss Egypt because of her striking good looks. With her blonde hair, porcelain skin, and enormous blue eyes, she was a real beauty, and something of a local celebrity as a result. The newspapers had been full of photographs of her, and the Jewish community had been very proud that one of their own had won the prize, especially considering the way things had been going lately. It was nice to have something to celebrate, even something as trivial as a beauty contest. Because of the victory, Claire had been invited to take part in a ball at the palace. In fact, King Farouk himself had sent one of his colonels, who served as chief of protocol, to go to the girl's house to deliver the invitation in person.

Claire's parents, Abraham and Astra, lived in a modest apartment in the Jewish Quarter—just three rooms with a bathroom that they had to share with two other families. They were quiet people who had never sought the limelight, and they liked to keep themselves to themselves. Abraham ran a stationery shop and Astra stayed home and took care of the house. Claire was their only child and their pride and joy. They were absolutely astonished when they answered a knock on the door to find the king's colonel standing there in full military regalia. He clicked his heels together and stood to attention.

"How can I help you?" asked Claire's astonished father. His first thought, on seeing the uniform, had been that maybe they were in trouble of some sort. After all, these were difficult times. But then the colonel saluted, so it must be something else. It was all very extraordinary.

"I have come to issue *this*," the colonel said and grandly handed over an envelope containing an invitation printed on a heavy embossed card edged with gold.

"What is it?" Abraham asked, gingerly accepted the card and passing it to Astra, who opened it and withdrew the card. She looked at it nervously, as though it might explode and kill them all.

"It's an invitation for your daughter, Claire, from His Majesty himself. She's to attend the Grand Ball as his guest of honour!"

"I don't think so," Abraham responded, attempting to return the business card. "We're simple people, and Claire is just a very young girl who has never gone anywhere without her parents. She would not know what to do at a grand ball nor how to talk to the king. We're not used to mixing with people like that, and Claire is not allowed to go out without her mother or me."

"If it's a question of money, don't worry," said the colonel. "The king will provide funds for her to buy a dress and whatever else she needs. He would be delighted to ensure that such a pretty girl is properly dressed for a grand occasion at the court!"

"Please tell him that we are deeply honoured, and very grateful, but the answer is still no. Claire is far too young to attend an event like this."

"I don't think you understand," the colonel said with an unpleasant grin. "This invitation is not optional. The king has seen your daughter, and he is *very* impressed by her, if you get my meaning. He wants to have her at the ball, and if he takes a liking to her, she will stay on afterwards, too. All you have to do is take the money, get her ready, and hand her over. It's not very difficult to understand, and I don't think that you are in a position to refuse him, do you? After all, he is the king, and you are nothing but a shopkeeper—and a *Jewish* shopkeeper, at that. If I were you, with all the things that people are saying about Jews at the moment, I would not want to annoy the king!"

Astra burst into tears and clapped her hands over her mouth. She understood perfectly well what was going on. The king, who was used to buying and selling whomever he took a fancy to, had decided that he wanted to have sex with their daughter. As she was from a Jewish family, and the situation of the Jews was increasingly precarious, despite the victory of the Allies, they were being tacitly threatened: hand your daughter over or else.

"I think we understand each other," the colonel said. "Don't we? I will tell His Majesty that he can look forward to having the company of your daughter at the ball … *and* after the guests have gone home. Don't worry; she'll be returned to you in one piece. You should both be very proud. This is a great honour that is bestowed on very few girls. Claire is a very lucky young lady indeed."

The colonel left, and Claire's mother and father urgently discussed what they needed to do next. King Farouk loved to cultivate a playboy lifestyle, and everyone knew about his reputation with women. Everyone in Cairo knew about the many mistresses he had; he liked to collect women as though they were trinkets and liked it best of all if the women "collected" could be stolen from someone else; their husbands, fiancés, or fathers.

Farouk's kleptomania in general had long been a national embarrassment. Instead of the national symbol he should have been, he was a constant source of shame. In his formal photographs, he invariably wore a fez—seen as the headwear of Egypt since its introduction, when Egypt had been under the rule of the Ottoman Empire—and represented himself as a national figurehead. In reality, most Egyptians just wished that he would simply disappear along with his wife, his children, and his mother, Nazli. He pilfered money and jewellery from the pockets and purses of visiting dignitaries, including Winston Churchill; had stolen a ceremonial sword, belt, and medals from the coffin of the deceased Shah of Persia, causing a rift in diplomatic relations between the two countries; and had hired a pickpocket to come to the palace and teach him how to steal.

When he ate in restaurants, he rolled his bread into little balls and threw it at the other diners. He liked to burp loudly in people's faces, simply to embarrass them, and when he had a number of nightmares about lions, he went straight to the Cairo Zoo and shot its lions dead in their cages. He didn't even pretend not to engage in many of the activities deemed unacceptable in Egypt. For instance, he loved playing cards and compounded the sin by cheating. He was said to have presented a hand, during a game of poker, consisting of three kings, and to have claimed that there were really four, because he himself was the third, and that therefore his was the winning hand.

Of him, people often commented that if God had identified seven deadly sins, Farouk was certainly capable of finding an eighth. Now he had set his sights on the virginity of a young girl from a respectable but humble family of the small, vulnerable Jewish community. If Claire went to the ball, it was obvious that it would be for one reason only. Afterwards, everyone would know that Claire was no longer a virgin—and, in her small, conservative community, that would spell disaster for her marriage prospects and her reputation, not to mention the trauma she would have suffered for being mistreated in this way.

"We can't let our daughter be dishonoured like this!" Astra insisted. "She's just a young girl, and she has her whole future at stake. Our Claire is no prostitute, to be sold to the highest bidder, even if he *is* the king. We'll have to protect her, whatever it takes."

"I'll go and speak to the rabbi," the girl's father decided. "He will know what to do."

"This is all your fault," said Astra, bursting into tears. "*You* let her accept that stupid Miss Egypt title, though I said she was too young and didn't need that sort of attention, turning her head and pushing her out into the world before she's ready for it. If she hadn't, then none of this would have happened. You were so proud of her because she's beautiful and wanted everyone to look at her and praise her for her looks, but see what's happened now! This is God punishing us for pushing her forward when we're just ordinary, quiet people who want to get on with our lives. We should have kept ourselves to ourselves like we usually do. We should have left Claire at school and found a husband for her quietly, from among our own people. There was no need for any of this."

Abraham said nothing. He left, slamming the door behind him, and went straight to the rabbi's office.

The rabbi listened carefully to Abraham's tale of woe.

"So, you see how it is," Abraham said, when he had finished explaining. "We've been asked to do something completely unacceptable, but we're afraid to say no, because King Farouk could do anything he wanted to us. You know how difficult things are for us Jews at the moment, and Astra and I are not wealthy or influential. I need your advice. How can we get Claire out of this situation without getting the whole family into trouble, and without her getting hurt or sullied in any way?"

"It's clearly a very difficult situation for you all," the rabbi said delicately. "A lovely girl like Claire. Of course, you want her to be safe and not mauled around ... you have her future to think about, and prospective husbands would not like to know that she had been manhandled in such a way ..."

"Of course ..."

"... but on the other hand ..."

"*What* other hand? There is no other hand!"

"On the other hand, do you have any idea how delicate things are for us Jews at the moment? Have you heard what has happened to the Jews of Europe? People are saying that most of them have been killed! Do you think things are going to turn out better for the Jews of Cairo? You can't possibly be so stupid! We were complacent for years, thinking that the people of Egypt accepted us, and even liked us, but now that it looks as though Israel might actually happen, everything's changing."

"Well yes, but ..."

"King Farouk himself wrote to Hitler, telling him that he would be welcomed here if he decided to invade. What do you think will happen to us if he takes against the Jews of Cairo? We'll be decimated, that's what. Maybe the war is over, but that doesn't mean that everything is all right again. Sometimes, a single person is called upon to make a great sacrifice for the good for their people. That's what is happening in this case. Claire is being called upon to sacrifice her virginity and honour in order to keep the rest of us safe. As you know, there is an important example in the Torah of women having to make great sacrifices for their people, and this could be another of those times. I think that you should be brave and let Claire fulfil her destiny."

The example to which the rabbi was referring was the well-known story of Queen Esther, whose feast day, Purim, was celebrated every year. Purim marked the delivery of the ancient Jews from Persia. Esther, a Jewish woman said to be the most beautiful woman in all of Persia, had been taken as a wife by King Ahasuerus after a competition to find the worthiest of all the women in the land. Esther was an orphan who had been raised by a man called Mordechai, who kept her Jewish identity secret, even within the palace precincts. Esther arranged for Mordechai to be taken as a Jewish advisor to the king. When Mordechai uncovered a plot to kill the king by courtiers who were angry about his appointment, he told her, and she alerted her husband, who was saved.

Later, the king, who was very impressed by his prime minister Haman's wealth, ordered all the people to bow down to him. The Jews could not do this, as Haman wore an idol around his neck, and they were forbidden to engage in idolatry, which had been identified to them as an abominable sin. Angered by the Jews, and by Mordechai's presence in the court, Haman devised a plot to have all the Jews in the land slaughtered. Esther—a secret Jew—pleaded for their safety. The king listened to her, and they were saved.

During the Purim festivities in Cairo, people ate sweets and cakes made in the form of the head of the villain of the story, Haman, with moulds that were sold especially for the purpose, and children had a good time throwing firecrackers on the floor. Girls celebrated by dressing up like Queen Esther, who had saved the Jews by giving herself to the king, Ahasuerus. While the Egyptians did not celebrate the day themselves, they had long looked forward to seeing it being celebrated in the Jewish communities, and small children of every sort had tremendous fun watching and listening to the firecrackers going off. Usually, Purim had nothing but positive associations for the Jews of Cairo, as it was a very popular annual festival. On this occasion, however, Abraham was not at all impressed to be reminded of it.

Abraham stared at the rabbi, and then he turned on his heel, slammed the door behind him, and went straight home to his wife. Maybe the rabbi was highly educated in matters of theology, but he clearly did not understand anything about what it meant to be a father.

"What's going on?" Astra asked. "Did the rabbi tell us what to do? Did you get an answer to our problem?"

"You don't want to know what he said," Abraham said grimly. "But I can tell you one thing: If we want our daughter to be safe, we're going to have to take care of her ourselves, because nobody else is going to do it."

That night, Claire and Astra boarded a ship to Italy under the cover of darkness. While many of the Italian Jews had suffered terribly during the war, the family hoped that they would be safe there, and at least Claire would be safe from the lecherous king. Abraham stayed behind to run his shop, taking the risk that he would be punished for what had happened.

King Farouk was furious when he found out that Claire had been allowed to slip away. News of the sequence of events circulated rapidly among the Jews of Cairo. Everyone had a different opinion on how the situation should have been handled. Some agreed with the rabbi, thinking that if Claire and her parents had only done what he wanted, maybe he would have looked kindlier on the Jews of Cairo and cracked down on the persecution they were suffering. Others, however, felt that Claire's parents had been put in an impossible situation and saw reflected in it the dilemma that was facing the entire Jewish community.

It was increasingly clear that Jews were no longer safe in Egypt, in Cairo. The beautiful city that had long been their home had turned on them. The neighbours with whom they had shared so much were no longer their friends, but people who could not be trusted. What good was a community that could no longer even keep its own people safe? If the king felt that he could buy and then discard an innocent girl like Claire, how could anyone else think that things would be different for them and their family?

Raphael did not know Claire personally, but like everyone else, he had heard the story of the terrible decision that she and her parents had had to make. He loved Cairo, but like the rest of the Jewish community, he could see that their future in it was running out. For now, he was still busy running his father's leather workshop, and he was not personally in any danger, but what was going to happen next? He was 15 now and quickly turning into a man. Was this how he was going to spend the rest of his days, living in a country and a city in which the Jews were second-class citizens, at best? When he grew up and married, was this the sort of society he would want to raise his children in? He didn't think so.

The Jewish community of Cairo was becoming depleted. Those remaining were seeing people who had just recently been friends and neighbours turning on them, suddenly spitting out anti-Jewish slogans they had heard at the mosque or read in the newspaper. People were packing up their belongings, selling homes that had been in their families for generations (often for a pittance), and leaving. Some, like Joseph and Flora before them, went to Sudan, still vaguely hoping that things would get better in Egypt and that one day they would be able to come back. Some went to the United States, Italy, or France. Others, feeling that the Jews would never be safe unless they had a homeland of their own, were going across the border to Israel, with the dream that one day they would be able to create a state in which they could live and raise their families in peace.

Raphael knew that, one day soon, he would have a very big decision to make. It weighed on his mind. Should he stay, or should he try to make his future elsewhere? Should he try to work to make Egypt a better, safer home for the Jews, or just give up and throw his lot in with the Israel project? The only person he discussed this with was his friend Robert. They had known one another for years, but because of their three-year age difference, they had grown close only when Joseph and Flora had left. Robert lived with his parents, John and Alice; his four sisters; and his younger brother. He had a busy life, as John was unwell and needed to be accompanied to the stock market where he worked every day. Like Raphael, Robert found relief from his busy life in the Jewish youth centre. They often went out with their friends, but sometimes they talked about their concerns for the future.

"At least your parents could see the writing on the wall," said Robert. "Mine are in complete denial. They think that everything is going to be fine. They're sure that all of this anti-Jewish stuff will die down and that my sisters and I will be able to raise our families here. There's no way … if my dad didn't depend on me so much, I'd be out of here like a shot. America, Canada … or maybe the Holy Land. Some people think we might actually be able to make a country there. Wouldn't that be amazing? A country where the Jews get to be in charge for a change! Recruits have been going there for a while now, trying to get it started. Wouldn't it be incredible if their optimism paid off?"

"I don't know," said Raphael. "I know everything is shit right now, but this is our home, too. Maybe your parents are right and things will get better. Do we really want to leave and lose everything we've worked so hard for? I know that a lot of people are leaving, but I don't like the idea. It's like admitting that we don't have the right to be here, when we absolutely do."

But even as he said those words, Raphael thought of all the times he had been shooed away from a grocery stand lately, called a "dirty

Jew" who was unwelcome in Egypt. There were only so many times someone could handle that before they had to take matters into their own hands. He thought bitterly about a conversation he'd had with a neighbour recently. He had always gotten along well with Hassan, so when Hassan had beckoned him over a few days ago, he had gone gladly.

"I just wanted to say," Hassan said, "that I don't hold anything against you. I know that you are a good guy. You're not at all like the rest of the Jews."

Hassan had seemed to have no idea what a terrible thing he had just said. He had genuinely believed that he was giving Raphael a compliment. Raphael knew that Hassan was not a bad person; it was just that now he was exposed to a constant barrage of negative misinformation about the Jews in the Middle East, and like so many Egyptians, he could not help but be influenced by it.

"Maybe," said Robert darkly, "it's time we took our future into our own hands and started fighting back and showing people we've had enough. Why should we put up with being pushed around, just because of who we are? After all, nobody chooses to be Jewish or Muslim. We just are what we are because of the families we're born into. I refuse to let anyone push me around because they are making assumptions about me on the basis of the family I was born into. My parents are good people. They raised all of us to respect everyone we meet. Why should I stand aside and put up with it when they are disrespected?"

Raphael looked at Robert thoughtfully. It sounded as though he had more to say on this topic, and Raphael wanted to hear it.

* * *

The months passed steadily and became a year, and then more. Raphael was nearly 16 now, and he had grown used to living alone. He heard from his family by letter now and again, but he felt increasingly disconnected from most of them. The only one he missed was his mother. He thought of her every time he became aware of the weight of the amulet around his neck. Work was going well, and the leather workshop was making money. Most of the time, Raphael was busy chasing orders and making sales, but life did get lonely sometimes—and, when it did, he remembered that he was not yet quite a man but a boy, with a boy's need for companionship and support.

He was a member of the local Jewish youth club, which catered to girls and boys who met to play basketball and tennis, to flirt, and to have a good time. Once in a while, it was fun to go there and just be young, to forget about the responsibilities he had at the workshop. And, while part of him still pined for Miss Mackzumi, he longed for female company and for the companionship of young people of his own age. He got sex from professional prostitutes, who were always kind and welcoming, but he wasn't fooling himself—with the exception of Maddy, to whom he had felt truly close, he knew they weren't really friends. When money changes hands, it's not a real friendship but a business arrangement.

At the club, Raphael had gotten to know Maxa and Renata, sisters who were close in age to each other and to him and lived not far from him. They were outgoing, friendly girls who found the fact that they still lived at home with their parents restrictive and annoying, despite the fact that their parents—who were originally from Greece—were much more liberal than most Jewish families in Cairo. The girls were very excited to find out that Raphael lived on his own and didn't have to do what he was told.

"You mean, you have the whole apartment to yourself?" Maxa asked, impressed. "With nobody there to tell you what to do? That's amazing! How did you manage to arrange that?"

"Yes," said Raphael. "I haven't even seen my family for ages. I'm on my own. So, in a way, it's my apartment now, so long as I keep getting the rent for Uncle Ali downstairs."

"I guess that means you can have your friends over whenever you want," said Renata. "Let's say, for example, if you had some friends who *never* got any time on their own in their house and needed a space to get away from their boring parents … and maybe wanted to let their hair down once in a while … like for instance when your Uncle Ali rents the courtyard out and there's a party going on down there. I bet that's fun to watch, and I'm sure that it's quite easy to get some of the treats on offer, too."

Raphael smiled broadly. "Well," he said, "I like you two so much, I'll give you a key of your own!"

From then on, Maxa and Renata used Raphael's home as if it were their own, popping over to his place to spend time with him, listen to music, and just enjoy the fact that there were no adults around. They took to calling in every day on their way home from their work in a department store. When Raphael announced that he was planning to redecorate his apartment, they volunteered to help. The three of them had great fun choosing the paint and applying it to the walls.

Raphael's apartment shared a terrace with Uncle Ali's, separated only by a glass dividing panel. While it was great to have such friendly neighbours—and Ali and his wife, Jasmine, were unfailingly kind and gracious—Raphael found the intimacy a little annoying sometimes, and he knew that Uncle Ali would not approve of him entertaining girls with no adult to chaperone. With a bucket of paint in his hands, he realised that he had a simple solution: he could paint the panel white and make it opaque. That way, he would have his privacy, and Uncle Ali would not know things about Raphael's life that were better kept secret. For the girls, it was a bit like playing house, but for Raphael, redecorating was a way of affirming that he was a man now, and that this was *his* home.

One day, Maxa let herself in. She was all dressed up for playing tennis in a white T-shirt and shorts, with her long brown legs on display.

"Hello, Maxa," said Raphael. "On your own today?"

"I was just playing tennis at the club," she said, throwing herself down on the sofa to sit beside him. "I'm *so* hot and sweaty, I feel like I must be melting. I could have gone straight home, but Mum and Dad and Renata are all in Alexandria, and I felt like having some company rather than going back to an empty apartment and being on my own."

"Well, you're always welcome here."

"I'm just fed up of my boring job and living at home with my parents. You're *so* lucky to be on your own. I wish I was a boy sometimes. You know, even though I've finished school and everything, my parents would go completely crazy if I tried to move out and live on my own, like you do. I'm actually old enough to be married, if I wanted, but they still treat me like a little girl and boss me around. It's so unfair."

"I guess they think you'd try to do something naughty if they weren't around to keep you in line," Raphael teased. "Maybe they don't trust you to be good, and maybe they're right!"

"Well, hm, they *might* be right about that, because there are lots of naughty things I like doing, and I don't mind admitting that I'm not a good girl at *all*. Quite the opposite, in fact!"

Provocatively, Maxa stretched out a long brown leg and let it lie against Raphael's.

"What's going on here?" Raphael asked.

"Oh, Raphael, don't be so silly! You must've noticed that I fancy you. I think you're gorgeous! I've just been waiting for Renata to be gone so that I could make my move."

"Really?" Raphael turned to look into Maxa's hazel eyes. It was August and searingly hot, even in the shade of the apartment. Tiny beads of sweat had formed along Maxa's upper lip, and he was suddenly full of the urge to lick them off.

"Go on," Maxa said. "Give me a kiss."

Maxa held her face up expectantly.

Well, thought Raphael. *She's always been more fun than Renata. I might as well give her what she wants.*

Raphael leaned forward towards Maxa's open mouth. He kissed her and felt her tongue penetrating his lips eagerly. Experimentally, he reached out a hand and cupped her breast. Maxa moaned. For several long minutes, Raphael and Maxa continued with this journey of mutual discovery, and then she pulled away.

"What are you doing to me?" she said. "I came in to cool down after a hot game of tennis, and now I am hotter and sweatier than ever."

"I don't mind," said Raphael, who had every intention of continuing what was proving to be a very interesting experience. "I like the smell of fresh sweat on your skin."

"Well, I think I should have a shower to freshen up. I'm all sticky. I'm a bit embarrassed about you touching me when I'm so grubby."

"Maybe you should, but what about me? I'm all hot and sweaty too. Shouldn't *I* be embarrassed? I'd better have a shower as well."

"Well, I'll go first," said Maxa. She stood up and started to walk towards the bathroom. Then she paused. "Unless," she added, "you think it would be a good idea for us to have a shower together."

"Together? Like, in the same shower at the same time?"

"Haven't you ever taken a shower with a girl before?"

"Of course I have!"

Raphael didn't mention that the last time he had been in a shower with a girl, they had both been under 3 years old.

"Come on then!"

Maxa stalked off to the shower, leaving a trail of discarded clothes as she went. Eagerly, Raphael followed her example. By the time they got to the bathroom, they were both naked.

"You're perfect," said Raphael, admiring Maxa's body, tanned a deep brown except for the white area that delineated her swimsuit. Against the whitewashed bathroom walls, she looked even browner than before. He admired her pretty breasts, which stood firmly out from her chest.

"So are you!"

Maxa turned on the shower and pulled Raphael under the stream of water. She picked up a bar of soap and worked up a froth by rubbing it all over his body. His nipples hardened as her hands passed over his chest, running across his amulet and down to his flat stomach.

"What's this?" Maxa teased when she reached Raphael's penis—which, unsurprisingly, was hard as a rock.

"I think you know ..."

Raphael couldn't stand to be teased any more. He picked Maxa up and carried her the short distance into the bedroom where his parents used to sleep. There, he laid her on the big matrimonial bed where he himself had been conceived, which was still made up with heavy linen sheets, ready for when his parents were able to return. This was a good occasion to use it, he thought. There would be more room for fun here than in his narrow single bed.

"Look at you ..." Raphael breathed. He reached for a towel and dried Maxa's body. "You're perfect."

"Look at you, too," Maxa said. "You look just as I imagined you would."

Sinuously, Maxa stretched out against the linen sheets. With her arms over her head, her breasts were high on her chest, with their light brown nipples pointing at the ceiling. Between her legs was a lightly dusting of hair, and he could see her inviting pink cleft, slick with moisture.

Raphael was excited but confused. He had never expected to be in this situation with Maxa, who had never been anything more than a friend, but in this moment, he desired her more than anything. He leaned over the bed and took her nipple into his mouth in a spirit of experiment. It hardened as his tongued played against it.

"Raphael," Maxa said. "I don't care if it's wrong, but I want to do it. So there's no need for you to hold back. I'm all yours. Let's go all the way."

Raphael lowered himself onto the bed and carefully laid his body over Maxa's, feeling the give of her soft flesh as it responded to his. Beneath his legs, her thighs started to open.

"Are you sure?" he asked. "You don't mind? You won't regret it afterwards?"

"I'm sure more than anything. I've been thinking about this for days. Come on, hurry up. I can hardly bear to wait a moment longer."

Raphael held his weight on his elbows as he slid into Maxa's body and moved above her, watching her pretty face contort in pleasure. When it was over, they lay side by side on the white counterpane.

"There's something I want to tell you, but I'm a bit shy," Maxa said.

"What is it?"

"I can't bring myself to say it out loud, so I am going to whisper it in your ear."

Maxa leaned over and put her lips to Raphael's ear.

"That was my first time," she whispered. "I was a virgin until a few moments ago. Everyone says it's supposed to hurt the first time, but that didn't hurt at all. It was amazing. I never knew that my body could feel that way."

Raphael rolled onto his elbow and kissed her on the forehead.

"It was lovely for me too," he said. "I'm honoured to have been the first. I feel very lucky."

As he spoke, his amulet swung forward.

"What's this?" Maxa asked curiously. "You wear it all the time, but you've never told me anything about it."

"Oh, it's just something my mum got for me when I was a baby."

Maxa held the amulet and looked at it carefully.

"I've seen a picture of this man before," he said. "It's Rambam, isn't it? The saint? I think my mum has a picture of him somewhere that she bought one time when we went to his mausoleum."

"Yes."

"Well, I didn't know you were religious."

"I'm not. Look, do you want to talk about something else …"

Raphael didn't want to talk to Maxa about the amulet. He knew it kept him safe, but he didn't want her to think that he was silly or superstitious. Anyway, it was nothing to do with her.

"Are you ready to go again?" he asked.

"Yes, but Raphael …"

"What?"

"You're not going to tell anyone … about us, are you?"

"Of course not."

Raphael knew that respectable girls like Maxa were supposed to stay virgins until their wedding night. If word got around that she had already had sex without a ring on her finger, it would be seriously frowned upon. She would get into awful trouble with her parents, and the consequences for her marriage prospects would be devastating. One day, Maxa would want to get married to a respectable Jewish man, and when that day came she would do what girls had been doing for generations, and act as though she had never been with anyone at all. She would pretend to be a little scared on her wedding night and convince her husband that she had never seen a man's naked body before. She would slip into the bathroom before they went to bed and scratch her private parts with a nail scissors so that there would be some blood on the sheets, reassuring him that this was her first time. Nobody would ever have to know.

"Well," Raphael said. "This will be our little secret. Nobody is going to hear about it from me, and you can take that as a promise."

A few days later, Raphael got home from work to find Renata perched on the sofa.

"I hear that you and Maxa have a secret," she said. She raised her eyebrows and looked at him suggestively.

"Em ..."

"Come on, she's my sister, and she tells me absolutely everything, so don't play dumb. It's not breaking a secret to tell *me*. I know all about what you two did together. Well, you should know that it was all my idea ..."

"What?"

"Yeah, I haven't been a virgin for ages, and I told Maxa how great sex is. We both think that you're really good looking, so I told her she should go for you. I was sure you'd know how to be discreet and not get her into trouble, and I thought you looked like you'd be good in bed."

"Well then, thanks ..."

"From what Maxa tells me, her first time was a lot more fun than mine, so I think maybe it's time that you and I had a little secret, too, because now I am curious about what you did to her. I've only been to bed with one man, and he's as boring with his clothes off as he is with them on. I think I chose the wrong guy to give my flower to ..."

Before Raphael could even respond, Renata had started removing her clothes until she stood in front of him, completely naked. She was a little taller and thinner than her sister, with smaller breasts, but they were very alike. He moved towards her and took her into an embrace while she got to work peeling off his clothes. Together, they moved towards the sofa and stumbled onto it, breathing heavily with excitement.

Just after Renata and Raphael had finished making love, the door to the living room opened and there stood Maxa, with a naughty twinkle in her eye.

"Now you've had us both!" she said. "Who's the best, me or Renata?"

"I really couldn't say," Raphael panted. "You're both amazing."

"Well, we're neither of us jealous girls, so as long as you can keep a secret about us both, there's no reason why we can't all have a secret for a looong time ..."

2017

"Grandad at it again!" said David happily. "With memories like his, no wonder he always has a twinkle in his eye!"

"Yep," said Richard. "Every generation thinks that they're the ones who invented sex, but young people everywhere are the same."

"And with all the uncertainty in their lives at the time," said Rebecca, "it's easy to see how social norms were being broken. I mean, as things were getting so difficult for the Jews in Cairo, I guess the young people probably felt that they might as well have sex, even if their elders wouldn't have approved. After all, they knew that anything might happen next."

"Funny you should say that," said Richard. "Because actually, a *lot* of things happened next … and Grandad was right in the thick of it all!"

CHAPTER 7

FIGHTING BACK

2017

"A lot of the Jews of Cairo had left by now," Richard said, "but a fairly sizable community still remained. Some of them were in denial about how tough things were getting, and others had business interests in the city that they didn't want to leave—and strong emotional ties to the place that had been their home for generations. The war had ended, the Allies had won, and in theory things should have been getting back to normal. In Europe, people were beginning to get their lives back on track and to recover after the war. But everything was still very complicated in the Middle East, and for the Jews of Cairo, it seemed as though their future was worse than ever."

"How difficult were things really?" asked Rebecca. "Was it that they were having to deal with rationing and stuff, or did they actually fear for their lives?"

"Well, Grandad's story tells it all."

"Go on then …"

1948

Raphael remained in Egypt, still running the leather workshop, which had expanded to take on more workers—and which was now making enough money to support both him and his family in Sudan.

He also sent merchandise to his grandfather in Sudan to be sold there, and he had to hire extra workers to handle the packing and shipping. Although some of the workers were in the Muslim Brotherhood, he was on friendly terms with them and still hoped that one day soon, the madness that was taking over Egypt would recede. At lunchtime, Raphael ate together with the workers and made small talk, hoping to show with his respectful attitude that he was not someone to be feared and resented but a friend. In general, this fostered a sense of collegiality among the workers, who almost all endeavoured to do their best every day.

One of the men, Mansour, was a hunchback, but this did not seem to impact on the quality of the work that he was able to produce; he was good with his hands and produced fine bags. None of the other men liked him very much, however, which Raphael put down at first to the fact that he was a little different. Then one day, the foreman, Fareed, came to him with a concerned expression on his face.

"I didn't want to say anything before," Fareed said, "but it seems that Mansour has been stealing leather. I've never liked the way he carries on. In the evening, everyone else leaves, and he's always the last one to go. Unless he's up to no good, that just doesn't make sense."

Fareed quickly explained that he thought that Mansour had been stealing pieces of crocodile leather, which was the most valuable of all the material they used. It seemed that he had been stuffing pieces into his shirt, bringing it home, and crafting items in his workshop at home to sell on the side. News had gotten around that one could purchase high-quality crocodile leather goods from Mansour at very low prices. There was only one possible explanation.

Raphael thought long and hard about what to do. He couldn't afford to have someone stealing from him, and the thought that a worker whom he had always treated fairly might be taking his things made him very angry—but on the other hand, he couldn't just sack someone without knowing for sure, still less a disabled man for whom it would be very difficult to find another job in an already difficult economic climate. Eventually, he decided to go and visit a local traditional profiler, a sort of fortune teller who helped people understand what was going on in others' minds.

Asim, who lived not far from Raphael's apartment, was a well-known local profiler, and Flora had visited him on various occasions for help and advice. Raphael trusted his mother's judgement and felt that if Asim had been able to help her, then Asim would help him, too. The next day, he waited until Mansour had gone out for lunch, and then he took a handkerchief Mansour had left on the desk. He brought the scrap of cloth to Asim's place, handed it over, and asked if Asim could provide any insights into the character of the owner.

Asim took the cloth and held it carefully in both hands, looking at and smelling it at length. "What is the initial of the person who owns this?" he asked eventually.

"His name begins with the letter *M*," Raphael said.

"Hmm," said Asim. "I am getting something about him. Does he work with you at the leather workshop? There's something wrong with him. No, don't tell me … a limp … no, a crooked back or something like that?"

"Yes," Raphael said. "What else are you seeing?"

"Well," said Asim, "he is cutting pieces of leather and taking them home. In short, he is stealing from you, and unless you do something to intervene, he's not going to stop. He has been doing it for several months now, and he's getting cocksure and arrogant. He thinks that you'll never suspect a thing!"

Raphael returned from Asim and instructed Fareed to watch Mansour very closely until they had some definitive proof of what he was doing. That afternoon, when Mansour was about to leave, Fareed and Raphael approached him, restrained him, and searched him carefully. They quickly found the large pieces of leather that he had hidden under his clothes.

"What's this?" said Raphael.

Mansour started to snivel.

"I'm sorry, boss," he said. "I just wanted to make a little extra money, and I didn't think that anyone would notice a few missing pieces. What are you going to do? Are you going to tell the police? It's just that I live all alone with my widowed mother, and she depends entirely on me, you know …"

"Just go home, Mansour," Raphael said wearily. "So long as you never show your face around here, I won't tell anyone."

"Thank you," Mansour grovelled. "You're a good man. God bless you. I'll pray for you …"

Raphael just turned his back and walked away. This was the first time he'd had to deal with a situation like this, and it didn't make him happy.

"Are you sure, boss?" said Fareed afterwards. "He probably got away with a lot of leather before we found him. You're being very generous, because I bet if the police searched his house, they'd find loads more leather and enough evidence to put him behind bars."

"I think losing his job is punishment enough," said Raphael. "God knows it won't be easy for him to find another one without a reference."

As several of the workers were Muslims, they paused at midday to go to the local mosque and say their prayers. The rest of the workers were Copts, and therefore Christian, but it made sense for them to take a break at the same time, so they typically went for lunch in a nearby café or brought their home-made sandwiches outside to eat them. When he didn't eat with the workers, Raphael used this time to catch up with his paperwork, because it was quieter than usual in the workshop, and he found it easier to concentrate without the noise of the men at work. He quite enjoyed these quiet times, focusing on the lists of numbers in the blue-lined ledger and figuring out what he had to do over the next few weeks to ensure that money kept coming in and the business continued to grow.

One day during prayer time, there was a sudden knock on the door. Raphael looked up from his bookkeeping and saw El-Sawi, one of the younger workers he had taken on recently as the demand for his products expanded. El-Sawi was a quiet, shy young man who had not yet found his feet at the workshop, but Raphael liked him and was worried to see that El-Sawi looked very upset about something.

"What's wrong?" Raphael said as he opened the door. "Did you get some bad news? Why aren't you at the mosque with the rest of the men?"

"Not me, boss, you …" El-Sawi panted. "I came as quickly as I could because I thought you needed to know … I don't want you left in the dark … you deserve to hear what's …"

"What do you mean? Calm down and catch your breath."

"I mean, I've got some bad news for *you*."

"What's going on?"

"People are just going crazy. I know it's been crazy since the start of the war, but this is new, and it's worse."

Quickly, El-Sawi explained that the anti-Jewish sentiment that had become increasingly common in Egypt was exploding into violence, abetted by the Young Egypt political party that fed on populism. Its leaders told the people of Egypt that all of the problems in the country were the Jews' fault. Five Jews had been murdered in Alexandria, and riotous mobs had burned down a synagogue. El-Sawi himself had just come from the local mosque, where the imam had been repeating these messages and urging the congregation to take matters into their own hands and attack the local Jewish population.

"The king and the prime minister said it was bad," El-Sawi said, "but then the prime minister also said that it was partly the Jews' fault for provoking people and trying to keep all the money, and now everyone is saying the same thing. Boss, honestly, I'm very worried for you. You're a good person. I don't want anything bad to happen to you just because you're Jewish. But there's a sort of madness out there on the streets these days, and I am worried that it could all go wrong. They started saying bad things in the mosque today, so I decided to run back and tell you, so that you could think about what you need to do."

"Bloody hell," said Raphael impatiently. "All I want to do is get on with business and make some money. I thought now that the war was over, things would calm down around here."

"Sorry, sir …"

"No, no, don't worry. I appreciate your support, and I know that none of it is your fault. Look, El-Sawi, could you go and make me a cup of tea while I think about all this?"

Obediently, El-Sawi went down the stairs to the basement, where there was a small kitchen. Moments later, Raphael heard a loud crash. *What now?* he wondered. *What's going on?* He raced down the stairs to find a huge hole in the wooden floor, with El-Sawi in the middle of it. Stunned, all El-Sawi could do was moan and flap his hands helplessly. Raphael reached over and pulled him out.

"Has the world gone mad?" Raphael asked rhetorically. "El-Sawi, you can go home. Today is not your day. Stay home for a few days until your scrapes and bruises are better. I'll pay you anyway … now I have to figure out why there's a great bloody hole in the floor, and how I'm going to fix it."

When El-Sawi had gone, Raphael started to explore the hole. He quickly realised that it was more of a tunnel. About two metres high, it went far enough in either direction that he couldn't even guess where it ended, and along the sides there were roughly-constructed shelves with provisions on them, such as dried bread and corked bottles of water. Further along, heading into the darkness, he saw weapons and ammunition.

Well, this is strange, Raphael thought. *One thing's for sure, though. I can't just leave it like this. Eventually, whoever owns it will realise that I know it's here, and then they'll have to do something about me.*

On the way home, Raphael called his friend Robert's house to discuss this new, strange development. He described the tunnel to Robert and asked his friend what might be happening under his workshop.

"I don't know exactly what's going on," said Robert. "But I have a fairly good idea, and I know someone who can fill us in exactly."

"What? Who?"

"Her name is Marcella, and she's in charge of my group. She's going to be really interested to hear about this."

"What group? What are you talking about, Robert?"

"Come with me, and you'll soon find out!"

"There's a woman in charge of a group?"

"Come on, what's wrong with that? This is the twentieth century. Women have had enough of being bossed around, and at least some of us think they should have as equal a chance to lead as anybody else."

"Fair enough."

Robert led Raphael through the streets until they reached a rundown house in a rough-ish neighbourhood, where rubbish filled the gutter and the barefoot kids playing in the street had their heads shaved to prevent them from getting lice. None of the children paid them the slightest bit of attention.

"This is where Marcella lives," Robert said, knocking on a door covered in green flaking paint. "I think you're going to like her; she's one in a million. I can guarantee that you've never met a woman like her before in your life."

They waited for a moment and then heard footsteps approaching.

"Who is it?" came a gruff female voice from behind the door. "Who's there?"

"It's me, Robert. You can open the door, Marcella."

The door opened a crack and a suspicious dark eye peered out.

"Who are you with?" the voice demanded to know. "I don't know him. I already told you not to call around here with people I don't know. This had better be good, or I'm going to be angry, and I know you don't like me when I'm angry."

"This is my friend Raphael. He's fine. You can trust him. He's someone I want you to meet."

"OK, if you say so. But you'd better be right."

The woman opened the door wider and let the boys in. They shuffled past her and stood in the hall until she gestured with her head for them to enter a small living area to the left.

"Sit down," she said abruptly.

Raphael and Robert did as she said, but Marcella remained standing, hands on her hips, looking down at them both with a rather fierce expression on her face. She had thick, black, curly hair and heavy, unplucked eyebrows in a typically Egyptian face, with a dark complexion and a wide mouth.

"So," she said, "what's going on? What's so urgent that you had to come and disturb me at home instead of waiting until the next meeting?"

"Raphael found a tunnel under the floor of his workshop, Marcella, and he says that someone has stored weapons in it," Robert said, getting straight to the point. "So I thought it was time to tell him everything. We need weapons, and if he agrees, we have access to some through his basement floor. I knew that you would want to hear about this."

"Can we trust him? Is he likely to panic and go to the police at the last minute? Because that's not the sort of person we can afford to have around."

"Absolutely. I've known him for ages. He's as straight as a die, and I'm sure he's going to be very interested in our work—and in a position to help us out."

"Hmm," said Marcella. "I certainly hope so. He looks very young."

"He's young, but he's clever. He's been running his dad's business on his own for a couple of years now. I think if you let him join in, you won't regret it."

Raphael looked at Marcella, who was about twelve years older than him. She was very different from most of the women he knew. Women like his mother wore an air of authority in the home, but elsewhere they usually deferred to their husbands, and they rarely spoke up in public when there was a man around. He couldn't imagine Marcella deferring to any man. With her stocky build and broad shoulders, she looked strong enough for any physical task, and her body language was decisive and bold. Clearly, Marcella was a leader. He was impressed.

"OK," said Marcella. "If he's with you, I'll trust him. How much does he know?"

"Not a lot," said Robert. "Well, nothing really. Just that there's a big fucking tunnel under his floor with guns and all sorts of things in it."

"Right, Raphael," said Marcella. "Here's how it works; well, the short version, at least. You know that things have been shit for the Jews for a while now, and they're only getting worse. Some of us have decided that we've had enough of being the doormats of Egypt and we're going to start standing up for our rights before we're all killed … or worse. So you say you found weapons under your workshop floor? I don't know exactly whose they are, although I have some ideas, but we can use them. First, I need to send someone around to your place with a carpenter who can fix up the floor, and then we'll need to figure out where the tunnel goes and who is using it. I'm going to arrange for a chap I trust called Saleem to meet you there so that he can do the carpentry work. I've used Saleem before, and he is completely reliable."

Raphael found it quite unusual at first to be addressed by a woman who held so much authority, but he liked it. Aside from his mum and the teachers in school, he'd never been spoken to like this by any woman. It wasn't that he thought it was wrong or inappropriate; it just seemed strange. Most of the women he knew were quite shy and retiring. Marcella was a born leader, and it was already obvious that anyone who met her fell into line and did as she said. Now that he thought about it, he liked the idea of a woman in charge. He had always preferred women and found them more honest and reliable than men. Even if this wasn't the usual set-up, why not?

Marcella called someone from inside the house and went out to the hall, where Raphael could hear her instructing the unseen figure to fetch Saleem and bring him to Raphael's workshop as quickly as possible. He noted that she did not need to check with Raphael for the address, and he was impressed; clearly, she knew Cairo like the back of her hand. He would soon learn that Marcella never went anywhere without a map of the city, and that she spent hours poring over it, studying all the streets and alleys in detail in the context of every plan they had made. She had memorised the names and the details of the surroundings of every single street in the city. If she heard of any relevant activity in a given area, she made queries about every single household around. Because of her dark complexion and Egyptian appearance, with the right clothes, it was easy for her to pass as a Muslim woman, and sometimes she dressed in a wrap so as to walk the streets in Muslim areas unnoticed, checking the situation out.

While they waited for Saleem, Marcella barked out instructions. Raphael was to make sure that the carpenter repaired the floor so that it looked exactly as it had before—but hinged, so that it could be easily accessed from the workshop. He also had to ensure that none of his workers knew about this, which was going to call for him to make up some excuse to forbid them from even visiting the basement.

As Robert and Raphael hurried back to the workshop, Robert turned to him with a grin.

"Welcome to the group," he said. "You're one of us now. You're a freedom fighter. You're in the Young Sentinels."

"I am?" said Raphael. "Things are going so fast. I don't even know what that really means."

"Well, unless you've had your head in the sand, you must see what's going on with the Jews."

"Head in the sand? Why do you think my family is all in Sudan right now? You'd have to be blind and deaf not to see the way things are going in Egypt these days. Just the other day, I tried to buy some onions and the man in the stall told me that he doesn't serve Jews."

"Exactly. Some people think that there's a future for the Jews here if we keep our heads down and don't bother anyone, but let's be serious: there isn't. After what happened in Europe … well, the same thing could happen here, definitely. We're getting the young Jews ready to leave Egypt and go to the Holy Land. You know, the idea is to create a Jewish homeland where people can finally feel safe and that they no longer have to worry about losing their businesses or being bullied into doing something they don't want to, just to keep themselves or their families out of trouble. People have been talking about it for generations, but it finally looks as though it might actually be possible!"

"How are you doing it?"

"Carefully! If we got caught, we'd be in massive trouble for sure. We're calling ourselves the Young Sentinels, like I said, and we take our inspiration from the Zionist cause, which is to create a safe homeland for Jews from all over the world. God knows they need one. We've set up a training camp about twenty-five kilometres outside the city. At a glance, it looks like it's been set up for the boy scouts or something, but the young people are learning how to be real revolutionaries there, not just how to tie knots and set a campfire. They're learning to use a full range of weapons, as well as getting fitter than they've ever been before, so that they'll be able to defend Israel when they get there. Every single weekend and during the holidays, they're out there, girls and boys together, getting ready to fight for a new Israel. One day, we're going to have the choice of living in a country where the Jews come out on top for a change."

Raphael was impressed. "That's amazing. I can't believe it's been going on all this time and I never even knew about it. I mean, I had heard some rumours, but that's all … I didn't even know how true they were."

"It's only the tip of iceberg. The plans are massive. Think about it. There are Jews all over the world, and most of them have been persecuted for hundreds of years. Imagine if young Jews from everywhere got together to create a brand-new country …"

"How would they even talk to one another? It'd be like a real-life Tower of Babel. There are Jews in every country in the world, and they all speak different languages."

The Jews in Cairo mostly spoke Arabic and European languages, and Raphael knew that many of the European Jews spoke Yiddish, as well as local languages like French and German. How on earth could such a disparate group of people found and run a country? It seemed to be a pipe dream.

"We've thought of that too! We're studying Hebrew, and so are young Jews all over the world. That way, when Israel becomes a reality, we'll have a way to communicate with one another."

"It all seems like a fantasy," commented Raphael. "So many things would have to fall into place in order to found a new country."

"Doesn't everything wonderful start with a fantasy? And for a lot of Jewish families around here, fantasy is all they've got these days. They've had their businesses taken away, they've been forced by the situation into subservient jobs, and they don't even know if they will be able to keep their families safe in the future. In those circumstances, don't you think it's worth a gamble?"

"You know what?" said Raphael. "I'm in. One hundred percent. I still think it sounds like a long shot, but you're right. A fantasy like that is worth fighting for. It would be amazing if the Jews had their own country."

"You need to take it very seriously," said Robert. "No playing around. I mean, we're all risking our lives here. The level of secrecy required is huge. Marcella is our leader, and we have to obey her unquestioningly, even when we think she might be making a wrong call. She liaises with trainers who are already in Israel, but she's the only one who knows who they are, and she's the only one who knows enough to run things. I know Marcella well, and I can tell that she likes you and thinks you're going to be a great asset to the group. Listen, I can see that this is all pretty new to you. Have you even heard of the Zionist movement?"

"I know the term, but I don't really know what it means."

"Well, a lot of us want to make a homeland for the Jews, but the Zionists are the ones who've made a religious deal out of it. They believe that the Holy Land is still the promised land for the Jews and that we've got a God-given right to it … most of them are actually in Europe, and they've just been through all the shit going on up there. To be honest, I'd say that their deep faith in God and His promise is probably the only thing that's got them through all they've endured. Here in Egypt, we're only starting to hear the details about this stuff now, because everything's been fine for us here until recently. But if we can learn anything from what happened in Europe, it's that everything can change extremely quickly."

"I really don't know anything about it," Raphael said, feeling a little humble. Robert was clearly much better informed than him.

"Well, I'm no expert," said Robert, "but I can tell you a bit about it. The whole thing started among some Jewish intellectuals in Europe in the last century, and it gradually grew until 1917, when the Balfour Declaration was made. That was the first time someone actually seriously suggested that the Jews could be given a homeland in their own area of origin. By then, it looked as though the British were going to win the war, and the British government made a formal commitment in support of the idea of creating a Jewish homeland in Palestine and sent news of it to the British Zionist Confederation. The funny thing is, they made the commitment partly because of just one man: a Jewish man called Weizmann who invented the gas mask and saved the lives of thousands of British soldiers in the war.

"Anyway, after that, the Zionist movement started to grow pretty quickly, because people began to feel that maybe it was a real possibility and not just a pipe dream. People from Poland and other countries in Eastern Europe started to move to Palestine about ten years ago, when they could see the way things were going in Europe. Many of them were educated people, well-to-do, and firmly committed to the whole Zionist ideology. They even learned Hebrew and started persuading people to move to the area from the Middle East too, with the idea of increasing the population and working towards having a viable state.

"A few people in Egypt started to get interested when Rommel was getting close a few years ago and it looked as though we were going to be taken over by the Germans. That's one side. The other side is that now the Egyptian government has started to realise that it could actually happen, and that's one of the main reasons why people are turning against us … along with the fact that, back when it looked as though the Germans were going to take Egypt, King Farouk was very attracted to the German way of doing things."

"I don't understand why Egypt even cares," said Raphael. "No matter what that stupid king thinks. What's their problem if the Jews have a state of their own? It's not going to make any difference to them, is it?"

"All the Arab nations are against the idea. The idea is that while it's OK for people not to be Muslims, Islam is the only acceptable basis for a state. They can put up with the non-Muslim states that already exist, but they are not going to tolerate the foundation of a state for Jews, in which Judaism is given a special place, right on their doorstep. Most of the Muslims have never had a problem with Jews, but now some of the imams are going berserk and spouting all sorts of nonsense; I'm sure you're aware of it. That's why feelings are running so high at the moment. It's because people's idea of what God wants have entered the equation … and they don't match up. But what I reckon is, we've got to look after our own. If we don't, who will?"

When Robert and Raphael reached the workshop, Saleem was already there with his box of tools. Raphael unlocked the door and let him in, and he got straight to work. When he had finished, the work was inspected by Frank, an engineer who worked with the Young Sentinels. Frank proclaimed Saleem's work satisfactory and then let himself into the tunnel to explore. When he emerged, he said that he had a good idea where the tunnel went and that he would be back presently to explain.

Later that evening, Robert and Raphael made their way to Robert's house to meet someone whom Robert said was crucial to their mission.

"This is my cousin Ralph," Robert said when they entered the tiny living room. "Ralph is an invaluable member of the team. He's got all the skills that paramilitaries need, and he's been teaching them to us."

Raphael shook hands with the older man, who had a paunchy body and salt-and-pepper hair and looked to be in his mid-fifties. The bent and battered fingers on his left hand showed that they had been broken and badly set at some point in the past. Ralph's big, ugly face was covered in pockmarks and scars that suggested he had seen a lot of violence in his lifetime. Still, he had a kind smile, and he greeted Raphael warmly.

"Ralph used to be in the communist party," Robert continued, "and he's a big help when it comes to defence, because he's had lots of experience with home-made weapons. I've told him that you are completely trustworthy and that he can tell you anything he feels you need to know."

"Nice to meet you," murmured Raphael.

"We usually meet Ralph in his garage," Robert explained. "He's a mechanic who fixes cars and trucks. Nobody can fix machines like him."

"That's enough about me," Ralph interjected. "Aren't you going to take me to this young man's workshop? I want to see what we've got on our hands."

The three men walked the short distance to the workshop, where Raphael unlocked the door, locked it behind them, and ushered Robert and Ralph downstairs to the basement.

After listening carefully with his ear to the floor to ensure that there was nobody in the tunnel at that moment, Ralph carefully lifted the trapdoor that Saleem had installed and made his way down the rope ladder that Saleem had also supplied. Robert and Raphael, brandishing torches, followed carefully behind.

"Hmm," said Ralph, looking carefully at the eggs that had been stored on the makeshift shelves. "These are filled with sulphuric acid. Don't be fooled by how innocent they look, because they're actually very dangerous. The rest … the guns and ammunition and all that … that's going to be very useful."

"What are the eggs for?" Raphael asked.

"For throwing at people," Ralph responded simply. "Sulphuric acid is very strong, and it'll melt a man's face right off his bones. Even if someone gets just a few splashes, they'll be in so much pain they won't be able to do anything other than claw at their face and scream. They won't be able to do any harm while they're disabled like that, and they'll never look the same again afterwards."

"Ralph used to get up to all sorts of things in his communist days," Robert explained. "He's seen it all."

Ralph rolled his eyes.

"For my sins," he said. "I was young and foolish then and didn't realise what a pipe dream communism was. I've learned my lesson since then. You young people have a much better goal than we ever did. We never had a chance of converting the world to Communism, but I think that you lot are going to give this Holy Land thing a good shot. If you don't make it, at least you'll die knowing that you tried, and that's an honourable way to go."

Raphael's mind was racing. The eggs were dangerous, for sure, but he could also see that they would be a very effective weapon in a guerrilla war. There was no money to spend on weapons, but with some organisation, a lot of acid-filled eggs could be prepared in a short space of time.

"Can you teach me how to make them?" he asked, indicating the eggs.

"If you want," said Ralph. "It's not that difficult."

That evening, Raphael and Ralph spent hours in Ralph's mechanic's workshop carefully blowing out eggs, using a syringe to fill them with lethal sulphuric acid, and sealing the holes with molten wax. It was delicate work and the stakes were high, because if the thin shells were to break, they could be badly hurt.

"If you ever need to defend yourself, these little things will really help," Ralph said. "It's a lot easier to get away from someone who is trying to kill you when he is screaming as his face melts off and falls onto the ground, although you'll never forget the sound of the screams." He looked thoughtful for a moment. "I still have dreams about them, you know," he added. "The screams."

"I'm sorry to hear that," Raphael said. "It must be hard."

"Ah well," responded Ralph cheerfully. "It's nothing I can't treat with a bottle of beer. At least it wasn't *me* screaming, that's how I look at it! I may be ugly, but I'd be a hell of a lot uglier if I'd been hit by one of these eggs."

Ralph brought Raphael up to speed with some of the most time-honoured techniques of guerrilla warfare, such as how to make firebombs with kerosene, a bottle, and a wick; how to remove the gunpower from firecrackers to use it for a more lethal purposes; and how an ordinary car tyre, set alight, can be tossed over a man's head to buy time to get away while he struggles to take it off or gets burned to death in the process.

"Do you think I'll ever have to actually do any of these things?" Raphael asked. "It all sounds horrible. I'd hate to see a man die in such a painful way and know that I was responsible."

Ralph shrugged. "It certainly doesn't hurt to know how," he replied. "And if it comes down to it, you might find yourself in the situation of not having much of a choice. When it's either you or the other guy, your self-defence instincts kick in and you'll do whatever it takes to get out of there alive. You'll worry about ethics and someone else's pain afterwards."

The following morning, Raphael was woken early by a knock on the door. He opened it in his pyjamas to find Frank, the engineer who had inspected Saleem's work the afternoon before.

"Can I come in?" asked Frank. "I've got something for you."

"What is it?"

Frank pushed through the door and walked into Raphael's living room. He opened the small briefcase he was carrying and pulled out a hand-drawn map, which he spread out on the coffee table.

"So," he said, "we know who built the tunnel under your workshop, and my contacts have given me enough information to draw up this map. I have to say that Marcella was a great help. She seems to know every corner of the city intimately. Anyway, the person responsible for the tunnel is a Jewish storekeeper who has a shop selling hunting equipment. His name is Zeke, and he's in with the anarchists, fighting to get rid of King Farouk and the rest of the royals. He doesn't care about the Holy Land project, assuming he even knows about it, but he's managed to stockpile a large number of weapons, hoping to take part in some sort of a communist uprising ..."

Raphael didn't know Zeke personally, but he had heard of him. The man had been involved in founding Egypt's first communist party in 1943. Raphael didn't agree with his aims but was impressed by the lengths he'd gone to. In fact, most of the leaders of the communist party in its early days had been Jewish, although the party itself was multi-ethnic. They were an organised group, and they had arranged to receive regular supplies of live arms, with the eventual aim of staging a communist uprising that would depose the king and establish a government along the lines of that in Soviet Russia. They had very little popular support from the people of Egypt but were extremely passionate about their goals.

"I know this is all moving really fast, Raphael," said Frank, "but the thing is, we've got to get all the weapons out of the tunnel, and we've got to do it tonight, before it's too late."

"*Tonight?*" exclaimed Raphael. "But why? Surely we've got all the time in the world. Now that the floor at the workshop has been fixed, there's no way of knowing that we found out about the tunnel."

"Marcella has a mole in the police," Frank explained. "She's found out that Zeke is going to be raided in the next day or two. The tunnel goes all the way to his shop, and it's likely that the police will find it. If they do, they'll take all the weapons and use them as evidence against him. This is our best chance to get our hands on some real guns and ammunition that would actually give us a fighting chance to defend ourselves, if it came to it—and the trapdoor in your workshop is the perfect way to do it. What do you need to do to make sure that we can get down there this morning?"

Raphael's mind was racing.

"I'll send a messenger to tell the workers that I'm being audited today," he planned, "so there's no need for them to come in. They've all been working really hard, so they'll be delighted to have the time off on full pay. That'll give us the whole day, which should be more than enough."

It occurred to Raphael that he should be very concerned about the tunnel. The government was cracking down hard on the communists, and the last thing he needed was for someone to come across it, see that it went right under his workshop, and assume that it had something to do with him. If they thought that he was a communist, he would be arrested and sent away for a very long time.

When Raphael got to work an hour later, two vans were waiting outside. Working as quickly as they could, Raphael, Robert, Frank, and Saleem removed all the guns and ammunition from the tunnel, along with the food supplies, and disguising each piece as leatherwork, loaded the vans. While the vans brought the goods to Marcella's, Saleem sealed the tunnel with bricks and mortar and then filled in the cavity under Raphael's floor until nobody would have guessed what had just happened—or even that there had ever been a tunnel at all.

When the work was done, Raphael proposed going out for a meal and a refreshing drink, but Robert shook his head.

"Maybe later," he said. "First, we've got to report to Marcella. She's got the stuff, and she's waiting for confirmation that we've sorted everything out here."

When Marcella let the men into her house, her usually severe expression was cracked by a wide smile as she closed the door behind them.

"Great work, boys!" she said. "We've got forty-two guns, all the ammunition we need for them, and the food supplies will certainly come in useful at some point. He won't thank us for it, but we probably saved Zeke from some serious jail time, too. The police found the tunnel under his shop, but there was nothing in it, so they don't have enough evidence to put him away for long. Raphael, you've been pushed in at the deep end, and I'm impressed that you managed not to lose your head. Provided that you accept how dangerous our work is, you can consider yourself one of us! Congratulations. You're in the Young Sentinels now!"

"Thanks! I am really excited to see how I can help."

"You're very vulnerable," Marcella advised Raphael. "Not just because you're Jewish, but because you're still very young, and yet you have your own successful business. People get jealous very easily. My advice to you is that you get yourself a bodyguard who can help you to stay safe."

Things were getting steadily worse in Cairo. One of the local imams had taken against the Jews and started preaching even more inflammatory sermons at the central mosque, telling the faithful that all the problems in Egypt were the fault of the Jews, and that if the Jews were gone, Egypt would quickly become a prosperous country and take its place among the great nations of the world. Marcella's concern was that someone would take offence at Raphael's business doing so well and start to spread the idea that he was stealing money from the Muslim community.

"Surely that's not necessary," Raphael protested in response to Marcella's advice. "I've been living here most of my life, and nothing bad has ever happened to me. My landlord Ali is a Muslim, and nobody's been kinder to me than him. I even call him 'Uncle'."

"Your parents didn't go to Sudan without a reason," Marcella pointed out. "Things are changing here, and they are getting worse all the time. You have the potential to be very useful to our group, and we don't want to see you getting hurt or killed. Now, there's a man I know who can help. He's one of the good guys."

Marcella gave Raphael the name and address of a Jewish man whom she said she trusted, and that evening, Raphael went to his home and knocked on the door. It was opened by a giant of a man who towered over him and enveloped his hand in a massive paw.

"Pleased to meet you," boomed Levi. "Marcella's told me all about you. Won't you come in?"

Levi stood aside and let Raphael pass into the narrow hall.

"This way," said Levi, and he led the way down a short narrow hall to a tiny living room. His head nearly reached the ceiling, and the scruffy armchair creaked under his weight as he lowered his considerable bulk into it.

"I hear you're looking for a bodyguard," Levi said.

"That's right," Raphael replied.

"Well, that's the sort of thing I do. My mother says I didn't grow this size for nothing. I was never one for my studies, so I do what I can with what I've got."

Raphael looked at Levi. His tiny home was in the poorest part of town, the Jewish Quarter, and the humble furnishings and the clothing Levi wore showed that he lived in desperate poverty. Most of the Jews in this area were physically tiny; they had been malnourished as children and suffered from diseases like rickets and repeated bouts of diarrhoea and cholera, as they lived in crowded quarters with no sanitation. Levi was not a wealthy man by far, but he was the picture of health. His hands looked big enough to crush someone's head, and his huge thighs rippled with muscles.

"You've got the job," Raphael announced. "If Marcella recommends you, then that's enough for me."

"Just like that?"

"Just like that."

"Well then, I guess we both agree that Marcella is one of a kind!"

From then on, Levi accompanied Raphael everywhere he went. The crowds parted before his huge, lumbering body. Although he looked menacing—so much so that people often crossed the street just to get away from him—Raphael soon discovered that his fearsome aspect hid a very soft centre. The older man was kind and generous and, despite his poor level of education, remarkably insightful.

"You're my guardian angel," Raphael told him one day, a month or so after hiring him. "You don't just keep me safe, you give me good advice too—and I consider you a friend."

Levi responded with a big smile. "I don't think most guardian angels look like me, boss!" he said. "I should think most people would be pretty scared if they saw their guardian angel and he turned out to be a big bruiser like me. Can you imagine?"

"That may be, Levi," said Raphael, "but I stand by my words. I'm glad to have you around."

Not long afterwards, Marcella's prescience was proven when a mob, inspired by the inflammatory sermons in the local mosque, assembled on Fouad Street in front of Cicurel's, a big department store owned and run by a prominent Jewish family. Cicurel's made most of its money selling luxury items to wealthy women, and it was an easy target for angry people who had been told that the Jews were stealing money that ought to belong to Muslim Egyptians. The crowd threw stones through the plate-glass windows and rushed inside, roaring in both anger and delight as they grabbed at the merchandise.

When the rioters had taken as much as they could carry, they set the store on fire. The shop assistants, who had been cowering in fear, fled in terror, and the looters moved on to other shops along the street, although the only one that went up in flames was Cicurel's. All of the Jewish businessmen in the area were in a state of alarm, including Raphael. They were all vulnerable to being looted—or even worse.

"Boss, don't worry," Levi said. "I took the liberty of taking some money out of the till, and I paid the leaders of the mob to stay away from the leather workshop. Nobody's going to bother us."

Raphael didn't like the fact that Levi had parted with the workshop's hard-earned money, but he accepted that it had been the right thing to do under the circumstances. Without Levi's quick thinking, the workshop would probably have gone up in flames.

Although the workshop continued to do well and bring in money, it was increasingly clear to Raphael that his future was not in Egypt. He was torn. On the one hand, this was where he and his family had chosen to make their home. How dare anyone, still less a mindless angry mob, try to prevent him from living and working here? He had always assumed that this was where he would grow up, make a home, get married, and eventually raise a family of his own—and now people were trying to tell him and the rest of the Jewish community that they were not real Egyptians, simply because of their faith.

Raphael had long counted on his amulet for protection, and now he had Levi too. But was this really the way he wanted things to be for the rest of his life? Everything seemed to indicate that the political situation was going to get worse. King Farouk, who had never been very popular to begin with, was being targeted on all sides by groups who disliked him, from the communists to the Muslim Brotherhood. The communists hated him because he represented all of the worst of capitalist excess, while the Muslim Brotherhood professed horror at the drinking, gambling, womanising lifestyle that showed him to be far from a good Muslim. Everyone resented how he seemed to do nothing but take from those who had far less than he, and his conduct on visits to other monarchs was nothing but an embarrassment.

The British, who had stayed on in Egypt since the end of the war, appeared to be planning to stay indefinitely and had made themselves comfortable in enormous military instalments along the Suez Canal, which had villas for the officers to share with their wives and children, beaches to play on, and shopping centres selling European goods, including the tinned Spam the English apparently couldn't bear to live without. The British forces maintained a sort of uneasy calm, which spilled over into violence only now and again. It was in everyone's interest to keep the canal open, as it was the channel through which oil was transported from the Arabian Gulf and also a channel of communication with the many colonised nations of Africa. Raphael asked himself if he really wanted to stay in a country in which the best chance of a more or less peaceful future lay in the hands of another nation—one that didn't really seem to care about the future of the Jews of Egypt. Although in general he preferred action to introspection, Raphael spent many evenings on the riverbank, Levi at a discreet distance, watching the water move slowly by and wondering about what his future held.

Increasingly, he could see the attraction of the vision held by Marcella and the Young Sentinels. They said that if Jews weren't welcome in Egypt, or indeed anywhere else in the region, there was only one thing to do. Whatever it took, even if they had to resort to violence, they would establish their own nation and make it into a place where every Jew in the world, regardless of how poor and how downtrodden, would be welcomed and given the opportunity to raise a family in peace, far from the threat of violence. Even if that prize had to be won at the point of a gun, it would be worth it. If they had learned only one thing from the war, it was that some people would stop at nothing to exterminate the scattered Jewish people. It was time for them to learn how to stand up for themselves, because nobody was going to do it for them.

That's it, Raphael thought. *I am going to do more than just help Marcella and the Young Sentinels. I'm going to put myself at the heart of it all. I am going to train and learn how to fight like a soldier. I'm going to work hard and try to get put in a position of leadership. I want to be able to stand up for my people and the dream we have of a future in which our children can be safe.*

The Young Sentinels trained on Sundays, as most of them either worked or attended school on the other days. A few years before, they had been children, and many of them had started their involvement in activism as kids. For very young people, the group was rather like the scouts but with much more serious ambitions. The trainers were local women and men who had, in their own turn, been trained by activists from Eastern Europe. They had learned not just paramilitary skills but also to respect the equal rights of women and men to serve as leaders for the Zionist cause. Raphael was a little nervous attending the first training session, but he was reassured when he encountered Maxa and Renata.

"What are you doing here?" he asked. "You never told me you were into this!"

Renata winked at him. "We've been Young Sentinels for some time," she said. "We don't have to tell you everything! As you know very well, we're both really good at keeping secrets!"

"Enough talking!" Marcella roared to the group. "We're not here for a picnic! If you've been here before, you know the ropes, and you can fall into line. If not, shut your mouth and do what you're told. This isn't a game, and I need you all to either take this seriously or fuck off back home!"

The group of girls and boys, forty-three in all, shuffled into a rough line and stood in a respectful silence, waiting for their orders.

"Adi and Benny here will take you lot in hand," Marcella informed them. "So make sure you do what they say."

Marcella withdrew, dismissing the group with a nod, and Avi assumed charge. He was a stocky, well-built young man with a barrel chest and strong, slightly bowed legs. His face was stern, without even a hint of a smile, as he surveyed the group. Then he noticed that Maxa was wearing leather shoes.

"What the hell were you thinking?" he shouted, pointing an accusatory finger at her shoes. "I made it perfectly clear that you should wear tennis shoes, and that's it. Take them off at once. If you are not going to do as you are told, you can go barefoot. Maybe next time you'll remember how much your feet hurt, and you'll do what you're instructed!"

Raphael winced in sympathy at the thought of Maxa's delicate pink feet against the dry, yellow, stony ground. They would be bruised and scratched within minutes.

Avi divided the group in two, assigning some of the youngsters to himself and the others to Benny. Raphael was put in section A, which meant that he would be under Avi's direction.

"Raphael is starting a bit later than some of the others," Marcella said, pointing him out to Avi. "So I want you to train him very intensively and get him up to speed as quickly as you can. I am going to use him for a mission soon, and I need him to be ready for it."

For the next two hours, Raphael and the rest of his group walked across the arid, stony ground under the burning sun. They were allowed to drink a few mouthfuls of water every two kilometres and completed twelve kilometres in that time.

"Some of you are very unfit," Avi criticised them when they paused for a rest. "You're going to have to start putting a lot more effort in if we're going to be able to use you for the cause. This just isn't good enough, you know."

Just as Raphael was wondering why they had stopped in this particular spot, two of the girls leaned down and started to brush at a clump of earth on the side of the road. After a few minutes, they had revealed a roughly made wooden door that one of them heaved open with a certain amount of difficulty. The door sealed a dug-out cellar that was filled with revolvers, rifles, and ammunition.

"OK, everybody take a weapon," Avi instructed the group, "and we'll start training. Hurry up, now. We don't have all day."

Impressed, Raphael watched as Renata and Maxa, along with the rest of the group, took out the weapons and handled them with familiarity and ease, loading the ammunition and setting up targets to shoot at along the side of the road. He took up a revolver and managed to load it. He was then pleased to note that he acquitted himself quite well, especially considering that this was his first time with a weapon.

"I want you all to imagine that you are shooting at real people," Avi instructed, "because that's how it's going to be at some point. You all know how the people of Cairo are turning on the Jews. Nobody in Egypt wants to see a Jewish-led Israel happen, and they will do everything they can to prevent us from reaching our goal. Envision the people you'll have to shoot at, because if it comes down to it, you'll have to be prepared to do it. Imagine their faces and the expressions on them. Imagine the lives they have at home and the people who care for them. Imagine all of that, and then harden your hearts against them, because that is what you are going to have to do when the shit hits the fan. Don't think for a moment that just because they have families and friends who love them that they wouldn't hurt you, because they would. They have been taught to think of the Jews as something other than fully human, so there's no time here for sentimentality."

Raphael held his weapon and pointed it at a tin can that someone had put on the side of the road for them to shoot at. He tried to imagine that there was a man standing there—a man like the many who had looted Cicurel's department store, shouting about bringing death to the Jews. Raphael pulled the trigger and felt the power as the bullet left the gun to fly towards the imaginary man. In his mind's eye, he could see the man stagger backwards, hands to his chest as he realised he had been hit, and then fall flat on his face while blood spurted everywhere. He shuddered. He knew he could do it if he had to, but he hated the thought of killing another human being, even one who wouldn't hesitate to do the same to him.

The group did target shooting for over an hour, and then Avi instructed the others to return the way they had come and go home.

"You stay here, Raphael," he said. "I need to talk to you in private."

Raphael did as he was told.

"Marcella has plans for you," Avi said. "Plans that are different than the ones she has for your friends. Whatever she or I tell you is a secret, not to be shared with Robert or any other friends. This is for their own sakes. The less they know, the safer they'll be. Is that perfectly clear?"

"OK," Raphael nodded.

"You might think this all seems like fun and games," Avi continued, "but it's deadly serious, and you should take it that way. Jews are literally fighting for their lives in Egypt today, and nobody really knows how bad it's going to get. We're all in danger anyway, but you're in even more danger now that you're with us. I know you've already got a bodyguard, but you're going to have to take extra precautions from now on. Never take the same route to anywhere two days in a row. Make sure that you have a means to defend yourself at all times, and be aware that violence—*serious* violence, much worse than anything we've seen in Cairo before—could break out at any time, and that you will be called to deal with it and may have to risk your life in the process."

"What are my instructions?" Raphael asked.

"You'll get them in due course. For now, focus on your training, secure your business, and make sure that you are safe from attack. I have a feeling that it's all going to kick off soon, and when that happens, I want you to be ready for it."

Avi and Raphael walked back together in silence until they caught up with the others. Raphael examined his thoughts and feelings. He was caught between excitement and fear, he decided, but the funny thing was, he was not afraid for himself at all. He was scared of losing a friend or of the business getting looted and damaged, but he was also quietly sure that he personally could not be hurt, because he had his amulet, and so long as that was the case, nothing truly bad could ever happen to him. At the same time, he felt driven to succeed as an activist. It was exciting to think of what they were trying to accomplish and how, and he felt sure that he could move through the ranks and maybe even be promoted to a leadership position.

2017

"God," said Rebecca with a shudder. "It really is no wonder the kids were growing up so quickly in those days. Didn't Grandad's parents have any idea of what he was up to? They can't have, or they'd surely have insisted that he go to Sudan."

"I don't think they knew," said Richard, "and I am sure he didn't tell them anything. He wouldn't have wanted his mother to worry, for a start. Can you imagine how frantic she would have been, if she'd known that her youngest boy was getting involved in activism at a time like that? She'd have been terrified for him."

"God," said David, "it's easy to forget now, all these years later, how difficult things had become in Egypt. These kids were mostly just teenagers, but they didn't feel like they had any choice. They had to take up weapons and learn how to defend themselves, because if they didn't, they knew they could be killed."

"Yes," said Richard grimly. "It all puts the foundation of Israel into perspective, doesn't it? The world had just seen what Europe had done to European Jews, and now those in Egypt were seeing their own compatriots turn on them. It must have been confusing and devastating for them. It's absolutely no wonder that young Jews in Egypt had the dream of establishing a country of their own, where they would be able to raise a family without the fear that had always been in the background of their own childhoods."

"I think a part of Grandad has always missed Egypt," said Rebecca. "I mean, he gets a certain look in his eye when he talks about his childhood there."

"Did he actually see any violence?" David wanted to know, "or was he just ready for it?"

"Oh, he saw a lot of things. Do you want to hear about it?"

To a chorus of assent, Richard continued to speak.

CHAPTER 8

TROUBLE IN EGYPT

2017

"So," continued Richard, "the atmosphere on the streets of Cairo was getting tenser by the day. There was more and more overt hostility to Jews who were just trying to run their businesses and get on with their lives. People were being yelled at on the street, shopkeepers were refusing to serve them, and businesses of all sorts were being vandalised. You could say that things were going from bad to worse … and on top of all that, Grandad was busier and busier with the Young Sentinels."

"He must have felt very alone at times," said Rebecca. "I mean, I am sure it was exciting and all, but who did he have to talk to?"

"I think he actually felt less alone than before," said Richard. "He had good friends, and he knew that he could count on the other activists to support him. But he was often stressed. He told me that even now, all these years later, he still sometimes dreams about those times."

"Well," urged David. "What are you waiting for? Tell us more about it!"

1948

Raphael was exhausted. He was training and planning for the future, and he also had a business to run. Thank God for Levi, who was tireless in keeping him safe, and who spent his nights at the leather workshop, making sure that would-be arsonists could not burn it down. Raphael had finally gotten around to getting the locks on his house changed. He had given new keys to Maxa, Renata, and Robert.

"Boss," said Levi one day, "things are getting very hot around here, you know. There was a gang of kids around here last night planning to break in, steal whatever they could, and burn the place down."

"Well, as the business is still standing," said Raphael, "I suppose you went out and frightened them off, as only you know how."

"I went out all right," said Levi, "and they started to scarper when they saw me, but I called them back. They were just children, really, caught up in the whole thing because they think it's exciting. Kids are stupid, aren't they? I persuaded them that I wasn't going to eat them, and eventually they let me buy them a snack and a drink. They promised not to try to do any damage again—and to tell the rest of their pals that the workshop is off limits. And I got some information out of them. The people who are out to get the Jews consider themselves anarchists, and they have this crazy idea that the Jews are really running the country or something, that Farouk is some sort of a puppet, and the rabbis are pulling his strings. Absolutely crazy nonsense, of course, but they seem to believe it. They won't be happy until every last Jewish business in Cairo has been either closed down or burned to the ground."

"Good work, Levi," said Raphael. "Keep it up, because the more we know about what they've got planned, the easier it'll be to fight back."

A few days later, Levi saw the kids again. He bought them some more treats, and in return they told him what Raphael and the rest of the Young Sentinels needed to know: the anti-Jewish "anarchists" were fomenting a plan to destroy all the Jewish-owned businesses in the city, starting in the Jewish Quarter. By telling the poor people of Cairo that the Jews were to blame for all their woes, they had a massive amount of support. They had also managed to rally some of the local imams to their cause, and these alleged men of God were using their mosques as a way to spread hatred and unquiet. The mosques had been responsible for spreading anti-Jewish sentiment for some time now, but it was getting steadily worse.

"At this point, we've got to prioritise," said Levi. "I've been sleeping at the workshop to keep it safe, but I think it's time I started spending the night at your apartment instead. I know you feel that you can look after yourself, but you're vulnerable. Important as it is, the workshop, along with all the leather and tools it contains, is replaceable. You, on the other hand, are not."

From then on, Levi spent the nights at Raphael's, leaving only when Maxa or Renata came so that Raphael could have some privacy with them.

A day or two later, Marcella called an urgent meeting to discuss what was going on in Cairo and what they should do next. They met at the Palmyra coffee house, which closed its doors and shutters for the purpose of the meeting. Robert was already there when Raphael arrived, and the two boys nodded at each other solemnly. Marcella quickly introduced Mireille, her second in command. Mireille attracted Raphael's attention straight away. With her stocky body, stern expression, and tomboyish clothes, she was not especially attractive in any immediately obvious sense, but there was something about her that commanded a second look. Mireille glared at Raphael as though she hated him, and he decided to keep his distance unless he absolutely had to interact with her.

"OK, Raphael," said Marcella. "People like to follow you and take your leadership, so I am going to give you a lot of responsibility. You should only answer to me, but if something happens to me—and something bad could happen to *any* of us at this point—you can report to Mireille, and she will tell you what to do next. Is that clear? In my absence, I want you to give her your complete and absolute obedience."

Raphael nodded his assent, and Marcella continued to issue directives.

"We've found out that there's going to be an anti-Jewish riot on Friday," she said. "The so-called anarchists are going to take to the streets in Cairo, and their plan is to destroy all the Jewish businesses they can. Our job is to protect our people and their livelihoods.

Robert, I want you to get a hundred and fifty men and go to the textile quarter, where most of the merchants are Jews. There are a lot of successful businesses in that area, and obviously a lot of money, so that is where we are expecting the worst of the violence to take place. Take up position in the apartments above the shops, and ...”

“Excuse me, Marcella,” Raphael interrupted. “But I have some intelligence that suggests they're going to start with the Jewish Quarter, not the textile quarter.”

Marcella did not like being interrupted. Raphael knew that she never planned anything unless she was completely sure what was going on. She always looked into every detail meticulously before signing off on an intervention. He had always admired her for that, and he trusted her as a leader—but on this particular occasion, he was also sure that the information he had received was accurate and that she needed to listen to him.

“Don't be ridiculous,” she said. “Why would they do that? The Jewish Quarter is a poor neighbourhood, and the Jews who live there don't have even two sticks to rub together. It just wouldn't make any sense for a bunch of looters to kick off there, because there's absolutely nothing to steal. At the end of the day, all they really care about is getting their hands on whatever they can manage to take. In the Jewish Quarter, all they're likely to get is a dose of the fleas!”

“That's right,” said Mireille. “Sounds like a daft idea to me. I mean, some of my friends grew up there and they actually had only one pair of shoes for all the girls in the family. They took it in turns to go to school because none of them wanted to attend class without shoes. What would be the point of attacking a place like that?”

“But I heard it from Levi,” Raphael insisted, “and he heard it from the rioters themselves. This is reliable information, Marcella! Seriously, I am sure that it's where it's going to start. I know the Jews there are poor, but that also means that they are vulnerable. They're an easy target, and the rioters are cowards. They're the sort who like to hit a man when he's down.”

“*Fine*,” said Marcella shortly. “If you're so sure of it, then I'll put you in charge of guarding the Jewish Quarter. It'll probably be an easy job for you, too, because I don't think you're going to see a lot of action. I suppose that's a good way to break you in. Perhaps you'll be more amenable to taking orders when you've had a nice quiet night."

Mireille stared at Raphael crossly from under her heavy brows. He had the distinct impression that she had taken a dislike to him.

"Do you have an actual plan, or are you just contradicting Marcella for the sake of it?" she asked. "If you don't have a plan, you're just wasting everyone's time with your nonsense, and that would be not just irresponsible but downright bloody annoying."

"I'll have a plan before it kicks off," Raphael said shortly. "Come to my place in three days, and I'll tell you all about it."

After the meeting, Raphael walked home thoughtfully. He realised that he had just put his reputation on the line by insisting that his information was accurate. If Levi's information was incorrect, and nothing did happen in the Jewish Quarter, nobody would ever take him seriously again, and he might even be kicked out of the Young Sentinels for insurrection.

For three days, Raphael talked it all over with Levi, Maxa, and Renata. Levi had an ear on the ground, and Maxa and Renata were shrewd young women who were completely committed to the cause; for the last couple of years, they had both devoted a huge amount of effort to persuading other young people that the time had come to move to Israel and start anew. It was a message that a lot of people, especially young men, found more palatable coming from two pretty girls.

Three days later, Raphael had a plan to present to Marcella. He was a little nervous, but he also felt confident that, if the Jewish Quarter was attacked, as he expected it to be, he and his fighters would be in a good position to defend it.

Renata and Maxa had made some snacks for Marcella, who bit approvingly into a cheese sandwich as soon as she arrived.

"This is good," she said, spraying crumbs everywhere. "I've been so busy lately, I hardly ever get time to eat."

"OK," said Raphael. "Well, while you're busy having your sandwich, let me explain the plan."

Raphael took out a hand-drawn map of the Jewish Quarter and laid it out on the table. He had spent ages making it, detailing all the shops and buildings along El Mouski Street, which formed the heart of the hardscrabble area, and Khan el Khalili Street, which largely hosted jewellery shops. Marcella had been perfectly correct when she had pointed out that most of the Jews in the area lived in poverty. The main street wasn't even paved, and the shops and houses on either side were tumble-down affairs. It was an area where children played barefoot in the dust and people preferred not to linger after dark, because you never knew what might happen there.

"We've got one very important thing going for us," Raphael explained. "There are only two ways in and out of the area, and they're both gated. This means that it would be hard for anyone to launch a surprise attack, and even if they come in great numbers, we should be able to manage the situation if we're properly prepared."

"If they come—and you know I think they probably won't—it probably *will* be in great numbers," Marcella said grimly, "because there are plenty of Jew-haters in Cairo; more with each day that passes. So how many personnel do you have?"

Raphael was very proud of how successful his efforts had been in the Jewish Quarter.

"Between boys and young men and women, we've got about 250 activists. Levi is from that area, and he knows everyone. He's been scouring the streets, explaining how it important it is for everyone to pull together to defend their homes. Right now, I've got them collecting old tyres ..."

"Old tyres?"

"We don't have weapons for everyone, obviously, so tyres are as good as it's going to get for most people. If they are put on fire, they can be thrown from the windows and roofs of the apartment buildings. Once a flaming tyre goes around someone's neck, he's not going to be able to think about anything else."

"That's a good point, if you think you can stomach the sight—and the smell."

"The gates that guard the entrances to the area are not in great shape, but we've stockpiled material like sandbags and old furniture to block them off to make it a lot harder for people to come in, and we've been in touch with the local funeral parlour, which is right beside the main gate. I've had twenty girls working in there day and night filling eggs with sulphuric acid and sealing them and making Molotov cocktails. We're storing everything in the coffins for safekeeping."

"I see," said Marcella, impressed. "So you're going to be in with a fighting chance if you do get attacked. That's good, at least."

"Well, that's the general idea. There are twelve thousand people living in that area, and even if they are mostly poor, it's their home, and I know that they're prepared to fight for it. We've armed them with home-made bombs stuffed with bolts and nuts. The fact that most of the fireworks are made in the Jewish Quarter, and that the Sham el-Nassim festival is coming up, did come in handy. We didn't have to go elsewhere to get the gunpowder, so no suspicions have been raised."

Sham el-Nassim was the spring holiday traditionally celebrated in Egypt with fireworks, and the gunpowder for the fireworks had been used to make the bombs, which would only be deployed if it was strictly necessary. Everyone was hoping that nobody would actually be killed.

Marcella slapped Raphael on the back in congratulations for his efforts.

"Well done," she said. "You're coming along really well. I still think it's most likely that nobody is actually going to attack tonight, but if they do, at least you'll be prepared for it. I don't think that anyone else would have been able to do any better. The Jewish Quarter is in good hands. Remember, though: we have to maintain the moral high ground. That means that any violence has to be strictly in self-defence. Make sure that none of your people attack anyone, because the last thing we want is to get a reputation as trouble-makers or to have innocent blood on our hands. We are not here to hurt anyone. All we want to do is protect our own."

2017

"Can you just remind me of what was going on politically at the time?" Rebecca asked. "Obviously, this was a very troubled period in the region, and I know Israel was founded in 1948 …"

"Basically, Britain was getting fed up of being in the area," Richard said. "And they wanted to go home. The war was over, and they needed to focus on rebuilding their own country. At the same time, Egypt wanted them gone. It was embarrassing for Egyptians, being told what to do in their own country. Also, there was a massive movement of Jews across all of Europe and the Middle East. Jews were already moving into what was then known as Palestine with the idea of founding a new Jewish state, but there was huge opposition from Egypt, which is one of the reasons why things got so hot for the Jewish community in Cairo. The Jews were in a lose–lose situation, in some ways. How could they stay, knowing that people whom they had once seen as friends and neighbours had started to turn on them? And yet, how could they go and leave their homes and businesses behind? Even if the future of an independent Israel looked very uncertain, it's easy to see why people were pinning all their hopes on the idea."

1948

Raphael was awash with conflicting emotions ahead of the defence of the Jewish Quarter. He was excited but also scared—although that was something he struggled to admit, even to himself. He was proud to be defending his people but also horrified by the awful reality that he might have to kill someone, perhaps even a young person who had simply got caught up in the mass hysteria and didn't really know what he was doing. Concerned that the propaganda machine could present the Jews' actions unfairly, he had contacted journalists from all the major newspapers to come to the Jewish Quarter to see for themselves what happened. He wanted to be sure that an accurate depiction of events was presented to the public rather than the usual propaganda.

The violence had been expected for Friday, the eve of the Jewish Sabbath, but by Thursday more than five thousand angry protestors had already swarmed to the gate that led to the Jewish Quarter.

This is really happening, thought Raphael as he and Levi rushed to take their positions. *Thank God for my amulet.*

As quickly as they could, they ran to the funeral parlour, which had become the local headquarters of the Young Sentinels and the Jewish resistance. The leaders of the resistance cells had already gathered for their orders. Most of them were boys still in their teens, but a few were young housewives determined to fight as hard as necessary to keep their children safe. They had already done a lot of work to get things set up, with tyres stuffed with cloth to be set on fire and thousands of eggs filled with acid piled up in the coffins.

"Remember," Raphael said, addressing the group. "We are here to defend your area, your homes, and your children. We are not here to hurt people unless we have to. This is a defence force, and we do not want to sink to the level of the people who are out to hurt us. Is that clear?"

As the day went on, the crowds at the gates dispersed. Clearly, the attack was to take place the following day. Raphael and Levi decided to sleep at the funeral parlour so that they would be available straight away.

That night, Raphael tossed and turned. He told himself that it was important to rest, that he needed to be refreshed for the following day, but he couldn't sleep. He went over and over the preparations in his head, although he knew that they were organised and as ready as they would ever be. He asked himself why the angry crowd wanted to hurt and kill the Jews in the first place. It didn't make any sense. The Jewish community had always been a part of Cairo. Why was everyone turning against them now?

At least I'm not a virgin, Raphael though. *Even if I do die tomorrow, at least I've had that experience. I'm so glad that I'm not going to die without having had sex.* Calmed by this thought, he finally managed to get some sleep.

The next morning started out deceptively calm. As they had been instructed, the residents of the Jewish Quarter went about their daily business as normal. Shabbat would start that evening, so it was a busy day for the housewives, who had to get their homes clean and prepare everything for the meal. By late morning, the shops had closed down, and the streets were quiet. Even the pigeons which nested in the eaves and on the rooftops of the rickety apartment buildings were quiet, as though they, too, knew that trouble was on the way.

At noon, the Muslim call to prayer could be heard emanating from the mosque that lay just beyond the walls of the Jewish Quarter. Everyone knew that this was also a call to arms, for both the militants who planned to attack today and the Jews who knew they had to fight as hard as they could to save their homes and possibly their lives.

Minutes later, the first crowds could be heard approaching, shouting their anger against the king, the British, and the Jews. Preaching in the mosque, their imam had told them that there was a place in heaven for every Muslim who killed a Jew.

Many of the men in the crowd, marching with their faces distorted in anger, had brought knives from their homes for the purpose of securing their places in heaven. Their voices seemed to grow and swell until they reached the gates. From his vantage point in the funeral parlour, Raphael could hear them chanting: "Death to the Jews! Death to the Jews!" He could only hope that the preparations he had overseen would be sufficient.

This is it, he thought. *This is my moment of truth. Am I really man enough to lead these people to safety? Can my amulet really keep me safe? Will I die today, or can I hope to live long enough to finish growing up, get married, and have a family of my own?*

He knew that the next hours would bring him answers to all of those questions.

The angry mob reached the gate, their furious screams rending the air. Just outside the gate, a local shopkeeper emerged from his store and made his way to the middle of the street. From his vantage point in the funeral home, Raphael could see that the man was deeply distressed. Dark patches of sweat stained his cotton suit, and his face was contorted with emotional pain.

"What in God's name are you doing?" the man shouted. "These people are our friends and neighbours; you know that! We've been living in harmony with them for generations. Go home, please; go home to your wives and children and stop this madness. You are behaving like animals. Can't you see that what you are doing is wrong? God will curse us all if this continues! True Muslims are peaceful, not violent—if you have been listening to men who say otherwise, they are doing the devil's work!"

All the activists in the funeral parlour and the journalists held their breaths to see what would happen next. Raphael could see a young woman near him wipe a tear from her eye.

"That's Hassan," she whispered to him. "He's a friend of my dad's, and I've known him all my life. He's a Muslim, but he's never had any problem doing business with Jews or anyone else. I went to school with his daughter, and she's always been a good friend of mine. It's so like him to try to stop the rioters. He's a real gentleman, and we all love him."

The crowd paused to look at the shopkeeper in the middle of the street, and for a fraction of a moment it seemed as though they might listen to him. But then a lone voice shouted "Kill the Jew!" and then they all joined in, chanting, "Kill the Jew!" over and over again, like an awful battle cry. Two beefy men brandishing butcher's knives detached themselves from the mob. One of them forced the elderly shopkeeper to his knees while the other held up his huge, shining knife.

"Allah Akbar," the crowd shouted in response to the sight of the flashing blade. "Kill the Jew!"

While his friend held the shopkeeper's head back, exposing his neck as though he were a lamb at the butcher's, the large man approached him from behind and, with a single expert slash, cut through Hassan's throat and severed his head. The crowd continued to chant and bay for blood as he held the head aloft by the hair, basking in their praise.

"God help us all," muttered Raphael. "We will be fighting not just for our community, but for our lives, if this is the sort of thing they are capable of!"

Raphael heard the dull thud as the murdered shopkeeper's head hit the ground. He looked out the window again and saw the widening pool of blood around his prostrate body, which twitched for a few moments before becoming slack and still. The crowd was advancing again, marching through the blood, which soaked into the hems of their garments.

Raphael kissed his amulet, silently asking it for help. He knew that the people of the Jewish Quarter were looking to him for leadership right now, and he prayed that he would be able to give it. His heart was racing, and he knew that he should be afraid, but from somewhere deep inside himself he sensed the certitude that, whatever happened, he would be all right.

"Set the gate on fire!" he ordered. "Quickly, before it's too late!"

Two young men dashed forward with torches and lit the gate, which had been stuffed with all the flammable material that the community had been able to get its hands on. Flames surged immediately, crackling and reaching towards the sky. The mob attempted to breach the barrier, but many of them were wearing loose cotton robes that caught on fire immediately, leaving them flailing and trying to extinguish the flames while their companions scattered, afraid to get too close. Those who managed to escape the flames focused on destroying the gate and succeeded in opening a hole, through which two men managed to climb.

"Use the tyres!" Raphael screamed. "Throw them around their necks; that's what they're for!"

The activists had prepared hundreds of tyres, stuffed with flammable material. Quickly, the teenage boys under Raphael's leadership lit them with their torches and threw them over the heads of anyone who managed to make it through the gates. The screams of the victims were unbearable, and so was the stench of their cooking flesh as they fell on the ground and flailed around, trying futilely to get the tyres off from around their necks. It was hard to watch. Within moments, their frantic movements stopped and they lay on the ground, their faces and upper bodies reduced to scraps of burned flesh attached to skeletons, with their teeth still bared in a silent shriek.

Raphael knew that, although these men had come here to kill the Jews, they were also just ordinary people who had somehow allowed themselves to be swept up in the hatred that was engulfing Egypt. Months before, he might have met them in his workshop or exchanged a smile with them on the street. How could they have allowed themselves to become such monsters? Raphael ordered the activists to keep using the tyres as long as anyone tried to breach the gate. Anyone who attempted to come in was immediately engulfed in devastating flames.

Meanwhile, Raphael could hear Levi, who was in charge of the first and second floors of the funeral parlour.

"Throw your missiles!" Levi instructed the girls and boys—some as young as 12 or 13—who were listening to him intently, pale-faced but filled with determination to do what they could to save their community. The filled eggs and bottles they flung shattered as they hit their targets, and the sulphuric acid immediately burned away flesh as it dropped down their faces, shoulders, and arms.

Within minutes of the first breach of the gate, the air was filled with the horrendous sound of screaming as the first flank of the mob lay on the ground. Some were already dead, others were dying, and yet more were horribly injured. They writhed and begged for help, their hands uselessly tugging at the burning tyres around their necks or clawing at their faces, disintegrating as the acid steadily dissolved through layers of skin, fat, and bone. It was a gruesome spectacle that nobody could have borne had it not been for the fact that all the Jewish activists knew that if they did not defend themselves, they would be the ones writhing on the floor in agony, because they were vastly outnumbered by a mob filled with hatred for them.

Sullen and silent, the mob that had been so intent on destroying the Jews disbanded and left. News came through from the other gate that the attempts to breach it had been less determined, and the mob there had been dissuaded by just a few strikes of sulphuric acid. Now that their death was no longer imminent, many of the activists started to shake and cry, utterly overwhelmed by the horrors they had seen and participated in.

Raphael knew that if he allowed himself to relax, he would cry too. He felt sick. He had never seen anyone writhing in agony and screaming before; he had never had a part to play in the destruction of another human life. Instead, by allowing himself not to dwell on the devastation, he focused on the business at hand, which was assessing the situation and figuring out who needed help. A few activists had been hurt, but none seriously, and they had used about a quarter of their ammunition and weapons over the course of an attempted invasion which had lasted nearly four hours.

As soon as they knew that the coast was clear, the journalists—pale and shocked—packed up their notepads and pencils and fled back to their safe offices. Hopefully, they would write accurate accounts of what had happened here and tell the world that the Jews had had to defend themselves from a bloodthirsty mob and had done nothing wrong.

"Boss," said Levi, approaching Raphael with a kind expression on his face. "Don't feel bad about what happened here today. You did what you had to. Nobody died who wasn't here to take life himself, and if we had not managed to repel them, there would have been hundreds more deaths. Remember that they came here to kill the Jews, and they wouldn't have cared who they slaughtered. They'd have killed woman, children, and even infants. I've heard that people have been saying that they are prepared to pick up Jewish children by the ankles and smash their brains out against the wall. It's not pretty, seeing a man die, but they got what was coming to them, and you rose to the occasion and behaved as a true man must. If you have the energy to feel anything but exhausted, let yourself experience some pride, because you have earned it."

"Thanks," said Raphael. He knew that one day he would have to somehow confront the reality of what he had seen and done. This, however, was not the time. The mob could return at any time, with more weapons and better prepared. It was perfectly clear that nobody in the Jewish Quarter, and indeed no Jew anywhere in Egypt, was safe.

The city authorities sent ambulances to collect the victims, dead and injured, and bring them to hospitals and morgues. Later that day, a senior police officer was sent to speak to the inhabitants of the Jewish Quarter, and he spoke at an assembly of the local leaders.

"I understand that you only did what you had to, to defend yourselves and your families," the officer said, "but at the same time, people are very angry and upset about the deaths and injuries. Believe me, the Egyptian police force is here to defend all of the country's citizens and residents, including the Jews. However, for your own sakes, I urge you to pay an indemnity to the victims and the families. Otherwise, the situation is just going to get even worse."

Angry voices arose from the crowd.

"Where were the police for the four hours we had to defend ourselves from the mob?" one man shouted. "The Egyptian police force didn't show any interest in protecting us then! God knows what would have happened if we had not been able to fend them off."

"What about the poor man who was killed in the street, like a sheep at the butcher's?" someone shouted. "He was a Muslim—one of your own. Where is the justice for him? That man was a hero. He gambled with his life when he tried to protect his friends and neighbours, and he lost. So are you going to make sure that he and his wife and family get the justice they deserve?"

The policeman looked very uncomfortable.

"Unfortunately," he said, "we have not been able to identify any reliable witnesses to that particular death, and it looks as though it will be impossible to track down who killed the victim you are referring to. Of course, no stone will be left unturned—it was a despicable act—but we do not feel optimistic that we will find the culprit."

An angry rumble went through the crowd as people started to complain about the fact that a cover-up was clearly already underway.

The police officer shrugged his shoulders and looked down at the floor. The simple reality was that if the Jews didn't look after themselves, nobody else was going to. This extended, too, to anyone who stepped up to help the Jews. It was perfectly clear that nobody was going to face charges for the murder of the brave shopkeeper who had tried to quell the madness of the crowd, despite the fact that there had been scores, if not hundreds, of witnesses.

*   *   *

Marcella looked exhausted at the emergency meeting of the Young Sentinels, held in the Palmyra Café. The meeting was attended by Mireille, her second in command, Robert, and Raphael.

"We're in a mess," Marcella said briefly. "My chief, Elia, is furious with me for letting the situation get so badly out of control. Raphael, he feels that you came on far too strong. What the hell were you thinking? Eighty of the mob were badly injured, and a small number died. This has seriously impacted how we're seen in Egypt. Now that they think that we're prepared to kill, we'll be hated even more. I thought I made it perfectly clear that you were supposed to act in self-defence only. Now the newspapers can make it look as though the Jews led the attack and started the violence … Raphael, I am asking you to defend yourself here, before we decide what we are going to do with you. What do you have to say for yourself?"

"Marcella, you weren't there," Raphael said, "and you didn't see what we had to deal with. We had literally no choice but to defend ourselves as violently as we did. Didn't you hear about how they started by killing an innocent shopkeeper, who wasn't even Jewish, but a local Muslim who called on them to stop the violence? He was a good man who was loved and will be missed by many in the Jewish Quarter. They cut off his head right there on the street in front of his shop, threw it on the ground, and waded through his blood to get to us. They were out to kill us all, and if we hadn't stood up for ourselves, we would all have been destroyed."

Marcella listened but said nothing.

"It was as though they'd all gone mad," Raphael continued. "Honestly, I had never seen anything like it in my life. I don't really believe in the devil, but it was like they were possessed by him. It was awful. But you don't have to believe me, I invited journalists from all the major newspapers, and they should be publishing their stories. If they tell the truth, then you'll see for yourself that what I am telling you is accurate."

"I didn't know you'd invited the journalists," said Marcella quietly. "That was clever. Please God, they will tell the truth and support your story. If they don't, it could mean the end for the Young Sentinels—and enormous trouble for all of us. Everyone, go home and try to get some rest. There's no point in doing anything until the newspapers come out. Once we see what they say, we can make a plan for our next steps."

The following day, all the major papers published stories on the riot that described the terrible actions of the mob, starting with the murder of the honest, good-hearted shopkeeper who had been brave enough to do his best to get them to leave. Robert and Raphael pored over the newspapers together. The coverage blamed the authorities for doing nothing to contain the violence, and—even though they had often published anti-Jewish material before—they did not blame the Jews for anything in this instance. Raphael did not hear from Marcella immediately, but he felt that he had been vindicated. He had done nothing wrong.

"Well done," said Robert. "Marcella and the higher-ups will see that you did all you could. Those crazies would have murdered you and everyone else if you hadn't given all you got. You know what this means, don't you? You'll get a promotion. You'll probably be put in charge of a cell."

There were small cells of activists all over Cairo. Cell leaders didn't know each other, but they all reported to a central authority, which coordinated their efforts and made sure that they were all fighting seamlessly towards a common cause.

"I don't know if I even *want* to be promoted," said Raphael. "Part of me feels like I've already done enough and should leave before it all gets even worse."

"Are you kidding? Look, you obviously know what you're doing. You don't get scared and freeze when you are fighting danger, and people want to do what you tell them."

"It's not that I'm scared. It's that I don't like hurting and killing people. I know sometimes it's necessary to defend ourselves, but at the same time … the other day, it was like they had all gone crazy. On another day, in other circumstances, they'd just have been ordinary men, drinking coffee, complaining about their wives, or following the football results. Something got into their heads and drove them insane."

"You can't waste time fretting about them," Robert urged. "They're not your problem now, OK?"

"OK, but …"

Just then, the door opened, and Maxa and Renata came in.

"You're not having a meeting or anything, are you?" asked Maxa.

"No, nothing like that."

"That's good, 'cause we really wanted to see you. We've been reading the papers, and we also heard about what you did. Raphael, you saved so many lives! Everyone in the Jewish Quarter is talking about you and what you did. You could have been killed defending our people."

"Oh, Maxa, I don't know …"

"She's right!" Renata interrupted. "I know, a couple of people were killed and loads more ended up in hospital, but what do you think would've happened if you hadn't been there? The Jewish Quarter would have been decimated. Loads more people would have died, and they would have been *our* people. I know that the attack took four hours. Where were the police all that time? Where was the army? The simple truth is that the government of Egypt doesn't give a shit about the Jews. If we don't take care of ourselves, nobody will."

"We should celebrate!" said Maxa. "Let's have a party."

Raphael had never felt anything but love for the two girls, but suddenly he was furious with them.

"What are you talking about?" he shouted. "Celebrate what, exactly? The fact that some people are dead and that I had something to do with it? I don't think that's anything to be happy about, do you? And even the men in the mob weren't the real ones to blame. They were all wound up by some of the imams, who tell them that Jews are to blame for everything that's not going well in Egypt."

"Oh, give it a rest," said Renata. "This is not the time for getting upset about the feelings and motivations of people who'd kill you the moment they got a chance. If we don't stand up for ourselves, every single Jew in Cairo is going to end up murdered. Don't you get it? Or are you still hoping for a happy ending here? I think we should celebrate when we can. We could all be dead tomorrow."

"Oh, it's easy for you middle-class girls who think the idea of Israel is so *romantic*," said Raphael with a touch of malice. "All you have to do is flutter your pretty eyelashes and tell everyone how great it's going to be, when we're all living in Israel and talking Hebrew to each other like there's no tomorrow. Try telling that to the housewives in the Jewish Quarter, who had to fight off the mob to protect the lives of their children and then go back to trying to find enough money to buy some bread for their families."

"But that's exactly who I *am* talking about, Raphael," said Renata, exasperated. "Those women you mention … if it hadn't been for you and the rest of the activists, what do you think the mob would've done to them? They'd have been raped and murdered and would have seen their kids being raped and murdered in front of their eyes first. *That's* what you prevented! *That's* what we should celebrate. The fact that all those women and children are alive to see another day. And yes, the fact that there might soon be a safe home for them in a free Israel."

"I think we all need to calm down," said Robert. "I agree that these are awful times, but I do think that we could all do with a beer."

"Agreed," said Raphael, Maxa, and Renata together.

Robert went to the kitchen and returned with four cold beers, which the four Young Sentinels drank in a somewhat uneasy silence.

"I have to go," Robert announced when the beer was finished. "Renata, want to come with me?"

"Sure," said Renata. "Maxa, I'll see you at home later. Raphael, take care of yourself, and I'll see you soon."

As the door closed behind Renata and Robert, Maxa turned to Raphael with a cheeky grin. "I know what *I* need," she said. "A nice shower. Coming?"

Under the soothing flow of water, Raphael ran his hands over Maxa's supple young body and was finally able to forget about what had happened. For as long as they were together, naked and playing with one another's bodies, his mind's eye was not tormented by the awful sights, sounds, and smells of the raid on the Jewish Quarter. As they reached climax together, their young voices raised in a glad, life-affirming cry, Raphael knew that, despite recent events, the world was not an altogether terrible place. There was room for happiness in it.

When they had finished making love and were relaxing on Raphael's parents' big double bed, Maxa played with the amulet around Raphael's neck.

"I have the feeling that this is what kept you safe in the Jewish Quarter," she said. "Is it true? I know you never take it off, and there's got to be a reason for that."

Raphael deflected the question by changing the subject.

"You I know I love you and Renata very much," he said. "I just worry that I might get in your way of a happy marriage later on …"

"I know, I know," said Maxa with a pout. "You're already promised to someone and you're going to marry her one day, blah, blah. We both know all about that, and we don't care. You're not the beginning and end of the world, you know, and neither of us thinks you're going to change your mind and marry one of us. We're happy to love you now and worry about the future later. With all that's going on in Egypt, what girl would want to remain a virgin? We could all be killed any day, and who wants to die without having had sex? Not me, that's for sure! Maybe men think that women don't care about sex, but that's not true. We can think about virtue and all that rubbish when the violence is over. Nobody knows what the future holds, but let's just enjoy ourselves for now, OK? One day I'll get married to someone else, and I'll pretend I'm a virgin if I have to. We girls have our little tricks."

She added, "Do you know what girls do? They empty a quail egg, just like you did with ordinary eggs to make the acid bombs, and they fill it with blood from an animal. They get married with the egg tucked inside so on the wedding night, presto—just enough blood on the sheets to convince a husband. For now, I think we've all got more important things on our minds than virginity, like staying alive, making our dream of a free Jewish Israel come true, and …"

The rest of Maxa's words were swallowed by Raphael's kiss as he lowered his body once more onto hers.

2017

"It's so easy to forget how hard things were back then," said Rebecca. "You can understand how the young people grew up so much faster than they did today. They literally didn't know if they were going to survive to be adults. Of course they all wanted to have sex and weren't afraid to get involved in defending the community. What choice did they have?"

"I still can't believe that Grandad's parents just went off to Sudan and left him behind with everything that was going on," said David. "I mean, what kind of parents do that, seriously?"

"His mum, Flora, knew that there was no point in trying to force him to do something he didn't want to," said Richard. "She could see for herself that his mind was made up. I am sure that if anything bad had happened, she would have been the first to rush back to take care of him. As for his dad, well, things weren't great between them. They never really had been. They rubbed each other up the wrong way. Joseph really struggled to accept that Raphael just wasn't going to be like his brothers and do what he was told. I imagine that for Joseph, there must have been an element of relief in getting a break from a boy who was always pushing the boundaries—and all his dad's buttons."

"And yet," said Rebecca, "even though he spent his young days challenging his dad and pushing for more independence, he never once doubted his identity, did he? I mean, despite all these relationships with girls and women, one constant in his young life was the fact that, one day, he would come back to the fold and marry Granny, right?"

"That's right," said Richard. "And I'm sure that his involvement in activism only served to cement his Jewish identity further."

"Holy shit, though!" said David. "I wish my teenage years had been a lot more like Grandad's! Nothing like that ever went on in the boy scouts!"

"Watch what you're saying!" laughed Rebecca. "You don't want me to go back and tell your wife you said that. I think she's still under the impression that she's always been the only woman for you."

"Renata and Maxa definitely gave him a taste for having multiple partners in love, that's for sure," said Richard. "It was a taste that he brought with him all the way to Nigeria. He learned how to juggle more than one woman as a kid, and as you know, he perfected the art during his reign as the King of the Crocodiles. But before he left Egypt and made his way to Nigeria, he was part of something really big."

"What sort of thing?" asked David.

"Well," said Richard, "it's no exaggeration to say that he was involved in making history. Those were difficult times, and some of the young people in Egypt decided that they would be better off trying to create their own destiny than passively waiting to see how things were going to turn out."

"Go on then," said Rebecca. "Tell us more."

CHAPTER 9

DOUBTS AND AFFIRMATIONS

2017

"Even though none of us has ever lived in Israel," said Richard, "I think it's fair to say that we're all glad it's there …"

The others assented. None of them were history buffs, but they all agreed that you don't have to be one to know that the international Jewish community had suffered more than its fair share of discrimination over the years.

"You don't have to know a lot about history to understand that the Jews have a lot of good reasons to want to have a homeland of their own," commented Rebecca. "That doesn't mean Israel's perfect or anything—just that it matters to us all."

"Right. That's why it's so mind-blowing to think that without people like Grandad, there wouldn't even be an Israel at all, and the world would be a very different place for Jews everywhere. It's easy to be blasé about it all now that it's happened, but back then, things could still have gone either way …"

1948

Everyone Raphael knew seemed to be delighted with how things had worked out at the Jewish Quarter, but he was not so sure. He kept having nightmares about the things he had seen, the things he had been involved in. The nightmares woke him and left him in a state of turmoil. He was disgusted when he thought about how he had ordered the flaming tyres to be thrown around the invaders' necks— and by his memories of the gruesome spectacle of them writhing on the ground, trying and failing to get the tyre off. A lot of the invaders had been young men of much the same age as him. He could easily have attended the madrasa with them or played football in the street with them when they were all younger.

He desperately wanted to talk to someone about the many awful things he had seen and done, but he didn't know who. His friends didn't want to know. Most of them were involved in trying to persuade the Jews of Cairo to leave for Israel and couldn't afford to entertain any doubts or uncertainties. They all seemed to see him as a strong person, and he didn't want to let them down or disappoint them by revealing that he often had doubts and anxieties.

I need someone to talk to, Raphael realised. *Someone who won't judge me for the things I've done. But who? If my mum was here, maybe I could talk to her, but she's far away in Sudan … and anyway, I don't want to worry her. She's got enough to deal with already.*

Then someone came to mind: Maddy. Sure, he had just been her client and he'd paid her money for sex, but he also loved and respected her. For her part, she had been almost maternal towards him—loving, sweet, and kind. He felt as though she was someone who genuinely cared for him. He had gone to her for help in becoming comfortable with his own sexuality, and now he would go to her for help with something else: unburdening his soul.

Now that his mind had been made up, Raphael headed straight for the red-light district where he had first met Maddy. He went straight to the brothel where she used to work, but it had become a coffee shop, and the new owners didn't know who she was. Disconsolately, Raphael went from brothel to brothel asking about her, but nobody seemed to have heard of her—and if they had, they weren't telling. Finally, he confided in Levi.

"You should have come to me first, boss!" Levi said. "I know the woman you're talking about. She's not on the game anymore. She always said she'd get out of the business before she left her early thirties. The money's good when they're young and pretty, but it's a hard life and nobody wants to pay a haggard whore to spread her legs, do they? Anyway, it's getting harder and harder to run a brothel in Cairo, because the authorities are really cracking down on them. The Muslim Brotherhood has more and more power these days, and they say that brothels are un-Islamic, even if their own members are among the customers. The good news is that your friend Maddy is doing OK; she got out in time, and she's clever enough to land on her feet. She got a job behind the bar at Shepheard's Hotel, and she's still as pretty as a picture."

Raphael was impressed. Shepheard's was one of the fanciest hotels in Cairo, with a reputation for luxury and for treating its staff well so that they wouldn't want to work anywhere else. All the high-ranking British army officials patronised the place, and even Winston Churchill had been known to go there for a gin and tonic when he was in Egypt. Raphael also remembered that his cousin Shalom worked there. He hadn't seen Shalom since his parents had left for Sudan, but this seemed like a good occasion to look him up.

"Thanks, Levi," Raphael said. "I'm going straight there."

After going home to put on some smarter clothes and dress his hair, Raphael hurried down to Shepheard's Hotel. Sure enough, he saw his cousin Shalom behind the bar counter.

"Raphael, is that you?" Shalom said, emerging from behind it to hug him. "I haven't seen you for ages! Look at you; you're not a kid anymore."

Shalom was a few years older than Raphael, so they hadn't ever been close, but now Raphael realised that the age gap didn't seem important anymore. They were both men now.

"I'm glad you came by, Raphael," said Shalom. "These are difficult times, and we're family. If there's anything I can do to help, you just have to ask. So, what have you been up to?"

Raphael thought of all the dangerous activities he had been involved in. If he told Shalom about any of it, the news would filter back through the family grapevine to Flora, and then she would be worried and upset. He couldn't let that happen.

"Oh, I haven't been up to much," he lied. "Just keeping the business ticking over so that there'll be something there for my parents to come back to when things settle down around here."

Raphael took in the lavish hotel surroundings. Shepheard's had been built in a British colonial style and was decorated with gilt and luxurious furniture and ornamentations that captured the essence of both East and West. The hotel looked onto the great Cairo Opera House, which was in reality mostly used for performances of Egyptian music and belly dancing. Most of the customers were formally dressed in a Western style, but the waiters wore fezzes and loose Egyptian clothing. The largely British clientele preferred it like that, because it looked exotic to them and made them feel as though the Empire was still in its heyday rather than on the way out.

Shalom, who was the bar manager, was wearing Western clothing, but he still stood out like a sore thumb among the rest of the staff because of his red hair, green eyes, and pale, freckled skin. On one of his visits, Churchill had asked him suspiciously if he was Irish, and smiled when he said that he was not.

"Good," Churchill had uttered. "I can't stand the Irish. Silly buggers point-blank refuse to be English."

"Anyway," Raphael said to his cousin, getting back to business. "I was wondering ... I'm looking for an old friend of mine who I've lost touch with, a woman called Maddy. Someone told me that she was working here."

"Maddy? Could you mean Madeleine? Sure, I know her; I hired her myself. She's great. One of the best we've got—a real pro. People like being served by a Frenchwoman. They think it adds a touch of class, and her accent is cute. I was really impressed by how quickly she picked everything up and fitted in around here, and I like speaking French with her. I don't get the chance to use my French every day, and I'd hate to think of it getting rusty."

"Can I see her? I've known her for years, but it's important ... we've been out of touch for a little while, and I need to ask her something urgently. She's really clever, Madeleine, and I value her judgement a lot …"

Briefly, Raphael wondered how Shalom and Maddy had met. The most likely scenario was that he, too, had been a customer of hers when she was still a working girl. Presumably their professional relationship had become a friendship, and he had been able to see that Maddy was capable of a great deal more than working in a brothel. Although Raphael didn't really know his cousin very well, realising that Shalom was broad-minded and open made Raphael like him very much.

"She's working at the moment," Shalom told him. "Could you come back after seven when she finishes her shift?"

"I'm in a bit of a rush. Sorry, Shalom, but I'd really like to see her, even if it's just for a moment."

Shalom could see that it was important for Raphael, so he relented. "OK. She's working in the bar at the front, and it's fairly quiet at the moment, so I suppose she can take a break. Just for a few minutes though, OK? It's a busy time of day around here, and business could pick up at any minute."

Shalom led Raphael around to the bar, where he had a few words with Maddy. Surprised, Maddy looked up and straight into Raphael's eyes. Her blonde hair was caught up in a high ponytail, and in her bar-staff uniform, she looked years younger than her actual age. She and Shalom exchanged a few words, and then she smiled at him, took off her apron, and walked around from inside the bar.

"Fancy meeting you here!" Maddy said. "You're a sight for sore eyes. It's been a long time. I can see that you're taller, and you look a lot older, more grown up."

"Maddy, I was wondering if I could see you in private later on," Raphael said. "Not like before … I know you work in the hotel now. It's just that I need someone to talk to, someone who'll really listen, and you came to mind."

"We always did have that special rapport," said Maddy. "Sure, we can meet up. But there's just one thing: can you call me Madeleine? I really prefer to go by Madeleine now. New life, new start … it's easier if I have a new name, too. It's not that I regret the past, but it's time to move on."

"Of course. Madeleine it is."

Madeleine gave Raphael her address, which was in an upmarket apartment building called Immobilia on one of the big avenues of Cairo, not far from the hotel. The building was quite new and many storeys high, which was still very unusual in Cairo—where in general, buildings never exceeded four or five floors with no elevators—and ensured that it was a landmark that could easily be seen even from quite far away.

"Don't look so surprised!" she said in response to his expression when she told him where she lived. "The hotel pays the rent. I just stay there. It's great; means that I'm able to put away a little every month so that eventually I'll be able to buy a small place of my own, maybe even that patisserie in France that I've always dreamt of. Look, I have to go back to work now, but I can meet you outside my place at seven."

Raphael paced the streets until seven. He had waited so long to unburden his soul to someone that he could hardly bear to wait another minute now. Eventually Madeleine appeared, her blonde ponytail swinging to and fro as she walked quickly up the street.

"There you are!" she said. "Come on in."

They walked into the lavish building together, went past the doorman whom Madeleine greeted as "Bawab", and took the elevator (a great luxury in Cairo) to the seventh floor, where Madeleine opened the door into a small but perfectly maintained studio apartment with a jug of fresh flowers on the little table in front of the window.

"Home sweet home," she said. "Take your shoes off, sit down, and make yourself comfortable."

Raphael did as she suggested and then sank into a soft armchair in the corner while Madeline filled a jug with fresh water and laid out two glasses.

"How can I help you?" Madeleine asked simply.

"I just need to talk."

To his embarrassment, Raphael felt tears welling into his eyes. He brushed them away with the back of his hand.

"Then talk."

After waiting for him to compose himself, Madeleine sat and listened while Raphael poured out his heart to her. He told her how proud he was of making the leather business work when his father had been ready to give up on it and even to sneak away without giving the workers fair notice of his plans; the fact that, at times, he missed his mother more than he wanted to admit to anyone, even himself; his fears for the future of the Jews in Cairo; and the nightmares he had suffered again and again since that awful day in the Jewish quarter.

"Raphael, look," Madeleine finally said. "I am so glad that you felt able to come and talk to me. I can see that you don't really need help. You're more than capable of looking after yourself, and you just need someone to talk to. But it's not crazy to be scared right now, and you definitely shouldn't be ashamed or embarrassed about your feelings. Cairo could descend into chaos any minute.

"I know I'm just a bargirl," she continued, "but I see everyone— Egyptian politicians, British army officers ... everyone. They have a few drinks at the bar, and they start to get indiscreet and blather about what's going on. It's a real mess around here, I can tell you that. The army hates the royal family, and the royal family hates the army. The Egyptians want the Brits to leave, but the Brits don't intend to go anywhere until they have to. Everyone agrees that it could all go up in flames here and that the Jews are right in the firing line. Because there aren't that many of you, you're easy to blame—and a few lunatic imams have started telling their even more lunatic followers that the Jews are to blame for all their problems."

"So, what's your advice?"

"Take care of yourself first," Madeleine replied. "From the sound of things, you have good friends. Keep the girls—Maxa and Renata, isn't it?—close to you, because I can tell from the way you talk about them that they are important to you and that they are strong-minded girls. I know you like women better than men, and I know it's not just because you love sex. There's something about you that women respond to, and in this macho society, women like a man who actually listens, really listens, to them."

"That sounds like good advice," Raphael conceded.

"I can help you too. I'll keep my ear to the ground at the hotel, and I'll let you know what all the politicians are saying. That way, you'll know as much as I do about which way the wind is blowing— and believe me, I know a lot."

"Thanks for letting me talk, Madeleine," Raphael said. "I feel like a weight has been lifted off my mind, I really do."

"It's my pleasure."

"There's just one other thing."

"What is it?"

"Can you hug me? It's been ages since I had a proper hug, and I am too embarrassed to ask my friends. They all think that I'm this tough guy who doesn't need anyone for anything. Nobody knows how often I feel alone and afraid."

"Oh, sweetie …"

Madeleine crossed the room and put her arms around him. Raphael lowered his head to her breast and enjoyed the embrace. Her body was soft and warm, and he felt loved and secure, as he once had as a small child in his mother's arms.

"There have been plenty of girls, just as you said there would be," he mumbled, "but none of them hugs me the way you used to."

Suddenly, to his mortification, Raphael realised that tears were flowing down his cheeks, and that this time there was nothing he could do to stop them. It was as though the plug that had been holding in his emotions for months had just been removed. He said nothing, hoping that Madeleine wouldn't notice, but soon the front of her blouse was wet, and still his tears kept coming.

"Sweetheart, what's wrong?" she asked, tenderly.

"I don't know," he said. "I'm just tired. I'm so tired all the time, and I can't show it, because people think of me as strong and determined. Sometimes it's hard having to be strong and determined all the time. Sometimes all I want to do is go to sleep and not wake up until things are better."

"Come on," Madeleine said. "Lie down beside me on the bed, just for a rest. I will keep my arms around you."

They lay on the bed together, and Raphael continued to talk. He told Madeleine about his involvement with the activists and how, although he liked to show a brave face, he was often afraid. He explained that he'd had to hire protection, and that while he liked Levi and appreciated the work the man did, the fact of having a bodyguard just served to remind him of how dangerous his life in Cairo had become.

"Sometimes I feel as though my friends don't even care about all the sacrifices I make," he said. "It's probably my own fault, because I never let anyone see that I have a weak side. I tell them that I'm perfectly fine about everything, and they take me at my word, but the truth is that there are times when I wonder if I've just made one mistake after another. Maybe I should have gone to Sudan after all."

"What sort of work are you doing, sweetheart?"

"You know how difficult things have gotten for the Jews in Cairo? Well, I'm in a group that is helping young people get into Israel and defending the Jewish community in the meantime. Remember a few weeks ago when the Jewish Quarter was attacked? I didn't tell you the whole story before. Well, I wasn't just there; I was in charge of the resistance, and now I'm doing everything I can to get the Jews into Israel."

"Wouldn't you get into a lot of trouble if you were found out? The Egyptian government is strongly opposed to the whole idea of Israel, I know that much."

"I certainly would. I wish I could tell you more about it, but if you knew more, then you could get into trouble too."

In fact, the Young Sentinels were so well-organised that even if Raphael had told Madeleine all he knew, it would have been difficult for the police to do more with the information than arrest the people in Raphael's immediate cell. Ordinary cell members like him knew only their closest peers and their local leader. They had no idea who else was involved and were ignorant of the identity of regional and national leaders. The whole system had been set up to minimise the risk of information leaking and to keep those involved as safe as they could possibly be under very difficult circumstances.

"Well, don't tell me anything, then," said Madeleine. "All I want to know is how I can support you. I hate to see you all worried and upset like this."

"If I can come and talk to you now and again, that would help me a lot," said Raphael. "And if I ever get into trouble, and there's a way you can help me, can I let you know?"

"I'll do whatever I can," said Madeleine simply. "All you have to do is ask."

Then they lay in silence, Madeleine's hand softly stroking his thick black hair, until he fell asleep.

When Raphael woke, hours later, Madeleine was sitting beside the bed watching him, with a sweet smile on her face.

"Hello, sleepyhead," she said. "How are you? I thought you'd never wake up!"

He stretched and sat up.

"I feel amazing," he said in surprise. "I haven't had such a refreshing sleep for months, or maybe even years."

"That's the benefit of a good cry," Madeleine said. "Don't let yourself get so worked up again. Come to me first. I will always be here for you when you need to talk. Will you remember that?"

"Thank you, Madeleine. I won't forget."

From then on, Raphael and Madeleine's friendship developed into a warm relationship between equals. Whenever work allowed him, he went to Shepheard's Hotel to see her when she was taking a break. She coached him on the correct way to eat in France and on European etiquette, which could be quite different to that of the Middle East.

In the Arab culture, it was normal—particularly among the working classes—for men to sit down without waiting to see if their wives were comfortable and to talk among themselves while ignoring any women in their company. In France, instead, polite manners dictated that women should be seated and served first and that they should be included in any conversation taking place. Arabs ate many of their meals with their hands, whereas in France most food was eaten with a fork and knife or spoon and eating with the hands was considered uncouth. Raphael was eager to know how to conduct himself like a European so that he would know exactly what to do when he visited the great cities of the West, like Paris and London, for himself.

Sometimes they met when Madeleine had finished working for the day, and they walked along the banks of the Nile together, occasionally stopping for an ice cream or a sherbet, or just to sit beneath Raphael's favourite bougainvillea to enjoy the view or look at the pretty houseboats, with names like Dahabia and Tarbouch, bobbing on the water. Many of the houseboats were fully habitable homes, lavishly decorated inside and out. Some of them were kept as weekend or holiday homes, and others were kept by wealthy businessmen as comfortable apartments where they could spend time with their mistresses, far away from the prying eyes of their wives.

Raphael had learned that, while male sexual escapades were widely accepted and women were held to a different standard of moral behaviour, the reality was not always as advertised. One night, he told Madeleine the story of a wealthy woman who had ordered a fancy handbag to be delivered to her houseboat on the Nile and insisted that Raphael deliver it in person. As she was prepared to pay considerably for this personal delivery, he brought it—and was pleasantly surprised when the attractive woman in her thirties suggested that he stay for a while and make an even more personal delivery to her. When he was leaving afterwards, she gave him a wink.

"I'm the wife of a very wealthy man," she said, "and he's happy to buy me all the handbags and dresses I want, so long as I show up and play happy families with him whenever he asks. The problem with him is that he's getting old, and he isn't really able to satisfy a woman in bed anymore. I don't think he'd mind about you, though I am definitely not going to tell him."

"Ha!" said Madeleine, amused. "I bet the wives of most of the men who used to come to see me … back in *those* days … might have had similar stories to tell. Men are so silly; they can't even do simple mathematics. If they are all going out every second night with their mistresses, who do they think are the mistresses of the other men? Their wives, of course! The only real difference between women and men when it comes to infidelity is that the women are better at keeping it under wraps."

Raphael was glad to see Madeleine enjoying her work at the hotel so much. Although he had himself visited her as a client, he had always hated to think of her lovely body being pawed by so many men's hands. Now Madeleine wasn't seeing anyone.

"I'll tell you the truth, darling," she said. "I'm through with men. Maybe one day I'll meet someone I really like, fall in love, and get married, but until that time, I'm not interested in having anything to do with any of them. I haven't let a man touch me since I stopped doing … *that* work, and I'm just not interested in that sort of thing anymore."

Levi always kept a discreet distance while they spoke at the hotel. He understood, without having to be told, that Raphael needed some time alone with his friend.

"Is he *always* with you?" asked Madeleine on the fourth or fifth occasion, amused. "I know that things are going from bad to worse, but is a full-time bodyguard really necessary ..."

Just as she spoke, Levi raced towards Raphael, picked him up in his huge, meaty hands, and placed him on the floor behind the armchair where he had been sitting, like a child playing with a doll.

"What the ...?"

But before Raphael had time to finish protesting, an Egyptian army officer tore into the room with a pistol in his hand and started to fire wildly in the general direction of another officer, who was enjoying a drink with the aggressor's wife. Before anyone was hurt, four large security men rushed into the room and disarmed the shooter, handcuffing him and marching him away.

Madeleine rose from behind the bar where she had instinctively run for shelter before the confusion had broken out.

"I suppose he *is* really necessary," she said. "How did he even know what was going to happen?"

"Levi has a second sight for trouble," Raphael said simply. "And this isn't the first time that I've been very grateful for it."

But Levi could not keep Raphael safe all the time, and his work in the Young Sentinels was getting more intensive.

"We've go to escalate," Marcella had told the group recently. "There's nothing and nobody in Egypt for the Jews. It's no longer enough just defending our people here and trying to persuade them to go to Israel. It's time to get as many people as possible out of here and into Israel before we have a bloodbath on our hands. We've got to be proactive and arrange the transport for them ourselves."

"I'll do whatever I can to help," said Raphael. He knew that things were getting serious, so when he heard that a meeting had been called the following week, he was expecting big news.

As usual, the meeting took place at Café Palmyra. Marcella, Mireille, Avi, and Benny were all there when Raphael arrived, sitting around a table and sipping cold sherbets. At a glance, they could have been four ordinary young people enjoying some time together, but on closer inspection, anyone could see that there was more going on than that. Their sombre expressions, and the dark circles beneath their eyes, showed that they had had many sleepless nights of late.

"Sit down and make yourself comfortable, Raphael," said Marcella. "We've got a lot to discuss."

Raphael sat down.

"Things are serious now," Marcella began. "We're moving on to the next step. Over three hundred volunteers are trained and ready to move to Israel, where they'll do whatever they have to to found a new country. Getting there is likely to be dangerous and difficult, especially if they travel as a group, which is what we are aiming for. We need them to cross the Suez Canal into Sinai. There are people waiting for them on the other side, ready to help them to settle into their new life and defend Israel."

"OK …" said Raphael.

"You're good at planning in a tight spot. I need you to come up with a plan of action to get them across. I know that the physical distance isn't that great, but it's still likely to be the most dangerous journey most of them have ever taken."

Raphael sighed. "I don't know if I can," he said simply. "I have a business to run … it's getting harder and harder, and I've had to hire new people to cover for when I'm not there. To be honest, I'd like to take a couple of steps back from the Young Sentinels for the moment."

Marcella furrowed her dark brows and glared at Raphael.

"No," she said. "That's just not good enough. I don't think you realise how difficult it was for us to find and train three hundred young recruits. They've got a long, hard road ahead of them, and we've got to get them across the canal and into Israel before they change their minds. A lot of people are depending on them—and on us!"

"Raphael," Avi interrupted. "It *has* to be you. We know that you provide leather goods to the British military camp … and we need someone on the inside there to help us. You've already shown us that you can cope under pressure. We trust you, and we know that you are not going to let us down."

"Oh, for God's sake," said Raphael, irritated. "Sure, I distribute things to the British, but that doesn't mean I can get my contact in the camp to do whatever I want. Do you think they don't have any proper security there? Believe me, their security measures are tighter than you can imagine. I can't just snap my fingers and get things to happen like some sort of magician."

"The thing is," said Avi, "access to the British military camp is essential to our plan. The idea is to smuggle the volunteers into Israel through there. If we can't get in, then the whole plan is in jeopardy. We're depending on you."

"Look at it this way," coaxed Mireille. "Today, we're inviting you to choose which side of history you want to be on: the side that helped Israel to be born or the other one. Think about how you would like to be remembered."

Raphael relented. "I'll see what I can do," he said. "But I can't achieve anything overnight. I'm going to need some time."

"How much?" Marcella asked.

"Give me a week."

"That's fine," Marcella said. "If it takes a week, it takes a week. Better things get done properly than not at all. You start getting the wheels into motion, and we'll get busy getting the volunteers ready."

Raphael took a deep breath. He was so tired—tired of working, tired of activism, tired of worrying about his future in a country that seemed to hate him. Sometimes he wished it would all go away.

I'll do this, he thought, *and then see how I feel. Maybe I can give up then.*

"Leave it with me," he said. "I'll talk to my contact at the camp, and then I'll get back in touch with you so that we can work on the plans."

The five of them finished their drinks, shook hands, and left the café, heading their separate ways.

Raphael started thinking. As well as having a contact at the British military camp, through whom he sold the British army supplies from the workshop, he knew Madeleine and Shalom at Shepheard's Hotel. He knew that he could trust them both, and he had seen for himself how the two of them had developed a close relationship and trusted one another as well. Lots of high-up British army types stayed in the hotel or drank gin and tonics on its terrace. A certain General Ross stayed there every weekend. Perhaps Shalom knew him, or at least knew something about him. Maybe Madeleine had chatted with him at the bar. Surely, with their help, he might be able to make contact?

With the beginning of a plan forming in his mind, he started to feel more positive. Hands jammed into his pockets, he headed straight for the hotel.

Raphael managed to get Shalom into a corner. "You know General Ross?" he said. "He stays here every weekend, right?"

"Yesss …" said Shalom cautiously. "I know him. What do you want with General Ross?"

"Would you say you know him well?"

Shalom laughed. "That guy's a law unto himself. He can't stop gambling. He gets paid plenty of money, as a senior officer, but he loses it all at the card tables. He's got unpaid bills all over Cairo, and just last week I had to lend him some money to help him out. He's a heavy drinker, too. One of these days, his bad habits are going to trip him up!"

"Really?"

"Yes. What are you looking so happy about? What difference does it make to you?"

"I guess you could say that General Ross owes you some favours then!"

"I suppose … but what's that got to do with you? Look, Raphael, I'm feeling a little uncomfortable about this whole conversation. This is where I work. I'm not supposed to gossip about the guests at the hotel. I know we're family, but …"

"This is *important*," Raphael insisted. "I need you to get General Ross a message. You say he has debts. How much do you think he owes?"

"Oh, at least five hundred pounds."

Five hundred pounds was a lot of money, equivalent to several months' salary for an army officer and much more than most Egyptians earned in a year.

"Right, well, I need you to get him a message. Tell him that I will give him enough money to clear his debts so long as he does me a small favour. I need to get some entry passes to the military camp for me, Levi, and a few other people. Can you arrange to have him meet me in person?"

"I suppose so. Raphael, what are you up to? You're not getting yourself into trouble, are you?" Shalom knew that Raphael had a leather workshop, but he knew nothing about his activism or any other activities he might be involved in.

Raphael thought fast. "I've gone into the building materials business," he lied, "and I'm supplying materials to builders in the camp. I just need to get in there to make sure that everything is going the way it should."

Shalom looked at Raphael for a long moment and decided to believe him. After all, it would be to his advantage if he was the one who found a way to get General Ross the money he needed.

"OK," said Shalom. "I'll talk to him. I'm sure there won't be a problem, because I know he's desperate to clear his debts. Be here the day after tomorrow, Friday, with the money. I'm putting my reputation with Ross on the line for you, so make sure you don't let me down."

"I won't," Raphael promised.

That Friday, Raphael made his way to the hotel with five hundred Egyptian pounds stuffed into the inside pocket of his jacket. He had been compelled to go to Marcella for the cash.

"Are you sure this is going to work?" Marcella asked. "That's a lot of money which we could otherwise have spent on ammunition."

"It's going to be fine," Raphael said firmly, although he was secretly far from sure. He knew that if this didn't work out, he'd be kicked out of the Young Sentinels in disgrace.

Shalom arrived, looking rather tense. "He's here, but I'm not sure about this whole thing. If you get caught trying to influence an army officer, we could both end up in huge trouble. I'd lose my job, for a start, and we could both be put in jail."

"I'll be careful," Raphael said. "Don't worry."

General Ross sauntered into the hotel bar. Like so many of the British army men, his complexion had been burned a bright red by the Egyptian sun. His nose was misshapen from his excessive alcohol consumption, but he had an upright military bearing and wore an impressive waxed moustache.

Shalom introduced Raphael and General Ross.

"Raphael," he said firmly, "I told General Ross that I trust you completely, and that you are a fair and honest businessman. I am sure that you will do nothing to let me down."

Shalom scurried away, back to the bar, and Raphael and General Ross engaged in a little small talk about the weather—a subject of which the English never seemed to bore, Raphael had noticed—before getting on to business.

"So, young man," General Ross said. "Shalom tells me that you have something of a proposition for me. Is that the case?"

"Yes, indeed," said Raphael. He had nearly said "sir" but checked himself at the last minute. He was doing his best to look older than his real age and to act like an established businessman. "The thing is, I want to apply to be an accredited builder to the military camp, and to the Suez Canal in general. As they are both under British control, I need to make sure that I get all my paperwork in order."

"Interesting," said General Ross. "Well, your timing is rather good, because the contract we have with a building company is about to expire, and we're looking for someone new. Shalom said that you can be trusted. Would you agree with that assessment?"

"Without wishing to blow my own trumpet," Raphael said, "I would. I am a man of my word, and you can count on me. If I say that I'll do something, I'll do it, and I know that you'll be pleased with the quality of the work."

"Well, we've got a lot of building to get done," General Ross said. "Big jobs and little jobs … we really need to establish a workforce of builders who'll come to the camp every day."

"My men are second to none," Raphael affirmed confidently, although of course he had no building company at all. "How many do you think you need?"

"Well, there's a lot to do, so I think we need three hundred or so. Let's say three hundred and twenty. I know you say your men are good, but the Egyptians work so very slowly. I've grown to accept that we always need more men than it would take to do the job in England, because you lot are lazy and keep taking breaks. Look—I like your face, young man, so I'm going to trust you do to the job. I'll arrange the security passes."

"Thank you," Raphael said. "You won't be disappointed."

General Ross leaned over towards Raphael and lowered his voice. "I gather Shalom explained about the, ahem, little *contribution* for the officers' mess," he said. "It's just the way things are done around here, you understand. Well, you're Egyptian. I'm sure you know about this sort of thing. I know it's second nature in your country. When in Rome, eh?"

"Indeed," Raphael replied without so much as blinking. "I have it right here."

Raphael reached into his inside pocket and removed the envelope full of money that he had brought as an unofficial payment to make things easier. Discreetly, he handed it to General Ross.

"I trust it's all there," General Ross said. "Five hundred pounds for the first payment. I presume I don't need to count."

"The *first* payment?"

Raphael was taken aback. Shalom hadn't said anything about his having to make more than one payment.

"Oh, I am sure that this seems like a lot of money to you," General Ross said with a little sneer, "but it's just a fraction of what is needed overall. Five hundred is a drop in the ocean. I know what you're really up to. You're Jewish, right? And the territories the Jews are going to are right across the water…"

"How much were you expecting?" Raphael asked. Marcella was going to be furious about this.

"For three hundred and twenty men? That's a lot of permits. You're going to have to come up with at least three thousand five hundred overall. You're not the only building contractor in Cairo, you know. If you don't want the 'work', I'm sure I can find someone else who does."

Raphael stared at him, feeling the blood draining from his face. How was he supposed to come up with that sort of cash? It had been hard enough getting the five hundred!

"Very well," he said. "But as you can imagine, I don't carry that sort of money on me. I can pay the balance in a week's time, next Friday. On Monday, I'll supply the names of the workers, and I would appreciate it if you could arrange the permits straight away."

General Ross peered at Raphael from beneath his heavy brows.

"All right then," he said. "I'll trust you. You're young, but you've got an honest face. Well, an honest face for an Egyptian, let's put it that way."

Raphael and General Ross shook hands and exchanged false smiles. Neither really trusted the other, but General Ross knew that if he didn't give Raphael the permits, he wouldn't get any money at all—much less the three thousand five hundred he wanted—and Raphael knew that General Ross represented his only opportunity to get the recruits out of Egypt and into Israel.

Tense and in need of both emotional support and physical release, Raphael spent the night with Madeleine, leaving her apartment early in the morning to head home and get ready for the day. When he got home, he turned the key in the lock and let himself into the living room.

"You absolute *beast*! You horrible boy! Sometimes I bloody well hate you!"

It was Maxa, who had clearly been there for several hours. She ran over to him and started hitting him on the chest with her fists.

"How *could* you stay out all night and only come in now? I was so worried about you! I thought that someone must have hurt you—or even killed you."

"Calm down!" Raphael said. "I didn't even know you were here!"

"Even still!"

"It's not like I'm your boyfriend and owe you an explanation," he reminded her. "We always said that what goes on between us is with no strings attached and that one day we'll go our separate ways."

"I know, I know," said Maxa. "I just got so scared. Never mind. Anyway, look. Marcella sent me here to bring you a message. We're to attend a meeting with the boss later this morning."

"What boss? Marcella is the boss."

"Marcella's boss Elia, I mean. Marcella's the only one who ever met him before, so this is obviously very important. Just be there, OK? Renata and I have to report on how we're getting new recruits to the Israel cause, and he's going to want to hear your plans about how you're going to move all the people."

At eleven, Raphael pushed open the door of Café Palmyra. Marcella was sitting in her usual spot, and beside her sat a slightly older man Raphael hadn't seen before. Tersely, Marcella introduced him as Elia. Elia was carefully groomed and dapper, with a sallow complexion and a trim moustache, and he appeared to be very confident. He looked Raphael up and down as Marcella started to speak to the small group, which included Robert, Avi, Benny, Mireille, and Maxa.

"We've reached a critical point of the operation," Marcella said. "And whether or not it succeeds—and indeed, whether or not we come out of this alive—depends on how we approach the next steps. Elia here is our regional leader, and I've reported all the actions we've taken to him. The orders you get from me are his orders. Now Elia has come to direct us about what to do next, and I want you all to listen carefully."

Elia coughed and clasped his hands.

"We, the regional leaders, are pleased with your group's achievements to date," he said. "The volunteers are well-trained, and we have a large number of young people in your area ready to move to Israel and do what it takes to defend her and build a Jewish nation. We also heard about the riot at the Jewish Quarter, Raphael, and were delighted to see how things worked out. Without such a tireless defence, there could have been a bloodbath."

"And now," Marcella interrupted, "we're here to talk about the next stage—getting the volunteers across the Suez Canal and into Israel: the Passover Operation. Without them, there isn't even going to *be* an Israel, so it's very important."

"Right," said Elia, taking back control of the meeting. "Raphael, Marcella tells me that you're going to give us an update."

"I've got an in to the British military camp at El Fayed," Raphael said, "but the costs are going to be an issue … I'll get back to that, but the camp is our best bet by far. If anyone is caught, at least they'll be caught and dealt with by the British rather than the Egyptian authorities. The camp is also as close to the other side as it gets, so the journey into Israel won't take too long."

"What about the Bedouins?" asked Robert. "They live around there, and they keep their eyes open. If we start moving large numbers of Jewish volunteers, they're bound to see that something's going on."

Raphael dismissed this with a shrug. "There's no love lost between the Bedouins and the authorities," he said. "And besides, they're good businessmen. If necessary, they can be easily paid off. There won't be a problem with them keeping their mouths shut if they know there's something in it for them."

"What about the English? How are you going to get over three hundred Jewish immigrants to Israel past them?"

Here, Raphael felt confident. He explained that he had made contact with General Ross, who was up to his eyes in debt and only too willing to accept a payment to offer Raphael the supposed building contract and look the other way while the Jewish migrants passed through the camp.

"And that's not all," he said. "I know at least twenty Jewish merchants in the area who will help. Three of them have transport vehicles, and one of them is the biggest subcontractor in Cairo. They're all delighted at the prospect of helping the Israel project and making some money at the same time."

"Well, that all sounds promising," said Elia slowly. "But there are still some issues we need to discuss. How are you going to deal with the British checkpoints? How are you going to get three hundred people through the British camp without anyone noticing? We're talking about three hundred young Jews, half of whom are women. How are we going to pass them all off as builders?"

"The British are a lot more corrupt than they like to think," Raphael said. "This General Ross is in it for as much as he can get and he knows what he's getting into. He's roped in a man called Colonel Reed, who is in charge of the checkpoint and traffic in and out of the camp. Reed is prepared to help out so long as he gets paid off, too."

Raphael could see that Marcella was looking rather irritated and was not surprised when she interjected.

"I see you've taken it upon yourself to make a lot of decisions you are not in a position to make," she said sourly. "The plan sounds great, but for one little detail. Where are we supposed to find all that money? Who gave you permission to start promising money we don't have to corrupt army types who don't deserve it?"

"I know it's a lot of money," Raphael said mildly. "Five hundred pounds … that's more than most Egyptians earn in a year. But I really think we can make this work, and I'm prepared to put up the money myself for now, because business is going well, and I want this to work. Ross is holding out for another three thousand five hundred, but I've persuaded him to wait a week for it. If we can get everyone into the camp and across the Suez to the Holy Land … well then, I think it will be worth it. Honestly, this is the safest way."

The group sat in silence for a few minutes, pondering this.

Finally, Elia spoke up. "It's a long shot, and it's not a perfect plan by any means. What does everyone think?"

"It's very risky," said Robert. "Especially for Raphael. If he was caught … well, between smuggling Jews into Israel and bribing British army officers, he'd be in big trouble. He'd be lucky to get out of prison before he turns forty … if at all. Most of the people who serve time in jail here only ever come out in a box."

"There's another big problem," said Mireille. "Everyone's talking about how to get the volunteers into the camp, but nobody's said anything about how they're going to get them out of there and into Israel. There's a bloody great canal in the way, in case you've all forgotten!"

"Right," said Marcella. "What's the plan for that?"

Just the day before, Raphael had been asking himself the same question. Then he remembered that a friend of his dad's, a Greek called Panayotti, had barges that he used to bring Muslim pilgrims to Saudi Arabian ports during the pilgrimage season and for cargo the rest of the year. Each barge could carry twenty-five passengers, or up to forty if they were prepared to be cramped and uncomfortable. Raphael had rushed to Panayotti's house and asked if he would be prepared to bring a group of passengers across the canal so that they could visit Mount Sinai.

"They're Copts," Raphael had said. "You know that they like to go on pilgrimage to Mount Sinai."

Panayotti had nodded. He didn't believe Raphael's explanation, but he didn't care. So long as he didn't know the full story, he could plead ignorance, and so long as he got paid, he was happy to take anyone anywhere.

Quickly, Raphael started to explain what he had planned. "I know it's not perfect," he said, opening his hands in a gesture of apology.

"The barge transport is going to cost more money again. I understand that this is all getting very expensive, but I honestly think that this is our best chance. If headquarters can cover the additional cost, on top of the five hundred that I have personally contributed as the accommodation for Ross, then I think we have an excellent chance of getting all of our young recruits into Israel, where they can start building new lives and a new country."

The group sat in silence for a few moments, thinking about it all. After having worked so hard to get to this point in time, now it was difficult to believe that they were close to achieving what they had set out to do. It was bittersweet. As with the hundreds of volunteers who were ready to settle in Israel, Egypt had always been their home, and it was going to be painfully difficult to leave it. On the other hand, things had been getting worse and worse for the Jews in Cairo. People were being harassed in the streets and called "Zionist dogs". Public places, like swimming pools and parks, had started to post notices stating that neither Jews nor dogs were permitted entry. As dogs were considered unclean animals by the Muslims, the message they were sending out was loud and clear.

The government had passed laws that limited employment in a wide range of settings to Egyptian citizens. Jews were not allowed to hold citizenship, which meant that many jobs were out of bounds for them. Along with the incrementally more frequent outbreaks of violence, if they stayed, they were looking at a future in which most of them would be poor. Already, many of the Jewish families with resources of their own and friends abroad had left. How long could the Jewish community hold on with things as they were? The ones who were really suffering now were mostly very low on funds. They simply did not have the resources to leave, and their best chance at securing a happy future for themselves and their children was to go to Israel.

"OK, Raphael," said Elia. "Your plan is a good one—and, more importantly, it's the only plan we've got. We'll do it. But I want you think about one thing."

"What is it?"

"You're supposed to be a member of a group, not some sort of big shot out on your own. That means that you are supposed to report back to the group, and above all to Marcella, who is your immediate superior. You're not supposed to make big decisions on your own, as you've been doing. We have a hierarchy here, and you have not been respecting it. That has to stop."

"I know," said Raphael. "It's just that there's really not that much time, and I felt that I had to make some snap decisions or I wouldn't manage to come up with a plan at all."

"I know how that feels," said Elia. "We'll let it go for now. I do appreciate the fact that you are clearly prepared to take personal risks for your people."

"We *all* are," interjected Marcella.

"Yes," said Elia. "Well, we have a plan now. Operation Passover is going to happen. Not only that, but it's going to coincide with the feast of Passover. Let's take that as a positive sign that God is watching over us and will help us deliver the young Jews into Israel, just as our ancestors were delivered into Israel all those years ago."

"Good idea," said Raphael. "Though I don't think we can count on the Red Sea opening up for us and then swallowing the Egyptian authorities. We'll definitely need the barges."

*　　*　　*

As Raphael walked back home from Café Palmyra, he sensed someone walking behind him. Paranoid, he continued walking for a while, and then he turned his head to see who was there. It was Mireille, walking about twenty metres behind him with her hands stuffed in her pockets.

"Mireille!" he exclaimed in surprise. "Are you *following* me? Why?"

"I'm just going the same way as you," Mireille said rather sullenly. "What's your problem? Think you own the street or something?" She kicked at a piece of rolled up newspaper in the gutter. "You're not the only person in the world, you know," she said. "Other people have things to do too. It doesn't all revolve around you, regardless of what you think."

Mireille had always seemed to dislike Raphael, glowering at him from underneath her dark brows. He had tended to ignore her, preferring to deal directly with Marcella, who could be a bit hard but was always straightforward and clear. He was about to brush Mireille off when he remembered Elia's remarks about the importance of working as a team rather than going off on his own.

Maybe, Raphael thought, *I should make a bigger effort with Mireille. She's probably OK when you get to know her.*

"If you're not busy," he said, "do you want to go for a drink with me? We've never really had time to talk, have we? We don't really know one another at all. Well, we've a little time now. So what do you say?"

"All right," said Mireille. "But I'm sick of Café Palmyra. We always go there for meetings, so I can never get relaxed there."

"I live near here. I could make you a coffee at my place, if you like?"

"Thanks."

Mireille matched her pace to Raphael's, and the two of them walked in a slightly awkward silence until they reached his place. He let her in and invited her to sit on the sofa while he made coffee for her and served it in one of his mother's best cups.

"It's so hot," said Mireille, sipping her drink. "Too hot for coffee!"

"I should've made lemonade. I'll open the window."

"Not *that* sort of hot."

"Excuse me?"

"Oh, come on, Raphael. You know exactly what I mean. Everyone knows you're pretty generous with your affections, as they say. I didn't come here for a drink, if you understand me."

"What do you mean?"

"Oh, for God's sake! How obvious do I have to be?"

Mireille reached forward and grabbed Raphael by the belt, pulling him closer.

"Women can ask for sex too, you know, and sometimes we've just got to have it or we'll go crazy. What about it?"

Raphael looked at Mireille. It had never really occurred to him to wonder whether he found her attractive or not. She had always just been this scowling presence beside Marcella. Now that he looked closely, she was quite sexy. She wasn't pretty, exactly, but something about her wide mouth and high cheekbones made her look like she would know her way around a man's body.

"What are you waiting for?" she asked. "Are you going to take off your clothes or not?"

Raphael leaned forward and gave Mireille an experimental kiss. He was rewarded by the familiar sensation of desire flooding through his body.

"Why not?" he said. "Considering what we're about to do, we could all be in jail soon anyway, or even worse."

"That's exactly what I was thinking."

Mireille peeled off her khaki shirt. Her small breasts required no brassiere and her lean arms were muscular and tanned. If it wasn't for her tiny waist, at a glance she might even have been taken for a boy.

"Don't just stand there watching! Take your shirt off too."

Raphael peeled off his shirt. Mireille dropped her trousers to the ground and stepped out of them. She wasn't wearing any underwear.

"Do you want to go to the bedroom?" he asked.

"I thought you'd never ask!"

"Better yet," he said, "how about a shower?"

Raphael had never been dominated by a woman as he was by Mireille. She never once let him take the lead but took over his body, grinding her pelvis against his and ensuring that she reached orgasm without a thought for him.

"Don't you want a turn?" she asked eventually.

"Sure, but not here. Let's go to the bedroom."

For an hour, the two young people made love as if it was their last day on earth. Afterwards, they lay together. Mireille put her arms around Raphael's waist and held him in a hug.

"Sometimes it's good just to be with someone else," she muttered against his shoulder.

They lay for a while and then started to chat.

"You and Marcella are amazing," Raphael said. "She's such a great leader, and I can see that she really trusts you."

"Oh, I do my best," said Mireille. "But Marcella's a real pro—head and shoulders above the rest of us. You know, she's been involved in this for years, since before anyone even heard about it. Her own family is involved. Her mum and dad are in it right up to their necks. The last five or six years, she goes away for training for a full month every year."

"What sort of training?"

Mireille looked vague. "I don't really know the details," she said, "and I don't know where she goes, but I think it might be France, because I know she speaks French, and she's let a few clues drop along the way. There are Jewish activists there who run training sessions for the leaders involved in the project. But even though I've been helping her for ages, I don't know much about her personal life. Nobody knows what sort of work she does, or how she supports herself, and she likes it like that. She prefers to keep her personal business personal.

"I'll tell you one thing, though," Mireille added. "Nobody is more committed to the cause of Israel than Marcella. She told me one day that if she had to, she would be prepared to have sex with a man she hated if she thought it would make it easier to get information that would be useful to her. I don't know if she's ever had to do it, but she definitely would, if she thought it was worth her while."

Mireille leapt from the bed and went around the apartment collecting her discarded items of clothing.

"If you ever tell anyone about this, I'll kill you," she said. "This never happened. Got it? It's strictly between you and me."

"Got it," said Raphael, amused, although he certainly did not doubt that Mireille was capable of doing what she said.

"Oh, and Raphael?" Mireille said as she opened the door to leave.

"What?"

"Thanks. That was just what I needed."

*   *   *

Just one week after Raphael started devising the plan, the group swung into action. Raphael had already collected the permits from General Ross, who just wanted his money and didn't care about what the supposed construction workers actually did. They bore the names of the three hundred and twenty youngsters who were about to take the voyage of their lifetimes. The distance from Egypt to Israel was tiny in one sense, but it was monumental in another. The Bedouins had been paid off, and the barges were ready to take the pioneers, five barges at a time, with forty passengers crammed into vessels that had been designed to take twenty-five.

After all the Young Sentinels' planning, the exercise went smoothly. The trip across the water was not long—it was a distance of about a kilometre at that point—but it was dangerous, especially because the crossings had to take place at night, under the cover of darkness. Thanks to the corruption of the British officers, at least they could be reasonably sure that they would not be disturbed by the army. Welcoming parties in Israel were waiting on the shoreline to receive them. The young immigrants were welcomed to their new country and helped to settle into their homeland. They were all immediately absorbed into the unofficial Jewish army known as *Haganah*, which had been founded to defend the recruits and would one day soon— they hoped—become the army of a free Israel.

The day after their plan had been realised, Raphael met up with Marcella and the others at Café Palmyra.

"We did it," Marcella said. "I keep pinching myself. It's actually real. I can't quite believe it."

"We did it," said Mireille, "but I think we owe extra thanks to Raphael. It was because of his plan that we were able to pull this one off. Now that we've got a system running smoothly, so long as we can keep General Ross in 'accommodations' so that he can pay off his gambling debts, we can keep transporting the Jews to Israel until they are all there."

"What's going to happen now?" asked Raphael.

"Ah," said Marcella. "That's the million-dollar question."

The obvious next step was for the Young Sentinels to themselves move to Israel. After all, a free Israel was what they had been working for all this time, and what they wanted, more than anything. One by one, they talked about their hopes and plans for their lives in the future, and their dreams of what life could be like for the Jews in a land where they faced no persecution.

"Imagine how wonderful it will be," said Marcella, "when Jews from all over the world can come together and know that we will be safe. I am so sick of Jews always being seen, and seeing themselves, as victims. It's time for *us* to be in charge for a change. Just think about that."

"Imagine ..." echoed Raphael. But, privately, he felt a little deflated. It was wonderful to know that the dream of a free Israel was beginning to come true at last. But for some reason, he could not see himself there. He couldn't pin down why, but he knew that his future lay somewhere else. Where, he was not yet entirely sure.

Back at the apartment, Levi had been thinking along similar lines. It was time for a change, but he wasn't sure what was going to come next.

"Boss," he said. "I'm so glad I was able to help you, in my little way, with your job of getting the recruits to Israel. People have been telling me that I should go there too. But something makes me feel that it's not the right place for me."

"Where would you like to go? Do you want to stay here?"

"There's no future for any of us here. I've been thinking of South America. There are lots of opportunities there for a man prepared to work hard, and I have never had a problem with hard work. The weather is good over there too, and I hear that the women are gorgeous. I've never managed to find a wife here, but I might have better luck over there. Over there, nobody needs to know that I grew up in the Jewish Quarter, the poorest end of town."

"So what's keeping you?"

Levi looked dolefully at the floor.

"I just don't have the money to go to Brazil," he said. "The fare is higher than I'll ever be able to save up."

Raphael looked at the older man and felt a warm surge of affection for him.

"I'll pay for your ticket," he said.

"I wasn't suggesting that you don't pay me enough!" said Levi, aghast at the thought that his words might be misinterpreted. "I've been very happy working for you, and I have no problem with the salary. It's more than fair."

"I know. You're the best, Levi. But I've realised that Israel is not the place for me, either. I don't know why, but I feel quite sure that my future is somewhere else, and that I am going to have a lot of good luck. Let me share some of it with you."

Not long after that, Levi left to seek his fortune. Raphael never heard from him again but would never forget him. Now Raphael had to decide what he would do next ...

2017

"That's amazing," said David. "Do people in Israel know about Grandad's involvement with the activists in those days?"

"Well, they know insofar as the work of the activists in Cairo is a matter of public record," said Richard. "A few of them went on to be well-known and to have involvement in the government of Israel, but most of the activists, like Grandad, were happy to do their bit without recognition. They got on with their lives afterwards, and very few people knew about their involvement. It was never supposed to be about getting noticed; it was about making a safe home for the Jews."

"Whew," said Rueben. "What a story. I wonder how many people Grandad helped get into Israel."

"Hundreds," said Richard. "And that was just the beginning for them. They all had to work together to defend the country and to build homes for the new families they started. It's an amazing history. Grandad didn't go on to live in Israel, obviously, but it's always been close to his heart, and he picked up an involvement with the country later on."

"What was that?" Rebecca asked curiously. "What did he do?"

"Let's say that he was always a friend to Israel and that he remained willing to go out on a limb to help."

"You know what?" said Rebecca. "We should all make arrangements to get to Israel with Grandad and Granny to celebrate his birthday. Knowing a little about what he had to do back then would make it really special."

"That's a great idea," said Richard. "And you're the organiser in the family, Rebecca. You're the woman who can make it happen. Now, does anyone want to know what happened next?"

CHAPTER 10

THE END OF THE BEGINNING

2017

"So," said Rebecca. "What did happen next? Isn't it funny that Grandad didn't decide to live in Israel after all that?"

"Well," said Richard, "the circumstances in his life were complicated at the time, and some of the things that influenced his decision were completely beyond his control."

"Like what?" asked David.

"Have another glass of wine," advised Richard, "and I'll tell you all about it."

1948

On 14 May 1948, David Ben-Gurion proclaimed the establishment of the State of Israel, and US President Harry S. Truman recognised the fledgling nation that very same day. History had been made, and Raphael and the rest of the Young Sentinels had played a part in it.

The day after Israel's declaration of independence, 15 May 1948, Egypt, Jordan, and Syria joined forces to invade the brand-new country. They invaded and seized control of the areas largely inhabited by Arabs, attacking Jewish forces and settlements, while tiny Jewish units managed to repel much bigger and better equipped factions of the Egyptian army, which provided the bulk of the forces. The invaders were denounced by both the United States and the Soviet Union, as well as the secretary-general of the United Nations.

King Farouk, who had showboated his way through the war and given military rank to all of his sisters, experienced a dramatic fall in popularity. The fighting continued, on and off, for a period of ten months and had a dramatic impact on the entire region. Over 700,000 Jews were expelled from the countries they had inhabited in the Middle East, while a similar number of Arabs left the new Jewish state.

The Jewish recruits, among them the young Cairenes whose flight had been assisted by Raphael, knew that they were in a precarious situation. The training they had done stood them in good stead, as they were all expected to serve in the army, the Haganah. The army grew as the Jewish population steadily increased, and from 26 May 1948, it was known as the Israel Defence Forces.

On 24 February 1949, Israel signed an armistice agreement with Egypt, with further agreements with Lebanon, Jordan, and Syria to follow. Israel now consisted of 21,000 square kilometres. About 1 per cent of the population of the young country had died in the war, of whom about a third had been survivors of the European Holocaust.

As time passed, there were fewer and fewer Jews left in Cairo. Many of those who departed cut off all their ties with the city and everyone they had known there. It was as if they had ever been there at all.

Raphael wondered what to do. Business was going well, but it seemed like it was only a matter of time before the anti-Jewish sentiment in the city started to have even more of an impact on him. He knew that a life in Israel was not the right choice for him, but he hated the thought of joining his family and losing the sense of independence he had grown to love.

With ever fewer friends to be spend time with, Raphael was visiting Shalom at Shepheard's more than before, always hoping that Madeleine—or Maddy, as he often still thought of her—would be free to talk. One day he arrived to find Madeleine working but in a state of great distress. It was easy to see that she had been crying not long before.

"What's wrong?" Raphael asked.

"It's Shalom," she said, starting to cry. "He's been arrested. It happened just this morning."

"Arrested? I can't believe it! For what? I thought he had something on every Egyptian politician and policeman and could never be arrested."

"He wasn't taken by the Egyptians but by the British. He's being held on accusation of being a spy."

"A *spy*? That's crazy! Who's he supposed to have spied on?"

"I don't know. They came and handcuffed him and led him away, and that's literally all I know. He's at the British embassy."

"You've got to know more than that! Come on, Madeline, think! It's important."

"I really don't ... except that it is supposed to be something to do with the assassination of Lord Moyne five years ago, in 1944."

"Lord Moyne?"

Lord Moyne was an Anglo-Irish politician who had served as the British minister of state in the Middle East until November 1944, when the Jewish paramilitary group Lehi assassinated him. The members of Lehi were dedicated to expelling the British authorities from Palestine by force, using whatever means they had at their disposal to facilitate the immigration of Jews and the founding of a dedicated Jewish state. They had fought against the British in Palestine throughout the Second World War. As the war progressed, they had tended more to the left and to supporting the Soviet Union under Stalin, coming out as a Bolshevik organisation in 1944, the same year Lord Moyne was killed by paramilitaries armed with guns because of his opposition to the establishment of Jewish army units in the Middle East and the foundation of a state for the Jews. Moyne did what he could to limit and prevent Jewish settlement in Palestine, including forbidding entry to Egypt of ships filled with Holocaust survivors.

"I don't understand," said Raphael. "They executed two men for that four years ago. How can it have anything to do with Shalom? Surely that's all done and dusted by now. Ships of Jews are entering freely now, too, from all over the place. The whole situation has changed completely, even in just the past few months."

"I do know that Shalom hated Lord Moyne," said Madeleine. "He told me that, during the war, General Eichmann from Germany, one of the top Nazis, rang Lord Moyne, said that he had a million Jews, and asked what he should do with them. Obviously, Lord Moyne could have arranged for them to be sent to British Palestine, where they would have been safe, but instead he just said, 'You can do whatever you want with them.' They were all sent to the concentration camps and murdered."

She added, "People say that Lord Moyne pretended to be a great man but that he really hated Jews as much as the Egyptian Muslim Brotherhood does. He also refused access to Palestine of a ship full of Jewish refugees, including lots of women and children, and they all drowned. That's why so many people were glad when Lehi killed him … and now they are saying that Shalom was in Lehi!"

Despite the Balfour Declaration of 1917, the British and the Saudi Arabians had reached an agreement that the population of Palestine would be limited and that no more Jews were to be allowed to enter and settle there. One of the ships subsequently sank, leading to the death of hundreds of Jews fleeing Europe, many of them women and children. The fledgling Jewish government in Palestine met and condemned Lord Moyne to death for his role in all these unnecessary deaths, and two killers were sent to shoot him. After his assassination, Lehi issued a formal statement that said, "We accuse Lord Moyne, and the government he represents, with murdering hundreds and thousands of our brethren; we accuse him of seizing our country and looting our possessions. We were forced to do justice and to fight." Two members of Lehi were tried, found guilty, and executed on 23 March 1945.

"I find this very hard to believe," said Raphael. "I mean, I know that Shalom supports Israel, but I would never have imagined that he was capable of this sort of thing."

"Well, I will keep my ear to the ground," said Madeleine. "Everyone comes here, and the bartender hears everything. I know Ahmad Mahfouz, the head of the police, and I'll ask him what he's heard. For a policeman, he's not a bad guy. He knows a little French, and sometimes he practices by chatting to me. As a matter of fact, we're on first-name terms. I know the police are tough on the Jewish activists, but he's an honest guy, and I trust him."

Through Madeleine, Raphael was kept apprised of Shalom's fate. The prisoner was taken to London and detained there for three months, after which he was released to the French authorities and finally let go.

Shortly after Shalom's release, police officers came to the leather workshop and arrested Raphael, refusing to explain what he was being taken in for or where they were taking him.

"You'll see when we get there," was all they said.

An hour or so later, Raphael was deposited at Camp Huckstep, part of a large military base in Cairo, where several hundred other young Jews were also being detained. He recognised a few of them. Most were members of Jewish sports centres or social clubs and had no involvement with activism at all. The guards treated them well and provided them with good food, and there was no sense that any of them were in danger.

A few days later, with no explanation given, Raphael was released and told that he was free to go. He went straight to Shepheard's Hotel, where a very worried Madeleine embraced him. She had heard about his internment from General Mahfouz and had been desperately worried about him.

"I'm absolutely fine!" Raphael reassured her. "Nothing bad happened at all. They have no evidence that I've ever done anything wrong, and they were just trying to scare me. I wouldn't take it too seriously, honestly! It was more like a summer camp than a jail."

"You're fine for now," Madeleine said, "but what about the next time and the time after that? I'm sure the authorities are watching you now. I don't know what you've been up to, but I know you, and I'm know you're involved in things the government doesn't approve of. Raphael, I'm worried about you. I know you think that you are completely invulnerable, but it's not really true. You're made of flesh and blood, and you can be hurt and killed as easily as anyone else."

Raphael brushed her concerns away. "Don't fret about me like you're my mother," he said with some irritation. "I've got everything under control!"

Raphael knew that his amulet made him feel safe, even when bad things were happening all around him. He wondered for a moment if he depended on it too much, but then he dismissed that thought. No; he was fine. Despite the arrest, he was sure nothing bad could happen to him.

That night, he got together with Robert, Marcella, Maxa, and Renata to celebrate his release. He had been hoping for a happy gathering, but the mood was sombre. Marcella grilled him—had he told anyone anything? Had he been tortured or bribed? Was he sure that he wasn't being followed?

"It's time you started to make your own plan," said Renata.

"What plan?"

"To get out of here, of course. Do you think that Maxa and I are going to stay here and wait for the government to take everything from us, arrest us, even kill us? The Muslim Brotherhood is taking over everything, and they hate the Jews."

"I'm leaving too," said Marcella. "It's Israel for me. I've been working for a free Israel for years. It's all I've ever dreamed of. I can't wait to be part of it."

"I won't be staying either," said Robert. "The girls are right. Egypt was our home once, but it isn't now, no matter how we feel about it. We're just going to have to grow up and accept that it is time to say goodbye."

"You're right," said Raphael. "I've been struggling to admit it … but yes. You girls"—he gestured towards Maxa and Renata—"you'll probably lose your jobs in the department store because you are Jews before too long. Even if the store is Jewish-owned now, it won't be for long. The government will take it over and give its management to an Egyptian citizen, or maybe close it down because they're down on the middle classes and think that we should all be socialists now. After that, who knows what will happen?"

"Can you help us get out?" asked Maxa. "You know we're descended from Greeks, so that should help us to get to Europe. Once we're there, we can get jobs and start saving for the future."

"I can arrange for you and your parents to leave on the *Esperia* on the next crossing."

Two weeks later, Raphael, Maxa, and Renata hugged their goodbyes while the girls' parents waited on the gangplank.

"I'm sure we'll see each other again one day," Raphael said to the girls. They smiled a little sadly but didn't answer.

Feeling bereft without his friends, Raphael made his way to Shepheard's and Madeleine. At least she was left. Usually she smiled when he walked into the bar, but this time she approached him in a state of great anxiety.

"Raphael," she said. "The chief of police, General Mahfouz, has been here, and he told me that he's after you. It's a warning, an opportunity to get out before you are arrested. He doesn't want to do it, but he has no choice, because his instructions are coming from higher up."

Raphael's heart sank. "I doubt I have time to get things ready before I have to go," he said. "What can I do?"

"Look, he's a good man and a friend of mine. I've asked him if he can get you out of the country in secret so that the whole thing can be avoided. He's said that he will help. I trust him. Please God, I am not making a mistake."

That afternoon, an official came to the leather workshop and informed Raphael that his property had been sequestered by the state. He was devastated but unsurprised. The same thing had already happened to countless Jewish-owned businesses all over Cairo, and it was happening to Muslim-owned businesses too. Naguib, the new leader, was a socialist and wanted everything to be run by the state. He had it in for entrepreneurs and the middle classes, especially when they were Jewish, and he was selling the idea that anyone who made a lot of money was a parasite on the working people. On top of all that, Raphael felt sure that someone had been following him lately, too, and that they knew about his activism. The net was closing in.

After a restless night, Raphael was awakened by a tap on the front door. He opened it to find a police officer standing there.

"You're under arrest," said the officer.

With a deep sigh, Raphael pulled on his clothes, put on his shoes, and followed the policeman outside.

Raphael was marched peremptorily to the chief police station in Cairo, where he was deposited, handcuffed, on a hard, wooden bench and told to wait his turn to be interviewed. Five hours later, his handcuffs were removed, and he was called into an office decorated with framed photographs of Egypt's most famous mosques and rulers, as well as a pair of crossed swords. He recognised the older man in front of him, on the other side of a heavy mahogany desk, as General Mahfouz, whom he had often seen in Shepheard's Hotel.

"I've been wondering when you would turn up," Mahfouz said. "I'm surprised it's taken this long. We've been keeping an eye on you for quite some time now, young man."

"I haven't done anything wrong," said Raphael. "I don't know why I'm here."

"We both know that's not true," said Mahfouz, pouring himself a glass of Johnnie Walker from a bottle that he removed from a desk drawer. "You've broken more laws than I can count."

Raphael said nothing.

"You're probably thinking that the worst that can happen to you is another stint in Huckstep, which is basically a summer camp for Jewish lawbreakers and overexcited youngsters, but I can send you to Abu Zaabel any time I want, and I can leave you there for as long as I see fit. I know a lot about you, and I know that you have very expensive tastes for a young man of your age. I don't think that you would enjoy spending time in Abu Zaabel."

Abu Zaabel, about half an hour's drive from Cairo, was a notorious prison that housed Egypt's worst criminals—murderers, rapists, and the like—and it was a byword for violence and corruption. Most of the people sent there didn't come out alive, and the few who did were never the same again.

Again, Raphael said nothing. There was nothing he could contribute to the conversation that would make things better.

"The only thing you've got going for you at the moment is the fact that we have a mutual friend. Madeleine down at Shepheard's says you're a decent lad, and I respect Madeleine's opinion. So I'm going to give you a choice. You can leave Egypt straight away and make a life for yourself somewhere else, or you can stay here and face the music. It's up to you."

"I need some time to think about it," Raphael protested. "I have a business here. I can't just turn my back on all the work I've done!"

"You've got two minutes."

"Two minutes! That's crazy. I can't make a decision that's going to affect the rest of my life in two minutes."

"You can if you know what's good for you."

Raphael let his face sink into his hands. It was so unfair. All the work he had done to get the leather workshop profitable again ... all for nothing! He had made himself into a businessman, and he would be leaving with nothing. Egypt was his home. On the other hand, he understood that he had absolutely no choice. The authorities were cracking down on all the Jews, even the ones who had done nothing to annoy them—and he had done plenty. The policeman was right. It was a choice between incarceration or death and the challenge of finding a new way to live somewhere else.

"I'll go," he said.

"Good. You're making a very wise decision. Now, Madeleine told me that you have family in Sudan, so that's the obvious place for you to go. I've prepared an official letter for you that will get you through the border at Haifa."

Mahfouz pushed the letter across the desk.

"Thank you," said Raphael.

"I want you to know that I've nothing personal against you or your people. These are just the times we live in. I'm just following orders."

"I know."

"Now go home and get your things together. It's time for you to get out of here."

Raphael walked home, his hands stuffed into his pockets. He walked past Uncle Ali's mechanic's workshop without saying hello and trudged upstairs. As he reached the door, he was suddenly alert to the sounds he could hear from inside the apartment. He put his key in the door and opened it to find his brother Avi.

"Hello, small stuff," said Avi. "Long time no see." Avi reached out and ruffled his younger brother's hair.

"What are you doing here?"

"I thought it was time for me to come back to Cairo. I'm a married man now, and there isn't much for me to do in Sudan. I'm going to take over the apartment."

"What? *My* apartment?"

"It's not yours, silly, it's Daddy's."

"OK, but I've been looking after it and paying the rent this whole time. I've had it repainted and everything."

"That's good, and we're all very grateful," said Avi impatiently. "But I'm your older brother, so by rights it belongs to me, not you. And I'm married now, as you know"—Raphael had not attended the wedding, but Flora had sent him photographs of it—"so I've come to take what's mine by rights. You can forget about any ideas you might have about me just being a caretaker for you. I'm the older brother, so it's only natural that I should be the boss. Dad said so."

"That's not fair! How can you just come in and take it when I've worked so hard?"

"I don't know what you're talking about," exclaimed Avi's wife, Sultana, coming through from the kitchen. "You've been lucky enough to have the place to yourself the past few years, and now you're complaining because your big brother is here to get what's rightfully his? You have some nerve!"

"Will you take care of my things?" Raphael asked. "I've bought a lot of furniture and other stuff for the apartment in the last few years."

"*Your* things?" Sultana sneered. "Seeing as how you bought them with money you earned from the workshop, which would be Avi's if the state hadn't taken it, they're really *our* things. I'll take care of them all right, but it won't be for you, because this is our home now."

"But I bought them with my own money and decorated the whole apartment with my own hands!"

"Oh yes? Well now you can just fuck off!"

Raphael went downstairs to tell Uncle Ali about the change in the situation and in the tenancy of the apartment. What else could he do? He felt utterly defeated. In the morning, he'd had a successful business and a comfortable home of his own. All of a sudden, it seemed that he had neither and that there was absolutely nothing to show for his years of hard work. He didn't even have enough money in his pocket to buy the food he would need for his trip to Sudan.

Somehow, when he got to the ground floor, the news that he was about to leave had reached the neighbours. One by one, they hugged him and wished him well.

Uncle Ali hugged Raphael tightly. "Don't let your brother get you down," he said. "If you were able to stand on your own two feet once, you'll be able to do it again. I know that you're going to do great things."

On going upstairs again to retrieve his personal belongings, Raphael looked around the apartment that had long been his home. He knew that he might never see it again. The doorjamb in the kitchen bore the notches his mother had made with a pencil when she measured each child on his birthday to see how much he had grown. He remembered all the happy times he had spent with his mother and with his siblings before they had all started to grow up and go their separate ways. He smiled as he thought about the many happy hours he had spent with Maxa and Renata, exploring their lithe young bodies and feeling their hearts beat against his own. Now it was all over.

He stuffed a few items of clothing into a cloth bag. He packed nothing else. This was going to be a fresh start, and there was no point in trying to bring the old life with him. All he really needed was his amulet. It would keep him safe.

"I've made you some sandwiches," said Jasmine when he came back downstairs. She handed him a little bundle wrapped in brown paper and tied with a string. "Just a little taste of Cairo to bring with you on your journey."

Raphael thought about calling in to Shepheard's to say goodbye to Madeleine but decided against it. He knew that she would be leaving soon too. Now that she had a respectable job, she had felt confident enough to write to her family in northern France and restore contact with them. While she had not told them about the years she had spent working in the red-light district, she told them that they had been right about her Egyptian lover, who had abandoned her as soon as he got what he wanted from her. They had written back to say that they still loved her and that they would support and help her to rebuild her life in France if she ever decided to come back again. Raphael knew that parting would be too difficult for them both and that they would start to cry, and he was afraid that if he started to cry, he would not be able to stop.

She would go back to France. Perhaps she would finally open the patisserie she had been dreaming of. Maybe one day, he would visit and taste her mille-feuille and see her with a husband and a family of her own. He smiled wryly to himself. He knew that he would never see her again, but he also knew that he would never forget her—and that she would always be one of his most cherished friends.

Raphael had not seen his family for four years, and the trip to Khartoum, the capital of Sudan, would take four days by sea and land. There was a symmetry there that he found pleasing. He would need all of those four days to process everything that had happened and to get used to the idea of being back with his family again after all this time. He very much looked forward to seeing his mother, Flora, but was anxious about how things would go with his father, Robert, and with Isaac, Elie, and Leon.

Raphael was used to running his own business and being his own boss, and he had just seen that Avi, at least, was not prepared to see him as his own person. Would Joseph expect him to buckle down and work for him now? He probably would. Joseph was very traditional in some ways. So far as he was concerned, all of his sons should be prepared to work for him and do what they were told, and each son should be expected to defer to the older ones, regardless of which one had a greater natural aptitude for business or authority.

Raphael knew that he would absolutely hate that, especially because he was the youngest of the boys and would be expected to defer to each and every one of his brothers and to respect them as his seniors. He could already imagine the rows and arguments that they would inevitably have. It would be stressful for everyone: for him, because he was sure that he would do best striking out on his own in life, and being his own boss; and for his older brothers, because every time he defied their wishes, they would interpret this as a threat or an insult and take it to heart.

When the boat arrived at Wadi Halfa, the letter Raphael had received from Mahfouz ensured that he was passed through the border with no difficulty or delay. He boarded a train that would take him through the Desert of Atbara on a twenty-four-hour journey to the capital. The trip was long and monotonous, but Raphael enjoyed looking out the window of the train at the desert passing by outside.

The air was still—thankfully, as a sandstorm would have delayed the train, possibly even for days—but the landscape was sculpted by the wind into dunes that captured the rays of the sun. Raphael began to feel more optimistic. After all, in one way, Sudan was his home.

Eventually, the train arrived at Khartoum. Stiff-legged from sitting for so many hours, Raphael climbed down from the carriage and walked the short distance to his family's house. It was midday and stiflingly hot. Few people were walking the streets, and just a small number of old men sat out of doors in the shade, mopping their brows with their handkerchiefs and sipping cool glasses of water while they played cards or exchanged gossip.

He passed through an area that served as a sort of red-light district. Here and there, in the shade, he could see the figures of women dressed in modest Muslim clothing, with even their faces obscured. Men hired these women, sight unseen, and brought them to hotels or other private places for sex, hoping that they would reveal themselves to be pretty and well-formed when the clothes came off. Rumour had it that many of these women were actually the well-to-do wives of important businessmen and politicians, who took advantage of the fact that their clothing hid their faces as well as their bodies to have sexual adventures with white men, far from the prying eyes of their extremely conservative society. Had any of their husbands found out, they would have been killed for their behaviour.

When he arrived at his parents' address, Raphael knocked on the door and waited for what seemed like a long time until he heard footsteps approaching and then someone jostling with the latch on the other side. Finally, the door opened, and Flora's surprised face took in the view of her youngest son. She looked older, he noted. There was more grey hair at her temples, and the lines at the corners of her eyes had grown deeper. But she was still beautiful.

"Mama," said Raphael as she opened her arms wide to take him into her embrace, "I'm home."

The two stood for a moment, their arms wrapped around one another, and then Flora turned and called for Joseph, who ambled out of a room that gave onto the courtyard of the small building. When he saw who it was, he rushed forward.

"Thank God you're here, son," he said. "We've been so worried about you."

"Thanks, Dad," said Raphael, thinking with a degree of amusement that they would have been a lot more worried if they had known the whole story. Nobody in the family had a clue that Raphael had been involved in activism and that he had come so close to being locked up in Cairo's most notorious prison. They didn't even know that he had spent a few days at Huckstep.

"Well, come on in," said Joseph. "Make yourself at home. Did you see Avi before you left? Did he and Sultana arrive?"

"Oh, they arrived all right," said Raphael bitterly. "And they are just fine."

"Good, good," said Joseph, oblivious to the displeasure in his youngest son's voice. "Well, hopefully they are settling in. We'll have something sorted out for you in no time."

Shouldering his small cloth bag, Raphael followed his father into the tiny courtyard. He was taken aback by how modest the house was—just a few rooms arranged around a shabby outdoor space furnished with rough-hewn wooden chairs and hemp beds. Despite the fact that his father Eli was a successful man who had given his sons every opportunity to succeed, Joseph had never had the success in business that he had dreamed of, despite managing a big company at one point. Had he finally given up completely? Was this what Raphael's life was going to look like from now on—shabby, humble, and unassuming?

Suddenly overcome by emotion, Raphael sank to the floor. His hands reached unthinkingly for a blanket on one of the hemp beds, which he pulled over himself as he lay down.

"If you're tired, darling, I can get a bed ready for you," said Flora. "You look thin. A good sleep, and then I'll cook something delicious for you. You'll be back to yourself in no time."

"No," said Raphael. "Leave me alone. I'll sleep here."

He pulled the blanket right over his head and closed his eyes. He didn't want to talk to anyone right now, not even his mother, and certainly not his father. He stayed in that position for forty-eight hours, only vaguely conscious of his mother approaching, trying to talk to him, and weeping, and of the comings and goings of his father and brothers. When he finally emerged from his long restorative sleep, he knew one thing for certain: he could not, and would not, remain in Khartoum with his family for one minute longer than was strictly necessary. He was determined to find his own path and continue to journey through life according to his own rules.

Raphael sat up, holding his amulet in his hand. *I'll go to Nigeria*, he decided. *Something tells me that things could really work out for me there.*

Of course, it did occur to Raphael to move to Israel, like so many others, but there were arguments against taking this step, and certainly at the moment it would be a very bad idea. He could not cross into Israel through Egypt or Egyptian waters, as if he was apprehended, he would be immediately captured and sent to prison. Even if he did manage to get through Egypt unscathed, it would be almost impossible for him to safely see his family again. Moving to Israel would mean accepting that he would be completely isolated from his family—and from his plan to one day marry his promised one—and that was not a price that he was prepared to pay. Moreover, something in his heart was telling him that he would be of more use to Israel if he made his life and his fortune outside it. He was quite convinced that he could only achieve his potential if he gave himself the opportunity to do so on his own, and that he had inherited his grandfather's unusual drive to succeed.

Before telling his family about his plans, Raphael spent some time getting back in touch with all the relatives in Sudan and renewing old friendships with the boys—now young men like himself, some of them already married—he had known since childhood. Through the family grapevine, he heard, to his great relief, that Shalom had gone from France to Italy. With the expertise he had acquired at Shepheard's, Raphael was sure that he would be able to find an excellent job at a fancy hotel in Rome.

In Khartoum, daily life was going on, in many ways much as it always had. The young Jewish men and women went to tennis. The women shopped and met for coffee, and the men met up and talked about business. They were all growing up and marriages were being arranged among his group of peers. What cultural life there was, aside from a handful of cinemas, was confined to social clubs set up to cater to each specific ethnic group.

Although the various ethnic groups had all got along well until recently, the deeper you looked, the more the divisions were apparent. At the British Sudan Club, while the members occasionally brought friends from different backgrounds, only the British-born were allowed to use facilities like the pool. Once in a while, a ball would be held at one of the social clubs, and everyone would get dressed up and go out to dance with the same people they worked, lived, and socialised with every single day of their lives. Under the watchful eyes of the community's matrons, it was very difficult for anyone to have a sex life outside of marriage. For this reason, the young men occasionally escaped from the strictures of their family homes and made their way to the small red-light district, where they were serviced by beautiful young women from Ethiopia and Egypt.

Raphael tried to imagine staying here and making his life in Sudan. Certainly there would be some good aspects to it. He knew that the girls liked him, and even if their parents would never let them be alone in a room with him, he enjoyed their admiration. He relished the company of the other young men and was struck by the fact that many of them were extremely ambitious—almost as ambitious as him. He liked the tightly knit Jewish community and the sense that everyone was pulling together and would help each other out in any way possible. A lot of people loved the fact that everyone knew each other and that they could always count on help and support. The Jewish community was so small, people had known each other since childhood, and mostly they wanted to see everyone do well.

As he was from the same sort of background as the others, it was easy for Raphael to communicate with his peers, and he found that people wanted to listen to him and hear what he had to say. He could see that, if he stayed, he would not find it difficult to establish a professional position for himself. He would soon be seen as a leader in the community, even if he was the youngest son of a large family.

On the other hand, the atmosphere was stifling, not just because of how small the Jewish community was but also because of the many stresses and strains in Sudan at the time. Everyone was trying to put a brave face on things, but life was actually getting quite difficult, much as it had in Egypt, and although the Jews of Sudan had worked very hard to create a community for themselves, it wasn't clear whether they would be able to keep it up. The anti-Jewish sentiment that was decimating the Jewish community in Cairo was getting stronger here, too, along with a general anti-white feeling. It was getting more difficult to do business, and all the Jewish mothers were upset about their children being bothered on the street.

It occurred to him that his relationship with his father was much the same as his relationship with Sudan. There was a great deal of love and respect there, which he was sure he would keep with him always, but at the same time he knew that he had to leave in order to reach his full potential. Whether in the shadow of his father or in the heart of the loving but stifling community of Sudan's Jews, he could never truly be himself. Still, he knew that one day he would marry a girl from Sudan—his Angel—and in this way forge a connection with both her family and their shared cultural background that they could take with them everywhere they went.

"What's going on with Lola?" Raphael asked his mother. He'd had no contact with Lola or her daughter, his future bride, for years.

"Lola's fine," Flora said. "She's as pretty as ever, and she loves being a mother. But Abraham is very gloomy about business."

Abraham, Lola's husband, owned a big property that housed offices and shops which he rented out, but so many Jews and other white businessmen were leaving Sudan that it was getting progressively harder to find tenants.

"Other than that," Flora continued, "everything is good. I try to see Lola as often as I can. You know how much I love her. Their house is lovely, you know. They have a big garden with a veranda, and Lola and the children all sleep outside when it's hot."

"What about Angel?"

"Your intended? Well, she's a delightful child. Do you want to see her? Maybe it would be a good idea for you two to start getting to know each other. She's very young still, but you can already see that she's going to be a gorgeous young woman when she grows up. She knows that she'll marry you when she leaves school; her mama makes sure that she is in no doubt about that! She's going to the nuns' school, but they're planning to move her to an English school for the next academic year. Her English needs to improve, and it will be nice for her to be able to walk the short distance home. I see her playing at the Jewish Club sometimes. She's a little darling."

"I don't really want to see her now," said Raphael. "What would I do with a little girl? It would be weird to spend time with a child and know that she'll be my wife one day. There'll be plenty of time for me to see her when she grows up."

"I thought you might be interested to see how she's coming along."

"I'll wait until she's older. She's still a child. I don't want to frighten her."

"It won't be *that* long, darling. You know how I feel about marriage. It's best to get married young. That way, the couple can grow together. Don't forget that I got married at 14 and had Avi when I was just 15. I might have some regrets about my life, but getting married young is definitely not one of them. Take my advice and marry your Angel just as soon as she is ready. Then all you have to do is love and respect her, and you are guaranteed a happy life!"

"OK, Mum, I will. But can you stop talking about Angel for the moment and tell me what your cousins' plans are? Are they going to stay here?"

"I don't know what Abraham and Lola are planning to do," Flora said. "Lots of people are leaving. Come to think of it, I don't know what we're going to do either. Your father hasn't decided yet."

"Well, he'll have to decide soon."

"It was hard leaving Cairo in some ways," Flora began, "but the wonderful thing here in Khartoum is how we all help each other out. You know, nobody ever lets anyone go through difficulties on their own. And not just the Jews, you know. People are so friendly: the Italians, the Greeks, the Armenians … we're all here for each other. But then it used to be like that in Cairo, too, and now, well, who knows what is going to happen?"

She continued, "All through the war, everyone was really happy to know that the British were here to keep Sudan safe from the Germans, but now that the war is over, people have taken against the British— and all of the other whites by association. Lola, and others too, tell me that their children can't even walk in the street anymore. If they are sent out to a shop or want to go to the cinema, people come up to them and pinch them and bother them. They say things like, 'Hey, whitey, guess what we're going to do to you!' They make it very clear that they would actually like to hurt the white people, just because they are white."

Flora shuddered. "Obviously, people are especially worried about the girls, because even if boys get chased and bothered more often, the girls are more vulnerable. That nice lad you used to play with, Aaron—his mum said he was chased all the way home last week by a group of boys calling him a 'dirty Jew', and now he says he wants to go to Israel and join the army just to get away from it all, and that he'll pretend to be 18 if he has to. He's still just 16. That's the kind of thing that's going on. Lola told me that Abraham is going to send Angel to boarding school in England as soon as she's old enough to get her away from all this."

She concluded, "At least business is going well for them, and they can afford it. It's good to know that your wife is going to be an educated woman, at least. She'll be able to support you and help you make decisions in a way that I was never able to for your father."

Soon, the family heard the sad but inevitable news that Raphael's grandfather Eli had died. He had worked right into his old age and still had a considerable business empire in Sudan, having started with nothing. When his son-in-law, rather than one of his own sons, took it over, it was a devastating blow for Joseph, who could see his own family's status and power diminishing before his eyes.

It was strange: Whereas Eli had been a wonderful businessman, perhaps he had not been such a great father. Surely a good father would have ensured that the family business would have been passed on to his own sons. On the other hand, Joseph, who had less interest in business, always did his best to ensure that his children were number one. Raphael decided that he would do his very best to combine the best qualities of each man in himself. Perhaps he wouldn't always achieve that goal, but at least it was something to work towards.

Shortly after his grandfather's death, Raphael heard that Avi and Sultana had given up the tenancy on the apartment in Cairo and were returning to Sudan. Avi had not managed to find a good job. Meanwhile, under state ownership, the leather workshop had gone bankrupt. All the men had been laid off, and they were due back-pay that they would never get because the money just wasn't there anymore.

In Egypt, Marcella had been caught, although the authorities did not know the full details of what she had done. She served some time in prison, as did Elia, the man who had been her immediate superior in the chain of command. Through the grapevine, Raphael heard that Marcella had had an affair with a German man—tall and handsome, which must have made it an easier task than it would otherwise have been—who had been part of the Nazi regime. He had been appointed as one of the intelligence people for the Egyptian Army, and through him she had received a huge amount of information that had greatly facilitated the establishment of Israel.

On her release, Marcella married Elia, and she and her husband continued to work as activists for Israel, which they made their home.

1951-67

In 1951—by which time Raphael was firmly entrenched in his own business in Nigeria—Joseph felt that, after all, he would make the move to Israel. When he got there, however, he was disappointed, and after just one year, he left. To the dismay of the Middle Eastern Jews, Israel had established a European elite, and citizens of places like Sudan—many of whom spoke Arabic as their first language—were very much looked down on as second-class citizens and considered uneducated and boorish. Their opportunities to get ahead in Israel were limited.

Like a lot of businessmen, Joseph was also dismayed by the socialist economic policies that Israel had adopted at that time, which seemed designed to shut down private enterprise. The many very poor Jews who had opted to leave their homes elsewhere and settle in Israel had decided, for now, that socialism was the best approach for them. With time, Israel would become more stable, affluent, and opportunity-rich.

In 1952, the corrupt and decadent King Farouk, then 32 years old, was finally deposed and the kingdom abolished by the army's coup d'état and the Egyptian Revolution. Together with his wife and children, their nanny and an aide—armed with a machine gun in case they had to defend themselves—the king fled from the army in his top-of-the-line Mercedes Benz packed with crates of gold bars that he would sell to maintain his luxurious lifestyle. The army, led by a man called Gamal Abdel Nasser, had decided that Egypt had been ruled for long enough by such an embarrassing and unworthy king. Although the United States disliked Farouk and shared the Egyptian army's view of him, the US authorities helped the family to escape what was rapidly becoming a deadly situation. Farouk abdicated in favour of his baby son, and on 26 July, the family left the country for good on the royal yacht.

The victorious army did not gloat about their successful coup but let the king leave with his dignity intact. The family settled into life in exile overseas. Farouk's sister, Fawzia, a strikingly beautiful woman, had married the Shah of Iran a few years earlier, and through her and his other contacts, Farouk had plenty of access to men of influence. His life outside Egypt remained comfortable and coddled.

For Egypt's minorities, however—and especially the Jews—the deposal of King Farouk was not good news. The intensely nationalist government that succeeded him under Naguib and then Nasser simply didn't want them and increasingly portrayed them as parasites on the ordinary people of Egypt, among whom anti-Semitism was already rather common. The political parties that had once competed with one another for the king's favours were now running the country and competing with one another over politics instead. Among them were groups that had radical Muslim views. So long as they were in positions of authority, Egypt would not be a comfortable home for a Jewish minority, nor would it be a friendly neighbour to tiny, newly founded Israel.

Nasser was an ambitious man who sought to seize control of the Suez Canal with a view to gaining control over the Arabian Gulf and establishing an Egyptian empire that would spread Arabic culture and language and the Muslim religion far and wide. The poor people of Egypt, who had been promised so much by the revolutionaries, remained just as poor as they had always been, and before long some of them had already started to feel nostalgic for the days of King Farouk. They remembered his corrupt regime as a "golden" period in Egypt's modern history, because at least there had been a greater degree of political stability at the time.

The British, meanwhile, had been busy getting everything ready for their departure. They set up Jordan with its king and Saudi Arabia with the Saudi family, while the Ottoman Empire had been banished from Palestine and the Shah of Iran was under their thumb until the Americans dethroned him. The British understood something that the Americans never did, which is that democracy simply doesn't work in some cultural contexts. Given the choice between instability and autocracy, the British had always tended to prefer autocracy. When the Americans gained the upper hand, they invariably flew the flag for democracy, even if it could only come at a huge cost.

Nasser would remain in place until 1967, when he waged war against Israel. By that time, the Jewish population of Egypt had dwindled to just about five thousand optimistic souls who thought that if they hung in for long enough, perhaps they could have successful lives. While Nasser himself was not a radical Muslim, Islamist extremism grew in Egypt on his watch, especially among the poor. The Egyptian middle and upper classes had always bent the rules when it came to following their religion, freely drinking alcohol and having affairs. As they had so few material goods, the poor had to content themselves with the idea that they were morally superior, and they were often very attracted to the notion that if they adhered to an extremely rigid version of Islam, they would be rewarded for it in the next life. In reality, people of all social classes saw their businesses suffer or had them confiscated on the grounds that the government was intending to nationalise all business.

Ultimately, the few remaining Jews had to escape from Egypt as refugees in a massive exodus of Jews from their homes all over the Middle East. The other minorities, although they were less persecuted, suffered too. Some in the Greek community were involved in growing tobacco and making cigarettes, and they were reluctant to leave what was then a very successful business. Ultimately, however, the decision was made for them. Steadily, all the minorities lost the influence they had had in Egypt. Because the Secret Service was everywhere, they were afraid to go out to restaurants, even if they could afford to, and all the restaurants closed or were given over to Egyptian managers.

While some business people struggled with Israel's economic socialism at that time, for most it was a much more comfortable environment to do business in and to live in. Radical Islam was growing in Egypt, although the government was not a theocracy, making it an ever more dangerous place for Jews to be.

2017

"Wow," said David. "It's crazy to think about Israel being so underdeveloped back in those days. I mean, I've been there, and it's one of the most modern countries I've ever visited—and the tech sector is second to none!"

"Things can change a lot very quickly," Rebecca pointed out. "And the Israelis have always been a very motivated people, for obvious reasons."

"Yes," said Richard, "and outside Israel, too, the country has always had its supporters doing what they can to ensure that it gets a fair chance. I know that Grandad has always done whatever he can for the country and that it is very dear to his heart. When he bought a second home there just a few years ago, it was a dream come true. I know that he feels strongly that we should all keep up the family links to Israel, even when he's gone."

CHAPTER 11

THE BIG TIME AT JUST NINETEEN

2017

"It might sound superstitious," said David, "but I think it's actually true that Grandad's amulet kept him safe through all those difficult times. Has he talked much about it? I know it's very important to him."

"Oh," said Richard with a laugh. "There are actually *loads* of stories about Grandad's adventures and how the amulet kept him safe through them. We could be here all night if you want to listen to them all—but I'm game if you are!"

"Yes, go on," urged Rebecca. "I'm not tired at all. Tell us a story about one of the times the amulet brought him luck!"

"All right then," said Richard. "There are so many to choose from. Let me see … OK, I've got an idea. Are you ready?"

"Yes!" said David.

"Definitely," said Rebecca.

"OK," said Richard. "Well, we'll get onto some of the wilder adventures later, but first of all, Grandad always said that his amulet is what brought him so much success in business. Remember how I was telling you that he had a successful business exporting crocodile skins from Africa when he was just 19 years old?"

"Nineteen!" exclaimed Rebecca. "Isn't it extraordinary? I was in my first year at uni. when I was 19, and I hardly knew how to tie my own shoelaces! I remember trying to cook pizza in the dormitory microwave and being surprised when it didn't come out nice and crisp."

"Perhaps things were different in those days," said Richard, "or maybe he's right, and it was the amulet after all. Anyway, you already know that he had some experience as a crocodile hunter, but Grandad was already making millions of pounds in the business before he even turned 20 ..."

"I always knew that Grandad had made a lot of money when he was still very young," said Rebecca. "But 19... most kids of 19 today can't take their heads out of their mobile phones, not even for a minute. All they want to do is watch stupid celebrities on YouTube and take selfies for their Instagram feed. I'm sure that, even back in those days, a lot of kids were still at home, doing what they were told. Actually, I'm surprised Grandad's parents even let him just go off and do his own thing at that age! Weren't they worried about him? *I* would have been! The war was just over a few years, he was little more than a kid at the time ... and he wanted to go and live miles away from them and fend for himself ..."

"From what he tells me," said Richard, "there would have been no way to stop him. He'd already been earning his own money on the streets of Cairo for a number of years, and he was determined to strike out on his own as soon as he could. Besides, he had the amulet, and he was quite convinced that this meant that he was destined to do well. With the amulet in his possession, nothing serious could go wrong."

1950

For as long as he could remember, Raphael had been attracted to money. First of all, he liked the fact that money offered security. There were many families in Egypt who were much worse off than his, but nonetheless, he was always aware as a child that there were many things his family could not afford because Dad was having difficulties of one sort or another in business—and because he was growing up in turbulent times, when Jews and their businesses were being targeted.

He and the rest of the children had often heard their parents talking about their money worries, even though they weren't supposed to. Things had never been easy for Joseph, and with the way the world was going … well, they were getting a lot more complicated.

But that wasn't the sole reason for Raphael's attraction to money. He also relished the sense of power it gave him. When he had money in his pocket, he became somehow more important and dynamic than when he didn't have any. Pragmatically, he understood from a very early age that, in many ways, money really *did* make the man. By the time he reached his late teens, Raphael had decided to be independent and do whatever was necessary not to need help from anyone else. He was determined not to ask his father or another relative for work but to forge his own path in the world and stand tall because of his own efforts and no one else's. His mother, Flora, who knew that he had been fiercely independent all his life, respected this urge.

"I trust you do to the right thing, dear," she said. "You know a mother always worries about her children, but I've seen since you were tiny that you need to be on your own. Go and do what you must, and know that I will always be here for you."

Joseph loved his son, but he had always found Raphael difficult. Unlike the other boys, Raphael constantly pushed the boundaries and challenged him, forcing Joseph to explore his own decision-making in ways that he did not always find very comfortable. If Joseph said something had to be done a certain way, his other sons generally accepted their father's edict and did what they were told without questioning his authority, but Raphael always asked "Why?" It was hard for Joseph, at first, to accept a child who didn't simply obey the way he was expected to, as was traditional in Cairene society at the time. But by the time Raphael had turned 19, Joseph had accepted that the boy would be going his own way from now on, and that there was little point in trying to exert any fatherly discipline. To do so was more likely to drive Raphael away completely than to bring him into line.

"You keep telling me you want to be on your own and to do your own thing," Joseph said. "And I am not going to fight against your will. If that's what you want, that's what you want. I have no problem leaving you alone. You can go and make your own mistakes—and hopefully have your own triumphs. We'll all be here waiting for you when you are ready to come back to us. We know that one day you will be ready to settle down and marry, but not yet."

Raphael was grateful to his parents for their understanding, but the fact was that he would have done his own thing regardless of what they said. At this point in his life, despite the fact that his future bride had already been chosen for him, Raphael really didn't want to hear about his family and their connections and plans. He didn't want to be like his father, always worrying about business and never making quite enough money to keep the family going. He didn't want to be like his brothers, falling into line behind their older male relatives as though they didn't have minds of their own. He wanted to work, and he wanted to make money—a *lot* of it.

He didn't want to scrimp and save or panic about where the rent for the next month was going to come from. He didn't want to hire servants only to have to let them go when there wasn't enough money to cover their salaries. When he was older and had a wife of his own, he wanted her to be able to dress in beautiful clothes—silks and satins every day if she wanted—and to wear expensive jewellery. He wanted her to know that her children would never want for anything. He wanted to live like a king. Not only that, but he had a plan, and he felt confident that he could achieve it.

Raphael had decided that he was going to leave his family and make his way to Nigeria in the western part of the African continent. He knew there was a lot of money to be made there from crocodile skins. So he packed a few items of clothing in a bag and carefully hung his beloved amulet around his neck, and after shaking his father's hand and squeezing his mother in a bear hug, he was on his way. The world was waiting for him.

2017

"Just like that, he decided to go to Nigeria?" asked Rebecca incredulously. "Without ever having been there before or knowing anything about the culture?"

"Well," said Richard, "that's the story he tells."

"After all he'd been through, you'd think he would have been ready to take it easy for a while!"

"Oh, come on," contributed David. "If there's one thing we all know about Grandad, it's that he doesn't take it easy. Never has, never will! When he does something, he goes all the way, whether it's business or wooing a woman …"

1950

The day Raphael left his home to travel to Nigeria, Joseph and Flora watched him walk away. For the first time in their lives, they felt old. Joseph put his arm around Flora's shoulder and held her tight as their boy strode towards the manhood that awaited. Raphael did not look back. Not even once.

After a long trip across the African continent, observing the changes in the landscape and the appearance of the people who filled it, Raphael arrived at his destination in Nigeria. He noted that the Nigerian people looked very different from the Egyptians. The men and women alike were often tall, with perfect posture, well-formed bodies, and black or dark brown skin. Whereas the Egyptians tended to dress in a limited range of colours and often in a conservative Western style, the Nigerians loved to wear vibrant colours and patterns. Many of the women were bare-breasted, showing their full breasts and large, dark nipples without a hint of embarrassment or shame.

As the climate was hot, little children were often stark naked or wearing just a ragged pair of shorts or a skirt below the waist. Here and there, one saw a European—a British member of the colonial administration, a businessman, or a teacher from Britain or another European country. In contrast to the native Nigerians, they looked very pale and very overdressed.

Most of the roads were unpaved, and because of the dry climate, great clouds of reddish dust rose up in the air whenever anyone drove on them. It often seemed as though everything in Nigeria was covered in a thin film of dust. Even the animals were dusty. There were herds of goats—sometimes even a herd of goats that had managed to climb into a tree to eat the tender leaves—and thin, rangy dogs whose ribs were as visible as if they were the bars of a xylophone.

African farmers used the roads to bring their products to market in the towns. Raphael could tell when he was nearing a town by an increase in the number of men riding battered bicycles with all manner of things piled up on them and women walking tall and erect with goods for sale or already purchased balanced on their heads. When he drove through the towns, flocks of tiny children would run after the car he was travelling in, partly because they were excited to see a car with white passengers drive by and partly because they hoped to be given a handful of coins they could bring home to their mothers. When passengers threw them coins, the children dived after them with great vigour, little caring about the scrapes and bruises they might suffer as they jostled with the other children for the bounty.

Maiduguri, Raphael's final destination, was a British colonial settlement that had been founded as a military outpost in the early part of the twentieth century. The British had chosen the location for the town on the basis of the attractive landscape, the abundant supply of water for both human and farming needs (a big, deep river flowed through the town providing all this, as well as a mode of transport for farmers living along its shores who needed to bring their produce to market), and the pleasant climate. They had done their best to create a little patch of England in Nigeria, with a degree of success. Certainly, Raphael reflected as he stepped down from the car, this town looked very different from the many small, dusty towns he had driven through on the way.

Raphael would soon learn that Maiduguri very much reflected the local status quo. There was the English town, where the English expatriates lived and worked in their comfortable, white-washed homes; another area where the non-English whites lived and worked (including a small Jewish community, among whom were a number of Raphael's relatives, although he did not intend to see them very much, as he was absolutely determined to go his own way); and then the areas inhabited by the native Africans, who were further divided along both tribal and religious lines, with corresponding linguistic differences. Many of the Nigerians in the area were Muslims, while others practised indigenous religions, Christianity, or a combination of the two.

The Muslim women in particular were easy to identify. While all the women wore clothing made from bright fabrics with vibrant designs, many of the non-Muslims were bare-breasted, and all of them kept their heads proudly uncovered, whereas the Muslim women invariably covered themselves with a blouse and wore an additional piece of fabric wound around their heads. They looked less comfortable in the intense heat than their scantily clad sisters, but it was important for them to make this public display of piety and modesty.

Every effort had been made to make the English town look as British as possible, despite the intense tropical sun and the very un-English vegetation that lined the streets and filled the gardens. The houses were built in a British style, and here and there a union flag fluttered in the breeze. The women who had come to live there as housewives—taking care of their husbands, who mostly worked in the civil service—wore English dresses with fitted bodices and flared skirts. They dressed their hair in styles that approximated those of the film stars they saw at the cinema as closely as possible.

In general, the married English women had very little to do. They had given up work on getting married, and in Africa it was cheap and easy to hire local women to do all the housework and take care of small children, while older children were generally shipped off to England to attend boarding school there. When he first arrived in Maiduguri, Raphael was mildly surprised to see the prominence given to bottles of good British gin in all the shops. He soon learned that drinking gin was one of the main pastimes of the English ladies, who could often be seen slightly the worse for wear, tripping their way home in their pretty dresses after another gin-soaked afternoon with their female friends.

An education system had been set up along British lines, and in each of the neighbourhoods, the local school tended to be among the more impressive of the buildings. The schools were generally segregated by race— this habit was not inscribed in law but tended to be observed nonetheless—but the same decent British education was available to anyone who wanted to partake in it. Whatever their colour, the schoolchildren wore crisp ironed uniforms and could be seen walking to and from school in the morning and the afternoon.

For educated Africans, it was frustrating to know that, despite their efforts, there were distinct limits to how far they were likely to travel in their career. The British paid lip service to the idea that everyone was treated equally according to his merits, but the reality was that it was unheard of for a native African to be given a job that would involve supervising white employees. This fact dissuaded some African families from investing in their children's education and kept the numbers of educated Africans lower than it should have been. Some other Africans stayed away from the British-run schools because of a misplaced sense of pride, thinking that they were letting down their own people if they had a European education and would be better off simply doing what their forefathers had always done.

Raphael had decided to set up a camp just outside of town, and he had brought sufficient funds to pay for the preliminary work to be done. He obtained a plot of land with a good aspect, prone to receiving a refreshing breeze, and hired local men to put up a fence and stake out areas for the erection of tents, showers, and everything he would need to live with a reasonable degree of comfort.

As soon as the camp had reached a rudimentary state of preparedness, with living quarters and buildings for cooking and for processing the skins, Raphael opened for business. He had exhausted the relatively meagre funds he had brought with him from Sudan and needed to start making money as quickly as possible. He felt confident that, if he could establish a reliable supply of crocodile skins, it would not be long before he was generating a decent income.

He started by going to the African area and making inquiries about which of the men with experience would be available to hunt for him. It would be dangerous, risky work, but there was good money to be made, and Raphael made it clear in all of his interactions with the men and their families that he respected the Africans just as much as he respected anybody else and that the men he employed would be paid fairly for their hard work. At that time, all the fashionable women in France (and therefore throughout the Western world) wanted to buy handbags and shoes made of crocodile skin, so there was a huge market supplying skins to the fashion industry. If Raphael played his cards right, he would make a lot of money, while the hunters who worked for him would benefit from secure employment and a decent wage.

As the word got out that there was someone looking for hunters—and that he was prepared to pay more than was usually on offer—more and more men came to see what Raphael was proposing. If they were surprised to see how young the new employer was, most of them managed to hide it. With little to go on but his gut instinct and the help of a local man called Jemperino, he made contact with a small army of extremely experienced crocodile hunters who knew how to kill the animals with minimal damage to the skins and who could be relied upon. Jemperino had a background of crocodile hunting in Lake Chad, and he knew how to find and work with all of the most competent men.

Raphael drew up a shortlist of candidates and offered them work. They would get paid strictly according to the number of skins they brought in, but he was prepared to pay generously so as to ensure that he found and kept the best hunters in the area. Soon, Raphael had a team of men working for him. They were hard-working and eager to please, knowing that the decent salaries they made would support their families and possibly even pay school fees so that they could educate their children and prepare them for a better life.

The men had great local knowledge of their area; they were all aware of the parts of the river and the water holes that harboured crocodiles; and they had no love of the beasts, which were sometimes known to kill people who strayed too close to the water. Most of the hunters knew at least one family that had been affected. They killed and skinned the crocodiles and brought the skins to Raphael's camp; they were free to dispose of the meat as they saw fit, so they brought it home to their wives. Crocodile meat was not considered a great delicacy, but it went against the grain in African families to waste any good food.

Raphael inspected the skins and oversaw their processing. The processing room contained a large table onto which the wet skins were thrown with a dull slap, their vaguely fishy and muddy smell filling the air. Raphael inspected them carefully, running his hands along every grain of the skin and using sight and touch to ascertain quality and freshness.

The value of the skin depended on many issues, including how badly it had been damaged when the animal was killed and whether or not the animal had experienced any scars or scratches during the various battles it had participated in during its lifetime. While the less experienced hunters often had to jab at a crocodile many times in order to kill it, a man who knew what he was doing could dispatch one with a single strike from his spear.

It was also important that Raphael receive the skins as soon as possible so that they could be wet-salted and preserved before they dried out or the natural process of decomposition impacted on their quality. A good clean kill would result in a high-quality skin and a good price from a buyer in Paris, who would be able to sell the whole skin to the fashion houses.

Once the skins had been cleared for sale, they would be wet-salted and packaged in bundles that were carefully sealed to ensure they suffered no damage during transit and storage. The bundles would be opened only when they arrived in Paris and the buyer inspected them carefully to ensure that he had acquired the quality and quantity promised. Potentially, the skins could remain wet-salted for a whole year without any damage occurring to them.

Now that he had established a steady supply of skins to his camp, Raphael needed to find a buyer, and he quickly did so through his contact with a local agent called Seeliger. The buyer in Paris was an older man called Monsieur Gravitz, who was originally from Marseille. Gravitz was in a position to make a lot of money from the skins, and he didn't care or comment when Seeliger explained that he was making contact on behalf of a very young businessman who had recently set up shop in Nigeria. All Gravitz was interested in was obtaining the skins on time and in the conditions that he had been promised, and Raphael was more of following through.

The first time Raphael supplied Gravitz with his product, he sent the skins on spec and without having received a deposit or payment of any sort. He included a note saying that he had such confidence in his product that he was sure Gravitz would not only pay for it but would order more immediately. Gravitz was delighted with the quality of the skins, and he paid for them promptly so as to ensure a constant supply.

From then on, Gravitz trusted Raphael to supply the materials and paid him without hesitation or delay.

Soon, Raphael was making the sort of money his father had only ever dreamed of and establishing a professional reputation that would make it easier for him to build the business going forward. He was happy that things were going so well, but at the same time, he was not surprised. After all, he had his amulet; he wore it around his neck every day, and he had always been sure that, so long as he did, he would prosper and no harm of any sort could come to him.

One day, Raphael overheard the hunters talking about him. He had acquired the nickname "King of the Crocodiles", and this was the term they were using to describe him. Nobody, they said, could understand how Raphael had managed to establish such a thriving business in a matter of a few months. None of them had ever had so much success in hunting before. It was, they said, as if there was magic at work. Surely some mysterious force was helping Raphael. He smiled and fingered the tiny gold charm that hung at his neck. He knew where his help came from.

Unlike many of the white businessmen in the area at the time, Raphael understood that it was just as important to build a good professional relationship with his suppliers and staff as with his customers. One of the biggest mistakes that many of the expatriate businessmen made in Nigeria was to underestimate the Africans and assume that they were less intelligent and shrewd than Europeans simply because of their dark skin and the different course that history had taken them on. The Englishmen in particular often spoke to the African men as though they were idiots, raising their voices and shouting at them as though to dim children who struggled to comprehend. Many of the English wives spent their afternoons with their friends, getting sozzled on gin while poorly paid African women tended to their homes and, often, did much of the work involved in raising their children. Understandably, this sort of attitude infuriated the African workers, and they often responded to it by becoming bullish and uncooperative—which, to the British, seemed to confirm the views they had acquired about their intellectual abilities or lack thereof.

Of course, most of the British employers failed to understand the relationship between their treatment of their staff and how effectively the men worked. In the wood-panelled rooms of their private clubs and in their tastefully wallpapered living rooms, they joked to one another about how difficult it was to get good help in Africa and told each other that the blacks would never be capable of running their own affairs and that the empire was undoubtedly safe for the foreseeable future, because it would all fall apart without some good old English efficiency. Raphael knew what it felt like to be looked down on, and he resolved to never be anything but respectful in his interactions with the hunters.

While anti-Semitism was not official policy in Nigeria, Raphael was aware that many of the British men were uncomfortable with Jews and with people from the Middle East in general, especially when they did well in business and showed that they were in no way the British men's social inferiors. They made their lack of ease abundantly clear. In fact, most of the English made it very clear to everyone they came into contact with that they considered themselves vastly superior not just to the native Africans (whom they largely regarded with a sort of paternalistic benevolence and treated like children) but also to all of the other people of non-European origins. Most of them, or at least most of the men, were not very inclined to be friendly to a young Jewish Egyptian with more confidence than they felt anybody of his age had a right to. They might be courteous to his face, but they were sure to bad-mouth him behind his back.

Despite the atrocities that had taken place in the recent war, many of them persisted with their anti-Semitic views and weren't at all ashamed of airing them—especially when they'd had a few drinks or were ensconced in the smug security of their English social clubs. Moreover, some of the British men were former army soldiers who had served in Palestine. Even if they paid lip-service to the idea that all men were created equal, in Palestine they had picked up anti-Semitic views that they often failed to disguise.

In the urban parts of the town, segregation between the races was not enforced by law but by tradition and by layer upon layer of social convention. If you weren't British, then you simply weren't welcome to live in a British area. You might be allowed to come if you were working in a service position, like many of the Africans, or on business, like Raphael or the other whites, but the British— and especially the English—maintained an air of faintly amused superiority that excluded all others and made the English town an unwelcoming place to be.

While Raphael was always polite and considerate in his dealings with the English, he also kept his distance from them emotionally. He knew that, despite his competence as a young businessman, most of them did not see him as an equal and could not be relied upon to provide a positive business environment to anyone outside their small circles. Raphael realised very soon that, while Englishmen might be happy to do business with him and provide his banking or accountancy needs, so far as they were concerned, he was a social inferior, simply because he was not an Anglo-Saxon. No matter how much money he made, it wouldn't make any difference. He would never be part of their society—and he didn't want to be.

After a while, news of how Raphael managed his African staff reached the ears of the English administration. When it was time for him to renew his residency permit, he was called in for an interview with the police. He was slightly nervous, as he was aware that the English authorities had the right to deny him a permit. On the other hand, he knew that he had done everything according to the book and that they welcomed the substantial taxes paid by businessmen who did well.

"Now, young man," said the British police officer, an officious older man who had introduced himself as Graham. "People are saying that you are paying your men too much and giving them … *ideas*. Now, I think that we can all agree that it's a very bad idea when Africans acquire ideas and notions of grandeur. They'll start wanting everyone to pay them the same amount you do, and that'll dig heavily into a lot of people's pocketbooks and wreak havoc with the local economy, don't you know."

Raphael made a stiff little nod that acknowledged the older man's words without accepting them. "With respect, sir," he said, "it is dangerous work, hunting crocodiles, and the men all have families to support. I don't think it would be reasonable to expect them to risk their lives without offering them sufficient reward to make it worth their while. I want the best hunters I can get, too, not men who will do a shoddy job and don't have any ambition."

"People don't like it," said Graham, impatiently tapping his pen against the desk. It was perfectly clear that by *people*, Graham meant *white people*, and above all, the English—for many of the English, only Britons were really seen as full human beings. "If one person starts paying more than the others, it wrecks the system for everybody. If the Africans start thinking that they are good enough to earn wages like that, it's only going to lead to social unrest and the end of our way of life here in Maiduguri. What next? Communism? Their wives will start wanting handbags and shoes and perfume and thinking that they are too good to do the laundry for the whites, and then where will we get our servants from? Do you think the Englishwomen will be happy about having to wash their own drawers? Look; we have a system in this town. It works very well for all concerned, as it has done for more years than you have been alive, and nobody wants a youngster like you coming in and wrecking it for the rest of us by giving the Africans … *ideas*."

"Sir," said Raphael, "if the system is as fragile as you seem to suggest, then it's not a very good system, is it? I expect the hunters I hire to work hard and bring me as many skins as they can, and I expect them to ensure that the skins are of a decent quality. If they don't work hard, I let them go, because I am not running a charity and I expect to get what I pay for. But in return for the fair wages I give them, most of them do excellent work and don't want to go near anyone else offering work. Not one of the hunters I employed has decided to go and work for somebody else. This makes me think that maybe some of the other businessmen in this town should ask themselves if they are paying enough."

"It's not just the issue of the wages, either," Graham said. "I hear that you have been fraternising with the Africans and treating them as drinking buddies."

"Not at all," said Raphael. "I observe the natural distance between employer and staff. Unless by 'fraternise' you mean 'treat with respect', in which case I can only plead guilty. I socialise with my own friends, but when I am working with my men at the camp, we eat together around my table. Do you think that I should treat them like animals and send them to take their meals outside on the ground? Is that how you treat your junior staff here in public office?"

"Just a word of advice, boy," the older man said unpleasantly. "You won't make many friends around here unless you learn to play by the rules that have been established by your elders and betters."

"Thank you," said Raphael blithely. "I will bear that in mind." He made a mental note to avoid Graham in future. What a pain the man was!

Raphael nodded politely to Graham—who did not return the courtesy—and left. Watching him depart, Graham's upper lip twisted in a sneer. Despite his great show of English superiority and rationality, when Graham had heard the rumours that Raphael owed his good fortune to a special amulet, he had believed it. How else, he reasoned, could such a young man, and a *Jew* at that, manage to do so well after arriving in Nigeria just a few months before? It didn't make any sense.

If only, Graham thought, *I could get my hands on his precious amulet. I could do with some of his good fortune. I'm sick of sitting on my arse behind a desk, waiting for my ship to come in. Some people have all the blasted luck …*

On some level, Raphael could understand the rationale behind the British approach to the Africans. They had all grown up with the knowledge that Britain headed an enormous empire. Unless they held onto their understanding of the British as naturally superior and at the top of some sort of evolutionary ladder, there was no excuse to maintain the colonies at all. Most of the senior civil servants had been born into families, and then educated in expensive private schools, that taught them that the British way of doing things was not just the best but the *only* acceptable way. They had been told that if they started to mix with local people and to see them as equals, then the empire would start to crumble and they would lose everything.

The fact was, in the 1950s, anyone with eyes in their head could see that the empire was already crumbling and that it would not take much for the system to begin to change utterly. In maintaining a segregated society, with white Englishmen at the top, all the British were doing was struggling to maintain the status quo. It was pitiful, in a way. How were they going to cope when the inevitable happened and most of them had to return to their small, cold, windswept island?

Would they have forgotten how to make their own afternoon tea after a lifetime of having things done for them by African servants?

Raphael resolved to always ensure that his taxes were paid fully and on time so that the English authorities could see that his business was of benefit to the area. He did not want to give the English any excuse to close him down, and it was very clear that this Graham would take great delight in causing him problems. He was also aware that, as a Jewish Egyptian, most of the English would never completely accept him as a member of society and their equal. To feel confident that he had done everything the right way, he hired a Scottish accountant who checked every penny so meticulously that the British never had anything to complain about. From then on, whenever he encountered Graham in the street, the two of them exchanged a formal nod. So far as Raphael was concerned, that was more than enough.

In the context of Maiduguri's divided society and the turmoil that rippled beneath an apparently tranquil surface (reminiscent of how the river water rippled when a crocodile swam just beneath the waves), Raphael's decision to set up his camp outside the town had been both pragmatic and symbolic. It was pragmatic, because he needed ample space to store and process the many crocodile skins he was planning to claim for export, and it was symbolic, because he wanted to make it perfectly clear to the local British ascendancy that, despite their snootiness and belief in themselves as innately superior, he had no desire to align himself with them. On the contrary, he felt that in many ways he had much more in common, and many more shared interests, with the African people the British so looked down on.

While Raphael was the boss and therefore could not allow himself to be overly familiar with his staff, he knew that they were all involved in a joint endeavour that depended on mutual cooperation and that he could not achieve anything without their support and help. He did not treat his African staff differently than anybody else. When, during working hours, meals were served in the camp—which was steadily becoming increasingly comfortable and sophisticated—everyone ate together and conversation flowed. As he had a knack for languages, Raphael had begun very quickly to understand and be able to speak in Hausa and some of the local tribal languages. In fact, he welcomed the opportunity to get to know people from a culture so very different to his own and to acquire new forms of wisdom. In the short time since he had left Egypt, he could already sense that he had become more mature and more aware of the world around him.

The camp food was prepared by a diminutive, light-skinned African man whose eyesight was so bad that he needed to wear thick spectacles—lending him his nickname, Gandhi. With his very poor eyesight, Gandhi was unsuited to most outdoor jobs, so it was lucky that he had a natural aptitude for the culinary arts. Raphael had also hired an assistant cook, a steward, and a cleaner, who all worked hard to keep the camp impeccably clean.

Gandhi and his assistant were adept at preparing and presenting food cooked in both the African and the blander English style, and they were open to learning about French cuisine, which Raphael liked best. Raphael often marvelled at how Gandhi was able to cook so well with such rudimentary equipment. Gandhi cooked on an open fire— which was so hot in the kitchen that he could wear little more than a loincloth—and he had nothing more sophisticated to use than basic pots and pans, a knife, and a wooden table to prepare food on.

Every morning, Gandhi rose early to buy fruit, vegetables, and meat in the local market, which was a colourful affair supplied by the farmers and hunters of the area. Women and men (the women often multitasking, attending to their infants and toddlers and breastfeeding while they worked) spread out colourful mats on the ground and arranged their wares on them attractively, piling up mounds of fresh produce and hanging bananas and plantains on strings that they suspended from their market stall, if they had one, or heaped in pyramids, if they did not. The fruit and vegetable vendors were interspersed with sellers offering items such as pots and pans; soap and cleaning equipment; basketwork (often with the vendor producing baskets by hand behind the stall, the rapid rhythmic movements coming together in the form of exquisitely produced handiwork); colourful fabric with imaginative, rich designs for making clothing; and everything deemed essential to the running of an African household.

There was a wide variety of fruits and vegetables, but the only meat generally available was goat. Live goats wandered here and there through the market, oblivious to the fact that their relatives were displayed for sale, cut into pieces. Cattle were kept by local farmers for the purpose of producing milk, but beef was rarely, if ever, available for purchase. Despite the lack of variety, Gandhi used his imagination to prepare the meat in a wide range of styles: stews, steaks, and minced meat for burgers and kebabs. In the African villages, bushmeat was eaten too, but this was rarely offered to the Europeans (although Raphael did sample crocodile on a number of occasions, confirming its reputation of tasting like something half-fish half-animal). All in all, Gandhi did an excellent job in feeding the busy camp and providing Raphael with the home comforts he needed.

As his business grew, so did Raphael's need for local banking services. At first, the managers of the local bank were puzzled by him, because he was so young and had so much money, but they soon learned to appreciate him. To ensure good service, Raphael brought gifts of champagne and other delicacies from France, which he had shipped in to Fort Lamy and delivered directly to the camp. In return, he was treated exceptionally well. He was never left waiting at a counter but always ushered into the manager's office for personal service. Nobody demurred when he requested large sums of money as bags of coins, because his African staff preferred to be paid in coins rather than paper money. The bank managers could see that Raphael was making a lot of money and had the potential to make a great deal more, and they did their best to ensure that he would stay with them.

The local Africans could also see that Raphael was successful, and just like the bank managers, they wanted him to look on them with favour. Raphael had learned to bring Maria Theresa Thaler dollar coins with him everywhere he went, because these were the coins that most Africans longed to have. The heavy silver coins bearing the characteristic imprint of the monarch's face had originally been made in Austria in the eighteenth century, but they were still in circulation in swathes of Africa and the Middle East,. The Nigerians trusted these coins far more than any currency, regarding them as not just valuable but also lucky.

Whenever he had business to attend to in a native village, Raphael brought some coins with him to present to the local chief. In return, many of the chiefs presented Raphael with young women, inviting him to use their services as concubines for as long as he wanted. Invariably, the young women climbed into the back of his truck, where they waited patiently for him to drive away. As it would have been grossly offensive to both the chief and the girls to make them dismount from the truck in front of the gathered villagers, Raphael developed a system of thanking the chief fulsomely for the gift of such beautiful girls and insisting on presenting more money while explaining that he could not take the girls with him, as he was already married and could not therefore sleep with them. This arrangement seemed to satisfy everyone. The girls and the chief got some money, and Raphael had the satisfaction of knowing that he was not like the many British functionaries who took advantage of such situations by sleeping with young African girls and then making the girls leave their homes by the back door because they were ashamed to be seen with black women.

*   *   *

After just a few months, Raphael decided to travel to Paris to meet Gravitz and consolidate their professional relationship face to face. He travelled to Cameroon and took a plane from there, exulting in the fact that he could afford to pay for first class. When the plane touched down in Paris, Raphael began a love affair with the beautiful city that would last for the rest of his life. He marvelled at the beautiful women, *très chics* in their elegant Parisian couture; at the architecture; at the way the light reflected off the Seine and the elegant glasswork in the apartment buildings and department shops; and at the exquisite French cuisine. He determined to come back as often as he could. Remembering with great fondness his dear friend Madeleine from Cairo, he looked for her on every street he walked upon, but she was nowhere to be seen. He could only hope that, somewhere, she was well and happy, and that she remembered him with the same affection that he had for her.

Too soon, it was time to return to Africa. Having packed his bag with delicacies for the camp, Raphael returned to the airport and boarded the plane, an American-built Constellation. The first Constellations had been made during the Second World War and had been used in the bombardments, but now they were being made for civilian use and were known for their comfort and good safety record.

Again, because he could afford it, Raphael had paid to be seated in first class. First class was located near the front of the plane and was dominated by white businessmen from diverse backgrounds—while the black travellers, who usually had less money, sat in economy. First class guaranteed the best service and food, and attentive smiles from the gorgeous French hostesses. Raphael enjoyed a lot of attention from the women in Maiduguri ...

("You're going to tell us all about it, right?" interrupted David. "Because even though I can't quite believe that Grandad had a love life apart from his marriage with Granny, I want to hear everything."

"Yes, yes, be patient," said Richard. "Don't worry. We'll get around to that in a bit. There is *plenty* to talk about when it comes to Grandad and women, believe me!")

... but he still liked to look at the pretty French hostesses, who were chosen by the airlines as much for their good looks and stylishness as for their competence in serving food and looking after the passengers. Like all the other men in first class, Raphael loved it when they bent over to serve drinks and knowingly offered a tantalising glimpse of their *décolletés*, but although he was sometimes tempted to turn on the charm, he knew that they were working and did not want to disturb their professionalism.

On this flight, however, there was a young lady who didn't seem able to stop looking at him. She was very pretty, with an olive complexion, glossy dark hair piled up high on her head, an upturned nose, and a cheeky expression. She kept making her way down to Raphael's seat to see if he wanted anything. On her third visit, she slipped him a note: "Hello, lover-boy," it read. "I can see that you are a bit of a rascal, just like me. Next time I come down the aisle, attract my attention and ask me to show you where the bathroom is."

Raphael raised his eyebrows as he read the note. Unless he was *very* mistaken—and he was pretty sure he wasn't—he had just been given an invitation that only a fool would turn down. He folded the note and slipped it into his breast pocket. For a few moments, he waited to see if anything would happen. Perhaps it had all been a joke, and the girl was giggling with her friends right now about how easy it had been to fool him. But no—here she came, sashaying down the aisle of the plane like a fashion model on a catwalk.

Raphael put up his hand to summon the hostess.

"Excuse me, miss," he said. "But would you be so kind as to show me to the bathroom?"

"Certainly, sir," she said demurely. "Right this way."

The young lady led Raphael up the aisle and through the heavy baize curtains at the top.

"Right in here," she purred. "I think you'll find everything you need."

Raphael stepped into the bathroom, still unsure as to what was going to happen next. With a quick glance left and right, the air hostess came in behind him and closed and locked the door.

"I *knew* you'd come," she said with satisfaction. "I could tell from the way you were looking at me that you were a ladies' man and know your way around. I bent over your seat and gave you a bit of an eyeful just to make sure that you were looking at me and could see the quality of the goods I have to offer. Well, now, here you are …"

"Is this what I think it is?" Raphael asked. "A gentleman doesn't like to assume …"

"Well now, I don't know," she teased, her fingers deftly undoing the buttons of her blouse. "What do *you* think it is? What do you think a girl like me would like to do with a boy like you? Hmm? Any ideas at all? Not even an inkling?"

Her small, shapely breasts fell forward as she leaned over to Raphael and began to unfasten the buckle on his belt. Her pointed pink tongue licked her lips as she achieved her goal, and Raphael could hear her breath growing faster as she became aroused.

"I see," she said. "What have we here …? Do you have a little surprise for me? No, I see that you don't … you have a *big* surprise! Well, aren't I the lucky girl?"

Mesmerised, Raphael put his hands on the girl's smooth, warm thighs. He pulled her fitted skirt up over her flared hips. She was wearing nothing underneath. Shamelessly, she parted her legs and showed him her sex, which glistened with moisture.

"See?" she whispered. "I'm ready for you. I'm ready in more ways than one. I've been ready since I saw you walk onto the plane."

In a moment, Raphael had entered her warm, waiting flesh and, despite the cramped space of the tiny airplane toilet, their two bodies soon were moving as one. When the plane hit a patch of turbulence, the hostess held herself in place by wedging her feet on the wall behind Raphael's back. Never once did her dark eyes close or look away from Raphael's face, even as her mouth twisted in ecstasy. She bit her lip until it bled, but she remained perfectly silent from start to finish; she would certainly have lost her job if they had been discovered, and she could not afford to cry out, much as she wanted to.

Half an hour later, having fixed her hair and tidied her uniform, the hostess cautiously let herself out of the bathroom. From inside, Raphael heard her ordering a waiting passenger back to his seat, citing the recent turbulence as a danger. He understood that she was clearing the way for him to leave the tiny bathroom discreetly, without making it obvious what they had been doing and causing a scandal. He wondered how often she had done something similar in the past; she certainly seemed to know what she was doing! Well, that was fine by him; he wasn't going to complain about the hostess's morals when he had been the beneficiary of her generosity.

When he was quite sure that there was nobody outside, Raphael let himself out of the narrow space (he wondered how they had managed to have sex in such a tiny closet and was grateful for the girl's flexibility) and returned quickly to his seat. For the remainder of the flight, the hostess served him and the rest of the passengers as calmly and coolly as if nothing had happened at all. The only sign that she had done anything not in her job description was the fact that her lower lip was slightly swollen, where she had bitten herself during her ecstasy.

2017

"I still can't believe Grandad made so much money when he was just nineteen," said Rebecca, "but I'm beginning to understand what sort of person he was back in those days. Not that different from how he is now, in some ways—though I do wonder if he ever told Granny about his amorous adventure with the air hostess … and how she reacted if he did!"

"Oh," said Richard, "I don't think there are any secrets between them. You know how close they are. I doubt she'd approve of that sort of carrying-on—but then again, it all happened long before they were married."

CHAPTER 12

A NEW LOVE, A NEW THREAT

2017

"So everything was great for Grandad. He had loads of money, loads of women, and was beginning to feel as though he might just stay in Nigeria forever," said Richard. "Of course, he knew that one day he would get married and settle down with the girl who had been chosen for him, but it seemed so far away that he couldn't really imagine it yet. The only thing that disturbed him was the lingering sensation that someone might steal his amulet or that he might somehow lose it, and then all his good fortune would disappear. He told himself that could never happen and tried to banish the thought from his mind. But there it stayed, at the back of his consciousness, all the time. He wore it around his neck day in, day out, feeling that this was the only way in which he could be sure that it was perfectly safe."

"Who did he think might take it?" asked David. "I mean, I'm sure he was always very careful of it."

"I don't think he really had any idea. It was gold, or at least it appeared to be gold, so I suppose it might have looked valuable, and a lot of the Africans were very poor, so it's easy to understand that there could have been a temptation. Maybe he was worried about the staff at the camp, who mostly came from very poor families, or perhaps he was worried about someone else. But the whole sense of concern seems to have started around the time someone new came into his life … perhaps because, for the first time, he let himself come close to falling in love."

1951–2

Raphael had expanded his business to include paying guests who stayed in luxury tented accommodation at his camp and enjoyed attending the wonderful parties he threw for them and the English teachers in the nearby town. He loved this aspect of the business on many counts: it provided him with additional funds, the presence of attractive female visitors who were not averse to having a little romance with their safari trip, and a chance to show off, which he always enjoyed more than he liked to admit. He relished it when people admired him and his achievements, especially when those people were women. Perhaps, he thought, it had something to do with the relationship he had had with his mother as a boy. Flora had taught Raphael to love, respect, and cherish women, and that they should never be seen simply as sexual objects. He was never happier than when he was surrounded by women.

By now, too, Raphael was one of the biggest exporters of crocodile skins in Nigeria, sending as many as eight tonnes a week to his buyers in Paris. As things were going so well, he decided to throw a huge New Year's Eve party to celebrate his great fortune and see the new year arrive in the company of his many friends in the area. He also had a point to make. He had tried to join the British social club, but his application had been blackballed—presumably by Graham, who made no secret of how much he disliked Raphael. The man had been heard drunkenly proclaiming that one day, Raphael would slip up, and then he, Graham the policeman, would be on hand to ensure that the young man got what was coming. Nothing would make Raphael happier than to know that his party was better than theirs.

In early December, Raphael had attended a party at the British club as the guest of some friends, John and Sheila Kremer, who were working in the area as anthropologists. When a drunk Englishman named Eric had asked the beautiful Sheila to dance, she had refused. Eric had taken offence and asked her why she had agreed to dance with a "dirty Jew" and not him, as she had danced with Raphael before being accosted. John had demanded and obtained an apology from Eric for both Sheila and Raphael, and the following day, Raphael had been called to a meeting with the High Commissioner, who had apologised for the event—but warned Raphael that his glamorous lifestyle and the fact that the English women all wanted to socialise with him was angering many of the Englishmen.

"They're saying that you are spoiling things for them. Before you came along, the girls didn't have such high expectations of our British men. They didn't expect fine dining and linen tablecloths in Africa, and they understood that the men out here can be a little rough and ready and not always perfectly *au fait* with the latest in elegant manners. Now they're all disappointed if they get asked out and the evening is not as fancy as having dinner at your camp."

"That's hardly my fault," Raphael objected mildly. "I haven't done anything wrong."

"I know. It's just that people get their noises out of joint when they are used to things being a certain way and then they change. Look, there are people in the community spreading rumours about you, saying that you're having orgies out there in the camp and the like, and that you have designs on other men's wives. I'd just lie low for a while, if I were you. Things will be easier if you don't stick your head above the parapet. That is how things are done around here, and it is easier for everyone if we stick to what works. It's the English way. I am sure that things are different in Egypt, but you're in the British Empire now, young man, and maybe it's time you started remembering it!"

Raphael was indignant. "Look," he said. "I am providing a lot of employment in the area. I have a lot of responsibilities, and sometimes I like to unwind. If people prefer coming to parties in my camp rather than in the English social club, that's a reflection on the social club and not me. I have never dismissed anyone as unworthy of my respect just because of who they are. I keep all of my affairs in order. I pay my taxes, and in return I get nothing but harassment from the English authorities, especially Graham, who seems to have a personal vendetta against me, and who has been getting drunk and going about town issuing threats. He's a disgrace to the police. I've tried very hard to be patient, but now my patience is wearing thin."

The High Commissioner sighed. "We've had a lot of trouble with Graham," he admitted. "I know that he has been harassing you under false pretences, and to tell the truth, he's become something of a liability and an embarrassment. How are we supposed to administer law to the darkies if our police officers behave like that? I'm in the process of having Graham relocated to a much more remote area to serve as the police officer there, where he won't bother you again. We've been having trouble with him too. There are rumours that the native chiefs have been letting him sleep with underage girls and that he's developed an appetite for that sort of thing. We can't have that going on around here. I know that the African girls often get married young, but what Graham gets up to … well, it's unacceptable. Disgusting, quite frankly, and not how we'd like to think an English police officer should behave."

"Thank you," said Raphael, somewhat mollified by this news. "That's good to hear. I don't want to bother anyone. I am just here to work and, from time to time, to enjoy an evening with friends. I can assure you that I will continue to do everything by the book."

The two men rose and shook hands, and Raphael took his leave.

I wish my mother could see me now, Raphael thought. *She'd be so proud of the fact that I am standing up for myself and our people.* He reached up his hand to touch the amulet that hung around his bronzed neck. He wore it every day, a constant reminder of his mother and her love for him.

Raphael decided to stop trying to infiltrate the British social scene. If they didn't want to have anything to do with him, he certainly didn't want to have anything to do with them. And, after all, what was the point? Some of them were anti-Semites, and almost all of the men were hopeless drunks with few or no social graces. It was as though Britain sent the worst of its men to work in the colonies—perhaps because they knew that the empire was in its last days and nothing that happened now was going to make any difference to that. Well, Raphael didn't care. He could make his own entertainment. He could throw the best party that Maiduguri had ever seen. He was sure that the English girls would all choose his party over a drunken shindig at the English club. They were all sick and tired of being pawed by grubby mid-level civil servants who thought that the career women were there only to provide them with sexual services until they went back to England and found girls who didn't know what pigs they were to marry.

Raphael went to Paris to see his buyers and arrange to have supplies shipped to his camp for the party: champagne, foie gras, French cheese, and countless other luxuries. He also made an appointment with his regular hairdresser, Marcelle.

While Marcelle snipped and pomaded Raphael's hair, he told her all about the plans for the New Year's Eve party.

"Sounds amazing," she said. "I can just imagine all of the glitz and glamour under the African sky. You're really going to give your friends a night to remember, aren't you?"

"I know, but I can't shake off the feeling that it should be better. I'd love to do something really special—something that my guests will be able to remember for the rest of their lives, something they'll want to tell their grandchildren about."

"Have you considered hiring a party organiser? Sometimes you need to bring in a professional to get things done. You don't let just anyone cut your hair, do you? The same should go for a party. How are you supposed to organise everything on your own when you work full time, after all?"

"I wouldn't even know where to find one, and I highly doubt that any such person actually exists in Maiduguri! It's not really that sort of town."

"Well, I wish *I* could go, but it's just not possible … but I know someone who'd be absolutely perfect. Her name is Nadine. She's a hairdresser like me, but she's more into the flash and dazzle than I am. She does the girls' hair at the *Folies Bergère* when they go on for their big shows. She knows all about costumes and style and all that razzmatazz, and she's got a real flair for the dramatic. If you like, I can introduce you. She's young and single, and I imagine she'd be able to arrange to take some time off and would enjoy the opportunity to have a bit of an adventure somewhere exotic. She's generally recovering from one love affair or another, and that's probably the case now, too. I'm sure she could arrange to take some time off."

"All right, can you arrange a meeting, and we'll see how it goes? I don't know if a professional would be interested in an event like this, but you never know, and I'd like to hear her ideas at minimum. Maybe she'd be able to help me make things really special."

The next day, Nadine called to the hotel where Raphael was staying. He had come downstairs to meet her and was waiting in the lobby when a slender young woman with long fair hair, a cute upturned nose, and lightly freckled skin came through the hotel's heavy doors. She looked imperiously around the room until her blue eyes alighted on Raphael.

"You must be my appointment!" she said as she approached. "Marcelle said that I would recognise you because you are so young."

"It's delightful to meet you," said Raphael, reaching out and shaking Nadine's hand. "I must say, Marcelle told me that you are interested in glamour, but she didn't mention how beautiful you are."

"You're too kind."

Raphael could tell that Nadine was used to receiving compliments and that she accepted comments on her beauty as her due. They exchanged the customary kiss on each cheek. Raphael could smell her perfume—something bright and floral—as they greeted one another, and beneath the floral scent something headier, a faint musky odour that he realised must come from Nadine herself. His heart rate accelerated and he could sense his breath quickening as he experienced a sudden rush of attraction that went beyond what he felt for just any pretty girl.

"Well," Nadine said, apparently oblivious to how she was affecting him, or possibly so accustomed to the impact that she had on men that it made no difference to her anymore, "it's lovely to meet you. Marcelle said that you were looking for a party organiser. I've done a lot of work in that line, and I've brought some photos and sketches to show you."

"Shall we?" Raphael said, indicating a table with two small chairs. "I would love to see them."

For the next hour, Nadine showed Raphael hundreds of photographs of the parties she had thrown before and of the many beautiful women she had styled and dressed for them. It was certainly very clear that she knew what she was doing and that if he hired her she would be able to create the most amazing party that any of the guests had ever experienced.

"Depending on how many guests you are planning to have," she explained, "I can arrange for costumes to be brought for them from the *Folies*. There are so many outfits, and I am well connected in there. And then I can do your female guests' hair and make-up, too. I can guarantee you one thing for sure: Africa will never have seen such style before. I can bring the *Folies Bergère* to your camp!"

As Nadine talked, her cheeks lightly flushed with animation and excitement, Raphael began to see the party she envisioned. How amazing it would be to see all his friends beautifully dressed under the velvet-dark African night sky! Those English girls would never have seen style like this before, and the men's mouths would drop open with such a parade of beauties—and he, Raphael, the boy who had spent so much of his childhood on the streets of Cairo, would be responsible for it all. Even just thinking about it, Raphael began to feel excited.

Nadine named her fee. It was more than Raphael had been expecting, but he agreed to it without haggling.

"There's just one thing," he said. "I'll need you to come straight away and possibly stay for a number of months to help me with the business, too, because I'm trying to build up the tourism and entertainment side, and I think you could really help me. Do you think that this will be possible? I mean, I know that you're a hairdresser, and I suppose you have your own responsibilities to attend to ... but perhaps ..."

Nadine looked at him with her penetrating dark eyes and smiled. As she did, Raphael felt as though a jolt of electricity had shot through him.

"I'm sure it can be arranged," she said. "People don't generally stand in my way when it comes to doing things as I want."

"I can understand that."

That night, Raphael returned to his hotel room with his mind full of Nadine. There was something about her that reminded him of himself. For such a pretty girl, she had a real air of ruthlessness. Although they had done nothing but talk business, he'd had the impression that she was someone who would let nothing stand in her way. Two emotions battled for supremacy in his head and in his heart: lust and concern. On the one hand, he was extremely attracted to Nadine. Who wouldn't be? She was beautiful. Any man would see her and want to touch her immediately. On the other, a small, quiet voice in the back of his mind warned him to stay away, that she represented trouble and that getting involved with her would be a big mistake. As usual, lust won that particular battle. Raphael suppressed his lingering concerns and went to bed wishing that Nadine were there to join him.

Usually, Raphael slept soundly, but that night he woke several times from vivid dreams that he could not quite bring to mind when his eyes opened. All he knew was that, when he awoke, he experienced a deep sense of loss, as though something precious had disappeared from his life. Telling himself that it was probably just a touch of indigestion, he forced himself back to sleep and ignored the sensation of unease.

*   *   *

Two weeks after Raphael's return to Africa, he went back to the airport to collect Nadine, who had countless packing cases filled with costumes from the theatre as well as her make-up cases and equipment for dressing hair. He watched her descend from the plane while the porters piled the luggage high on their trolleys and brought it over to his waiting car. Her slim feet were encased in dainty sandals as she walked down the plane's staircase with grace and elegance, one hand holding her hair out of her face as she walked.

"Welcome to Africa!" he said, extending his hand to help her down the last step. "I hope that you are going to like it here."

"I'm sure I will," Nadine said, her eyes coolly surveying the scene. "Goodness, isn't it hot? It's so nice after the winter weather in Paris; it gets so boring having to go around the place dressed in heavy woollens. I got dressed in summer clothes for the flight because I knew I was coming here, but I nearly froze on the way from my apartment to the airport. I've always thought that I would enjoy the tropics and not having to hide under layers of warm clothes for eight months of the year."

"You look absolutely delightful," said Raphael. "Don't look now, but I am sure that all the men in the airport are staring at you. I think any man would find it very difficult to tear his eyes away from you!"

Nadine was wearing a simple tea dress in a blue and white print. It was belted tightly at the waist, which showed off her slim figure, and the top button was undone, hinting at a delightful décolletage that remained just out of sight.

On the journey home, Raphael remained professional, discussing the plans for the party with Nadine, who had plenty of ideas of her own. His mind wandered, however. With such delightful company, was he really going to be able to keep things professional for long? Not if he knew himself ...

Nadine fitted seamlessly into the camp straight away, proclaiming herself delighted with the luxurious sleeping accommodation, the showers and sanitary arrangements, and the easy, respectful relationship between Raphael and the staff. She unpacked all the costumes and hung them up in her tent to get rid of any creases that remained from the packing. She got all her make-up and hairdressing equipment ready. She explored the camp and introduced herself to the staff, and she even poked her nose into the room where Raphael sorted the skins.

"It's such a fantastic setting," she gushed. "*So* evocative. And the warm breeze and the smell of flowers in the air are so sensual. It's just how I dreamed Africa would be. This is going to be a party to remember!"

"Well, I am sure that you will do your work well. If it all goes according to plan, I will have to arrange a special treat to say thank you for all your efforts."

"Oh, Raphael," cried Nadine. "Thank you so much! I've been hoping that you would say something like that, and actually, there is one thing I would absolutely *love* to do, and I think that you would be the perfect man to help. I've been *dying* to go on a hunting trip in Africa ever since I was a little girl. I get excited just thinking about what it must feel like to have a big gun in my hands and know that I have the power to kill. It would just be *so* thrilling to be able to tell my friends back in Paris that I have been on a real hunting trip in the African bush! So, can you take me? Please say yes. It would absolutely make my day!"

Raphael had never been able to resist the requests of a pretty woman. What could he say, other than yes? He said yes again a moment later when Nadine asked him for a kiss. Moments later, he no longer had to wonder about the body that she kept hidden beneath her pretty dresses, as he could see it all for himself. She was absolutely beautiful—slim but with curves in all the right places and a certain delicacy of feature that he found delightful. They fell onto the bed and explored each other's bodies with as much familiarity as if they had known one another for years. Nadine was perfectly comfortable with her body and his, and she took her pleasure with satisfaction.

"Do you mind taking it off?" Nadine asked as they lay in each other's arms afterwards. She was gesturing towards the amulet, which as usual Raphael wore on a gold chain around his neck.

"My amulet? I never take it off." Raphael's hand went reflexively to the amulet, as though just talking about it might cause it to come loose. "No, sorry; it's going to have to stay on."

"It's very pretty. It's just that I want to see you completely naked, not even wearing your jewellery. I can take out my earrings if you want me to do the same."

"I'm sorry, sweetheart, but my amulet doesn't come off for anyone, not even a girl as pretty as you."

"How strange! I don't usually see men wearing jewellery."

"This is not just jewellery, it's a special amulet that was given to me before I was born."

"Really? Well then, tell me all about it!"

Suddenly, as though he had known her forever, Raphael was telling Nadine all about his mother's difficult pregnancy and how she had been warned that she and the baby were at risk, and of the extraordinary circumstances in which the amulet had come into his possession, even before he had left his mother's body. Nadine was the first person outside the family with whom he had shared the story, and he was surprised to find how very easy she was to talk to.

"It probably all sounds a bit silly and superstitious to you," Raphael said. "I know that you French pride yourselves on being rational at all times. But, to me, it really matters. It's something that comes from my mother and, in a way, maybe even from God himself. I can't prove it, but I still dread the thought of losing it. If the amulet was gone, perhaps I would lose everything else too."

"Well, it does all sound quite un-French," said Nadine. "But that's fine. If I wanted to be with French people, I'd be in France, not here with you. Anyway, it's all right. I understand that you don't want to take it off. I usually like my men completely naked, but for you, I can make an exception."

She reached out a long, slender finger and played with the amulet where it lay on Raphael's chest.

"It's lovely, isn't it?" she said. "Too bad *I'll* never get a chance to try it on."

A sense of foreboding rose up in Raphael's chest, but he ignored it. How could he think of anything but lovemaking with this beautiful, naked woman in his bed? Nadine was half upright, supporting her pretty face in the cup of her hand while she leaned over him to inspect the amulet. Her small, pointed breast was close to his face, the brownish-pink nipple grazing gently against his skin as she moved. Raphael opened his mouth to receive it, and all thoughts of the amulet left both their minds.

* * *

The female guests were the first to arrive on the night of the party. They had been talking about it for days. Raphael had told them to come in their everyday clothes, because Parisian costumes and professional hair and make-up would be provided. He smiled widely as he opened the gates and they poured in, as full of excitement as little girls on their birthdays.

Eileen, the English teacher who had been helping Raphael to acquire a greater knowledge of European history and culture—and who had been a beloved of his for a year—had chosen the music for the night and was busy with the record player, having arrived earlier. Raphael and Eileen had enjoyed many nights together, and he cared for her deeply, although he had made sure from the outset that she knew that marriage or a serious relationship would never be a possibility for him. She had seemed to accept this, although he was not always sure what went on in her heart. Eileen smiled as the music played, and Raphael's heart filled with affection for her as he watched from the other side of the room. From Nadine's tent, they could both hear the squeals of the girls as they explored the costumes Nadine had brought and argued playfully about who would wear what.

"I'll always care for you, Eileen," Raphael was suddenly moved to say. "No matter what happens in the future."

Eileen smiled sadly. "You've told me many times that you are determined to marry among your own people and that your bride has already been chosen for you," she said. "I am under no illusions about our relationship. One day whatever we have between us will be over, and I'll be just your teacher and friend again. I know that, and most of the time, I accept it."

Raphael didn't say anything. What Eileen had said was correct; there was no point in contradicting what they both knew to be true.

"Anyway," said Eileen, abruptly changing the topic. "I think the girls are nearly ready for the party. It's time to change the music." She stopped the needle, took off the jazz record she had been playing, and put on *Scheherazade*.

The women paraded into the centre of the camp in their splendid costumes while the music played and the male guests watched them with delight evident on their faces.

Look at them, thought Raphael. *All young, all beautiful, and all excited. And they are all here for me. I did this. All with my own efforts.*

That night, Raphael felt like the king of the world. Look what he had managed to achieve: a beautiful French dinner party in his camp. All of the most beautiful women in the town were with him. He imagined the scene at the New Year's Eve party at the English social club when the men gradually realised that they had been snubbed for the "dirty Jew" so many of them loved to dismiss and belittle behind his back.

I don't know if it's that I am doing something right, Raphael thought, *but certainly luck is on my side. Who knows—maybe it really is all because of the amulet!*

The party continued until the dawn was beginning to brighten the sky and the party-goers finally began to feel tired. One by one, the guests exchanged their glamorous costumes for their simple dresses and made their way home. Nadine retired to her tent, and Eileen and Raphael to his.

"I feel like I am losing you, Raphael," said Eileen as they lay down.

"You're not losing me," he said. "I'm right here." He reached his arm around her and gave her a hug. But he felt a pang of guilt. Despite his warm, loving relationship with Eileen, he had continued to pursue other women, and now that Nadine was here … well, Nadine was a minx. She didn't care about the feelings of Eileen or, indeed, anyone else. She was comfortable in her body and unashamed of her sexuality and her voracious appetites, as Raphael had already learned. While Eileen was just as beautiful, or even more so, there was something about Nadine that was bewitching, and he found himself unable to stay away from her. That night, Raphael and Eileen's lovemaking had a poignant edge, as though they had already started to say goodbye.

Afterwards, Raphael fell into a restless sleep, half-waking at times, thinking he could see strange shadows chasing across the walls of the tent. In the morning, he felt unrefreshed. Something was wrong, but he wasn't sure what it was. He should be happy; after all, the party had been a great success. He had achieved everything he wanted to by this age, and everything seemed to come to him so easily. So, what was wrong? What was causing him to experience these negative emotions?

When Eileen stirred and turned towards him to hold him in her arms and ask him to show her how he loved her, he forgot these difficult questions and fulfilled her desires. He knew that one day soon his relationship with Eileen would end, as she wanted more than he could give, but that time had not yet come.

After his morning shower, Raphael had an unexpected visitor: Mrs Gilchrist, the principal of the girls' school where Eileen and several of the other young women guests worked. Mrs Gilchrist stormed into the camp. Ignoring the admonishments of Raphael's staff, she demanded to know where his tent was. When they refused to tell her, she barged her way into each tent until she found the right one.

"Can I help you?"

Raphael was dressed only in his underwear, while Eileen sat on the edge of his bed in her nightclothes.

"Young man, I have come to tell you that you are a complete disgrace! The whole town is talking about it. All of my teachers were over here last night with you, getting up to God knows what, and here you are, openly consorting with another of the girls, apparently with no intention of making an honourable woman of her! Well, I have a certain responsibility for not just the safety but also the morals of my staff, and I won't stand for it anymore."

"Mrs Gilchrist," Eileen interrupted. "I'm not a girl, I'm a woman, and Raphael isn't making me do anything. I'm here of my own free will."

"Your free will is neither here nor there, young lady! As the teacher in an all-girls' school, you have a responsibility to set a good example to the students. How can we teach them to be chaste young women when you are the rest of the staff are gallivanting about with this … this … We are *English* women, not savages or Continental decadents! We're supposed to set the Africans a good example, not give them the impression that English girls will drop their drawers for any handsome stranger!"

"I think we've heard enough," said Raphael decisively. "It's time for you to go. And, I might remind you, you have just stormed uninvited into the bedroom of a man you don't even know. I hardly think that *you* are setting anyone a good example at the moment, do you?"

Mrs Gilchrist left in umbrage, and Raphael tried to laugh off her incursion, though he was concerned that there might be negative repercussions for Eileen's career. Eileen tossed her head and said that she didn't care what Mrs Gilchrist thought. But Raphael was left with a certain amount of anxiety. He didn't care a fig for the British sense of propriety. He was doing nothing wrong, and he had never set out to mislead anybody. But he was concerned about Eileen. After all, she had to go back to work at that school, and even if the rules of behaviour were ridiculous, perhaps she would be risking her job if she did not observe them. The last thing he wanted was for their relationship to cause problems for her. One day soon he would be gone from her life, and it was important for her to have a career.

Suddenly, Nadine bounded into the tent.

"The party was a huge success!" she said, ignoring Eileen as though Eileen wasn't there at all. "So, do I get my reward? Are you going to take me hunting, like you promised? I'm turned on just thinking about it!"

As Raphael watched the devastation dawn on Eileen's face, he realised that he had not told her about the hunting trip and, now that the matter was raised, that she could see perfectly clearly what was going on between him and Nadine.

"Eileen …" he said. "Let me explain."

"You don't have to explain anything to me," Eileen said tightly. "I see the sort of man you are. And as for *you*—" here she addressed herself to Nadine "—you're a fucking bitch. How dare you come here and take him from under my nose?"

"He wouldn't have come if he didn't want to," Nadine snapped back. "Maybe he needed a bit of Parisian style for a change. Some nice, ripe camembert instead of a stodgy Yorkshire pudding."

"Eileen …" Raphael said again, approaching her. He had always been honest with her about his intentions and did not feel that he had done anything wrong, but he was very upset to see how sad he had made her. It was not at all like Eileen to swear or use strong language, and he could see that she was moved to these extremes by the intensity of her emotions.

"Raphael," Eileen said, containing herself. "You always say that you have a charmed life, that you are lucky, that your precious amulet is keeping you safe. I don't know whether all of that is true or not, or whether or not you believe those stories, but I can tell you that if you treat people as playthings, at some point your luck will turn and bad things will start happening. Maybe God has blessed you, like you say, but that doesn't mean that He always will. I can also confirm to you that people are not always exactly what they seem. You may be trusting people in your life who have done nothing to earn that trust!"

"We're still going on the trip, aren't we?" asked Nadine. "You're not going to cancel it just because she's having a tantrum?"

Raphael gestured to Nadine to leave for now and, with a toss of her head, she left his sleeping quarters.

"Just hug me, Raphael," Eileen asked, wearily. "Hold me in your arms and let me pretend that none of this is happening."

Raphael did as Eileen asked, and while he held her in his embrace, he loved her, although he knew that he would never stay away from Nadine—or indeed from the many other women who attracted him. Her face pressed against his shoulder, Eileen fell asleep. Raphael stroked her hair and thought of what she had said about his amulet. Could there be some truth to it? He had never considered the possibility that the good luck and power that the amulet gave him might be conditional on his treatment of others, or that anyone other than himself might be able to influence it.

2017

"Good for Grandad!" David laughed. "Two women fighting over him!"

"Well, *I* don't think it's good!" snapped Rebecca. "Think about their feelings! Did he have no concern for poor Eileen? I mean, you haven't told us how she came into his life, and we don't know how it ended, but she sounds like a sweet girl. Wasn't he playing with her emotions?"

"He didn't mean to, I think," said Richard. "He always says that in the moment of being with a woman, he loved her more than anyone else. The problem was that there were always other women and other moments—and don't forget, he was still very young. One thing that happened to Grandad that really helped him to start growing up was when he acquired the responsibilities of a father, long before he married Granny."

"*What?*" Richard's siblings all exclaimed in unison.

"Do you want to hear it?" he asked.

"Of course!"

"All right, then," said Richard. "Here follows the story of little Sunday, the boy genius, and how it came to be that he ended up working in Grandad's compound …"

CHAPTER 13

THE BOY GENIUS AND THE PURSUIT OF KNOWLEDGE

2017

"Grandad told me that he had his first experience of fatherhood when he was just 20, years before any of our parents were born," said Richard. "It was something that he wasn't expecting to happen, but you never know what's going to turn up in life, right? And that's especially true of someone like Grandad, who's always been one for adventure. He never knew what was going to happen next."

"Please don't tell me that Nadine or some random air hostess had a child by him and there's a whole branch of the family we don't even know!" said Rebecca, aghast. "I don't think I could cope with that! Not to mention Granny. How would she react if she suddenly found out that there was another family of Grandad's somewhere? She'd be devastated! And once we knew, we'd have to go to all the fuss and bother of getting to know them. I don't think I have the energy for that."

"No, no, don't worry. It's nothing like that. I'm pretty sure that somehow Grandad managed not to get any of his girlfriends pregnant! Maybe his precious amulet helped him out in that area too!"

"Well then," said David, with more than a hint of impatience, "tell the story!"

1952

Although the hunting was dangerous work, the hunters were skilled and very brave. The best of them were able to kill several crocodiles in a single day, remove the skins, and deliver them to Raphael at the camp or to one of the agents based in the villages who gathered the skins together to deliver to the camp in bulk. Raphael paid the hunters quickly and generously by local standards, and it was rewarding for him to see how their standard of living had started to improve as a result. He had noticed that the men could afford to wear better clothes than they had when he met them, as could their wives and children. More than one of them had mentioned that he was saving some of his salary so as to be able to send his children to a good secondary school, where they would get a decent education. Raphael was impressed that, despite the prejudice and racism Africans often suffered from the English, so many of his employees were still determined to make things better for their families. As their own lives were tough and challenging, most of them wanted to invest in an easier future for their children, and only a few spent their money on beer and having a good time behind their wives' backs.

"It's like this," one of the men said. "I am happy to catch crocodiles for you so that none of my sons will ever have to. I don't mind risking my life so long as I know it's for a good reason."

Then something dreadful happened. Raphael was attending to paperwork in his office when he became aware of a woman crying outside. Leaving the office, he found an African woman, her eyes swollen with tears and her face smeared with dust. She was seated on the ground, rocking back and forth slightly, and giving every appearance of being absolutely distraught. Raphael looked around to see if anyone was dealing with her, but there was no one.

"What's going on?" Raphael asked the woman gently. "Has someone hurt you? Can you tell me about it?"

His mind quickly ran through the possibilities. He was sure that none of the men working at the camp would have hurt a woman; they were decent men, not the sort to do something like that. Could she be mentally deranged or confused? Was it all an act, a show, intended to make him feel so sympathetic that he would give her a job or a handout? Whatever the case, he was not going to leave a woman weeping, unaided, on the ground outside his office.

Raphael reached out his hand, and the woman took it. He helped her to rise to her feet. She wiped her eyes and nose with a rag and began to speak softly in her native Yoruba, pausing occasionally to catch her breath through her sobs. As she spoke, Raphael could see that she was still young and that, if her face had not been so ravaged by grief, she would have been quite attractive. He listened attentively to her story; he had not mastered the Yoruba language to the extent that he had Hausa, but by paying careful attention, he was able to follow along. The story behind the woman's distress was a truly awful one.

"Master," she began, "King of the Crocodiles, I am the wife of Amiru."

Amiru … who was Amiru? Raphael combed his mind and then remembered. Yes, Amiru was one of his hunters, a tall handsome man in his early thirties who worked under a foreman called Mustafa. While Raphael had never known him beyond seeing him come with the skins and giving him his wages, he knew that Amiru was a hard worker, among the best of all the hunters he had.

"And what's wrong, wife of Amiru?"

This innocent question gave rise to renewed weeping. Eventually, the woman composed herself enough to speak.

"Sir, Amiru was very proud of working for you. He used to tell everyone that now he was working for the King of the Crocodiles and that some of your blessed good luck had rubbed off on him. But even without a white man's magic, he was good at what he did, and some weeks he was able to bring in as many as thirty skins. He was one of Mustafa's best hunters, and he was hoping to become a foreman one day. He was already earning more than twice what he had made before, and we all thought that he had a good future."

"Was? What do you mean, *was*?"

"Sir, something terrible has happened to him. It was two weeks ago. He decided to go out at night with his friend Alyu. I'll never understand why Amiru was careless that night, even though he knew everything about crocodiles. He knew that they should be approached after they have eaten rather than before because then they are slow and lazy and easier to catch. But he had been showing off, boasting to his friends about how many skins he was able to get in a week, and he had been safe for so long that he was sure nothing could happen to him. Maybe he'd had a beer or two. He didn't usually drink, but once in a while his friends persuaded him to have a glass. He asked Alyu to go out with him at night with a lamp and went into a part of the lake where the biggest, fiercest crocodiles are, saying that he was not afraid.

"When Alyu pointed the lamp at the animals, they got so agitated, it seemed as though the water was boiling or possessed by demons. There were so many of them, and they were so big! Amiru shouted, 'Go back! Go back!' to Alyu, and Alyu started to paddle the boat as hard as he could, but it was too late; there was no way they could go fast enough to get away. All the other hunters saw exactly what happened from where they were waiting on the shore, but they couldn't do anything expect stand and stare.

"About twenty crocodiles came swimming towards them, and one of them was absolutely enormous. Amiru and Alyu were screaming for help, but there was nothing anyone could do. The huge crocodile rose up in the air and smashed down on the canoe, which snapped in half as if it was just a twig. They tried to swim, and Alyu managed to get near the shore where the others dragged him out and pulled him to safety, but my husband—" here she broke again into sobs, and Raphael patted her gently on the arm until she composed herself enough to talk "—my husband disappeared beneath the waves. The last anyone saw of him was his terrified face just above the water and his hand gesturing for help before the enormous jaws of the crocodile closed around him."

"I am so sorry," Raphael said gently. "Nobody told me anything. I had no idea."

"Sir, just a few days ago one of my neighbours came running. A man's leg was found on the shoreline of the lake. It could only belong to Amiru, so as it was all I had left of my husband, I buried it in the graveyard, and we prayed over him. Now I am a widow, and I have not even been able to give my man the proper funeral he deserves because his body is somewhere in the belly of a crocodile. Sir, some people say that the crocodile that killed my husband was not an ordinary animal but some sort of a spirit or monster, or that a witch was responsible for what happened, or that someone had cast the evil eye on Amiru because of his success and the good money he was making working for you. Whatever the truth of it, all our hopes for the future have been destroyed. He was a good man. He never beat me, and he was good to our son. He didn't deserve to be taken like that."

Moved by the poor woman's situation, Raphael had already decided that he would help her in any way he could—and that he would have a talk with all the hunters about the importance of not taking unnecessary risks. Almost without exception, they were married men with children. No crocodile was worth doing something stupid. It was different for him; he knew on some deep level that he could neither explain nor justify that he would always be all right. All these men had was their own experience and instincts—and sometimes, as Amiru's wife had just explained so eloquently, that was not enough.

Before Raphael could ask the woman what she needed and how he could help her in her distress, he noticed a little boy sitting under a tree some distance away. The woman observed that Raphael had seen him and gestured to the child to come over. The little boy got to his feet and made his way to his mother's side, where he stood clutching her hand and looking at the floor shyly. He peeked up at Raphael every now and again, only to look away when Raphael's glance met his eye.

"Sir," she said. "This is my little boy, Sunday. He is my only child. He's just 10 years old. God did not choose to bless my husband and me with a big family, so this is the only one we have. I can tell you that he is such a good boy, I have never even regretted the fact that we didn't have more."

Raphael looked at the child, his heart full of sorrow. Losing a father at such an early age was going to make the boy's life much more difficult, and things were never easy for the native Africans anyway. Without a breadwinner in the family, Sunday would have to work, which meant the end of his education at a very early age. There wasn't a lot of work for African women, and even those who did find work as laundry-women or maids were so badly paid they could never support a household with their own efforts. At 10, Sunday was now the man of the house, until or unless his mother found a new husband. It was a very heavy burden for such narrow shoulders to carry.

"Sunday is a very good boy," the woman continued. "I am sure that you will be very pleased with him. He will be able to help you with your work."

"What a minute," Raphael said. "What do you mean, 'help me with my work'? What sort of help are you talking about?"

"I have nothing and no one," the woman said simply. "I have no way to earn a living on my own here, so I am returning to my people. God willing, one day I will find another husband and move into his house. But for now, I have to think of what is best for me and my child, and I have decided to give the boy to you. People say that you are a good man, and I know that my son is a very clever boy and that you will appreciate his gifts. My husband and I never learned how to read and write, but Sunday is the best student in his class, and the teacher often said that it is a shame we have no money, because if we did, he could even go on to the university when he finishes school. We are Christians, and the minister tells us that we need to have faith in God and ask for his help, but God has not done very much for us. I would rather put my faith in a man whom people say is good to the Africans."

Raphael looked at child, who in turn looked down at his bare, dusty feet. He was a skinny little boy with jet-black skin and big, round eyes. At 10, he was just beginning to leave his childhood behind and enter into the awkward years of adolescence. He was wearing a pair of ragged shorts that were several sizes too big for him and had been pulled in at the waist with a piece of string. Over this, he wore a grubby striped T-shirt made for a smaller child. His arms and legs were so thin that his knees and elbows protruded.

Despite Sunday's slender frame, however, it was clear that this was a child who was loved and well cared-for. His skin was glossy and healthy, and his eyes were clear and bright. On his forehead, he bore the tribal cicatrices of the Yoruba tribe. Raphael knew that Amiru would have made these marks on his son's face when Sunday was small and that they signified a sense of belonging and the tribesman's natural pride in his culture, language, and heritage. It was sad that Amiru would never see his boy grown into manhood. But what was Raphael to do about it?

He turned to the woman and said, "Wait a minute. I am certainly prepared to help you, but I can't take your child in, and I sincerely hope that nobody has been giving false expectations in that respect. I have no facilities here to care for a child and no wife to provide him with a mother's care. A child needs a woman to take care of him, not a busy bachelor like me. The women who stay in my compound are otherwise engaged and don't have time for a little boy. Don't you have any relatives who can help? I am sure you don't want to see him raised by someone outside the family if you can avoid it."

"My parents were opposed to my marriage to Amiru," she explained, "and they have never accepted our child as a member of the family. I know he is a child, but he's not an *ordinary* child. He can do work with his head that even most adults can't do. It's hard to explain, but soon you will see it for yourself."

The woman reached for her son's hand and pulled him to her side. She bent slightly to look him in the eye and then pulled him in close to her in a fierce embrace.

"My darling boy," she said. "Know that I will always love you. One day we will be back together again. For now, you are the son of the King of Crocodiles, and I want you to promise to do whatever he says. Be a good boy for him, just as you always were for you own father."

Dry-eyed, the little boy nodded his assent.

"Wait …" said Raphael weakly. He wanted to protest again that he couldn't keep the boy, but the woman was already leaving with the erect posture of someone who is certain that she has just done the right thing. He knew it had been painfully difficult for her to leave her child and that she was only doing the best she could under the circumstances. Exploring his soul, Raphael had to admit that, on some level, he also felt guilty about what had happened. Had he pushed the men too hard? Was the competitive atmosphere he fostered among the hunters responsible for Amiru's death? Nobody had even told him about the accident. Was the foreman loath to admit that the business was partly to blame?

Ultimately, of course, Amiru had died because he had been careless and had chosen to ignore one of the most basic rules of crocodile hunting: go after them when they have already been fed. Yet Raphael couldn't shake off the feeling that maybe he had contributed in some way. Perhaps the sense of security he'd always felt himself led him to be reckless about others.

Sunday was regarding Raphael with steady eyes and wore an expression on his face that spoke of maturity far beyond his years. With a deep sigh, Raphael put his arm around the boy's shoulders.

"Well, you had better come in," he said, "at least until we have figured out what to do with you."

Raphael called for Sum Sum and briefly explained the situation. Sum Sum looked at Sunday with great sympathy.

"My father died when I was a boy too," he said. "My mother remarried, and I never liked her second husband; he was jealous because he and my mother only had daughters and he wanted to have a son. He used to hit me all the time and tried to stop my mother from giving me food. It is a terrible thing, losing a father at such an early age, but it happens a lot, especially with men who do dangerous work like hunting."

"Well," said Raphael, "I don't know how long Sunday will be with us, but we had better take care of him so long as he is. I'll try to figure out some way to get this sorted out. Perhaps there are authorities or an orphanage that can make the necessary arrangements. Can you find him somewhere to sleep and ask Gandhi to make sure that he has all the food and drink he needs? Later on, I'll give you some money, and you can take him to the market and get him some shorts and shirts so that he is properly dressed. I'm responsible for him for now, and I can't have him running about the place like a little ragamuffin."

Finally, Sunday spoke.

"Sir," he said, "my mother told me that I am to consider you my father now. It is very strange for me to have a white father, but she said that you are a good man, and I will do my best to be a good son. You're my papa now."

With a sinking feeling, Raphael realised that it was not going to be easy for him to persuade little Sunday to live anywhere else.

Before long, Raphael learned that when Sunday's mother had described her child as particularly gifted, it had not just been a mother's pride speaking, as he had assumed. At just 10, Sunday understood numbers and mathematics better than Raphael—and better than any of the accountants he had met in Maiduguri. Soon, they fell into a routine. Raphael rose in the morning and took his breakfast, which generally consisted of just a cup of tea. While he sipped his tea, Sunday ate a huge bowl of semolina porridge that Gandhi had prepared for him and drank a glass of goat milk. As the slight chill of the night receded and the rays of the sun gradually penetrated and warmed every corner of the camp, they sat in a companionable silence until Raphael decided that it was time to work.

Sunday returned his bowl to Gandhi, and then the two of them made their way to the storage area known as the Godown. This was where Raphael kept the skins; counted and sorted them; and received the new skins coming in. Usually, the skins were delivered by his various agents in the village, who carried out an initial sort there after receiving them from the hunters. The agents paid the hunters and delivered the skins in large bundles. Raphael resorted them for export and measured each one carefully, as the price he received depended largely on size.

Raphael had discovered that Sunday had an absolutely remarkable memory. Whereas Raphael had to write down the number of skins and the individual measurements of each one, Sunday was, with no apparent effort, able to record all of that information to memory and repeat it correctly when all the skins had been measured. He could add up long lists of numbers in his head and always got the right answer without ever having to resort to a pencil and paper.

"How one earth did you learn how to do this, Sunday?" Raphael asked. He had seen the dusty, overcrowded, poorly equipped schools that were all that poorer Africans had. Attendance was patchy because the children often had to stay out of school to help their parents with work. It was a wonder that any of them managed to learn anything— and yet here was this child, just 10 years old, who seemed to be capable of anything.

"I don't know," Sunday shrugged. "It's just easy."

Gradually, Raphael started to give Sunday more and more responsibility. The boy was not just extraordinarily bright, he was also honest and trustworthy. He started to take the measurements of the skins, to categorise them by weight, and to number and order them. Meticulously, he prepared the export records and brought them to Raphael for approval. They were invariably perfect. When Raphael went to the bank to collect the hunters' salaries, he brought the child with him. Sunday was able to count coins into bags more quickly and accurately than anyone else, and soon he was in charge of making sure that each hunter received exactly what he had earned.

After a month or so, Sunday had made himself indispensable, and a warm, affectionate relationship had developed between man and boy. Raphael looked forward to seeing Sunday's huge smile first thing in the morning, and Sunday had taken to calling Raphael "Papa," in acknowledgement of the fact that he was filling a father's role. Despite the enormous burden of grief that Sunday carried, he seemed to laugh and smile all day long, and nothing made him happier than working with his beloved numbers. What most people experienced as difficult, arduous mental work—poring over rows of numbers, trying to balance the books—was nothing but child's play for him. In accordance with local tradition, out of respect, Sunday sat cross-legged on the floor when Raphael entered the room and rose only when he had been given permission to do so.

Sunday's mother had returned to her people, as she had said, but she was not far away, and Sunday was able to visit her on weekends. As they were Christians, sometimes they attended church together. Although she blamed God for not protecting her husband, their faith was important to them. Proudly, Sunday was able to bring her the money he had earned from Raphael and buy her an ice cream or another small treat after they had attended their house of worship. Raphael occasionally saw them, mother and child, sitting together in the small park in the centre of town, but he kept his distance. He knew that, even if he did his best, he could not replace a father's love—and that one day, he would leave Africa, and Sunday would have to go back to his own people.

As his affection for Sunday grew, so did Raphael's sense of responsibility towards the boy. Perhaps he had never really wanted or planned to adopt a son, but he was there now. Raphael began to feel a little guilty about seeing the boy work so hard when other children were just playing around. With a talent like his, Sunday deserved a proper education.

Raphael knew that he could send Sunday back to the dusty school that most of the other native African children attended, but everyone knew how bad the quality of teaching was there. The teachers themselves were poorly trained and were often so corrupt that they didn't turn up every day or came into school drunk. Most of the children emerged from school almost as illiterate as they had been when they went in, and there was little will to change anything. Besides, all the Africans knew that even a highly educated African man could only go so far under the British regime, while it suited most of the English to keep the Africans ignorant, as this appeared to justify the presence of colonial rule. It was amazing that Sunday had achieved as much as he had considering the fact that he had not had a better education.

Gradually, an idea formed in Raphael's mind. He had often wanted to improve his own education, too. All his life, he had been obsessed with making money, and he had started trying to earn as much as he could as soon as possible. His education had been cut short when he was 14 by his desire to enter adult life. There had been little time for thinking about less concrete things, like literature, music, and philosophy. Much of Raphael's education had taken place on the streets and markets of Cairo, where he had learned how to do business. But important as money was, there was more to life than that.

Sometimes, when Raphael had his European friends over to the compound for dinner, he felt left out when they talked about literature and music in a way that he couldn't. He would grow silent while they talked about this great author or that marvellous composer, often assuming that he knew and understood exactly what they were talking about. Although nobody ever deliberately made him feel bad, this made him seem to be at a disadvantage, and that was a sensation he absolutely hated.

Now that he had so much money to spend, it occurred to Raphael that he could use some of it to hire tutors who would be able to teach both him and Sunday. Sunday would get an excellent education and would be able to go to university one day, and Raphael would acquire the knowledge he needed to fit into European society, as he wanted. He too would be able to talk about this author or that composer and would participate in his friends' learned conversations as their equal. This would be a way in which they could both improve their lives.

Raphael felt that he had a duty to ensure that, one day, Sunday would be able to support himself, his mother, and any family he might have. As for Raphael, he was always ready for a new challenge. The business was going well, and while he would always have to work very hard to ensure that that remained the case, he had a little more breathing space than before and liked the idea of enhancing his academic understanding as much as he could. He had no doubt that he was up for the challenge. It was just a question of spending the time, and time was something he had finally managed to earn.

Raphael made inquiries about where to find tutors who would be able to teach both him and Sunday. He needed teachers who were flexible enough to deal with a boy genius as well as an adult man who had a business to run but who wished to improve his general knowledge. The perfect tutors came in the form of retired lecturing staff from Nigeria's best university, which was connected to an important college in London and had a history of teaching the elite of Nigeria. They were delighted at the prospect of what sounded like an easy job relative to the task of educating hundreds of young minds at the same time. Raphael quickly hired four to teach him economics and philosophy, as well as the finer points of language and grammar, and to give young Sunday an excellent general education.

Now that the decision had been made, Raphael was excited about learning. Since his travels to Paris and his exposure to a range of European cultures among the expatriate community in Africa, he had realised that he felt particularly attracted to European culture. His education in Cairo had included some European history, but he did not feel equipped to immerse himself in European culture the way he wanted to. He had a knack for languages, but he wanted to be able to speak French, English, and Italian like a gentleman, not like a ruffian who had grown up on the streets. He had grown up learning about Rambam's great contributions to philosophy—although, if he was honest, he knew much more about the legends and tales about Rambam than the great man's intellectual contributions—but he knew nothing about Plato or Aristotle or any of the major thinkers of European civilisation.

Raphael invited the tutors to come and live at the compound so that they would be on hand to teach him and Sunday whenever they were free. As they were to be very well paid, they all accepted this minor inconvenience. The day all four arrived, they ate with Raphael in the cooking area and proclaimed themselves impressed with Gandhi's efforts. The teaching began the following day.

While Raphael had often been bored and restless at school as a child, this time he experienced learning in a completely different way. It was as though his mind was a parched, arid field, and the teachers' knowledge a very welcome shower of rain that fell on it and turned it once again into fertile soil. Raphael loved all the subjects, but he especially liked learning about Western history and identifying the great men of history, whose achievements were something he could aspire towards.

Soon, he had a hero: the great English politician who had won the war, Winston Churchill. Of course, Raphael remembered seeing and hearing Churchill in the Pathé films and radio broadcasts that were released during the war and in the newspapers published at the time, but only now did he realise that the famous politician was also a great philosopher, orator, and statesman. And like Raphael, he was the son of a beautiful woman. That was something they had in common!

Hungrily, Raphael read everything that Churchill had ever written, amazed by the ferocity with which the man was determined to defend not only his own people but all of Western civilisation against some of the biggest threats it had ever seen. At the start of the war, not all of the British people were admirers of Churchill, but he had brought them together as one nonetheless. When the war ended, the British people were ready to work together for a better society and a better future. While Raphael had reservations about some aspects of British culture, based on what he saw of the behaviour of the expatriates in Maiduguri, he realised that they could not be all bad if they had managed to produce a statesman of Churchill's ilk. He acquired new respect for the British and their way of life.

Because Sunday's educational needs were different to Raphael's, the little boy was taught separately. When the arrangement was first explained to the tutors, Raphael could see that they were cynical about the child's capacity to learn. Would a shy little boy from a poor background really understand the value of a good Western education?

Would he really be able to concentrate? Wouldn't he rather kick a football around in the dust with other children?

Within just a day or two, the four men had all informed Raphael that Sunday was no ordinary child but an extremely gifted one—the most gifted child any of them had ever met. Despite the patchy education he had had so far and his parents' complete illiteracy, Sunday was able to grasp complex concepts very quickly and was able to concentrate on the material they gave him better than most adults.

"He's a lucky boy," was the consensus. "With a proper education, he'll become a young man who will go far."

Raphael nodded with satisfaction on hearing those words. He had not doubted Sunday, having seen for himself how talented the boy was, but it felt good to hear the tutors confirm what he already knew. He had given up on the idea of finding an orphanage to take the boy in and had accepted that fate had brought Sunday to him. While it was undoubtedly a tragedy that the boy's father had died, Raphael swore to ensure that Sunday would grow up to have every opportunity to develop his unusual mind.

2017

"Wow," said Rebecca. "That's quite a story. I'm amazed I never heard it before. Why have we never met Sunday? After all, I suppose he is sort of like an adopted member of the family. A kind of uncle, in a way."

"This part of the story has a bit of a sad ending," said Richard. "Well, not *really* sad, because Sunday ended up doing fine in life, but he also ended up hurting Grandad's feelings, and I think Grandad has always regretted the way things turned out in the end. In fact, I think that the reason he hasn't spoken about Sunday much is the fact that there is still some hurt there that has never fully been resolved. You know what a strong person Grandad is. He hates to admit it when someone or something gets under his skin. I think that's why he didn't tell us about Sunday."

"Why?" asked David. "What happened?"

"Let me tell you …"

1954-63

After three years of studying alongside Raphael in the compound, Sunday was ready for secondary school, and after graduating from secondary school at a very young age with extraordinary results, he was accepted as an undergraduate at the University of Ibadan. As there were no scholarships available, Raphael paid both his fees and a living stipend. He was determined that Sunday should have the best opportunity available to develop his remarkable mind even further. People like Sunday were not common, and that sort of talent needed to be nurtured and cherished. Again, he graduated with extraordinary results, having impressed the university staff with both his natural talents and his capacity and hunger for learning.

Shortly after his graduation, Sunday came to visit Raphael, the man he had always called Papa. He was a tall, handsome man in his twenties now—he looked just like his father, Amiru—and Raphael was in his thirties, married and with children of his own. Raphael held his arms wide when his former ward came into the room, expecting a warm and respectful embrace. But something had changed for Sunday. Rather than acknowledging Raphael with affection, as he had always done before, he remained standing stiffly near the door, giving the impression that he would really prefer to be almost anywhere else.

"What's going on, Sunday?" Raphael asked. "Aren't you going to greet me the way you have always done?"

Sunday was cold and angry. "I no longer trust white people," he said. "And I am afraid that this includes you. I've learned a lot about Europeans and how they take advantage of Africans and earn money off the backs of African labour."

Sunday went on to say that he had expected Raphael to put him in charge of a factory (Raphael's business interests had grown and expanded in the meantime) but that instead he had been offered a more junior role, which had disappointed him.

"There can only be one reason for his," he said, "and is that I am a black African and that you are as prejudiced as the English or any other white man. A racist, in other words. You think that I am not good enough to work as a manager because I am black. Despite all your fine words about education, in the end I'm nothing to you."

Uselessly, Raphael tried to protest that this was not the case. He wanted nothing but the best for Sunday and would help him in any way he could. But it was clear that something had happened that had altered the nature of their relationship forever. Eventually, his heart full of regret, he bid Sunday goodbye and saw the young man walk out of the door and out of his life.

Sunday's words had hurt him more deeply than he wanted to admit, even to himself, because he had grown to love the boy as a child, and because all the time he was in Africa, and in any of his subsequent dealings with Africans, he had always striven to accept each person on his or her own terms and not to be influenced by race in any way. After all, as a Jew among white Europeans, Raphael was no stranger to prejudice or to being dismissed without basis. He knew what it felt like to be looked down on, regardless of his achievements or efforts, just because of who he was. For this reason, he had always felt closer to the Africans than the Europeans in many ways, and he had looked forward to following Sunday's career and seeing the young man grow, flourish, get married, and start a family.

Some months after that dreadful encounter, an envelope addressed in Sunday's characteristic handwriting landed on Raphael's desk. Inside, Sunday had written that he was very sorry about what had happened. He regretted the things he had said, realised that he was wrong, and hoped they could be friends again. Although he was tempted to respond, Raphael realised that the best thing for Sunday was to be set free from any sense of obligation or duty. Sunday had grown up feeling indebted to Raphael for paying for the excellent education he had received, and nobody likes to feel indebted. This sensation had become a sort of weight that Sunday had been carrying around for years, even though there was absolutely no need for it; nobody had forced Raphael into doing anything. He had invested in Sunday's future because he wanted to. Well, Sunday was a highly educated man now, more than capable of making his own way in the world.

Raphael tore the letter up and threw it in the wastepaper basket. From then on, he would follow Sunday's career and wish him well from a distance.

2017

"Wow," said Rebecca. "Well, I can see why Grandad hasn't introduced him to us. That's heart-breaking. I'm surprised that he was able to talk to you about it at all."

"You have to put it into context, I think," said Richard. "By the time Sunday behaved like that, the African colonies were beginning to establish themselves as independent nations for the first time since they were conquered. There was a huge amount of resentment towards the colonising forces, and whites in general, and people were lashing out amid all the negative publicity they were reading. And let's not forget that a lot of Africans did have to put up with racism all their lives. Sunday was a young man finding his way—he realised that he had made a mistake, and he apologised for it, so I know Grandad didn't feel angry for long.

"On the other hand, I guess I can also understand why Grandad felt he had to cut Sunday loose. If he had renewed the friendship, Sunday might never have lost that feeling of indebtedness, and he might never have realised how much he was capable of on his own. I just wish he knew how Grandad has followed his career all these years and how proud he has always been of his role in helping Sunday when he was young.

"Sunday went on to do very well. Grandad said that he used to see Sunday's name in the business section of the African newspapers and that he rose through the ranks and ended up as the CEO of a big pharmaceutical company. He had a happy family life too, by all accounts, married to a wonderful woman who gave him four or five kids. He's retired now and lives in a nice suburb of Lagos. So, ultimately, it was a happy ending."

CHAPTER 14

MATTERS OF
PHILOSOPHY,
OLD AND NEW

2017

"Something I've always found fascinating about Grandad," Rebecca ruminated, "is the fact that he is able to understand people the moment he meets them. He doesn't need to know their background or their life story to be able to tune in to who they really are, at the most basic level. He just *gets* it. It doesn't matter what age or sex they are, or where they come from. Know what I mean? I've never been able to understand that gift. I certainly wish I had it. I've seen him use it in all sorts of circumstances—with business colleagues, waiters in restaurants, all sorts of people. He just has to see them and maybe exchange a couple of words, and then he knows exactly the sort of person they are."

"I think it all stems back to his time in Africa," Richard said. "Back to those days when he was working with the tutors and getting to meet all sorts of people from all different types of background. He often says that Africa provided him with a much broader education than he would ever have received in university."

"Kind of ironic," David butted in, "given how proud he was when all of us graduated from college!"

"I wouldn't have minded getting an education from the likes of Nadine and Eileen," offers David. "Or one of those horny air hostesses …"

"*Excuse* me, boys," said Rebecca, pretending to be shocked. "There's a lady present, don't you know?"

"Getting back to the topic at hand," Richard interjected. "Let me tell you all about how Grandad acquired his famous ability to read people. It's actually pretty interesting …"

1952

Now that he had given himself the time and space he needed to acquire his education, Raphael entered a period of introspection for the first time in his life. His driving force had always been the desire to make money, and that had not gone away; but for the first time, he was in the luxurious situation of having time to spend on exploring and understanding himself and the world around him in a clearer, more nuanced way than before. He had time to look at it not just in terms of new ways to make money and get ahead in life but simply as a wonderful collection of unexplained objects and circumstances, all waiting for someone to understand and explore them.

Raphael kept the tutors on, even when he had completed the equivalent of a bachelor's degree, as he wanted to continue learning from them for as long as he could—and they were still teaching young Sunday, who was like a sponge for knowledge and a joy to instruct— but he also increasingly realised how much there was to learn from all the people around him and that great wisdom was often found in the most surprising places.

First of all, the Europeans in Maiduguri, even the English, were a great source of potential learning, as many of them had been to university and had access to a rigorous academic education. Raphael had made friends with a number of the teachers, young English women who had come to Africa to further their careers and have an adventure before settling down. Life was often quite dull for these vibrant young women in the English quarter—not the adventure they thought they had signed up for at all. None of the married women wanted to socialise with the younger ladies, because they didn't trust their husbands to keep their hands to themselves. Socialising with the Africans was considered out of the question for young English ladies. White men could take African women as lovers, but if a white woman had done something of the sort, she would have been considered a pariah. Because they were teachers, the schools where they worked expected them to set a "good example" to the girls they taught, and they were told to dress and behave modestly at all times, including in their time off.

Raphael's camp, where he frequently held dinner parties for the young, beautiful people of Maiduguri, became a popular place to go. As it was outside the boundaries of the town and outside the strictures of British society, it was somewhere the young teachers could let their hair down, have fun, talk about whatever they wanted, and finally feel as though they were having the African adventure they longed for. But these were not just girls out to have a good time in the tropics; they were also educated women who had attended some of Britain's best universities and who talked about learned matters with the carelessness of people who had always been able to take a good, rounded education for granted. In that respect, Raphael envied them. He had been so busy hustling since the age of 12 that he'd had little time for book learning.

Of all the young women teachers, Eileen was the one to whom Raphael felt closest, and not just because of the sexual relationship they enjoyed. Whereas some of Eileen's friends were a little giddy and foolish—carried away with the excitement of not living with their parents for the first time and the prospect of carrying on love affairs far away from home—she had an air of mature dignity, and her calm grey eyes regarded the world with a sort of amused curiosity. Whereas even many of the nicest English tended to assume that the Africans were "a bit dim" or "childlike", as they put it, Raphael could see that Eileen had no such prejudices but respected everyone she met, unless she had a specific reason to do otherwise. (She didn't like Nadine, of course, but then she did have a reason for that.)

Realising that Raphael's education in the area of European history was, in fact, quite deficient despite the efforts that he was going to with his tutors, Eileen gently started to teach him about the cultural aspects of Europe. In their many long conversations, Raphael started to learn about things he had never even wondered about before. Eileen was so engaging, he often didn't even realise that he was learning, although he was often humbled by how much this woman knew.

As he found out more about the role of forces such as Christianity in shaping European history—and continuing to inform its modern society—he also began to think more about his own background and heritage. What did it really *mean* to be a Cairene Jew in a society on the cusp of dramatic change? How had his childhood shaped him and made him into the person he was today? Growing up, he had felt secure and loved in his family, and he had known that his wider community would always be place where he was cherished. As he became older, he often found the security of belonging stifling, and he had longed to get away from it—to go to Nigeria and stand on his own two feet. But he also realised that he loved knowing that his community was there for him, and he valued the sense of security, tradition, and gravitas that belonging to it gave him. And now the tides of history were sweeping away the Jews of Cairo, who were making homes in other places. Would they be able to retain their sense of togetherness and identity, even now?

"Something I like about you, Raphael," Eileen said one day, "is the fact that you're not afraid to admit it when you don't know something and you understand that everyone is a potential teacher. For someone who can be quite arrogant—no, don't pretend it's not true, because you know perfectly well that it is, it's one of the things that people like about you—it's a surprisingly humble, refreshing quality."

"Well, thank you," said Raphael. "I will take that as a compliment."

"You don't see much of it around here. I don't think I realised how class-ridden British society is until I got here and saw it in its distilled form in Maiduguri. God, we Brits can be insufferable at times!"

"You know what?" Raphael said. "I never really thought about it, but when I look back now, I can see that it's a gift from my dad, Joseph. We haven't always had the easiest relationship, and sometimes I've got so frustrated with him, but if you met him, you'd see how open-minded he is. And believe me, Egypt can be just as stuffy and class-ridden as England. My dad always told me that nobody can help the family they're born into, and we should take everyone on their merits. That's the way he brought us up, and I was glad of it, because not everyone was as open-minded as him."

While it would be unfair to say that Raphael looked down on his father, he had often felt impatient with Joseph's lack of ambition and what Raphael saw as a failure to provide for the family as well as they deserved. As he was so close to Flora, his mother, Raphael had always seen things from her point of view, and he knew that she had often found it stressful to get by on the income Joseph brought home from his leather workshop or the various other enterprises he had been involved in.

Raphael had often wondered why Joseph didn't seem to care about money and why he didn't have as much of a drive to achieve as Raphael did, especially considering the fact that Joseph was the son of a very successful man. It had made Raphael angry to see his mother wearing a shabby dress when he felt she should be able to dress like a queen. However, looking back at the decisions Joseph had taken with regard to his children's education, Raphael could see that, in his own way, he had done his best to prepare them for the wider world.

The Jewish community in Cairo was small and beleaguered, even before open hostilities broke out, and in Sudan it was suffocating, self-contained, and insular. Anyone who wanted to get on in life would have to know how to operate with people from very different backgrounds and cultures, because refusing to do so meant closing themselves off even further and making it even more difficult to engage in business and enterprise. While some of the Jewish families had responded to the growing tensions and strains around them by becoming ever more inward-looking, Joseph had insisted that his sons integrate into society and mingle freely with people from very different backgrounds to their own, even if it occasionally made them feel a little uncomfortable or prompted them to explore their own assumptions.

Looking back now, Raphael could see that some of his thoughts about his father had been disloyal and unfair. Joseph had been broad-minded and forward-thinking in ensuring such a varied education for his children, regardless of the family's limited resources. Thanks to Raphael's time at the madrasa, he understood Islam and the role it played in shaping culture and attitudes to business wherever it was found. This made it easier for him to understand the African Muslims, for whom Islam was a central part of their identity. Thanks to his studies under the Catholic priests, Raphael had learnt the fundamental tenets of Catholicism, and again, this gave him insights into European culture and how Europeans approached business and relationships with others.

Thanks to his experience of being educated beyond the comfort zone of family and community, he had learned that mixing with people who were different from him was something to be embraced, not feared. Without this very early exposure to people who were different from his family members and friends, Raphael realised, it would have been much more difficult to come to Africa and integrate himself so quickly into a diverse society in which intercultural tensions were always not far below the surface. In giving him this gift of open-mindedness, Joseph had done more for him than Raphael had realised until now.

At the same time, even as he got to know a wider variety of people in Africa and to appreciate both African and European culture, Raphael's own personal sense of cultural identity never wavered. Aside from Flora's simple faith in saints and prayer, his family was not very religious. Sure, they celebrated the high days and holidays, but for the most part, that was it.

"You'll be sure to look up your relatives in Africa?" Flora had asked Raphael nervously when he was about to leave. "There are some Jews in Maiduguri, including your cousin Albert. Go and talk to them as soon as you arrive. They can introduce you to the community there and make sure that you are never lonely. I'd like to think that you are getting some home cooking once in a while, darling!"

"Sure, Mama," he had said, seeking to reassure her. "Don't worry. I'll definitely look them up when I get there, no problem. I will tell them that you sent your regards."

But the reality was that Raphael did not feel any need to seek out and cleave to the tiny Jewish community in Maiduguri. He didn't care about going to the synagogue and knew that his own Jewish identity did not depend on matters of religious observance. His only concession to tradition was to sacrifice a chicken on the eve of Yom Kippur, a religious day when Jews fast, neither eating nor drinking, for twenty-seven hours. He reasoned that there would be plenty of time to explore his Jewish faith in more detail later on, perhaps when he was married. For now, he was perfectly secure about who and what he was.

Raphael was bemused to learn how little respect many of the Europeans had for African culture. Because most African wisdom was transmitted orally, rather than written down, they seemed to feel that it didn't really count in the same way as the sort of wisdom they could read about or study at the university. African beliefs were seen as mere superstition, their legends and myths as fairy tales rather than narratives on a par with the mythology of ancient Greece and Rome, and their music barbaric and primitive compared to European symphony orchestras. The reality was that very few of the Europeans ever really took time to listen to African people, and they overlooked the fact that African culture had, directly and indirectly, contributed to European culture in many more ways than they imagined. For example, a lot of the young Europeans were crazy about jazz. They never even paused to consider how its sounds and rhythms had their origins in the African music the slaves had brought to America when they were imported to work there, all those years before.

Most of the teachers working in the better local schools felt that European culture was simply superior in every way and looked down on the Africans as their inferiors. The men who held government positions and worked in business were generally happy to take African women as lovers on the sly but had little or no regard for what those same women cared and thought about. They arranged for the women to be delivered to the back doors of their homes, used them for sex, and then sent them out the way they came.

While Raphael was very happy about furthering his education with his four Western-taught tutors, he also knew that there was a lot to learn from the teachings of native Africans. A man called Alhaji Jibril, a Hausa speaker, emerged as one of Raphael's most important and influential teachers. Alhaji was an older man; his dark, tightly curled hair was just beginning to turn grey at the temples, and Africans tend to go grey much later than white people. He was sombre, serious, and well regarded by everyone who knew him. Raphael had quickly learned that Alhaji was scrupulously honest and could be entrusted with anything.

After the two men had known each other for some time, Alhaji approached Raphael one day. "Sir," he said, "I know that you are studying a lot with your Western teachers, and I would like to offer you the opportunity to learn a little African philosophy."

At first, Raphael was amused. His tutors all held doctorates from some of Britain's most highly regarded universities. For all the respect he had for Alhaji, he also knew that this was not an educated man. What on earth did Alhaji think he would be able to teach Raphael? But rather than dismissing Alhaji, he decided to give the man a chance.

"I will come tomorrow when you are finished with your white teachers," Alhaji informed him, "and you can learn about African wisdom for an hour or two!"

The following day, Raphael and Alhaji sat together under a tree in the compound, and Alhaji explained in great detail how one can tell all about a person simply from looking at them and figuring out which animal they most closely resemble.

Alhaji gave examples, "Look at Graham," he said, "the English policeman who works in an office and tells people what they can and can't do. Think carefully about what he looks like, and then tell me what you think."

Raphael thought carefully. Graham had a large pink face, small shiny eyes, and a hairline that started far back on his forehead. The fact was, he looked a lot like a pig.

I'm probably being unfair, he thought to himself. *I'm letting my personal dislike of the man cloud my judgement.*

"He looks like a pig!" Alhaji said triumphantly, echoing Raphael's thoughts. "I know that you are thinking it; you don't have to tell me! I gave you an easy one to get you started. Well, the fact that he looks so much like a pig tells you all you need to know about him. He is clever and shrewd, but he is also greedy, vicious, and venial. It's just a pity that someone like him is in a position of authority, because a man like that is bound to abuse it."

"That sounds like a perfect description," Raphael agreed grimly. "I disliked that man from the moment I saw him, but I wasn't sure why at first. He's someone who just takes what he wants."

Alhaji lowered his voice. "Sir," he said, "you don't know the half of it. He's a *bad* man, I can assure you. I have heard that he sends out to the villages for African girls as young as 8 or 9 years old to share his bed, and he does what he wants with them, if you know what I mean. Unfortunately, there are always some parents who are so poor, they will look the other way; and the police don't care what happens to poor girls, because they're only interested in keeping down the militants and protecting the interests of the English."

Over time, Alhaji pointed out to Raphael that this person or that one looked like a certain animal or another. Invariably, their personality traits matched that of the animal. It didn't matter whether the individual in question was black or white; with this way of seeing things, it became progressively quicker to figure out what they were really like.

Raphael gazed at himself in the mirror, trying to figure out which sort of animal he most resembled. Sometimes he thought he was like a dog and told himself that this reflected his well-developed sense of loyalty and the great importance he gave to friendship. Whatever else he did, he never abandoned his friends or his people. Other times, he looked in the mirror and fancied that he resembled a crocodile—slow to react at first, but fast and furious in action. When he confessed to Alhaji that he had been trying to read himself, the older man just laughed.

"That's one thing nobody can do," he said. "Try as we might, we can't tell which animal we most resemble ourselves."

"You tell me what you see, then," Raphael begged. "I know that you have already made up your mind about it."

Alhaji just tapped the side of his nose and looked knowing. "That, sir, is for me to know and you to find out."

As well as teaching Raphael how to understand people better, Alhaji taught him many of the best qualities of African cultures.

"If you don't mind me saying so, sir," he commented mildly one day, "you're not really a very *patient* person, are you? When you're doing something, you're already thinking about the next thing. You send off one load of skins to France, and then you start worrying about the next one before the first one has even left for the airport. You have one pretty girl to take around, and you're already considering what it would be like to be with a different one. Maybe sometimes there are good reasons to be impatient, but other times it just gets people worried and makes them sick."

He continued, "Think about how slowly things happen here. Maybe a bus or a canoe is supposed to come at seven, but it doesn't arrive until nine. You don't see the Africans waiting for it getting all stressed. We know that it will come when it comes and that there's nothing we can do about it, so there's no point in worrying. We spend our whole lives waiting patiently—for the rains to come, for our children to recover from illness, for the English to leave and go back to their own country. We wait and wait, and eventually what happens, happens."

Raphael was silent, trying to absorb the information in Alhaji's message. He had to admit, he struggled a bit with it. He had never been a patient person, it was true. His mother had often told him how, even before he was born, he had tormented her with his furious, angry movements, as though he could not wait to escape the fleshy confines of her body and take his place in the world. He had also noticed the great patience of the African people. He had often noticed that, when something happened, they didn't react straight away, as he would have done. Instead, they sat and waited to see how things would pan out and reacted only when they were completely sure of what was going on. Europeans often found this very challenging. They were used to their own ways and didn't understand that there could be a different approach.

Raphael could only agree with another of Alhaji's lessons, which was that each failure should be seen not as a setback but as a stepping stone.

"There is no man on God's earth who gets things right every single time," said Alhaji. "We all make mistakes. A foolish man gets upset when he makes a mistake. He might get some beer and get drunk and then go wailing home to his wife about how miserable he is. There's absolutely no sense in that. In the morning, he'll wake up with a bad headache and an angry wife, and he won't have learned anything at all from the experience. Instead, a wise man accepts his failures and learns from them. In fact, we all learn a lot more from our mistakes than from our successes. And then we come back to what

I was saying before about patience. Patience is never as important as when we've gone wrong or things haven't worked out as we hoped. We might be tempted to try to fix things straight away, but if we do, we're doing so with a hot head and an intemperate heart. It is better to let things cool down, go to bed and have a nice sleep, and then wake up in the morning to think about it all again. Often, the thing that was annoying us so much turns out not to be so very important, after all."

Raphael laughed. "Alhaji, you are reminding me of my mother," he said. "She always told me that sleep is a great healer—that sleep can heal all wounds. When I was a little boy, she told me, 'Count your blessings before you go to sleep, and in the morning, you will add to them.' When I was a little boy, she taught me to make a list, counting my eyes, nose, ears, and breathing as my blessings, and to keep adding to the list. I never got to the end of the list. I always fell asleep before I could stop thinking of them."

"Your mother was a very wise woman," said Alhaji. "For that matter, my mother was a wise woman too. She gave the exact same advice to me!"

The two men sat in silence together for a few minutes, each contemplating his boyhood.

"Isn't it funny," Alhaji said at last, "that two people can be so different and have mothers who gave the same advice?"

"I suppose mothers are the same all over the world."

"Thank God for that."

Raphael found Alhaji very interesting and tried to share some of his teachings with Nadine. To his surprise, she was immediately very hostile to the idea.

"I don't know why you are spending so much time hanging around with that boring negro," she said with an imperious toss of her pretty head. "How can you bear to spend so much time with an uneducated African? Sometimes I think you like him better than me. You say he gives you advice. Do you think that *I* can't give you advice? I have seen a thing or two in my day, believe me, and I know more than you can imagine."

"It's not like you to be so prejudiced," Raphael said with a mild note of admonishment in his voice. "You usually accept people for who they are."

"Oh, that one just gets up my nose! He thinks he knows all about everyone with his stupid see-what-animal-they-resemble nonsense! I hate it! The other day, I caught him looking at me like I was some sort of specimen under the microscope. Then he said that I look like a squirrel, always looking around me to see what I can hide away for later. I can't stand him. I wish you'd make him go away."

Raphael was surprised by Nadine's outburst. She was usually so even-tempered. He considered discontinuing his conversations with Alhaji, just to keep her in a good mood—he found it so very difficult not to do what she wanted—but something told him to just stay quiet and do nothing. He thought about Alhaji's assessment of Nadine as a squirrel and smiled to himself as he realised that it made sense. On the surface, it seemed like a strange word to describe such a beautiful woman, but then he thought of Nadine's bright, darting eyes. They moved around all the time, taking in everything around her, assessing all she saw, and determining whether or not it was useful or relevant to her. Her small hands were always busy, too. Nadine liked to touch things, to feel their contour and figure out how they worked—and how she might be able to use them to her own advantage.

Sometimes Raphael felt as though Alhaji was trying to warn him about something but didn't feel quite able to get out the words. One day in particular, Alhaji said, seemingly apropos of nothing: "You know, sir, I have found it very useful to stop thinking of people as either bad or good, because even people who do terrible things generally have something good about them. It's easier to divide people into two categories: good and less good. That makes it easier for us to forgive those who have done us wrong and understand what has happened when someone we thought was good does something bad,"

Something in Alhaji's eyes made Raphael wonder if he was thinking about someone in particular.

"Do you have someone in mind?" he asked.

"No, sir."

But Alhaji's gaze had wandered to the side of the compound where Raphael spent his afternoons in the blissful company of Nadine. Could Alhaji think that she could wish Raphael harm, that she might do something to hurt him? Surely not!

Not long afterwards, Alhaji announced that he was going to provide Raphael with some vital lessons about women. Raphael was amused by this. He was sure that he had had more contact with women than the rather austere older man, even if he was much younger.

"Do go on, Alhaji," he said. "But remember that European women are much more difficult to handle than African ones!"

"Well, sir," he said, "I know that you like to have more than one woman at the same time. As you are in Africa, that is perfectly fine. In fact, it is how many African families do things, and we think that there's nothing wrong with a man having more than one wife, so long as he has sufficient resources to support them all, along with their families. But it's not enough to just give them money. You also have to respect each one of them and take care not to hurt her feelings. The fact is, while a lot of men like the idea of having two or more wives, there are very few men who are able to keep more than one woman happy. All women are different, and they all have different needs, so it's better to avoid getting into a tricky situation. My advice to you is to stick with one woman at a time, unless you are sure you're not going to get yourself into difficulties!"

"I'll bear that in mind," said Raphael, amused. "Are there any other pearls of wisdom that you would like to share?"

"Well, sir, when you do get married and settle down, I would like you to remember that money can make your wife into a housewife, and it can also make her into a prostitute."

"Watch your mouth, Alhaji," Raphael rebuked him. "I can assure you that when I get married, my wife will *never* be a prostitute."

"That depends on you. If you give her the money she needs to take care of the house and your children, then she will be a happy wife and mother, but if you deny her that requirement, she will be forced to do whatever it takes. Most women will do anything before they see their children go hungry, even give themselves to a man for money."

"You know, Alhaji," Raphael said, "there's a lot to be said for this African philosophy of yours. I think it should be studied in the schools."

It was hard for Raphael to share his newfound passion for African philosophy with his friends, because even the most broad-minded of them struggled to consider African learning on a par with European. Only Eileen seemed to be interested. She listened to Raphael every time he spoke about what he had learned from Alhaji.

"That's all really interesting," she said, "but don't overlook book-learning. I think that if you combine what you learn from Alhaji with what you can read in books, you'll know a lot. You'll have the best of both worlds."

"Aside from the books my tutors give me to study, I don't know where to start," Raphael confessed. "I wish someone would just take me in hand and tell me what to read."

"I can do it!" Eileen said. "I absolutely love reading, and I can arrange for you to get all the books you need."

Eileen arranged for her friends to send books in the post, and she explored the library sections of all the local department stores for books.

"The best learning is learning you do on your own," she advised Raphael. "I know that you have been taught a great deal by your tutors, but you can build on it very quickly by reading on your own."

"If I find the time!"

"If you really care about learning," Eileen said with a hint of severity, "you'll just *make* the time. Anyway, it'll be fun."

Between his long conversations with Alhaji, his lessons, and the reading that Eileen supplied him with, Raphael felt that he had really improved his education, and he decided that he would make learning an essential part of his lifestyle. There was no reason for anyone to stop learning, whatever their age, he decided. Years later, however, he would look back and see that the lessons that taught him the most of all were those of Alhaji, who showed him how to see people how they really are, how to understand what was in his own heart, and how to embrace the quality of patience.

From Alhaji and the other Africans he knew, he also discovered aspects of African culture that he found less useful. The Africans venerated age and the wisdom that comes with it, but they did so to such an extent that it could stifle the young and stop them from achieving all they were capable of, because they felt unable to do anything that had not been approved by an elder. Raphael recognised that there was a degree of this in his own culture, too. His father had wanted and expected all of his sons to grow up to work for him and do what they were told without question. This had led to tension between Raphael and Joseph, and eventually Raphael had left.

He could see that things were different in Europe. Young Europeans were, by and large, much freer to do their own thing. Even the women were encouraged to get a good education and explore the world. This, he decided, was a better approach than the one he had grown up with and the one he saw around him in Nigeria. He was also attracted to the great freedom of expression enjoyed by Europeans. In the conservative African society, anyone who spoke out and challenged the accepted status quo was likely to be ostracised, or even worse.

Raphael was also uncomfortable with the way women were treated in African society, even if—as he had to admit—he benefitted from this in some ways. He loved and respected women and thought of them as superior to men in many ways. While Raphael was saving his heart for the woman he would marry one day, he cherished his relationships with the women in his life now and tried to treat them all like princesses. He would never get used to how, in African homes, men sat down and enjoyed their meal while their wives stood and served them.

Throughout his period of learning, Raphael was always conscious of the fact that he had lost his amulet and could no longer count on the great good fortune that he was sure it had conferred on him.

("What, what?" interjected Rebecca. "What are you talking about?"

"Hold your horses," said Richard. "I'm getting to it ...")

The loss of the amulet was one of the reasons he felt so strongly about becoming more knowledgeable. Without a touch of supernatural help, he would have to know how to stand on his own two feet. And yet ... there were days when he felt as though it was near him, nonetheless, days when it seemed as though he was still benefitting from its peculiar powers. He tried to tell himself to forget it, but it still haunted his dreams. He woke at night with visions of the amulet, its gold chain and the portrait of Rambam—sure, at least for a moment, that it was somewhere within reach.

2017

"Richard," said David, "you never told us Grandad lost the amulet! We know how he got it—and obviously, he got it back, because he has it in his safe now—but now you're telling us that it was lost. Do you know what happened to it?"

"Of course I do. I know the whole story, and as soon as I've opened another bottle of wine, I'm going to share it with you all. It's a good story, too. Several of the people I've already mentioned come into it. You're going to feel like I'm telling you the plot of an action movie!"

"Well, then, hurry up!"

CHAPTER 15

THE DEVASTATING LOSS

2017

"OK, so you know that the amulet was missing for a while ..." Richard started.

"Yes," said David. "What the hell happened there? Grandad loves that thing so much and says that he owes all his good fortune to it. He's had it since he was a tiny baby, and it's a link to his childhood past in Cairo on top of everything else. It's hard to believe that he let it out of his sight ... and even harder to understand how he got it back again after losing it."

"Also, why did he never tell us?" wondered Rebecca. "He talks about his precious amulet all the time. I mean, you'd think the subject would've come up at some point."

"It's a complicated thing, really," said Richard, "and I think it's quite a difficult one for him to talk about, because it brings up so many conflicting feelings, even now. But I know the whole story."

"Well, go on, then," urged David. "What are you waiting for? Tell us!"

1952

Nadine, who had come to the camp ostensibly just to provide costumes, hairdos, and make-up for the New Year's Eve party, had decided to stay on for an indefinite period. She was so pretty, and so enthusiastic about spending her afternoons in bed with Raphael, that he had no intention of asking her to leave, at least for now. He was very glad to have her around, although balancing her needs and demands with those of the other women in his life—such as the lovely Eileen—could be a challenge sometimes, especially as he also had to work.

Aside from the welcome presence of Nadine, there was a lot of good news to celebrate. Business was going better than ever, and Alhaji told him that Graham, the policeman who had been harassing him since his arrival, had been dispatched from the area.

"Remember Graham, the Englishman who looks like a pig?" Alhaji said. "Well, he's been sent to live in a village a long way from here—a punishment for the way he's been behaving around here, not just with you, but with everyone. He's a useless, corrupt policeman, and he always has been. It's good news for you, but don't think your troubles with him are over. Remember how I told you that pigs are clever? Well, Graham is clever too. He hates you, and I've heard that he blames you for his having been sent to such an uncomfortable place and has sworn to get his revenge on you. Before he went, he got drunk and went around the place saying that you would be sorry you ever came to Maiduguri and that you got on his nerves and were going to learn your lesson."

Raphael was inclined to laugh this off. He felt confident that he was able to protect himself from whatever Graham tried to dish out. Who was Graham, anyway? Just a pathetic, low-level functionary who didn't impress anyone.

"Oh, Alhaji," he said. "What on earth can Graham do to me from over there? I know the sort of place you mean. There's probably nothing there but a few mud huts, a couple of shops, and a cement office for Graham to work in. He'll most likely get sick of it before long and decide to go back to England. I expect we'll never see him again."

"Sir," said Alhaji, "mark my words, he is still a very dangerous man, and I would urge you not to underestimate him and the threat he poses. Like all pigs, now that he has been wounded, he's even more dangerous. Pigs will do whatever they can to make their lives more comfortable, and if he feels that what he needs to do is remove you, then that is what he's going to try to do."

"Well," said Raphael, "I don't feel worried at all. I've got armed guards here, and I'm on excellent terms with the locals. I don't think there's going to be a problem."

"I hope that you are right. Because he's also been telling people that you have a good-luck charm that makes your life easier, and that by rights it ought to belong to him. He says he's got a plan in mind to get his hands on it."

A momentary cloud of concern darkened Raphael's good mood, but then he dismissed it. Who cared if Graham knew about the amulet? So long as he never took it off, Raphael was sure that there could be no problem.

In fact, Graham was quite happy in his new posting. Of course, it was effectively a demotion, which had stung, but there certainly were some benefits, from his point of view. He was living in a very corrupt local community, and the first thing the chief had done was ask him what sort of girls he liked. When Graham told him that he liked them very young, the chief had arranged for a selection of pretty girls to be sent to Graham's house for him to do what he wanted with. In return, all Graham had to do was look the other way when laws were broken and old traditions, long thought to be suppressed, were restored. Graham fitted right in with the people he was now living amongst, and he had made many friends among the natives while also staying in contact with his cronies back in Maiduguri, who kept him well-informed about Raphael's movements and the rumours they had heard about goings-on at his camp.

Graham was not even slightly perturbed by some of the strange local customs. While most of the people in Nigeria were peaceful and law-abiding, that could not be said of the Jinja people at his new posting. Theirs was a bellicose, violent culture. The men frequently got drunk and beat their wives and children. The women got drunk and beat their children and each other. The children observed the adults and learned from them how they should behave when they were older. Ever since the British had arrived in the area, they had tried to persuade the Jinja people to live in a different way, but all to no avail. The rest of the native peoples generally did their best to avoid them.

Graham felt that there was no point in trying to change the local customs—and anyway, the chaos here suited him. It was easy for him to pay people off and do whatever he wanted, because that sort of behaviour was already the local custom. He didn't even care about the fact that human sacrifice was still practised among the Jinja, despite the fact that the official line was that there hadn't been a sacrifice for years. Before leaving Maiduguri, Graham had been informed that it had once been commonplace, but now it had been stamped out. He had quickly learned that it had not been stamped out at all but was merely hidden from the British authorities, who were prepared to look the other way so long as the practice did not inconvenience or embarrass them by coming under investigation.

But there was one thing that kept bothering Graham, and that was the fact that Raphael was still in Maiduguri, where his business was going from strength to strength—and that nobody seemed to be able to stop him.

I'll make sure that filthy, stinking Jew learns a lesson, Graham told himself, *if it's the last thing I do. Perhaps if someone took that blasted amulet away from him, the one he's so damn proud about, it would take the wind out of his sails. Perhaps if I had it instead, I might see some better luck in my life!*

And then Graham had an idea …

* * *

Back at the camp, Raphael and Nadine were getting ready for the camping trip he had promised to take her on. Nadine was so excited, she couldn't stop chattering about it. She told everyone that she was sure she was going to kill some fearsome beast all on her own and that she wouldn't be scared, because Raphael would be right there with her all the time.

"Not just me," Raphael reminded her. "Sum Sum and Rajibu will be there too."

"Well, exactly my point," she said. "It's going to be perfectly safe, because you've got everything organised. Now all I need is for the animals to turn up. We're bringing a camera, aren't we? Because I want to be sure that it is all caught on film—otherwise my friends at home might never believe me!"

Raphael laughed at her girlish excitement.

"I can't guarantee we'll catch anything that amazing," he said, "but at the very least, we'll kill something for our dinner. And if all else fails, you can always hunt down and catch *me*; I won't mind at all!"

At four in the afternoon, Raphael and Nadine, together with the two guards, climbed into the vehicle he had planned to use for the hunting trip. The car was loaded with everything they would need and more, including tents, water, petrol, food, and other provisions— and, of course, Nadine's make-up bag. She was planning to have photographs taken when she bagged her kill so that she could show them to her friends back in Paris—and she wanted to look good in them.

"Excited?" Raphael asked her as the car left the camp and set down the road leaving Maiduguri.

"More than you can imagine!"

By the time they had travelled for half an hour, dusk had begun to fall, and the road they had taken had deteriorated to little more than a dirt track. The jeep jolted violently from side to side on the rutted surface. Even in the fading light, it was easy to see the reddish colour of the dry soil on which scrubby bushes and trees appeared here and there. The sound of crickets filled the air, along with the rustles made by the nocturnal animals coming out for the night.

Raphael and Nadine sat together in the back seat of the jeep. On his advice, she had dressed herself carefully against the mosquitoes, as had he. They both wore shirts and trousers that fastened with elastic around wrists and ankles to keep the malaria-carrying insects at bay, and long knee socks. Nadine's hat had a net fringe that hung down over her face. It was a practical item of clothing, but it made her look prettier than ever.

As though she could read his thoughts, Nadine took Raphael's arm and squeezed it.

"It's *so* exciting going out into the bush with you," she said in a low voice. "I can't wait to start hunting, but I am even more excited about spending the night in the wilderness with you. I know that you have other women, and I don't really care, but I think that *I* am the special one, and I am sure that tonight is going to be very memorable."

Raphael smiled at the promise of the carnal delights that Nadine was offering.

"I'll certainly do my best to make it a night to remember," he said. "Perhaps you would like it if I …"

This delightful conversation was interrupted by a violent jolt, and Nadine let out a little scream as the car shuddered to a halt. Rajibu jumped down to investigate.

"Don't worry, boss," he called out. "We just hit a deer than ran across the road too quickly for us to see. It's still alive but badly hurt, so I'll kill it and we can have it for dinner. We might as well eat here as anywhere else."

Sum Sum drove the jeep off the road, and he made himself busy setting up the tents while Rajibu slaughtered, skinned, and butchered the deer.

"Ready to start hunting, Nadine?" Raphael asked.

"What, right now?"

"It's as good a time as any other," he said. "Maybe you'll manage to kill something while the men are getting dinner ready. At least you can get a bit of practice in before the real hunt starts tomorrow."

Raphael took out the equipment they would need—torches, shotguns, and rifles—and the two of them began to explore the brushy forest the road drove through.

Although it was night, the forest was alive with sounds, and in the darkness, they seemed far more prominent than they would have been by day. Raphael and Nadine could hear twigs snap not only under their own feet but also under the feet of heavy animals moving through the undergrowth just out of reach. From above them in the trees came the noise of birds and animals settling down to sleep for the night. Further up, the full moon shone at an oblique angle, casting black shadows on the grey ground.

"It's so thrilling," Nadine whispered. "It feels dangerous, like something could happen at any minute."

"Something *could* happen at any minute," Raphael confirmed. "So I hope you've got your gun ready."

Just as he spoke, Raphael became aware of the sound of something large and heavy moving through the forest to their left.

"Slowly, Nadine," he said in a quiet, steady voice. "I think that you are going to get your chance to go for the kill. It's probably a boar, and then we can add some boar steaks to the menu for this evening."

Cautiously, the two of them moved closer to the sound.

"Try a shot now," he urged her. "You might hit it."

Although she could only see the vague outline of a shadow among the trees, Nadine raised her gun and shot. The report of the gun rang out loudly in the darkness, and they heard the sound of something falling heavily.

They waited for a moment to see what would happen next, but there was complete silence. Either the large animal had died or it was badly injured and unable to move. Even the rest of the animals and birds around them seemed to have sunk into a shocked silence, waiting to see what would happen next and if the evident danger was likely to impact on them.

Cautiously, Raphael and Nadine walked in the direction of the shot, shining their torches ahead of them as they went.

"Is that what I think it is?" Nadine marvelled when her torchlight fell on a dappled pelt.

"It is!" Raphael exclaimed. "Congratulations, Nadine! Somehow you managed to get a cheetah with your first hit. Now, that's something that doesn't happen very often! Either it's beginner's luck or you have a natural talent for hunting."

They approached the animal and saw that the bullet had gone right into its head, killing it instantly.

"It's so big!" Nadine said. "They don't look so big in photographs."

"It's just as well you shot when you did. These big cats can move really quickly and pounce before you know what's happening. It could easily have killed us both before the men were able to get to us."

"I can't believe it!"

"Well, you're going to have a beautiful trophy to bring home. Now, let's go back to the fire and eat. Rajibu can skin it for you to take back to the camp."

It only took Rajibu a moment to skin the slain cheetah, and then he joined the rest of them at the campfire, where they tucked into the delicious steaks of venison.

* * *

Two hours further up the road, a small group of men waited impatiently. Among them was a tall, somewhat overweight Englishman with a red face. It was, of course, none other than Graham.

"Where are they?" he impatiently asked an African companion. "I thought they would be here by now. I'm going to be furious if things don't go according to plan."

"They're supposed to be," the man said. "I heard that they were expected to make their camp after dark. I paid a boy to sneak around to his place in Maiduguri and find out what the plans were. We switched the signposts so they'd come here instead of the spot they had in mind."

"Well, he'd better turn up like I was told, or there'll be trouble," said Graham petulantly. He lit up a cigarette and had a few puffs and then threw the rest of it on the ground, stubbing it out with his heel. "I've been planning to get my own back on that wretch and his bloody amulet for a long time," he added, "so I'll wait a few more hours if I have to, but I'm going to be really fuming if the information I've been given turns out to be incorrect."

"They'll be here," the African man said. "You just wait and see. It's all going to go like clockwork."

* * *

"Everything packed?" Raphael checked as they reloaded the car and took care to extinguish the last traces of the fire. "Then let's get going. We still have a couple of hours to go, and I don't want to be too late."

"Don't forget my trophy!" called Nadine. "Without it, nobody is going to believe that I managed to kill a cheetah on my first try."

"Don't worry, miss," Rajibu assured her. "It's already packed, and we'll take care of it when we get to the camp so that it's preserved properly."

Everyone was getting tired as the jeep bumped its way along the uneven road. After an hour or so, they reached a fork in the road. The headlights lit up the sign which indicated directions, but Sum Sum halted the jeep by the side of the road and got out to double-check.

"It says 'Sokoto' on the left," he said. "So we should be there soon."

"On the left?" Raphael asked. "That's strange. For some reason, I thought we'd be turning right here. Oh well, never mind; I must have been mistaken."

They drove along an increasingly pocked road for about forty-five minutes, travelling very slowly because even a jeep could not rush along such an uneven surface. Raphael was anxious, although he was not sure exactly why. He did not want to upset Nadine, so he fingered his amulet and kept his concerns to himself. After a while, he took out his compass and inspected it. Suddenly, he realised that they must have been going the wrong way.

"Something's up!" he said. He explained that they should be going north, and instead they were heading south-west. "The signpost must have been switched. I can't think of any other explanation for it. Let's stop here and figure out what's going on and what we should do next."

Sum Sum pulled the car into the side of the road and waited for further directions.

"Each of the men will take a gun and go and scope out the area," Raphael decided. "If it's safe and suitable for camping, I suppose we'll have to stay here for the night. It's getting very late at this point, so we might be better off waiting until daylight and deciding what to do then."

"What will *I* do?" asked Nadine.

"You'd better wait here. Keep the windows rolled up and the doors closed. I'm sure you won't see anyone, but if you do, don't open the car. Just be patient, and we'll be back soon with a plan. And don't worry; there's no reason to assume that anything bad is going to happen."

Sum Sum headed west. Before long, he was aware that the animals in the brush were making a lot of noise and were clearly disturbed. Before he had time to figure out why that might be the case, seven men leapt on him and tied him up. They wound a rope around his ankles and dragged him back to the car, where Nadine was waiting for the men to return. Sum Sum struggled all the way and yelled at them to let him go, but as he was just one man and they were seven, there was little he could do. Eventually, one of the men slapped Sum Sum so hard about the head that he sank into unconsciousness.

While Nadine screamed in terror, one of the men broke the window of the jeep with his bare hands, not even flinching in pain as the glass penetrated his skin. Expressionless, he reached in and opened the door and then pulled Nadine out onto the ground. She fell heavily on her hip. In shock, she stopped screaming and stared at the men in terror. They loomed over her, speaking to one another in a language that she was unable to understand, although their leering expressions gave some indication of what they would like to do to her.

Too far away to hear the commotion going on back at the car, Raphael had no idea what was happening. He proceeded in the opposite direction to the one Sum Sum had taken, exploring to see if he could find his bearings and figure out where they had gone wrong. After a while, he saw a light turning on and off in the near distance. Assuming that it was Rajibu signalling to him, he approached it. Instead of finding Rajibu, he found a small mud hut with a very elderly woman dressed in rags, crouching in the doorway.

"What do you want?" the woman addressed him in Hausa. "It is very late in the night for a white man to be walking about this area on his own. What is a man like you doing in a place like this?"

Raphael explained that he was looking for someone and had expected to see Rajibu when he moved towards the flickering light.

"I'll find the man for you," the woman said. "Give me your torch. He was right around here a few minutes ago. Stay here, and I'll go and get him for you."

Raphael handed the woman the torch, and she instructed him to wait in her tiny house while she went to get the man.

"I'll be back in a few minutes," she said. "He's right over here."

Raphael sat and waited. After a few minutes, he realised that something strange was going on. Feeling around in the darkness, he felt a few household implements—and then his hand landed on the side of a ceramic basin and slipped inside. He felt a roughly spherical object, soft on the outside but hard inside. When his finger slipped into the parted mouth, he realised to his revulsion that he was feeling the severed head of a child.

So, he thought, with gathering fear, *the rumours are true. They do kill children here. What sort of people are these?*

In that moment, he realised that the old lady was not just the innocent bystander she seemed but that she had gone to inform someone who wished him ill of his whereabouts. Raphael's mind raced. What should he do, and how could he ensure that he, Nadine, and the men left safely? The last thing he had said to Nadine was that there was no reason for her to worry. How could things have gone so wrong, so quickly? Without his torch, he could not make his way back to the car in pitch blackness. He felt in his pocket and was reassured to find some coins.

I can always try to pay my way out of this situation, he thought. *These are poor people, they might be willing to back off if there's something in it for them.*

Then he thought of his amulet, which as usual he wore on a chain around his neck.

I'll give them whatever they want, he thought, *but they are not getting this.* For the first time in years, he unfastened the clasp and let the heavy medallion fall into his hands.

Where can I hide it? he wondered. *I can't just put it in my pocket. If that old woman has gone to get someone, the first thing they'll do is go through my clothes to see if I have anything of value, and if they do that, my amulet is the first thing they'll find.*

With no other option that he could think of, Raphael put the amulet into the basin containing the severed head. With his heart in his throat, he decided to leave the hut—reasoning that if he was going to be hurt or captured, he might as well face his destiny like a man rather than cowering in an old woman's hut and wondering what was going to happen next.

Without the comforting weight of the amulet around his neck, Raphael walked outside. He had not gone further than a hundred metres when a group of men emerged from the darkness, kicked his feet out from under him, and tied him up. One of them kicked him hard on the side of the head. Then they proceed to tie him to a stretcher, which they used to transport him to the centre of the village.

The last thing Raphael heard before he sank into unconsciousness was one man saying to another: "This is the one we came for. The boss-man will be pleased we've got him, and he'll be sure to give us what he promised now."

Back near the car, Sum Sum had been prodded back to consciousness by his captors, while Nadine had been tied up. The two of them lay on the dusty ground, unable to move and too frightened to talk.

Now that they had captured their pray, the Jinja men seemed almost bored.

"Well," one of them said. "What are we supposed to do with them now? I'd like to have some fun with the woman—I've never had a white woman—but we're not allowed."

"Bring them back to the village?"

"We could just kill him"—the speaker gave Sum Sum a hefty kick for emphasis— "and keep the woman. I'm sure that someone will be prepared to pay a ransom for a white woman like her."

The men agreed that, for the time being, they would break the car's fan belt and carburettor, which would give them some time to unload its contents before anyone could try to take it away, and that they would bring Nadine back to the village, where she could be given food and water while they decided what to do with her.

In the meantime, Rajibu, who had become lost and disoriented, was reassured when he heard someone singing. *Where there's life, there's hope,* he thought. *Finally, someone who can tell us where we are and how to get out of here.*

Always cautious, Rajibu drew near to the sound of the voices. To his dismay, he saw Nadine bound and tied onto a stretcher. She looked confused and upset and was moaning in fear. The singing was coming from the men who were carrying her, who looked very pleased with themselves for having captured such a valuable trophy.

If they have got the naster's woman, he thought, *they must have captured everyone else, too.*

Unsure as to whether Raphael and the other men were dead or alive, Rajibu felt that there was nothing he could do but follow the men as they carried Nadine on a stretcher. Rajibu had grown up in a rural location just like this, and he knew how to track someone without being seen. He stripped off his clothes and hastily rubbed mud on his skin for camouflage, and then he started to track behind the group as they returned to their village. They walked for an hour until they reached their destination.

The Jinja town was an accretion of mud huts arranged in series of twenty or so around courtyards that were shared by a number of families, where housewives processed food, cared for children, and exchanged news. In the middle of the settlement, there was a sort of central plaza which was used for markets and for the annual parade, held to celebrate the sorghum harvest, as sorghum was the primary local crop on which all the people depended for sustenance.

The men carrying Raphael and those who had captured Nadine and Sum Sum all arrived at much the same time, and they gathered in the centre of the marketplace to discuss what to do next. In the very centre, underneath a spreading palm tree, there was a podium on which the local chief sat during parades and ceremonies. The men brought Raphael, Nadine, and Sum Sum to the podium and dumped them there in a heap.

"Well, we've got them, and we've delivered them," one said. "What's going to happen next?"

"They can stay here while we go and tell the boss-man," another, clearly the leader of the little group, decided. "Nobody's going to take them now. They're not going anywhere."

As soon as the captors had left, Rajibu approached from the shadows in which he had been hiding.

"Sir," he whispered. "It's me, Rajibu. I can untie you ..."

"They could come back at any moment," Raphael whispered back. He was conscious now and alert, but his head throbbed terribly, and his legs, arms, and back were painful and bruised from being dragged across the rock-strewn ground. "Even if you have time to untie me and we get away, it's dangerous. They'd probably execute Nadine ... and then they'll catch up with us and get us too."

Nadine was conscious now too, and Raphael was grateful that she could not understand the Hausa that he was using to speak. He hoped that she did not understand the extent of the danger she was in.

"I can't just leave you here and do nothing!"

"No. Look, Rajibu, the best thing you can do is get back to the car. I'm sure they damaged it, but there's a toolbox near the chassis. Get it patched up as best you can and go back to the camp for help. Tell Levalier to come as quickly as he can and to bring two big boxes of coins. I know they like those big Maria Theresa Thaler coins; they consider them lucky charms Money talks, and so does belief, so we can use money to pay our way out of this situation. I'll tell them someone is on the way with the coins, and I'll do my best to negotiate us out of this."

"But sir, it could take me as much as two days to get to the camp and back with the coins. What if they hurt you and madam?"

"It's our best chance. I'm relying on you. Look; Sum Sum is awake now, and he looks okay. Untie him and take him with you. They probably won't bother coming after you, because Nadine and I are the ones they really want."

Swiftly, Sum Sum and Rajibu left the village and raced back to the car, which they managed to repair and get back onto the road before the men came.

Now that he was more alert, with the terrible pain in his head receding slightly, Raphael managed to lurch into a seated position and assess the situation. Things were not looking good. There were very few Europeans in this area. There had been some in the past, but it was not an easy place to live in, and with the suggestion that Nigerian independence was on the way, most of them had retreated to town, leaving the police forces and all the other administrative positions in the hands of the local Africans, all of whom belonged to the fearsome Jinja tribe. In fact, the only white man in the area was Graham, and everyone knew how he felt about Raphael.

Graham. As soon as the name came into Raphael's mind, he understood who was behind his capture. Of course. Hadn't Alhaji warned him that Graham was more dangerous than Raphael could have imagined? Once again, it appeared that Alhaji had been correct.

In his cement house, Graham was waiting on news from his local friends. He was impatient and restless, snapping at the young girls he lived with and pacing up and down. He wanted to see Raphael hurt, and he also wanted to get his fat hands on the amulet, hoping that its power would help him to achieve his goals.

Eventually, a small posse of men from among those who had captured Raphael and Nadine arrived.

"Well," Graham shouted. "Do you have him?"

"He's tied up and waiting for you in the marketplace," one of them said with a laugh. "You can decide his fate for yourself."

"And where's the amulet? Did you bring me the amulet like I told you? That's the most important thing. Without the amulet, there's no point in going to all this effort."

The men exchanged uneasy glances. Graham had told them to bring him an amulet that hung on a gold chain around Raphael's neck, but although they had checked carefully while he lay unconscious on the ground, they had found nothing of the sort.

"Boss, there was no amulet," they said. "We looked everywhere, but there was nothing like you said."

"What the hell am I paying you for?" Graham screamed. "I said perfectly clearly that I wanted the amulet!"

"He's offered to give us Maria Theresa Thaler coins," one of them stated. "He says he has loads of them at his place near the town. We can get him to send someone for them and then kill him anyway. Those are supposed to bring good luck, so it's more or less the same thing anyway."

"It's not the same thing at all!" Graham was shrieking now, sounding and looking increasingly hysterical. "I need the amulet!" he shouted. "Without the amulet, this whole exercise has been completely pointless!"

"We'll find it, sir," the Jinja men said, and they began their return to the place of Raphael's captivity.

Behind them, Graham punched the wall and then turned to take his wrath out on one of the African girls who lived with him. With Raphael's amulet in his possession, he was sure that he could achieve whatever he wanted. Without it, was he doomed to stay in this lousy backwater forever while the man he hated continued to go from strength to strength?

Back in the Jinja town, dawn was breaking, and the local women had awakened to find Raphael and Nadine tied up in the middle of the town. Many of them had never seen a white woman before, and they found Nadine fascinating. They approached her and started to touch her clothes and skin.

"Don't let her go!" one of the older women barked. "If they've been brought here tied up, there's probably a good reason for it. We'll be in trouble if we let them go."

Without any obvious malice, the women untied just Nadine's feet and led her to a chair a short distance from the centre, on which they put her sitting upright. One by one, they removed her clothing until she was wearing nothing but her underwear. At first, Nadine was alarmed and protested against this indignity, but after a few minutes she realised that the women just wanted her clothes. They giggled and admired each other like women in a Parisian boutique as they took turns trying on her blouse, jacket, and shorts. From where he sat, tied to a tree, Raphael could see that Nadine was being brave and managing not to cry, despite the terrifying situation she was in. How he wished he could be free and save her! For now, their only hope of survival was if Sum Sum and Rajibu managed to get back to the camp and alert Levalier on time.

With no care for their comfort, Sum Sum and Rajibu drove the jeep as quickly as they could down the rutted roads. They managed to reach the camp in just under six hours, where they found a very surprised Levalier. As quickly as they could, the two men explained the situation to Levalier, whose visage darkened as he realised just how much trouble Raphael and Nadine were in.

"Boss," said Sum Sum, "I think the situation might be even worse than it seems. The men who captured them kept talking about the amulet—you know, the one that Sir always wears around his neck. That's why they were sent to capture him. Somebody really wants the amulet, and they don't care if they have to kill to get it."

* * *

"What do you want us to do with them?" the Jinja chief asked Graham of Raphael and Nadine. "We can't keep them here forever. Eventually, someone will come looking for them."

The chief was happy with the money Graham had paid him to arrange to have Raphael and his crew taken captive, but he knew that if word got out about it, eventually the British would send police forces to rescue the captives, and then there'd be nothing but trouble.

"I told you," Graham said shortly. "As soon as I've got what I want, you can feed him to the crocodiles. God knows, he's killed enough of them. The crocodile god will be very happy to have him as a sacrifice. You can kill the woman too, though I'd like to have some fun with her first. But nobody is getting killed until I've got what I want."

"The men have looked everywhere …"

"What I say goes," Graham interrupted. "If it comes down to it, who do you think the police are going to believe? You or a white man? I'm a senior member of the police force. Believe me, people would take me a lot more seriously than they would you. Let them be killed when I have got my amulet, and not before."

*   *   *

While Levalier led a group of men to save Raphael and Nadine—the car loaded with boxes of Maria Theresa Thaler coins to use as a ransom—Alhaji rushed to the home of the governor of the region, an African man called Murjan. Hastily, Alhaji explained the situation.

"That's a very problematic area," Murjan said when he heard where Raphael and Nadine were being kept. "Even if they support me politically, it's a backward, difficult sort of a place. The chief there …"

"In this instance," Alhaji interrupted, "I am concerned that the real problem is not the chief or indeed any of the locals but a certain English policeman called Graham who hates Raphael and wants to hurt him. I've heard it said that Graham is encouraging them to return to their old ways and enact human sacrifices, although official policy has always been to stamp out that sort of thing. Sir, I am concerned that, if we don't get there quickly enough, the next sacrifices will be Raphael and his woman companion. There'll be big trouble for you if white people are killed in that way …"

"You're right," the governor said decisively. "It suited the British to turn a blind eye to practices like that because, so long as they went on, they had the excuse they wanted to keep ruling us, pointing to the behaviour of a few fringe elements and suggesting that they are typical of Nigeria. Well, I won't have it!"

With Alhaji still there, the governor called for his aide and ordered him to arrange for troops of soldiers to descend on Graham's region and save the captives.

*   *   *

Raphael and Nadine had been tied up for hours. She had been fed a few bananas and given water, but he had been left largely alone. His face and arms were swollen from all the insect bites he had received. As he sank into delirium, he heard people talking with some excitement about an event that had been planned for later that day.

"There's going to be a parade," one man said. "Dancers, music, and everything. After he's been thrown to the crocodiles, there's going to be a wonderful feast. I can't wait; we haven't had a party like this since the sorghum festival. I'm going to get so drunk …"

Raphael's eyes snapped open, and he was suddenly alert. A parade was planned to celebrate his sacrifice later that day? How could they talk about throwing him to the crocodiles so casually? He was not a religious man, but in that moment, he prayed for his own life and for that of Nadine.

Without the amulet, I am nothing, he thought despairingly. *If only I had it, I know I would be able to get out of this somehow.*

A few hours later, the dancing began. The men were wearing ceremonial costumes and helping themselves to handfuls of food and bottles of sorghum beer that had been laid out for them on tables. As they became progressively drunker, they danced around him in circles, clutching spears that they used as props and singing wildly. The women watched them dance, clapping and occasionally raising their voices in song. Small children ran here and there, wild with the excitement of it all.

Raphael looked around. Where was Nadine? The women had not been treating her too roughly. Perhaps she was all right. No; as his eyes searched for her, they found her. She was being led to a pole in the middle of the marketplace opposite him. Her long hair had been hacked off, and she had blood running down her face from where the knife had scratched her skin. She looked heartbreakingly young and very afraid.

The dancing escalated and then slowed for a moment as a new figure entered the arena—a familiar figure wearing a police uniform onto which an improbable number of medals had been pinned. Graham! With his fat, red face twisted in a sneer, Graham approached Raphael.

"How are you feeling now?" he asked. "Not quite so cocky here, outside your area of influence, are you? You little son of a bitch. I told you not to mess with me. Well, you're in quite a pickle now, aren't you? Who do you think is going to save you now?"

Raphael mustered the strength to spit in Graham's direction. Graham ignored this token gesture of defiance and leaned in to whisper in his ear.

"They worship me here, you know. They treat me like a fucking god. I can get you out of this. All you have to do is tell me where your amulet is, and I will make sure you are freed."

Raphael said nothing. *Is it worth it?* he wondered. *If I tell him where it is, will it save me one more time?*

Then he realised that he was not even sure that the amulet was where he had left it. For all he knew, the basin with the severed head had already been presented to the chief, and the amulet was long gone. Moreover, once he had the amulet, Graham had no reason to keep him alive. Released, Raphael would go to the authorities and tell them what Graham had done. Instead, so long as Graham did not have the amulet, he had a reason not to allow Raphael's sacrifice.

"I'm not telling you where it is," Raphael said defiantly. "If I die now, at least it is with the satisfaction that you have not got what you want."

Graham slapped Raphael across the face.

"I always thought you were stupid," he sneered. "Well, at least I'll get to see you eaten by crocodiles and to have some fun with your lady friend before she meets the same fate. She's not looking so stuck-up now, is she? Usually someone like her wouldn't be interested in a chap like me, but I'm sure she'll be only too happy to do whatever I want if she thinks it's going to keep her alive."

Graham took a seat of honour on the central platform beside the chief, who began to utter a long list of offences that Raphael was said to have committed, from killing the crocodile god to the theft of what he described as a hoard of Maria Theresa Thaler coins.

Wait a moment, Raphael thought. *The chief is trying to tell me something. He is telling me that he doesn't care about the amulet or some stupid story about a crocodile god. All he really wants is a ransom, paid in the form of Maria Theresa Thalers.*

Raphael knew—or hoped—that help was on its way in the form of Levalier and his men, and that they had been instructed to bring a large number of the coveted coins. Perhaps there was a way out after all.

Graham tapped his fingers impatiently on his knee. He wanted to see Raphael slaughtered, but the chief announced that he was going to hold a trial to see if he was really guilty of what he had been accused of. First of all, Nadine was called forward to testify. Addressing her in English, the chief asked if she had seen Raphael kill any crocodiles or steal any coins. Of course, she answered no to both of these questions.

"That's enough," said the chief, clearly annoyed by this turn in the proceedings. "Let's get onto the next phase."

Four men walked forward, gingerly carrying a beehive, while two more approached with a large vat of honey. They smeared the honey all over Raphael's body and then gave the beehive a good kick. Thousands of furious bees swarmed out and began to sting Raphael all over.

"Ha, ha!" Graham laughed as though he was at the theatre to watch a particularly entertaining spectacle. "I've always loved this one!"

Raphael squirmed in pain as every part of his body started to swell and burn in reaction to the beestings. Although he wanted to scream, he forced himself to keep his mouth closed, as he knew that if he opened it, hundreds of bees would swarm inside. If they stung his tongue it would swell, and he would be unable to breathe.

Men danced in a swirling mass around Raphael while the bees stung him. He could hear the steady beat of the drums getting faster and feel the wind created by their grass skirts when they turned in time to the music. He felt as though he was trapped in a nightmare.

Suddenly, Raphael was aware of the sky growing darker. As if from nowhere, a tropical storm began. The heavy rain dispersed the bees, and the cool water relieved his suffering somewhat.

As soon as the rain had abated, the chief ordered his men to rub otter grease all over Raphael's body. While this made the beestings hurt a little less, Raphael's heart sank. He knew that the crocodiles would be attracted to the grease when he was thrown in the water and that he was being prepared for sacrifice.

Then Graham approached again.

"If you've had enough," he said to Raphael with a sadistic smile, "you can always tell me where your amulet is. Like I told you, I might be able to get you out of this if I had it."

"Go to hell," Raphael said. "That's one thing you'll never know. I'd rather die than give you the satisfaction."

Somehow, he found the strength to spit in Graham's face for a second time. The Englishman wiped his face with the back of his hand and gave Raphael a kick.

"Maybe *this* will change your mind," Graham said. He gestured to a space about ten metres away to which Nadine had been dragged. She had been stripped naked and tied to a stretcher, and some of the chief's men were running their daggers down her side—not enough to hurt her badly but breaking the skin just enough to make her bleed. Nadine was being brave, refusing to cry, but Raphael could see that she was terrified.

"Come here, Graham," he said wearily. "I'll tell you where it is …"

Greedily, Graham approached, but just before Raphael was about to speak, gunshots rang out, and Levalier and a small group of heavily armed men stormed the marketplace, the dancers dropping their spears and fleeing as they did.

"Are you all right?" It was Levalier, who had gone straight to Raphael and started to untie him.

"Nadine?" was all Raphael said. "How is Nadine?"

"She's fine. Sum Sum is taking care of her."

Raphael looked over and saw that Sum Sum was tending to Nadine's wounds and that he had pulled a sheet over her to preserve her modesty.

"You got here just in time," Raphael said. "They were about to throw me to the crocodiles."

"I know," Levalier answered grimly. "Even just a few minutes later, and it might have been too late."

Behind Levalier, Graham twisted and writhed in the grip of three armed men.

"It was all him," Raphael said, pointing at Graham. "He wanted to have my amulet, and he got the people here all worked up, telling them that I had stolen this, that, and the other. He's a dangerous piece of shit."

"We were just fooling around!" Graham panted. "Nobody was actually going to feed you to the crocodiles, like they said. It was just a bit of fun, just to get back at you for having me exiled to this arsehole of nowhere place."

The chief was clearly very concerned that he was going to get into trouble.

"What are you going to do with him?" he asked Levalier, indicating Graham. "Is he going to stand trial?"

Levalier looked to Raphael for guidance. All Raphael wanted was for this sorry episode to end.

"We're not going to do anything," Raphael said, "so long as you ensure that he never works here again. I think it's time for him to go back home to England."

"I'll go, I'll go," Graham blubbered. "Just please don't hurt me, I beg you."

At a nod from Raphael, two of Levalier's men approached carrying a heavy box, which they laid carefully on the ground in front of the chief.

Raphael spoke again.

"Your majesty," he said formally, "while neither I nor my people have ever stolen anything from you or yours, we would like to offer you this box containing one hundred Maria Theresa Thaler coins in thanks for our safe release."

The chief nodded solemnly and collected the coins. "You are free to go," he said grandly, as though he had not been arranging to have Raphael thrown to the crocodiles just a few minutes before.

As soon as he could, Raphael rushed to the hut where he had left his amulet. He looked all over the room, but the basin containing the head was gone—and so was the amulet.

"God damn it to hell!"

Raphael had managed to stay strong during the whole ordeal but now, for the first time in years, he felt like crying.

The old woman must have found the amulet and told someone, he thought. *It's gone.*

Outside, Raphael could see that Nadine had been brought clothes. She was dressed, and while she still looked pale and frightened, he could see that she was already beginning to feel better. She was a resilient woman. Before too long, this horrible ordeal would have become a wonderful story to tell her friends. Raphael could only hope that he would be able to recover as quickly as he knew she would.

"Where is Graham?" Raphael asked the chief.

"He's already left, and I will send a messenger to Maiduguri to tell the governor that we no longer accept him in our area. If he ever comes back here, we will see that he is expelled immediately … or worse."

"Your highness," said Raphael, "I ask your permission to examine Graham's quarters. I have good reason to think that he has something that belongs to me, and I want to get it back before I go."

Now that he had his Maria Theresa Thaler coins, the chief was all smiles and very inclined to help. "Of course, of course!" he said. "Anything you want!"

"I'm coming with you, Raphael," said Nadine. "I don't want to be away from you at the moment."

"That's fine."

"I'll come too, boss," said Sum Sum.

The chief ordered one of the men to bring Raphael, Nadine, and Sum Sum to Graham's house, and they were led across the square to a low concrete building that had served as both his home and his office. The little girls he lived with had fled, and inside, it was a squalid mess, with empty beer bottles everywhere and large black flies buzzing over half-eaten plates of food. A crumpled letter on the table bore a heading in Arabic. Raphael picked it up and scanned it quickly. Someone from Saudi Arabia had been writing to Graham, but the contents of the letter were vague, referring to a package that Graham was supposed to send his correspondent. The page was smeared with grease and food remnants from Graham's last meal. Raphael remembered Alhaji's comments about Graham being just like a pig. It seemed that he was a pig in more ways than one. He threw the letter back onto the table in disgust.

"What are we looking for, boss?" Sum Sum asked.

Raphael did not want to tell him that he was searching for the amulet.

"I just want to make sure that everything is in order," he said. "Let's start looking in this room."

Raphael and Sum Sum began opening every drawer and searching in every nook and cranny while Nadine explored the rest of the house. Raphael heard her move around, pause, and then, after a moment, scream.

"Come here!" she shouted. "Graham is here … and I think he's dead!"

Raphael rushed into the filthy living room and saw for himself that Graham was lying on the floor, face down, with a knife buried in his back. Quickly, he felt to see if there was a pulse in the large man's neck. Nothing.

"We're going to have to report this murder," Raphael said. "Along with the fact that these people have apparently been practicing human sacrifice at Graham's behest. The usual formalities will have to be observed, but I don't think anyone is going to miss him very much."

Then Raphael noticed something glittering in Graham's hand. Could it be …? Was it possible that he had found his precious amulet after all? He bent down and removed the shiny object from Graham's stiffening fingers.

"What is it, Raphael?" Nadine asked. "Did you find something you were looking for?"

"No," said Raphael grimly. "It's nothing."

He pocketed the gold chain. It was his chain, all right, but the precious amulet that usually hung from it was gone. Someone else had been here first, presumably one of the chief's men, gathering the amulet before Raphael could find it.

"Let's get out of here," Raphael said. "I want to go home."

"Me too," said Nadine, shuddering. "I never want to see this awful place again. I think I've got over my interest in hunting."

Hand in hand, Raphael and Nadine left Graham's house and began their journey back to the safety of the camp.

"I think I rather like my hair short," said Nadine. "I might just tidy it up and keep it this way after all."

2017

"Wow," said Rebecca. "So that's how he lost it. Sounds like a film or something."

"Yes," said Richard. "It's hard to believe that human sacrifice was still going on in the 1950s. But who knows? Maybe there are still some parts of the world where it happens today."

"Hang on," said David. "That explains how the amulet was stolen, but how long was it gone for, and when did he get it back?"

"Ah," said Richard. "Now that's another story. But while we're talking about Africa, I was thinking of another topic ... Grandad's complicated relationship with love ..."

1953

After what had happened among the Jinja, Raphael felt uneasy. He couldn't shake off the feeling that there was an enemy in his midst. Things had changed between him and Nadine, too. She didn't give him the space he needed and followed him everywhere. Gradually, he realised that it was time for things to change.

Raphael did not want to embarrass Nadine by sending her away, so he suggested that the two of them visit the south of France for a short holiday.

"That's just what we need after all we've been through," said Nadine, delighted. "I love the south of France!"

The next week, the two flew to Paris and took a train to Cannes, where Raphael secured a driver and a car to take them up and down the beautiful azure coast. They stayed in the finest hotels and dined on the best French food. Nadine looked lovely in the white sleeveless dresses she liked to wear in the warm southern climate, and they made love every night. It should all have been wonderful, but Raphael felt uneasy. He was impatient with himself for missing his amulet as he did; he considered himself a rational man, and he didn't like to think of the loss of an object holding so much sway over his mood. He also knew that he had to break up with Nadine, and he was dreading it— partly because he knew that he would miss her, but also because he was afraid how she would react.

He couldn't shake off the feeling that something was wrong, and it was hard for him to separate his feelings of anxiety about Nadine with the more general sense of loss he had been suffering since his amulet had been stolen. One night he dreamt that an unseen force picked up his bed and sent him flying through the air. He was immobile, powerless to move. From nowhere, a voice proclaimed: "Your amulet is with you. It's there."

"No," Raphael said in the dream. "I don't have it."

"No, it's there with you," the voice replied.

With a start, he woke up, bathed in sweat, his heart beating wildly. *It's nothing,* he told himself. *Just a dream. It doesn't mean anything.*

But he got no more sleep that night. When she woke, Raphael told Nadine his dream. She looked impatient.

"It's time for you to let go of the whole thing," she said, almost crossly. "It's in the past now. Just get on with your life. It's just a little piece of jewellery, after all. It's not really important."

On the last night of their holiday, Raphael arranged for them to stay in a particularly lovely hotel with a view of the blue Mediterranean Sea. Little waves lapped against the beach, and the scent of jasmine filled the air as they enjoyed their meal. Nadine was looking as lovely as always, with a flower tucked behind her ear, but Raphael had lost his appetite and found it hard to make conversation.

"What's wrong, darling?" Nadine asked solicitously. "You are so quiet. Are you upset because it's the last day of the holiday?"

"I'm fine," he lied. "Let's just finish our meal and get to the train station."

Raphael had arranged for Nadine to take the overnight train to Paris. She thought that he would be joining her, but she would be travelling on her own. When she got to the capital, she would find that all of her belongings from Africa had been packed and sent to her apartment. Raphael was going to stay in the south of France for a few more days before flying back to Nigeria. He could let her find out that he had left her when she got to Paris and saw all her possessions, or he could do the honourable thing and tell her his intentions before that. He decided that he didn't want to spoil their last meal together and that he didn't want to be underhanded. They would have that difficult conversation at the train station.

A taxi took them to the station. Nadine stepped out of the car and straightened her dress while Raphael paid for the fare. They made their way to the luggage office, to which he had arranged for Nadine's cases to be brought from their hotel.

"Where are your things, Raphael?" asked Nadine as he retrieved the cases and motioned for a porter to bring them to the train.

"I'm not coming, Nadine," said Raphael simply. "I'm going back to Nigeria on my own. Our story has come to an end."

Nadine stared at him.

"What are you talking about?" she said in a very quiet voice. "Are you losing your mind?"

"I've always been straight with you. I'm not looking for a serious relationship; you've known that from the start. I'm going to marry a girl from among my own people one day. We've had a lot of fun, and we've been through a great deal together, but it's all just getting to be too much. It's not fair to either of us to let things go on as they are."

Nadine dissolved into tears. Raphael took her into his embrace and steeled himself not to relent. He knew that she wanted him to change his mind, and it took all his willpower not to do so.

"You can't do this to me!" Nadine sobbed. "How dare you take me on holiday and pretend that everything is fine when you were planning this all along!"

"I'm not doing anything to you," he said. "I'll always remember you fondly. I just wanted to give you a special experience to end our relationship."

"You complete and utter *bastard*!" she screamed, suddenly furious. "How dare you lead me on like this!"

"I didn't …" he protested. "I've always been perfectly honest."

"Well, let me tell you this," she said. "You haven't seen the last of me. I know you think that this is over, but there's no way. what we have is special. You'll come back to me; I know you will."

"Darling, I won't …" said Raphael.

But Nadine, drying her tears from her face with the back of her hand, was already walking away from him.

1953-4

Back in Nigeria, Raphael did whatever he could to shake off his yearning for Nadine and to manage the suspicions that overcame him from time to time about all the people he had cared for and respected since coming to Nigeria: Levalier, Sum Sum, Rajibu, and even Ghandi. He immersed himself in his work and accepted every social invitation he was offered, while hosting many more. In his quiet alone times, he could not help thinking of Nadine and how much he missed her, so he made sure he had as few of those as possible. Above all, he accepted almost every invitation he received to make love with the women of the expatriate community of Maiduguri. And there were many.

An impotent man, tortured because he found himself unable to make love to his new wife, committed suicide. The widow sought solace with Raphael before returning to her home country. Afterwards, a man with similar issue came to Raphael for help. He was petrified at the thought of deflowering his virgin bride and unable to perform. Once she had spent a night with Raphael, his anxieties abated, and the marriage was able to continue normally. Another lover was a married woman from Ireland whose husband was Scottish. Maire was quite clear what she wanted: access to a young man who would make love to her, because her husband was useless in bed.

So far as Raphael was concerned, these women were a gift from God. He let them take advantage of his young body and his natural lust as often as they wanted; it distracted him from the ache in his heart that he had suffered ever since he had sent Nadine away. He knew that he had done the right thing, but it still hurt far more than he had expected. He focused as hard as he could on making money and took some pleasure in seeing his bank accounts swell, telling himself that when he had proved himself, he would be ready to marry and settle down. For now, he just had to get on with things.

2017

"Well," said David. "That Nadine did quite a number on poor old Grandad. I mean, obviously he eventually managed to get over her, but it's almost like she had cast a spell on him."

"I can't help seeing it from her point of view as well, though," said Rebecca. "She loved him. She probably thought he'd get married to her one day. She must have been devastated when he sent her back to Paris."

"He had been honest with her from day one," Richard reminded his sister. "He never told her that he would marry her. She should have known better than to let herself get so involved."

"Even still. When a woman's in love, she'll see signs of commitment even if there aren't really any," Rebecca replied. If you're saying that she did a number on him—well, to be fair, he did a number on her too."

CHAPTER 16

THE IRRESISTIBLE ALLURE OF NADINE

2017

"OK," said Richard. "So, as you've gathered, Grandad was *quite* the man for the ladies back in the day, to say the least! He knew that one day he would be getting married to the girl who had been chosen for him—no, I won't forget to tell that story, I'm getting around to it—but while he was in Nigeria, he was young, good-looking, and far from the prying eyes of his relatives and the conservative mores of the community in which he had grown up. So he figured, why not have as much fun as he could in the meantime? And who can blame him? Not me! Africa was a playground for a guy like him at the time. Really, there were girls of every type; someone for every possible taste. The idea was to play around and not to get too attached, but he couldn't get Nadine out of his mind."

"I wonder what she had that was so special?" asked David. "I mean, what made her so much better than all the other pretty girls living in Maiduguri? I'm sure there wasn't exactly a shortage of them!"

"Well, Grandad did give a glowing description of her looks and abilities in bed, but in addition to that, she seemed to have some sort of a hold on him that he could never understand …"

1954–5

Raphael hadn't seen Nadine for a whole year, but for some reason she was always on his mind. He had been worried about getting too close to her, perturbed by the way she was able to manipulate him, and concerned about the fact that none of his close associates in the compound seemed to like and trust her very much. But after she had gone, he dreamt of her at night, and often during the day her face and the timbre of her voice came to mind when he was busy working and should have been concentrating on what he was doing. He had been determined not to get too close to her because he didn't want to have a serious relationship, and when she had left he had been determined never to see her again. But this girl … this girl seemed to be different. His memories of Nadine were like a ghost haunting and surrounding him with its fragrant presence—and no matter how hard he tried, he did not seem to be able to banish her from his mind or his heart.

Raphael kept himself busy with work and other women in and around the camp in Maiduguri, but when a trip to Paris came up, it seemed as though destiny was telling him that he just had to see Nadine again. It was as though she was a magnet and he the metal ore that was irresistibly drawn to it. She was the north pole, and he was the compass. It was almost as though she had cast a spell on him. Had he believed in witchcraft, he could easily have swallowed the notion that she was a mistress of the dark arts.

Raphael made a reservation at the Grand Hotel, telling himself that this choice had nothing to do with the fact that Nadine's hair salon was located on the ground floor of the same building. *It's one of the finest hotels in Paris,* he told himself. *I'm giving myself a treat because I can afford it, and because I've been working so hard. It's nothing to do with Nadine. I'm done with her. I probably won't even drop in on her at all. I'm through with her!* But even as he said those words to himself, he knew they were a lie. He was as drawn to her as a moth to a flame and while he did have some business to attend to in Paris, it was nothing that could not have been done remotely. Nadine was the real reason for the trip.

Raphael arrived at the hotel and checked in. He went to his room, where he took a long hot shower and changed from his crumpled travel clothes into a smart French suit. He looked at himself in the mirror as he carefully dressed his hair and felt confident that he looked more than good enough to strut the streets of Paris and find himself some female company.

You could have any woman you want tonight, he told himself. *Just go out and meet someone pretty. It's easy in Paris. There are loads of pretty girls, and most of them aren't averse to having an adventure with a handsome stranger, even if they are married. You've done it before. There's no need for you to go chasing after Nadine. She's yesterday's news. You'd be better off leaving her in the past.*

But even as he gave himself a pep talk, Raphael knew that he was going to Nadine before he did anything else. He had known it since he planned the trip to Paris, which had always been about her and his burning desire to see her and be buried in her flesh. He had the strangest feeling that she was expecting him or might even know that he was already in Paris. He finished adjusting his hair and went downstairs to the salon.

Raphael pushed open the door to the warm, fragrant room where Nadine was attending to the hair of an expensively dressed woman who was perusing the latest edition of a top-end fashion magazine. Nadine was wearing a plain black blouse and a slim pair of Capri pants that showed her beautiful figure off to perfection. Her fair hair, which had grown back after being hacked off during the kidnapping, was tied up on the back of her head in an elaborate knot, fastened with a pretty mother-of-pearl pin that glistened against her silky locks.

As soon as she heard the door, Nadine dropped the scissors she was holding and ran to Raphael, her arms outstretched. To the immense surprise of the lady whose coiffure she had been tending, she rushed across the room and wrapped first her arms around his neck and then her legs around his waist in a double embrace. It did not escape his attention that, despite the thin layers of fabric between them, her genitals were now directly over his, reminding him of the many times they had been even closer to one another. He closed his arms around her, relishing the sensation of her warm weight against his body.

"I *knew* you would come back to me," she cried. "I just knew it. Nothing could have kept you from me. Even after a whole year apart,

I have never stopped thinking of you and feeling sure that you would return to me. I didn't doubt it for a moment."

Raphael's heart glowed. He had been sure that he would never see Nadine again, but now that he could feel her wrapped around him, he wondered where that conviction was coming from. Why would he not want to be with this glorious woman? To sink into her, body and soul, and to wake in the morning to see her beautiful face on the pillow beside him? Deep inside, a little voice told him to be careful, that she could be dangerous to him and his plans, but he was also filled with the overpowering urge to be with her; to see, feel, and smell her; and to possess that body he remembered so well with every part of himself.

"How did you know that you would see me again?" Raphael asked as Nadine covered his face in kisses. "When we parted the last time, I told you that it was the last time you would see me—and I meant it, too. I'm not even sure why I came here tonight. I wasn't really planning to."

"Oh, don't worry about that," said Nadine, climbing down from their embrace and gesturing to let her client know that she would return in a moment, just as soon as she had concluded her personal business. "I just knew, all right? And here you are now, and that is all that matters. I was right. Look at you! You are as handsome as ever— even more handsome, in fact! I guess you must just get better with each year that passes! It's true what they say: a handsome man is like a great vintage of wine."

At the back of his mind, Raphael felt uneasy. He sensed that Nadine had some sort of power over him, but he didn't understand what or why. Right now, he just knew that he wanted her more than anything else in the world. For now, he pushed the uneasy feeling to the back of his mind. He told himself that it was not rational and decided not to think about it.

"Let me finish here," said Nadine, indicating her customer. "And then I will cancel the rest of today's reservations, my darling, and dedicate myself entirely to you. You must be exhausted after travelling all the way from Africa! Let me do what I can to make you comfortable in true Parisian style."

"There's no need for that," Raphael demurred, although he didn't really mean it. "I don't want to interfere with your plans."

"Interfere? How could you interfere? At this moment, Raphael, nothing is more important than you! Honestly, for as long as you are here, I want you to know that you will be the absolute centre of my world."

The pair arranged to meet in a couple of hours when Nadine had finished taking care of her customer, and Raphael went to attend to business. As he left, she had picked her scissors back up again and bent over the head of her client, who looked as though she had enjoyed the unscheduled entertainment.

Nadine was stunning in a simple black sheath dress and pearls when she met Raphael in the lobby of the hotel that evening. He felt proud when she walked across to the room to him and all the men around could see that she was with him. He could see the envy on their faces and sensed their eyes on him and Nadine as they embraced and got ready to leave the lobby.

"I'm staying for a week," he told her as they left through the heavy front doors of the hotel. "Do you think you can spare a little time to look around Paris with me?"

"I've already taken the week off," she purred. "I was hoping that you would be here for a while."

That night, they dined on steak at the Café de Paris and then retired to Raphael's room to renew their acquaintance on a more intimate level. He had spent the whole evening looking forward to the moment when they would be alone together, so much so that he had barely tasted a morsel of the delicious food at the restaurant. The taste he really wanted to feel on his lips was that of Nadine.

"I feel a little shy," said Nadine when they were alone together at last. She perched on the edge of the enormous hotel bed and looked up at him with her huge blue eyes. "It has been so long, hasn't it? What if you don't like me anymore? Have you forgotten what my body looks like? Perhaps it is no longer to your taste. Maybe you prefer the dark-skinned African girls now, or those English ladies who go around in Maiduguri looking for fun and will do anything after a few cocktails too many. You don't need to ask the same of me. I remember the feel of your arms and the taste of your mouth as though I had experienced both yesterday. But you—you're a man, and everybody knows that men are far fickler than women."

"You are even more beautiful than you were when I saw you last," Raphael reassured her. "And all evening, the only thing that I have been able to think of is what you look like under that dress. Believe me, I remember the feel and shape of your body very well. I just wonder if anything has changed or if it is all as I recall. At the risk of sounding bold, I am hoping that you are going to let me find out."

"Well then," said Nadine. "Perhaps you had better unzip me and see what you discover. I think that you won't be disappointed."

She turned around and presented her slim back and shapely derriere, covered in the fine black linen of her dress. Her hair was piled up on her head, and the nape of her neck was slender and looked impossibly fragile with the string of pearls around it. Raphael started to unbutton the long row of small mother-of-pearl buttons that fastened her dress at the back, wondering how she had managed to get into it by herself. Nadine stood perfectly still as he worked, but he could sense the changing intensity of her breathing and the fact that she was getting quite aroused.

When the last of her buttons had been undone, Nadine stood before Raphael in her underwear. She turned around to face him and stood, her arms hanging down by her sides and her slim feet turned slightly inwards, like a small child waiting for her bath to be drawn.

"Well," she said. "What do you think? Do you still like me?"

His eyes explored her body: her small pointed breasts with delicate pink nipples, so firm and dainty that she had no need to wear a brassière; slim thighs and arms; and the flimsy piece of red silk that was the only thing that concealed her sex. She raised her arms and removed the pins that were holding her hair in place, letting the thick blonde locks tumble around her pretty shoulders.

"You are literally the only thing I want to look at right now," he said, his voice thick with desire and longing. "Right now, you are my everything."

Raphael moved as if to go towards her, but she put out a finger in admonishment.

"Don't move a muscle," she said. "Just stay there and let me come to you. I know how to take care of you, and I remember exactly what you need."

With deft fingers, Nadine removed Raphael's clothes until he was wearing as little as she was. Even if he had wanted to conceal his intentions, his body betrayed him. It was very clear how aroused Raphael was feeling as Nadine removed the rest of his clothing and pressed her warm, lithe body against his.

"Welcome home," Nadine whispered. "Now I am yours and you are mine, and nobody can tear us apart."

Hours later, Nadine lay in Raphael's arms. The curtains were open, and the faint light from the streetlamps outside caressed both their bodies—which, dewy with perspiration after their feverish lovemaking, lay atop the heavy linen sheets. The high-ceilinged room seemed to still resonate with the sounds of their passionate cries and moans. Raphael had renewed his acquaintance with every centimetre of Nadine's glorious body, and it was just as perfect as it had been a year ago, while the lovemaking was even better, as though they were now connecting on a level that went far beyond the merely physical.

"This reminds me of what it was like before," said Raphael. "Just you and me, always so much at ease with one another. Do you remember? We never had to speak to each other to ask what the other wanted; we just knew. We both know that we are not made for each other to have forever, but at least for now, everything is perfect."

"How could I forget what it was like before? You know that I left a big piece of my heart with you, Raphael. I have been waiting for this moment since we left, and I never stopped doubting that you would return to me. It is a dream come true having you back here with me now. I can't believe that you are here for a whole week. Just think of what we can do in a week!"

Nadine pointedly ignored Raphael's final comment. He had often told her that when the time came for him to get married, it would be to one of his own people. While she had never asked him to marry her, she still seemed to find this finality difficult to accept. He hoped that there wouldn't be another scene like the one in the train station a year ago and decided to simply not think about it.

Eventually, they both slept. Nadine sank into the deep and dreamless sleep of a small child, but despite his exertions, Raphael was restless. He tossed and turned in the thin strip of light that fell across the bed—they had left the curtains open and a street lamp burned dimly outside—never quite waking but tantalised by glimpses of his lost amulet that he was at pains to understand.

Raphael had various meetings to attend that week, but he was free to spend most of his time with Nadine. All that week, Paris was their playground—and what a playground it was! Raphael had loved Paris since his first visit, but the more he saw of it, the more he felt that this was a city he had really taken to his heart. It seemed to have everything—elegance, style, wonderful cuisine, and gorgeous women as far as the eye could see. When he glimpsed a beauty wearing a crocodile-skin court shoe or carrying a crocodile-skin bag, he could not help but wonder if the skin had come from his camp in Maiduguri. How extraordinary that a creature as stupid and vicious as a crocodile could be used to make such fragile and dainty symbols of Parisian femininity!

Two nights in a row, Nadine and Raphael went to the *Folies Bergère*, the French theatre of such great renown, where the stage was filled with beautiful women of all colours and backgrounds whose costumes revealed far more than they concealed. Raphael felt quite sure that none was even nearly as beautiful as his gorgeous companion. Nadine's beautiful little breasts—one perfectly filled his cupped hand—were far perter and prettier than those on the stage, he thought, and her behind ... well, a poet might write a sonnet about it, or a theologian might find in it proof of the existence of God!

Nadine enjoyed looking at the beautiful women just as much as he did. While some women might have been jealous of a man who relished looking at scantily clad lovelies, she knew that she could easily compete with the beauties on the stage, and she found a sensual delight in admiring the other women's curves and long, sleek limbs.

The young pair went to the Left Bank, where they joined the throngs of young people flocking to soak in the bohemian atmosphere and enjoy the paintings of the many artists who exhibited in the area. No matter how hard he tried, Raphael could not get enough of Nadine's honeyed lips. If an hour had passed without a kiss, he began to feel quite frantic until he had remedied the situation. They walked hand in hand, their fingers entwined, and their pace perfectly matched. In the evenings, they feasted on the most marvellous meals Paris had to offer, and by night they feasted on one another.

After five days, with Raphael's week in Paris drawing to a close, the pair decided to visit Barbizon, where they picnicked on the river, rented a boat to row on the water, and watched the Parisians on a day out, all dressed beautifully. There were parents flying kites with their children, grand old ladies taking small dogs for a walk at the end of elegant long leashes, and courting couples who had eyes only for each other. It was all exquisite.

After an afternoon of fun, Raphael and Nadine spread their picnic blanket out under a tree and sat down on the ground for a rest. Nadine lay her head in Raphael's lap, and he looked down at her pretty face, noticing how the dapples of sunlight on her skin moved when the breeze fluttered the leaves on the tree overhead. *Women are God's masterpiece*, he thought to himself. *Look at her; she's absolutely perfect.*

"These days have gone by so quickly," said Raphael. "When I arrived in Paris, a week seemed like ever such a long time stretching out in front of us. But now this week is nearly over, and in a couple of days I will be flying back to the heat and dust of Africa, to my hunters and crocodile skins, to my camp and my hours of work, and to the constant quest to make as much money as I can. And you will be returning to your perfumes and powders and your elegant ladies with their expensive coiffures."

"Well," said Nadine, "if you just say the word, it doesn't have to be like that. We could decide to do things a little differently."

"What do you mean?"

"I mean that I could come back to Africa again. I could ask my partner to take care of the salon for a while and come and stay with you. We don't have to be restricted to just a week. We can spend as long as we want. You know, since we were last together, I have been involved with a man. There have been times when I felt as though I loved him, but he's not good for me. He's married, and he is never going to leave his wife. He says he loves me, but I know that she's really the one for him and that he's only playing around with me and my feelings because he's bored of being a husband and father and is using me to have a little fun. To tell you the truth, it would be good to go to Africa to forget about him—and, above all, to spend more time with you, my only darling. It would be a dream come true."

Raphael had resolved not to get too close to Nadine, but as she looked up at him, so earnestly and with so much longing in her face, he could feel his resolve weaken. *After all,* he thought, *what harm could it do? She knows that I will never be able to marry her, but I care for her so much. Who could resent us having the opportunity to spend more time together?*

"Come back to Africa?" he asked, stalling for time. "Are you sure that's what you want to do?"

"More than anything. I know that one day you will be marrying one of your own people, and I understand that, but imagine how lovely it would be if I could just stay with you for longer. We would be able to do everything together. Raphael, it would be wonderful. You know it would. Say that I can come, and I will be the happiest woman in Paris."

"Aren't you afraid after what happened the last time? I thought you'd never want to go to Africa again after all that."

"Afraid, me? Pfffff." Nadine dismissed this notion with a toss of her hand. "In the end, nothing happened, did it? And what did happen was all because of Graham, and now Graham is dead and can't hurt us anymore. I'd love to come back to Africa with you. In fact, I'd give my right breast for it, if I didn't think you'd miss it too much."

What is this strange power she has over me? Raphael wondered. *I know that it is not a good idea to get too close, and yet I do not seem to be able to resist. She only has to say what she wants, and I feel immediately bound to do it.*

"Well then," he said, "let's do it. I'm not married yet, and I would certainly enjoy the opportunity to keep you in my embrace for a little longer."

Two days later, a triumphant Nadine swung her handbag as she crossed the tarmac at the Charles de Gaulle airport, hand in hand with Raphael. He had agreed to her proposal to bring her to Africa and had purchased for her a one-way ticket, as it seemed likely that she would stay for quite some time. Their luggage had been collected from the hotel earlier that day, and they were on their way to Maiduguri. Nadine was happy, her face glowing with a wide smile, as though she had won a prize. It occurred to Raphael to wonder how she had managed to convince him so quickly to do what she wanted, but he pushed that thought to one side. It felt good to see all the men at the airport watch them together and know that he was envied by each and every one.

Raphael had arranged for them to fly with *Union Aéromaritime de Transport*, a French airline that he had taken before. He always enjoyed VIP treatment with UAT because he was a regular client of their first-class service—and because he knew the CEO of the company and had dined with him in Paris on various occasions. He knew that Nadine would enjoy the special treatment that he was guaranteed on board. As soon as Nadine and Raphael took their seats, a smiling hostess brought them each a glass of champagne and offered it to them on a tray, along with a heavy linen napkin that they could use to wipe their mouths after drinking.

"It is very nice to have you on board, sir," said the smiling girl. "And if there is anything that you or madame need, you only have to ask. I've been told that you are a regular customer and that we are to take very special care of you. Just remember that we're here to serve! It doesn't matter how small or big your request is, we will do our best to ensure that it is fulfilled."

"Why, Raphael," Nadine whispered. "It's as if they know you or think that you are some kind of famous actor or something. I feel as though I am a celebrity too!"

Nadine drained her champagne in one greedy mouthful and, with a cheeky grin, summoned the hostess and asked for more.

The plane journey passed quickly. Raphael and Nadine held hands and talked about their plans for Africa, each of them carefully avoiding the topic of how long they could expect to stay together.

When the plane touched down in Fort Lamy, Nadine was further astonished when the local French customs officials greeted Raphael with warm smiles and handshakes and, instead of asking to see his passport, said, "Welcome to the country, sir," and waved him on with a considerable degree of pomp and ceremony. There was no customs building, as the airport was so tiny, so the officials came to the planes as they landed to stamp passports and grant permission to enter. Seeing that Nadine was with him, they did not ask for her passport either.

Raphael strode through the airport like a king. As he knew that someone was taking care of his luggage, they made their way straight to the waiting car. If he had been alone, he would have spent a night at a local hotel run by a distant relative, but now that Nadine was with him, he wanted to get back to the camp as soon as possible, to show her all that he had achieved in her absence and to enjoy her wonderful body in the surroundings of his own property.

"I can't believe it, Raphael," said Nadine. "What have you done to these people to make them all respect you so much? Have you been made king or something and not told me?"

"I'm a *patron*," explained Raphael. "I make money and provide jobs in the area, so in return the people treat me, and by extension you, with respect and honour."

Raphael was not boasting, just describing the reality of the situation, but he had to admit—if only to himself—that it felt very good.

"Well," Nadine said, "I definitely feel like a princess right now, and I could certainly get used to this treatment very quickly!"

"You *are* a princess," Raphael reassured her. "At least so far as I'm concerned. But while the camp is more comfortable than ever, it's not exactly a palace. You'll have to help me make it even better by introducing some of your Parisian style. We've slipped a little in that regard since you were here last."

Raphael and Nadine sat into the back seat of the waiting car, and he ordered the driver to take them to Maiduguri. He felt expansive and stretched his arm across the back of the seat, nestling it protectively against Nadine. He was with his woman—or at least his woman for now—and life was good. He had made a conscious decision not to explore the extraordinary hold she had over him and his affections. He didn't know what it meant, but he didn't feel ready to look into it right now.

As they drove, Raphael told Nadine what life was like in the compound now.

"It is so comfortable, you won't miss the luxuries of Paris," he assured her. "I have the best linen and tableware, and Gandhi is very competent, though I would appreciate it if you would teach him some more French recipes, as his repertoire is still a bit limited. I know that he would like to learn too; considering the conditions that he is used to working in, it is obvious that he has a real talent for the kitchen. He does his best, and I'm sure he's more than capable of getting even better."

"I'd be delighted!" said Nadine. "You know how I love fine food, and it's exciting, teaching an African man all about French cuisine. Maybe we can even invent some new recipes, like goat *a l'orange*! I do remember how much goat people eat in Africa. I'm looking forward to some, actually, although I got sick of it eventually the last time."

Raphael was astonished when, as the car approached the main gates to Maiduguri—the town was accessed by a dirt road and there was a wide-open gate through which all vehicles had to pass—Sum Sum and Rajibu came rushing towards him with expressions of great concern on their faces as they waved the car down.

"Sir, sir!" they panted. "You got here just in time. There's big trouble at the compound. They've taken the staff hostage and now they are demanding money, saying that otherwise they are going to kill them all, starting with Ghandi!"

Nadine went pale.

"Raphael," she said, "what is happening? I thought you told me that the compound is safe. This doesn't sound safe at all. Don't tell me that we're going to get kidnapped again!"

"Slow down," Raphael instructed the agitated men. "Explain to me exactly what is going on."

Sum Sum quickly explained that armed men—militants from the local countryside, armed with machetes—had stormed into the camp, threatened all of the staff, and tied them all up. Now they were rampaging around the camp with machetes, demanding enormous ransoms in return for the hostages. The implicit threat was that they would rape, kill, or maim anyone who was not paid for.

"I'm not standing for this," said Raphael. "This can't be. We'll have to take control back straight away. Where is Levalier?" Raphael asked the men. "Why wasn't he there watching over the camp?"

They explained that it was Levalier's day off and that he had gone to a nearby village where there was a woman he liked. So far as they knew, he had no idea what was happening. In fact, they themselves were supposed to have been on watch, but they had let their guard down.

Deciding to deal with Sum Sum and Rajibu later on, when he knew exactly what had happened, Raphael arranged for the driver to take Nadine to the home of a friend of his in the town, where she would be safe until the situation had returned to normal, and then he and the two African men rushed to Levalier to tell him what had happened and put together a plan to regain control of the compound and oust the usurpers.

"Listen," Raphael said after filling in Levalier on the situation back at the camp. "I have three guns, and I know that you have one. We're not going to be able to get our hands on more at short notice, so grab all the ammunition you can get and let's go. We'll get the police to back us up, but we won't rely on them to do everything. They have no skin in the game, and I'm damned if I am going to let the militants take everything I have worked for and hurt my staff in the process."

Raphael sent Sum Sum and Rajibu to the native town to summon the police as backup, and the police quickly assembled a team of thirty men with guns who joined Raphael and Levalier as they headed towards the camp. As they approached, they shot into the air to let the attackers know that they were arriving. The absence of a return volley of shots was proof that the attackers had no guns but were armed with just machetes.

"Well," said Raphael. "At least that is some good news. Hopefully we will be able to overpower them before they manage to hurt anyone."

Without hesitating, Raphael and Levalier, accompanied by the thirty men who had been assembled by the police, stormed into the camp, shooting as they went. The apparent leader of the men stood on the roof and shouted that they would not give in without a hefty ransom, but he was shot immediately and died on the spot. His body jerked in response to the bullets that hit and penetrated it. He stood still for a moment and then plummeted to the ground, removing several slates from the roof in the process. The body hit the ground with a heavy thud and then lay still in a grotesque position that would have been impossible for anyone still alive. The militants did not stand a chance with just their machetes. Two more were badly injured, and all of the rest were taken into custody and sent to prison.

Surveying the situation in the camp, Raphael was glad to see that few things had been broken and that the intruders had not interfered with the crocodile skins (he also noted happily that the hunters had continued to deliver skins while he was in Paris and that he only needed a few more to reach a full shipment). Even more importantly, the hostages were restrained and frightened but had not been harmed. Sum Sum and Rajibu rushed to untie the staff members.

Gradually, the full story of the raid emerged. The camp had been quiet, because Raphael had not returned yet from Paris, and Levalier was taking a day off. The women were taking care of the washing and were cleaning the house, and Sum Sum and Rajibu were on watch—or at least they were supposed to be. But things had been so quiet in the area for so long that Sum Sum and Rajibu had let their guard down, and when the marauders came, they were not paying attention. In fact, they had wandered off to chat to some of their friends, and the first they heard of the trouble was when the neighbours informed them that marauders had taken over the camp.

Panicked, Sum Sum and Rajibu had returned to the area to find out exactly what was going on. They quickly learned that the men had speeded up to the camp in a jeep and, on finding it unattended, leapt down and quickly subdued the small staff inside with their machetes. They had tied them up—the women, Gandhi, and his assistant—and had issued their demands to the general neighbourhood from the rooftop. Then they had started to explore the camp while they waited for their demands to be met. Thankfully, Raphael, Levalier, and the police had been able to intercept them before anyone was badly hurt.

This would never have happened if I still had the amulet, Raphael told himself. *I know that the amulet would have kept the camp and the staff safe. I suppose I should count myself blessed that things didn't turn out worse, under the circumstances.*

As soon as Raphael was sure that the staff were all right, he sent for Nadine. From the comfort of his friend's home in town, Nadine had stopped being frightened and was now quite thrilled at the thought of the raid and how Raphael and Levalier had daringly overcome the captors alongside the police. She had taken the opportunity to shower, to put in a comfortable cotton trouser suit, and to freshen her make-up. As always, she looked absolutely stunning.

Nadine walked into the camp as though she were the queen of all she surveyed. With an imperial expression on her face, she looked around and pronounced herself pleased with what she saw.

"It's all just lovely, Raphael," she said. "Even better than it was before. I think I will be very happy here."

Raphael retreated, saying that he would give Nadine a little time to settle in. He went back over everything in the compound and gave a pep talk to the staff, thanking them for being brave and promising that he would give them the time they needed to recover from their ordeal. He spoke with some severity to Sum Sum and Rajibu, reminding them that things could have ended up much worse if he had not returned when he did and that they had been negligent in their duty. They were paid to guard the compound, and instead they had wandered off and chatted to the neighbours.

"You let yourselves get lulled into a false sense of security," he said, "because nothing bad had ever happened around here. You forgot that the reason why nothing bad has happened is the fact that there was *always* someone on guard. With all the crocodile skins and money we've got lying around the place, it's important to remember that we are always vulnerable here. Now, I could fire you both right now, and nobody would blame me, because I have every right to, but I am not going to do that. I am going to give you both a second chance, because everybody deserves a second chance. I am sure that you have learned your lesson and will not let me down again."

"No sir, thank you sir," both men said with great humility. "We will never disappoint you again."

When Raphael returned to his room later that afternoon, he found a most delightful surprise. Nadine had drawn the mosquito net over his big bed and lain down for a rest. Removing his clothing, Raphael slipped in beside her.

After that first glorious night, Raphael and Nadine fell into a routine. He rose early in the morning and attended to his work, sometimes with Nadine by his side. At lunch, they ate together, along with the staff. Nadine had started to teach Gandhi some more sophisticated French cooking techniques, and despite the fact that he was still restricted to working on an open fire, his culinary repertoire was growing quickly. As Raphael had predicted, he proved to be a quick and able student. Often, walking by the kitchen, Raphael overheard Nadine and Gandhi discussing the latest recipe, sometimes among gales of laughter.

After lunch, in the full heat of the day, everybody had a siesta. For Raphael and Nadine, this was a time for fun. Raphael greatly preferred to make love during daylight. For one thing, there were far fewer mosquitos than at night, and for another, it was easier for him to see Nadine's beautiful body.

When they had finished lovemaking, Nadine demanded to know everything that Raphael had done, felt, and thought in the course of the day so far—and his reassurance that she was his number one. As Raphael felt powerless to resist her, he invariably complied, leaving Nadine satisfied in the knowledge that she knew things about him that everybody else did not.

After a long, love-filled siesta, it was time for Raphael to return to work. Levalier and the rest of the male staff must have known how Raphael filled his afternoons, but they never passed any remark or gave any indication of jealousy at all. Levalier had his own romances with attractive girls from the African part of town—Raphael had no objection to him entertaining them in the guest house—and the love lives of Sum Sum and Rajibu were none of Raphael's business, as his was none of theirs.

Raphael had everything a young man dreamed of: his own business, plenty of money, and all the sex he wanted with a beautiful woman, as intelligent as she was gorgeous, with the knowledge that he could also have any one of the other women who attracted him. When Raphael was at work, Nadine took the car, drove to the local high street, and explored the shops, which stocked everything from basic food supplies to guns and ammunition. She enjoyed pottering through the goods on offer and often came home with a new lipstick or perfume to try out. Nadine taught Ghandi how to inspect the foods on offer and choose the best ingredients to make the French food that Raphael enjoyed most of all. With Nadine's participation, Raphael was now hosting dinner parties every Friday night. In theory, he had everything a man would want for happiness, but he still could not shake off a lingering sense of anxiety.

"There's one thing I have been wondering," Nadine said one day. "I mean, I know that one day you will go back to your people and get married. I understand that this means that our love story will come to an end at some point and I accept it now, though thinking about it does make me feel sad sometimes. I won't get upset and cry the way I did before. But how do you think it will make me feel?"

"You'll always be fine, Nadine," Raphael said. "You've got a ruthless streak. You're pragmatic, and you know how to take care of yourself."

"You say 'ruthless' like it's a good thing!"

"It is, isn't it?"

2017

"Oh my *God*," said Rebecca. "Seriously, I don't know how I am going to look at Grandad the next time I see him! I can't believe all this! And what age was he at the time? Twenty-two? It's so funny – I always thought of him as quite strait-laced, and now you are telling me all this!"

"I know," said Richard with a naughty smile. "It's hard to think of people we've only known in their later years as being so young and so naughty, but that's just the way he was at the time. They say that the 1950s was a time of sexual repression, but all I can say is, not for Grandad, and certainly not for Nadine!"

"Not to mention the air hostess you told us about earlier!"

"Yes, indeed!"

"This Nadine was quite a character," said Rebecca. "I suppose she was taking a big risk, in a way, leaving her business and going to Africa on short notice like that."

"Well," said Richard, suddenly quite serious, "there was more to Nadine than meets the eye. I think that she was a beautiful woman on the outside but possibly not quite so beautiful on the inside. That's another story I have to share, but I'll get to it in good time. Nadine was absolutely obsessed with the idea that she had to know literally everything about Grandad, and when they weren't making love, she was asking him questions about his childhood and his past in Egypt. There were things he had not told anyone that he shared with her, including information that would have made him very vulnerable if anyone in authority had found out about it. For some reason, he just couldn't stop himself from telling her everything."

CHAPTER 17

RETURN TO EGYPT AND A FINAL GOODBYE

2017

"When Grandad left Egypt for Sudan, he assumed that he would never go back there again—or at least not for a very long time," said Richard. "But actually just seven years had passed when he made the first of several return journeys."

"Wasn't he scared?" asked David. "Couldn't the police have picked him up and thrown him in jail? I don't think they were any happier about the Israeli state than they had been a few years earlier!"

"I suppose they could have," said Richard, "but the fact is that he had been offered the chance to participate in an extraordinary business opportunity and—knowing him as we do—that would have made him comfortable with the risk."

1956

Over the past few months, Raphael had had a visitor who just happened to be a cousin of a senior politician in Egypt. This man, Aziz, was in frequent contact with his relative and knew what was going on at the top levels of government and business.

"Look," Aziz said one day, "I found out about something that I think you'll find very interesting. My cousin told me that the government wants someone to do some exploratory work to see if there's oil in a particular spot. He needs to find someone who can handle the job as well as provide some cash upfront to pay off a bunch of people. You know Egypt and how things work there. Would you be interested?"

Raphael's mind raced. Business had been going very well lately, and he had a huge amount of money in the bank—the equivalent of several million Egyptian pounds. It was true that he had left Egypt a few years before because the alternative had been being slammed up in jail. On the other hand, business was business, and this sounded like an opportunity to make a really big profit—and if he was there as the contact of a senior politician, surely that would protect him against getting in trouble with the police.

"You know what?" he said impulsively. "I'm in. The business sounds really interesting, and I'd like to see Egypt again. It's been too long. I'll bring Nadine, too. She's always pestering me to tell her details about my childhood, and this way I can show her where I used to live."

Over the course of the next few days, Raphael arranged for his business in Nigeria to keep ticking over while he was away. He decided to make the long journey by car. That way, he could bring a convoy. Much of the route would be the same as the one he had taken from Sudan a number of years ago. Then, it had been a voyage into the unknown, and he had been preoccupied with thoughts of what was going to come next. Now that he was an established businessman, he would be able to relax more and enjoy the beautiful African landscapes they passed through.

Of course, he was still searching for his amulet and hoping against hope that it would turn up. That meant that he could not count on its protection on the trip ... but something told him that, as long as he brought Nadine with him, he would be all right. Besides, he had the impression that Graham had not been working alone. He wanted the amulet for himself, for sure, but perhaps he also thought that he could share it with others. Perhaps the trail would lead him all the way to Egypt; who knew? At the very least, it was worth looking into.

"So what do you think?" Raphael asked Nadine after explaining the plan to her.

"I think it's *wonderful*," she enthused. "I've been longing to see Egypt and where you were a kid, and now at last I will. I'm so excited, you have no idea!"

It took a week to get the trip organised, and then Raphael, Nadine, and Levalier set off in an old army jeep with tyres thick enough to move across the sand dunes that they would certainly encounter. Behind them drove an open-backed truck capable of carrying five tonnes, onto which Sum Sum had laden provisions, spare parts, extra tyres, and everything they would need for the journey. Behind that again was another vehicle carrying two mechanics and a driver.

The trip started with the relatively short drive to Fort Lamy, where Raphael purchased canned French food so that they would be able to eat well on their journey and consulted his friends about the route ahead. It was important to know if there were bandits or marauders in the area, as in that case he would have to take due caution. Then, they took off.

The further they got from the European settlements, the wilder the landscape became. There were little villages dotted along the roads, and they stopped to explore each one. The group's mood was buoyant. Nadine was excited about going to Egypt, Raphael was filled with emotion at the thought of seeing Cairo again and perhaps some of his old friends, and Levalier, although his usual taciturn self, seemed to be feeling positive about the journey. He was always interested in travelling, having caught the bug in his days in the French Foreign Legion.

While Raphael was happy to be on the trip, he was also tired and anxious, as though someone was chasing him, and he had to take care to always remain a few steps ahead. He was finding it difficult to sleep and was experiencing nightmares. It had been well over a year since he had lost his precious amulet, and although he had tried to get over it, he couldn't help suspecting different people of having stolen it. For a while, he had suspected Levalier, but then he had started to wonder if it could really have been one of the Africans working for him. On the other hand, Nadine had been there when they found Graham's body, so perhaps it had been her. But no, he couldn't believe it ... she would never betray him in such a way. She was always telling him that she loved him, and people do not steal things from those they love.

He also had doubts about the wisdom of visiting Egypt just a few years after he had been compelled to leave. As he was listed in the police records as a Zionist, would they chase him down and throw him in jail as soon as he crossed the border? Or would they accuse him of coming back to Egypt to steal archaeological artefacts to sell to foreigners, as so many people had done before? If that happened, too, he'd be lucky to get away with ten years behind bars.

Then again, he didn't want to let anyone, not even the Egyptian state, stand between him and a promising business deal. And he was excited at the prospect of seeing familiar faces and showing Nadine around the dusty streets where he had grown up. He knew that some things would be very different. The Jewish Quarter had been completely destroyed and replaced with housing for Muslim citizens. All that was left of the Jewish infrastructure was the synagogue of Rambam and a couple of other synagogues, which the authorities maintained in good condition in the hope that foreign tourists would pay to come and see them—and to show (despite the abundant evidence to the contrary) that Egypt was very hospitable to its Jewish minority, or at least the few Jews who remained after years of violence.

The landscape grew progressively sandier as they approached the Sahara. As the dunes closed in around them, Nadine hopped up in her seat to have a better look.

"It's so beautiful!" she said. "I didn't know it would be beautiful. I always thought that there wasn't really anything in the desert, but now I can see that that's not true."

"You might find it less beautiful when we've been driving through it for several days," Raphael teased. "The sand gets everywhere ... and I mean *everywhere*."

It was hard work driving through the desert. The wind picked up the sand and blew it everywhere, and it was often quite difficult to figure out where the road was. There were times when sandstorms blew up, and the convoy had to stop and wait for up to two hours for them to pass before it was safe to travel again.

Although the desert seemed barren, it was home to nomadic peoples who were known in the region as the People of the Veil, because they covered their faces to keep the sand away. These people lived by herding goats, sheep, and camels, and they made their home in the oases that could be found here and there in the desert. Levalier had travelled this region extensively, and he knew where all the oases were. Most of them were exceedingly humble settlements, with a number of tents around a well that was both the water source and the focal point of any given village. The people wore simple white clothing and had few possessions, because of their need to be able to pack up their belongings and leave at short notice. They had a simple lifestyle that had remained fundamentally unchanged for thousands of years.

Their cuisine was simple too: milk from the sheep and goats, sweet dates from the palm trees, and occasional meat when a cherished camel died young or the male sheep and goats were slaughtered. They were resourceful with the few ingredients they had. They prepared dates in a range of ways, and with the milk, they made cheese and creams, which were often paired with their Arabic coffee, heavily laced with goat milk and sugar—salt and sugar were the only foodstuffs the desert people had to buy from outside.

They were also hospitable to strangers. On their third day in the Sahara, Raphael's convoy was passing through a village close to night, so they decided to stop and stay there. The locals provided them with tents to sleep in—one for Raphael and Nadine, one for Levalier, and one for Sum Sum (Raphael had left the camp in the care of some other local men whom he trusted). With gestures to indicate their gratitude, they took their places for the night.

Raphael woke early in the morning. Eager to get on the road again as soon as possible, he made his way to Sum Sum's tent to wake him and tell him to get things ready. When he pushed the door of the tent open, his heart leapt, because he immediately saw a scorpion perched on Sum Sum's shoulder. Sum Sum was sleeping deeply, utterly oblivious to the danger he was in. Raphael knew that a single prick from the creature could kill Sum Sum immediately and that he would need to act fast. He thought quickly and then pulled his scarf from his neck and used it to drag the insect onto the floor, where he stamped on it and killed it.

Sum Sum woke up and opened a sleepy eye.

"What's going on, boss?" he asked.

"Sum Sum," said Raphael, "I just saved your life." He showed him the squashed scorpion on the ground. "Now, I need you to get the car ready."

"Boss," Sum Sum called out as Raphael turned to go. "My people say that when someone saves your life, you have to do something in return. Seeing what's happened, there's something I need to tell you. I've been thinking about it for a long time. There's a risk you'll be angry with me, but I think you need to know, and I'm prepared to take it."

"What's that?"

"Well, sir, I think you need to watch Miss Nadine carefully. I know that she is your girlfriend, but I think she has been treating you wrong. Forgive me if I am stepping out of line, but I don't think that you should trust her. Don't you think that she might be the one who has your amulet? Hasn't that ever occurred to you? After all, she was the person who found Graham's body that day ..."

"I'm sure she doesn't," Raphael said. "She wouldn't keep something like that from me."

But as he said it, a doubt entered his mind. What if Sum Sum was right? That would explain the strength of his feelings for Nadine, despite the fact that he knew he should not let the relationship go on.

Raphael returned to his tent, determined to ask Nadine if she knew more about the amulet than she was admitting. When he pushed the door open, he saw her inside doing her daily exercises, and his heart melted. How could someone like this, so lovely in many ways and so strong in others, treat him as Sum Sum was suggesting? Was this the reason why, no matter how hard he tried to leave her, he never seemed to be able to? No, it was impossible! She was a good person, he was sure of it. She was so protective of him—she would never do anything to hurt him!

As if to prove that thought, later that day, when they had bid goodbye to their hosts and moved on, the convoy came across a group of small-time bandits who approached them and made threatening gestures, indicating that they wanted to take their money. Of all the people in the convoy, Nadine was the first to reach for her gun and shoot it in the air, scattering them. She was as close to fearless as any woman Raphael had ever met, and he could not stop himself from admiring her.

After travelling for a week, Raphael's convoy crossed the border without mishap and was immediately met by a local official, Shamseddine, who had come from Cairo to talk them through what was needed. Shamseddine led the way to a small village near the border where they were going to stay for the night. Before unpacking any of their things, he directed them to park in a clear space and invited Raphael to talk with him about the project.

"We've had geologists in the area," he explained, "and they've confirmed that there's petrol under the ground." He spread the geologists' plan out on the bonnet of the jeep. "It's right here," he said, indicating the spot. "Loads of it. That's where you come in. If you can supply the capital to get it out, we'll all be in business. There's a lot of money to be made."

"What do you mean, 'we'll all'?" Raphael asked suspiciously. "How many people are involved in this?"

"Not many. Don't worry, you're going to make a lot of money on this deal. There is another man, though. Actually, here he comes now."

A tall, blond man loped around the corner. At first, Raphael could not believe his eyes.

"*Hans*?" he said. "Is that really you? I can't believe it!"

"Raphael!"

The two men embraced.

"What the hell are you doing here?" Raphael asked. "I thought you'd have gone back to Germany years ago."

"I could ask you the same thing," Hans laughed. "I was really surprised when Shamseddine told me that you were coming back after all this time. We lost touch … I left Egypt for a while, and when I came back, I heard you'd gone to Nigeria and hit the jackpot. You know, I wasn't surprised at all to hear how well you're doing. You've always had it in you."

"I don't get it," Raphael said. "If you're already in on the deal, then what do you need me for? You could just do everything on your own."

"When I heard Aziz was staying with you," Hans explained, "I realised that it was a great opportunity to get you involved. He wrote to tell me that he'd got to know you, and I advised him to bring you here straight away. I told him not to tell you about me; I wanted it to be a surprise. Besides, I can't do it without you. We need a big injection of capital to get started, and I just don't have it."

Before long, Hans and Raphael had agreed that Raphael would advance all the money necessary to open the concession. It was a large sum of money that represented most of Raphael's savings, but when Hans told him that he would make it back many times over, Raphael trusted him. Hans had always been a good friend and a great businessman, and Raphael knew that he could not stay in Nigeria forever and would need to diversify if he was going to secure his future.

"Here's how it's going to work," Hans explained. "You'll buy the concession for the oil in your name, and then you'll hire me to organise people for drilling, exploring, and extracting the oil. I've already got a bunch of people lined up, Americans ... I didn't go to them straight away because I knew they'd try to stop me from getting a piece of the pie. I know that I can trust you not to cut me out of the deal."

"How much money do we need for 'accommodations'?" Raphael was pragmatic when it came to business. He knew that nothing would get done without the odd backhander. That was simply how things were done in Egypt.

"A solid 10 per cent. You provide it, and I'll make sure it gets to the right hands without a fuss."

Raphael and Hans shook hands on their agreement, and Hans promised to have the contracts ready the following day. He gave Raphael directions to a good local hotel where he could spend the night.

That evening over dinner, Raphael explained the deal he had made with Hans to Nadine. He expected to make a profit of a few million pounds on top of owning the royalty for the concession for ten years.

"That's great," said Nadine. "Well done. Can I come to your meetings?"

"If you like."

As he said the words, Raphael wondered why he seemed powerless to go against Nadine. Whatever she wanted, she got. There was absolutely no reason for her to go to any meetings with him—in fact, it wasn't really appropriate for him to bring a girlfriend to meetings—and yet, now that she had asked to come, he felt that he had to give her what she wanted and that he needed to have her near him all the time.

What's going on? Raphael wondered to himself. *I'm very fond of her, and she's great in bed, but I don't love her, and I'm not going to marry her. It doesn't make any sense. Why do I just let her do whatever she wants?*

The sensation of being controlled by a woman made Raphael feel uneasy. It made him feel dependent on her, and he had always hated the sensation of being dependent on anyone.

The next day, the convoy headed in the direction of Cairo, where Raphael would be able to access funds and revisit the past while he showed Nadine around. He had booked them into a fine hotel—not Shepheard's, that would have felt too strange—with whitewashed walls and wide arches stretching across an elegant veranda. To celebrate the deal, he had booked a suite with two bedrooms, and because he was feeling anxious for some reason that he could not quite pin down, he had booked a room for Levalier next door and asked him to serve as bodyguard. Shortly afterwards, on reaching the hotel, Raphael checked in, and he and Nadine made their way to his room. He was surprised to find that the room had been set up precisely as he liked it, with a bathrobe laid out on the bed, even though bathrobes were not usually supplied in Egyptian hotels.

"That's odd," he said. "What's a bathrobe doing here? Egyptian hotels never have bathrobes."

"Does it matter?" said Nadine. "You should be pleased. You always like to have a bathrobe."

But something about what ostensibly appeared to be a simple gesture did not sit right with him. It was as if someone at the hotel had been reading his thoughts. He popped out and checked in the room next door, which was unlocked. No bathrobe. Could it be a sign that someone knew that he was coming and was hoping to watch his movements? He couldn't prove anything and knew that he would sound crazy if he went to the concierge with his concerns, so he put these thoughts to the back of his mind for now. Instead, he went to reception and requested another room. The manager looked anxious, and after ostentatiously checking the books, insisted that Raphael and

Nadine had been given the only free room. With no option, he went back upstairs, telling himself that he was imagining things.

Nadine and Raphael refreshed themselves in their room and then, clapping her hands together like a little girl, she demanded that he take her out and show her around Cairo.

"I know that this is your city," she said, "and I think that if I can understand it better, I'll understand you better, too. Let's go! I can't wait to see all the places you knew when you were a child."

They ventured out and he took her to a shopping district so that she could start to get acquainted with Egypt. At one point, Nadine went into a shop to look at some pretty scarves and Levalier, who had been following them at a discreet distance, approached Raphael and asked him if he wanted to meet some working girls and enjoy the company of Egyptian women for a change. Raphael demurred, as he was with Nadine.

"You go if you want," Raphael told Levalier. "Take some time off. I know Cairo so well, I can take care of myself."

Back at the hotel, Raphael tried to convince himself once more that there was nothing to worry about; by dismissing Levalier, he had hoped to show himself that everything was just fine. He and Nadine went to their room and had started preparing themselves for the night when there was a knock on the door, and a man entered with a tray bearing two cups of steaming liquid.

"Your tea, sir," the man said, bending to place the tray on a side table.

"I didn't order any tea," said Raphael sharply. "Did you, Nadine?"

"Not me," she said. "All I want to do is go to bed."

Suddenly the situation took a dramatic turn. Rather than placing the tea down, the man threw the tray, cups and all, at Raphael. Raphael tried to catch him, but before he could, two more men had entered the room. The two new arrivals grappled Raphael to the floor and tied his hands behind his back, while the third restrained Nadine.

"What the hell is going on?" Raphael demanded to know, his face pressed uncomfortably against the floor. A dark thought overtook him. Was all of this Nadine's doing? Sum Sum had communicated the men's concern that she was the one behind the theft of the amulet, and despite his feelings for her, he had begun to wonder if he might be right. Was Levalier next door? If he was, couldn't he hear what was going on? No; Raphael had given him the rest of the day off. He was probably out having fun.

"You'll find out soon enough," one of his assailants answered in Arabic.

"Raphael," Nadine called out. "What's going on?"

But before Raphael could answer, both of them were gagged with lengths of grubby white cotton that smelled as bad as it tasted.

What the hell is this? Raphael thought. *Why would they tie up and gag Nadine if she was behind all this?* He could see her face, and she looked absolutely terrified. Nobody could feign terror so convincingly; not even someone as clever and manipulative as Nadine. Someone else must be behind it. But with Graham dead, who could it be?

The men started to search the room, turning cases and bags upside-down, upending the mattress, and throwing all the sheets and blankets onto the floor.

"Where the hell is it?" one of them said to the other, essentially confirming Raphael's suspicion that they were looking for the amulet. If only he wasn't gagged, he would be able to tell them that it had been stolen months before! Raphael was relieved that the men kept their hands off Nadine. Clearly, they were devout Muslims, and even if that didn't stop them from trying to steal his most precious possession, they intended to respect his woman. At least that was one thing he wouldn't have to worry about. Eventually, muttering curses under their breath, they stopped searching, gave Raphael a half-hearted kick, and left the room.

Raphael worked his hands behind his back. In their haste, the would-be burglars had not tied him very well, and little by little, he was able to release himself and then Nadine.

"Oh my God, Raphael," gasped Nadine. "What the hell is going on here?"

"That's what I am going to find out," he said grimly. "Lock the door behind me, and don't let anyone in."

Raphael went to the room next door to see if Levalier was there. He knocked, but there was no answer. *Damn it,* he thought, *he's probably having himself entertained at a brothel. I did tell him that he could take some time off, because I'd be fine here on familiar ground. Well, I'll just have to handle this situation on my own.*

Raphael took to the streets of Cairo that had once been as familiar to him as the back of his own hand. He made his way quickly on foot to the area where he had lived. To his great relief, Uncle Ali was still there. They embraced, and Raphael asked him for help, briefly explaining the situation.

"Bring the woman here," Uncle Ali said. "We'll keep her safe until you can get to the bottom of this."

Raphael rushed back to the hotel and told Nadine the plan. She looked at him pathetically.

"But I don't want to leave you," she said. "I want to stay with you, wherever you go."

As he experienced a flash of anger, Raphael realised that, if he had ever loved Nadine, his love for her had gone. Something was rotten between them. He was sick and tired of the way she tried to control and manipulate him, and often succeeded. Her manipulative behaviour had escalated recently, too—so much so that his first thought on being knocked to the ground and tied up had been that she could be behind it. Something was clearly not right.

"You're not coming with me," he said coldly. "Either stay with this family I know or you're on your own. You can make your way back to France however you like."

Nadine said nothing as they made their way to Raphael's old neighbourhood. Uncle Ali opened his door and let them into his home, which shared premises with his mechanic's workshop. Off the workshop was a simply furnished room with a bed.

"You can stay here until you're sorted out," he said. "Jasmine will bring you something to eat in the morning, and the bathroom is right down the hall."

Raphael and Nadine were both sweaty and grubby after their ordeal. He showered and dressed in clean clothes first, and then, while she took her time in the bathroom, he inspected her clothes and case, unsure whether he was hoping to find evidence of her involvement in the attack or dreading it. He found nothing.

As soon as she had returned from the bathroom, Raphael turned to Nadine and instructed her to stay put while he went back out to try to track down some old friends who might be able to get to the bottom of the situation.

"Don't do this to me!" Nadine sobbed. "Don't leave me on my own. I can't bear to be without you, and I know that you need me too."

She dropped to her knees and kissed his feet, and then she rose to her feet again. She took his hands in hers and covered them in kisses, her tears falling onto his skin. She raised her face to his and kissed him on the cheeks. He was astonished to find himself utterly unmoved by this display of devotion.

It's strange, he thought. *I've been obsessed with her for years, and yet I feel nothing for her now. But I can't find any evidence that she has been causing me problems or that she has stolen the amulet. Maybe she's perfectly innocent, and I've just fallen out of love.*

"Darling," Nadine said, "you're not looking at me the way that you usually do. Please, let's make love. I am sure that will change everything."

Throwing off her clothes, Nadine pressed her body against his and held him tightly. Although he had not intended to, he began to respond and eventually to return her kisses. The kisses turned into passionate love-making, and the two of them tumbled onto the mattress in the almost bare room, their limbs entangled. Afterwards, as they lay together, he regretted the thoughts he'd had not long before. After all, she was a wonderful woman. Of course, he would never marry her, but they had been through so much together, and she had given him so much of herself.

"I'm sorry about before, sweetheart," he said. "I know that I was tough on you. I think I'm just stressed because of what's going on. I came back to Egypt for a business deal. I didn't think that all of the shit we went through in Nigeria was going to follow us back here. I didn't think I'd need Levalier here, once we'd crossed the desert."

"I don't mind," Nadine said. "You weren't being bad to me. I understand how you are feeling. It's just all a bit much for both of us at the moment. I can't believe it either. After what we've been through before, it's awful that it seems to be happening again, now that we are here."

"Damn right."

"Let's try to get to the bottom of it," she said. "Let's go out and see if we can figure it out."

They got dressed and left the room. Walking the quiet streets of Cairo at night, they came across a Nigerian pilgrim on his way to Mecca, dressed in the pilgrim's characteristic robes. He looked familiar.

"That's strange!" said Raphael. "That's Rashido. He's one of my hunters. What are the odds that we would run into each other like this?"

Raphael ran over to say hello. Expressing great surprise, Rashido shook his hand warmly.

"I was sorry to hear what happened to you and Madam before," said Rashido, referring to their kidnapping in Nigeria. "I heard about it just before I left. By then, I had saved enough money from what I earned from you to start my pilgrimage, but I've run out now, and I'm trying to make some money in Cairo so that I can complete the journey and get back home to my wife and children."

"Make sure you don't stay away too long," Raphael advised him. "Religion is important, but family is more so."

"By the way, sir," said Rashido, "where is your amulet? Is it true that someone took it?"

This is all very strange, thought Raphael. *Is it really possible that it's just a coincidence, us meeting like this? What are the chances that I would just happen upon someone from my own area of Nigeria just a few hundred metres from my childhood home in Cairo? And now he wants to know about the amulet? Something very fishy is going on here!*

"Why do you ask?" Raphael said.

"No reason, no reason … I just remember that you used to wear it around your neck, and now I see that you don't have it at all."

Raphael pushed Rashido against the wall and held his arm tightly against his neck, making him gasp for air. Rashido was strong and wiry, but he was not a big man, and it was easy to restrain him.

"Listen," Raphael said, "I'm not buying this. You're not just here by coincidence. Now, tell me what's going on or I'll kill you. Don't think that I won't do it. It's the middle of the night, there's nobody around, and nobody's going to give a shit if the body of some pilgrim from

Nigeria is found on the street in the morning. You'll just get thrown out with the trash."

"I can't tell you."

"What's your problem?" Raphael punched him in the face, drawing blood from his lips.

"OK, fine. Look: there's a Saudi prince who has heard about you and your amulet, and he wants to have it for himself because he knows how much luck it brought you. He already knew Graham from before and had offered him a lot of money if he got it from you. He told me and someone in Egypt that he knew you were coming and that he's prepared to pay lots of money for the amulet. I thought that I might just be able to get it off your neck … I never planned on hurting you, boss. I know that you're a good man, and I'm no murderer."

"Show me who these people are," Raphael insisted. "Take me to their place."

"I can't! I don't know where they live or work. They've just come to me, not the other way around."

Raphael didn't know what to do. He was, frankly, terrified by what Rashido was telling him. He had known that Graham would stop at nothing to get the amulet but had not imagined that the conspiracy could be so far-reaching. He couldn't spend the rest of his life staying in a different place every night because someone was following him. Somehow, he had to put an end to all this. He released Rashido with a growl.

"If you know what's good for you," he said, "you'll stay well away from me and my affairs. You can forget about ever hunting for me again, and you can tell whoever hired you that he's wasting his time, because I don't have the amulet, and I haven't had it for a long time."

Rubbing his sore neck, Rashido backed off, mumbling thanks to Raphael for having been so merciful to him and looking quite abashed about having been caught out in such an underhanded business.

Over the next few days, Raphael tried to behave as if everything was normal, taking Nadine around Cairo, showing her the sights, and experiencing some nostalgia for his boyhood. However, he couldn't shake the feeling that someone was watching him at all times and that they weren't safe. Three days after the unsettling encounter with Rashido, he and Nadine were sitting on the terrace of Café Groppi, a café owned by a local Greek entrepreneur that was very popular with expatriates in Egypt, who crowded up to the glass-fronted counter to choose from one of the many fancy French-style pastries on offer or from a selection of ice creams, meringues, and other dainties. The sweets were served by pretty Egyptian girls wearing colourful aprons and headdresses. He looked at Nadine, who was tucking with relish into an ice cream in a tall glass. The traumatic events of a few days ago didn't seem to be troubling her at all anymore. Her ability to recover from even a very stressful experience was impressive.

He smiled at her when he caught her eye, but he did not share her sense of ease. He couldn't stop thinking about the amulet. When he had failed to retrieve it on that dreadful day when Graham was killed, and he came so close, he had assumed that he would never see it again and that, somehow, he would have to get used to living without it. But now people were following him all over Cairo trying to get their hands on it, even though he did not have it anymore. None of it made sense. What was going on?

Suddenly, Raphael felt a strong tug at his chair and turned to see two large men who had approached them at the corner of the terrace where they sat. One of them made a threatening gesture to him. Raphael could see that he was holding a knife and that his companion, who had now reached Nadine, was holding a gun against her ribs. With a sideways flick of his head, the one holding Nadine indicated that they should leave the terrace by the back steps, which led into a small alley behind the café. Slowly, for fear of angering their captors, they did as they were told. Once the men were sure that they could not be seen by anyone in the café, they bundled Raphael and Nadine into the back of a waiting truck, tied them up, and drove off.

"I can't believe this is happening again!" Nadine moaned. "What's going on, Raphael?"

"I have no idea," Raphael said grimly. "We both know that someone is chasing after me because he wants my amulet, but I haven't seen it for months. It could be anywhere by now. Even if I was prepared to give it to someone, I don't have it to give."

Nadine looked at the floor, chewing her lip.

They travelled for about an hour and then they could feel the truck slow, turn, and back carefully through what was presumably a gate. The back door of the truck was opened, and a man's voice barked at them to get out.

Awkwardly, because their hands were tied behind their backs, Nadine and Raphael got down from the truck. Nadine had started to cry, and her mascara was running down her face.

"What the hell is going on here?" Raphael blustered. "I don't have anything that you want."

"*We'll* be the judge of that," one of the men sneered. "And you'd better do what you're told if you know what's good for you!" He prodded them with his gun in the direction of a door, and the two of them stumbled towards and then into a small, dark room.

"Help! Help!" Nadine shouted. "I have it, I have it!"

She was panicking now, breathing quickly, struggling against the ropes that held her wrists painfully together, and looking around wildly in the hope of finding an escape route.

"What are you talking about, Nadine?" Raphael asked. "What do you have?"

"The amulet!" she sobbed. "I have it. I've had it all this time. I'm so sorry."

"Where is it?"

"I put it in my suitcase, and I left it behind in Nigeria."

"What?"

"Yes. You wanted me to go away, so I took it when I saw it in Graham's hand, and I kept it. I put it in my suitcase, and you stopped telling me you wanted me to leave. So long as I had it, I knew that I could keep you. I wasn't expecting any of *this* to happen. I'm so sorry."

Raphael's mind raced. What was he supposed to do now? They had been kidnapped again, presumably on behalf of the Saudi prince who had been having him chased, and neither he nor Nadine had the amulet in their possession. Would its absence persuade the prince that the chase was pointless and that he should let them go, or would he simply become enraged and kill them both? With the limited information at his disposal, it was impossible to tell.

"But why did you take it in the first place? Did you really think that it would change my mind and that I would marry you? I've always been perfectly honest with you about my intentions."

"It worked, didn't it?" said Nadine sulkily. "I'm still here. If it hadn't been for the amulet, I'd have been sent back to Paris long ago."

"You say you love me, but taking the amulet is not a loving act. You knew very well how much it matters to me. My mother got it for me before I was even born, and I have been upset every day since I lost it. How could you treat me this way?"

"I'm so sorry. I know it was wrong, but I only did it because I love you, honestly. Please forgive me. I beg you. If we get out of this alive, I'll do whatever it takes to make it up to you."

Nadine knelt down and held Raphael around the legs.

"Truly, I'll let you do anything to show you that I really mean it," she said. "You can kill me or whatever you want. All I have ever wanted is for you to love me."

"Stop being stupid. I don't want to kill you. I just want to get us out of this bloody mess, and then I want you to give me what you have stolen. After that, I want to send you home to France so that I don't have to deal with you and your nonsense anymore."

Raphael thought quickly. If he told his captors that neither of them had the amulet, surely, they would kill him. Then again, how could he give it to them when it was far away in Nigeria?

After an uncomfortable night, the men opened the room in which Raphael and Nadine had been confined. The room stank. They had both been forced to relieve themselves in a bucket in the corner of the room, and there was no way to wash their bodies, which smelled of fear and sweat.

"Get out," said one of the men, apparently the leader.

Raphael walked out, trying to look as calm as possible.

"Look," he said, "you're an Egyptian and so am I. Despite the circumstances in which we are meeting, I am sure that you are an honourable man, and I trust you. Please, let us go. We are exhausted, and you can't keep us in this situation for long. Do you want to have to deal with two dead bodies? We don't have what you are looking for. You can see that for yourselves. It was stolen from me a long time ago, and by this stage, it could be literally anywhere."

The man shrugged, looking slightly embarrassed.

"We had to take you in," he said. "Our Saudi customer already paid for us to have you brought here so that we could see if you had the amulet and check through your luggage. We haven't found anything, but we've taken pictures of you tied up in the room that at least show that we did what we were paid for and tried to find it. I'm going to let you go. No hard feelings?"

A car pulled up to the house, and Raphael and Nadine were parcelled into it and told that they could ask it to take them anywhere. They returned to Uncle Ali's house, collected their belongings, and checked into a hotel, where they both enjoyed long hot showers and put on clean clothes after throwing out their old ones. Raphael sent a telegram to Levalier at the old hotel, instructing him to stay put until he was ready to make the return journey to Nigeria.

When they were both clean and freshly dressed, Raphael asked Nadine to sit down.

"We have to talk," he said.

"I know," she said. "This is all my fault. I understand that, and I am just really sorry that I got messed up in it. I just want you to know that whatever I did, it was from a place of love. I know that you are promised to marry someone else, but I thought that maybe if I had the amulet, at least for a while, you might realise that *I* am the one you really love and marry me instead."

"That was never going to happen, amulet or no amulet. We have had a beautiful love affair, but by stealing my possession, you've sullied what could have been a wonderful memory for us both. I will never trust you again, and to be honest, I don't know if I can ever trust any woman again. I can see now that I have been quite naïve."

Raphael had thought long and hard about his relationship with women. His first sustained sexual relationship had been with Maddy, and although she had been a professional and he had paid her, he had grown to love and trust her, almost as much as he loved and trusted his mother. Sex and trust had become intertwined in his head, and he had found it impossible to think of any women he slept with in a disrespectful or suspicious manner. Now he realised that all of this was going to have to change. He would never again allow himself the luxury of trusting a woman—not until he was married with a wife of his own.

"So what's going to happen now?"

"It's time for you to go."

Nadine sat in silence, a tear trickling slowly down her cheek.

"I understand," she said. "And I'm so sorry for what I did. I'm sorrier than you can ever imagine."

Nadine packed her bags to return to France, and Raphael sent a telegram to Nigeria instructing that the rest of her belongings should be carefully packed and shipped to Paris. She had explained precisely where the amulet was, and he arranged for it to be removed from her case and placed in his safe. He swore never again to be in a situation in which it might be taken from him.

With the knowledge that Nadine was going to leave, Raphael felt as though an enormous weight had been lifted from his shoulders. The relationship had gone on for far too long, and it had been suffocating him. He knew that, back in Sudan, Angel was growing up and that she would soon be old enough to get married. He needed to start getting himself ready for family life. At the same time, he still harboured considerable tenderness for Nadine and knew that, although she had done something dreadful, she had done it out of love. He wanted to do something that would change her life for the better and that would make it easier for her to move on. He decided that they would end their relationship on a high note and arranged to take her all over Cairo, showing her why—despite everything—he still loved this wonderful, frustrating city.

Over the next few days, Raphael showed Nadine where he had lived as a boy; Café Palmyra, where he had attended the secret meetings under the leadership of Marcella; and where all the young people had trained in the suburbs of Cairo prior to their defence of the Jewish Quarter and their exodus to Israel. They did the tourist sights, too, visiting the pyramids and the archaeological museum. Raphael enjoyed explaining how the pyramids had been built, all those years ago, evoking images of the workers of the ancient Pharaohs somehow managing to transport the great cut blocks of stone all the way from Luxor, in the south of the country, just to make the pyramids, in which the earthly remains of those pharaohs were to be placed for all eternity. Perhaps the Pharaohs' arrogance was misplaced, because all great cultures one day crumble—but at least the pyramids were still standing and testifying to their achievements. Many of the men who had carried out the back-breaking work involved in their construction had been from among the Jewish people, actual and spiritual ancestors of Raphael and his family and of the huge diaspora of Jews all over the world.

He related to Nadine the story of how the Jews had suffered under the Pharaoh until Moses led them to the Promised Land with the thrilling words, "Let my people go." It was a narrative that every Jew knew well, from prayers and from reading the Torah. This story reminded him of the annual Passover celebration, when Jews dined on unleavened bread in memory of their ancestors who brought such bread with them on their journey all those years ago—and of the much later exodus, Operation Passover, still underway, of Jews from Egypt and all over the world to Israel.

Nadine was familiar with the old Bible stories, but nonetheless she enjoyed hearing Raphael relate the account of how the Red Sea parted to let the Jews flee from Pharaoh's army, only to swallow the chariots that pursued them. For the Jewish people, this story showed how God loved them, even though he had allowed them to suffer under the Pharaohs in Egypt for generations. Those early Jews had lived a nomadic existence in the desert for forty years, led by their prophet, Moses, who received the ten commandments by which all Jews everywhere are urged to live their lives. Religious Jews, who were waiting for the arrival of their Messiah in Israel, still believed that the torment their remote ancestors suffered, followed by their deliverance across the Red Sea to the Promised Land, had been part of God's design to teach them collectively how to endure the many hardships they would face in the world, how to strive for the advancement of knowledge and science, and how to know that there is only one God and that He alone is deserving of their worship and praise.

While Raphael was not himself religious, his background had given him some insight into how devout Jews think, and he tried to explain to Nadine how their faith influenced all their views of the world and how each major world event was interpreted in the light of their belief in God and understanding of the Torah. For as long as the Jews had existed as a distinct people, everything they did, said, and thought occurred against the backdrop of their long and troubled past. Would the new state of Israel last and join the other nations of the world, or would it be wiped out like every previous attempt at establishing a Jewish state? Only time would tell.

"I'm glad you've told me these stories," Nadine said. "Although it's going to be very hard to say goodbye, I think that I am starting to understand why you feel so strongly about marrying one of your own people."

Leaving the pyramids, the pair visited Old Cairo, on a hill above the modern city, where an ancient synagogue and Christian church had been built side by side with an interconnecting door, symbolising the fact that both faiths recognised their common origins despite the many differences between them. Raphael and Nadine looked also at the huge esplanades of the mosques in the area, which were very characteristic of the architecture of Cairo. Going back down the hill, past Nasser's barracks, they visited the Egyptian museum with its ancient artefacts and mummies, and they looked at shops all over the city, including the site of the leather workshop that he had run as a teenager and of the various department stores that Jewish families had run in Cairo until just a few years earlier—and that in some cases they still held.

Nadine was surprised by the number of donkey-drawn carts she saw in the city, carrying goods of all kinds. There were carts laden high with furniture, with fruits and vegetables, and really with everything one could imagine needing or wanting. Some of the carts were used for passengers, and especially for washerwomen, who travelled around the city doing laundry for the households that could afford to pay for home help. They were sturdy women, with muscles that bulged from the hard work of handling vast pans of hot water and heavy, dripping clothes, and rubbing them on their washboards to get the dirt out. Other vehicles were pulled by horses—particularly glazed, gilded hearses pulled by six or eight horses to carry the dead from home to their final resting place in the cemetery. They passed by a reception room holding a traditional Egyptian wedding, with the bride and groom mounted on a podium while the guests brought them gifts and danced in celebration. Belly dancers and singers had been hired to entertain the crowd, with the singer creating a customised song featuring the names of the bride and groom.

In the evening, Nadine and Raphael had a traditional Egyptian meal of foul (made of fava beans, tahine, and olive oil), freshly baked bread, fava bean falafel, and rice and molokhia leaves cooked with lamb stock—all dishes that Raphael had enjoyed as a child, served now by a woman wearing the traditional beaded headdress that the women of Cairo, of all ethnic backgrounds, wore when they were cooking and going about their daily activities to keep their hair out of the way and prevent it from smelling of fried food.

When the meal was over, and it was time to leave, the smiling woman wished them, "Goodbye, with God's will," the traditional Egyptian words of farewell.

"I wish I'd brought my camera," said Nadine. "I'd love to have taken photographs of everything I've seen. I'll just have to imprint it all on my memory. I know I'll never forget these days with you. I feel like I understand you better than I ever did before. I never really understood until now why being Jewish was so important to you, as you're not religious, or why you love Egypt as you do, considering how the Egyptian government treated your people. Now I think I'm beginning to see why you are as you are."

It had been a wonderful few days that reminded him of their time together in Paris, but with a poignancy lent by the fact that soon their relationship would end and they would never see one another again. Raphael was no longer angry with Nadine for her theft of the amulet, not even a little bit. In fact, he was thankful to her not only for the many wonderful days and nights they had spent together but also for her strength in enduring and surviving the various traumatic experiences they had experienced.

Their holiday in Egypt over and their brief kidnapping increasingly no more than a fading memory, it was time for the love affair to end. When Nadine arrived in Paris, she discovered that Raphael had purchased her partner's share in her salon and registered the business in her name. They never saw one another again.

Before leaving Egypt, Raphael and Hans consolidated their business arrangement. The oil project wasn't going anywhere for now, but Egypt needed to import a wide range of goods and produce of all types, and there was huge money to be made. With Raphael's investment of capital, the two men set up an import/export business that would reap huge dividends over the coming years and make Raphael a very rich man indeed. Knowing that he had done a great deal to secure his financial future, Raphael realised that he finally felt read to start planning for family life.

2017

"Just to remind you," said Richard, "Grandad was still only 24 or thereabouts at this stage. Nowadays, a young man of that age would be seen as barely more than an adolescent—but he had already become a millionaire several times over."

"I know," said David. "It's really very impressive. And I know that all of our lives have been made easier by the legacy he established for the family. I think it's important to remember that."

"Don't forget about Granny," Rebecca reminded them. "I know women didn't usually have flashy careers back then, but she's been just as much an influence in our lives as he has."

"Well, I'll tell you one thing," said Richard. "Grandad has never underestimated her. He wouldn't dare."

EPILOGUE

LOVE, MARRIAGE, AND HAPPY EVER AFTER

2017

"I suppose you're finally going to tell us about Granny and Grandad's wedding, right?" Rebecca asked impatiently. "I know I've heard this story before, but I never get tired of it. It's so romantic."

"Right," added David. "So what happened next?"

"Hold your horses," said Richard, refilling everyone's glasses. "And I'll tell you everything."

1957

Despite his financial and social success, Raphael was increasingly frustrated with life in Nigeria. He had always known that he wouldn't stay forever, but it was ever more obvious that it was time for him to move on. For one thing, he would never be fully accepted into the European set; the British, in particular, would never accept a Jew as their social equal, any more than they did the Africans. It didn't matter how much money he made. They'd be happy to take his taxes and even to do business with him if there was something in it for them, but they'd never let him be a member of their social club—not that he wanted to be.

For another, it was perfectly obvious that Nigeria was heading for independence, and nobody could tell how things would work out at first. The Nigerians weren't used to running a modern country on their own, and it seemed likely that there would be chaos for a few years while they figured it out. It was easier just to go. He decided to start wrapping things up and preparing for departure.

At 25, Raphael was also of a good age to get married. He wrote initially to his parents and his brother Leon to ask them to make a formal request of Angel's hand in marriage. Of course, it had been arranged since he was 10 and she was just a tiny baby, but it was still important to observe the niceties. Leon and Lola were on very friendly terms, and it was easy for him to tactfully inquire as to whether the marriage was still in the cards. When the response was positive, Raphael wondered if it would be possible for him to visit his intended and get to know her a little. He wrote to Abraham to see if this was possible.

Angel still had to finish a year of school in England, but Raphael was allowed to visit her during the school holidays and timed a trip to Sudan to coincide with them. Angel was delightful: sweet, clever, and just as pretty as her mother had been at the same age. Of course, a meeting in private was not appropriate, but he was allowed to take her out to the local hotel, the Grand Hotel, for a lemonade so that they could talk to and get to know one another, and to one of the few local restaurants for a meal. Angel was charming but shy, only looking at him directly when she thought he was looking away. He told her about some of his adventures in Nigeria, and she listened with interest.

"Someday we'll get to travel the world together," Raphael said. "And I'll be able to show you all sorts of wonderful things."

"I'd love that," she said. "I've only ever been where Mum and Dad let me go. Even in England, we're mostly just at the school, and I haven't really seen that much. I can't wait to have the opportunity to travel."

Raphael was delighted when Abraham pulled him aside to confirm that Angel herself was happy to proceed with the marriage, and that she already loved Raphael very much. Although the marriage had been arranged, he would never have gone through with it if she had not been perfectly happy about it. Abraham said that Angel was ready to get married any time and asked Raphael if he had a particular date in mind.

Raphael thought about it. He didn't feel quite ready to get married yet. To tell the truth, he felt dirty and sullied. He'd had so many affairs and one-night stands with so many women. How could he take himself to his marriage bed like this? He decided to go through a period of a year when he would have no sex at all—and try not to even think about it—so that he could approach his bride as a new man. He knew that Angel was young, fresh, and pure, and he did not want to contaminate that purity in any way. Somehow, he felt that the amulet made it easier for him to endure what would be a very different way of life.

Flora was positively delighted that, at last, her Raphael was getting ready to marry his promised one and settle down. She had always hoped for all her children that they would marry young to someone from within the Jewish community. But she had some advice for her youngest boy, which she put to paper.

"Darling," Flora wrote, "don't get offended with me, but you need to know that you can be a bit of a flirt, especially with your eyes. You can make women and girls think that you mean something that you really don't, just by playing with your eyes. It's not fair when you do that, so be careful. Keep your gaze just for your beloved, and you will have a much happier marriage than those silly men who let their glances go astray!"

The formal engagement was made in September 1958 via a series of letters between Raphael and Abraham, and then Raphael was able to start writing to Angel. He poured his heart and soul into those letters, promising her that he would love her, cherish her, and be faithful to her all the days of their shared life. Gradually, through their letters, they got to know one another better.

Finally, the wedding day came. Raphael had bought himself a handsome suit, and Angel's mother had helped her to choose a pretty dress. In her white gown, with a sheer veil over her face, she was like a luscious rose. The entire community, clad in their best clothes, packed into the synagogue to see them get married and celebrate with them.

Raphael was very aware that his lovely new bride was much younger than him. She was wise and mature for her years, but she was still in her teens. It was up to him to provide her, and the children they would have, with a comfortable and stable home. He decided that they would move to Geneva, Switzerland. They both spoke French, and he was confident that he would be able to grow his business there. There were fewer and fewer Jews left in Sudan all the time. Soon, they would all be gone.

Of course, he considered moving to Israel, where he had many friends. However, at that time, Israel was not the place to be for a man of considerable financial ambitions. It was still being run along socialist, almost communist, lines. Flora and Joseph had tried to settle there when they joined the Jewish exodus from Sudan, but they soon ran into problems. At that time, the easiest way to transfer wealth was to convert it to gold and bring it in as bullion. Joseph liquidised all the capital he could and brought it to Israel as gold, hoping to use it to set himself and Flora up in their new home. When he declared it to the customs authorities, they confiscated it and assured him that he would be paid market value for it. Six months later, no money had arrived, and even when they contacted the Prime Minister, Ben Gurion, they received no help—they were told that as Israel needed all the money it could get, they would have to wait for two years before they receive their recompense.

With nothing to live on, they had no choice but to leave again. They returned in frustration, and the whole family agreed that they would continue to support Israel from outside but that it was not yet time to move there. Many Jews made the same choice, and as history unfolded, their support would be influential in building Israel into the country it is today.

At just 25, Raphael knew that he and his Angel had many years together ahead of them. His main task now was to make her as happy as he could—and it seemed that that meant making a home for her outside Israel, where he could feel confident that the wealth and comforts he accrued would be available to her and to their children. He was determined to do whatever it took to make her content.

"And they *have* been happy, haven't they?" said Rebecca with a smile. "I think we'd all be lucky to have a marriage like theirs."

"They certainly have," said Richard. "Not many people nowadays settle down as young as they did, but there's a lot to be said for it. They had a similar background and similar values. It was very important to them both that their kids be raised as members of the Jewish community and know about their roots and heritage. It's a legacy that's been passed on to us all."

"Well, and it's something that I would want to pass on to my kids too," said David. "Sure, I'm not really religious ... but there's something deeply special about having a connection to the past like that."

"I'll drink to that!"

And, as the evening drew to a close, the three siblings raised their glasses in a toast to their grandad, his Angel, and the heritage that they had treasured and passed on to their family.

*   *   *

Egypt lost wars against Israel in 1948, 1956, and 1967. This made the government lose face and put Israel in an even more precarious situation. Surrounded by states that didn't want it to exist, Israel had to fight hard so as not to lose anything. The Arab League met, and all the Arab nations agreed not to recognise Israel in any way.

Largely because of the position taken by the Arab League, it was getting steadily more difficult for all the Jews in the Middle East, and one by one, those who remained left—either for Israel or for somewhere else. By this point, many of the Sudanese Jews wanted to leave, but because they were a financial asset, the government made it very difficult for them to get the papers they needed. Often, they had to resort to leaving under false pretences.

In 1968, a prisoner exchange programme saw Jewish activists released to Israel while their Arab counterparts were returned to Egypt and other countries in the region. In 1973, the United States got involved in the Middle East, and the British and French withdrew in the face of American pressure to leave them there to get on with it. American Secretary of State Henry Kissinger arranged for Egypt to take part of Sinai, giving the country back a sense of honour and making the situation between Israel and Egypt somewhat easier, to the extent that Israel and Egypt agreed to peace terms. In fact, even when relations were at their worst, Egypt never sank to the levels of extreme violence and hatred that would be seen elsewhere in the Middle East.

Meanwhile, Israel was growing in confidence as a state, and at the same time becoming an even more complex society than it already was. In theory, the Jewish citizens were bound together by their common religion. Up to a point, that was true, but some of the arrivals from Eastern Europe had a very different, and much stricter, interpretation of Judaism than the one that Raphael had grown up with. They didn't mix with the others, married only within their group, and had very restricted ideas on the role of women in society. It was often quite difficult for them to get along with the Jews who had grown up in the Middle East, who had not experienced the trauma of the Holocaust, and who often had a much more emancipated worldview.

In fact, the most devoted and disciplined of the Middle Eastern activists involved in the foundation of Israel were often not religious at all. For them, their Judaism was largely a matter of cultural identity. They wanted a safe home for all Jews but did not believe that their mission had anything to do with God. There was an immediate clash of interests with the much more fundamentalist Jews, who were almost exclusively European. The wealthiest and most influential people in Israel were mostly Europeans. Many of them looked down on their Middle Eastern counterparts and gave recruits from the Middle Eastern areas poor accommodation, limited access to anything but the most basic foods, and limited work opportunities.

Throughout these years, Raphael, now living in Geneva, kept up his connection with Israel and continued to serve her needs in his own way. He knew that Israel wasn't perfect, but he also knew that for a lot of Jews, especially those with scarce resources, it was the best opportunity they had to live in peace. As a well-to-do Swiss businessman, he was in a position to arrange for local hotels to be wiretapped when members of the Arab League were in town. This provided Israel with vital intelligence that helped it to protect its borders and keep its people safe. Raphael received his instructions from time to time from junior Israeli intelligence officers who came to visit him in Switzerland to tell him what they needed him to do.

He continued to serve the Israeli state throughout his working life and, when he could, to invest in property and development in the young country. As such, he built close relationships with politicians and decision-makers at every level of the Israeli government and business world. He was also in a position to provide intelligence from the many countries in which he worked, including west Africa, where he maintained both a professional and a personal interest. Angel knew about and supported his activities in this area, but they both agreed to protect their children—they had three sons—from this information, feeling that the boys needed the opportunity to grow up as happy and carefree as possible.

In 1988, the General Assembly of the United Nations held a special session in Geneva to accommodate Yasir Arafat, who was then forbidden from entering the United States. While Arafat had been an enemy of Israel for many years, he did have admirable leadership qualities. Ultimately, these led to an improved situation in Israel.

Raphael maintained a close interest in west Africa throughout these years, too. For some, the transition to independence in the former European colonies was easier than others. Many emerging African nations struggled in the early years with violence and civil unrest. However, because of the many contacts he had made in the area and his knowledge of African languages and culture, Raphael was able to continue working in the region and to enjoy friendships and business relationships with Africans.

Raphael's personal fortune grew, and he developed a large company with many employees—one that he firmly intended to pass on to his children and grandchildren when the time came. He also felt strongly that he should share his good fortune and used his funds to support a clinic for heart disease in Israel, treating Israelis of all ethnic and religious backgrounds, as well as providing some funding for Israel agents who worked hard to track down people who had targeted and killed Jews, both before and after the foundation of the State.

Over the years, Israeli state policy changed. It abandoned its communist ideals and became a thriving modern state and a leader in the area of technology. Many years after his initial involvement in the settling of the country, Raphael purchased a home in the bustling city of Tel Aviv.

One day, Raphael and Angel were in a small diner in a market in Tel Aviv. He enjoyed the hustle and bustle of the crowd, and they both needed a drink and a snack. The diner was a simple one, but the pastries on offer looked inviting. A number of old photos were pinned to the wall, and Raphael looked them over as he waited for his order. Suddenly, a face in one of the old black and white photographs stood out: it was the face of a middle-aged man from the old Jewish Quarter in Cairo.

For a moment, Raphael wracked his brains to remember the man's name. Then it came to him.

"That's Ozone," he said, pointing at the picture. "I remember him."

"That's right," the lady working in the diner said as she approached with coffee and pastries. "But how do you know Ozone?"

"I was the one who got him out of Cairo and into Israel," said Raphael. "Along with a lot of others. I remember him because he was already middle-aged when most of the recruits were young and because he was travelling with his family."

The woman rushed out from behind the counter, swinging her tea towel at Raphael. She swatted him with it.

"That's for bringing me to Israel," she said. "If it wasn't for you, I wouldn't have ended up in this lousy diner!"

Then she opened her arms for a hug.

"You helped to save my life," she said. "I'm one of Ozone's children, and I travelled with him that day. I was a little girl of just 9 at the time, and I have been here ever since."

2017

"Wow," said David. "That's all pretty amazing, really. I knew he was fond of Israel, but I'd never heard any of the details why, and I didn't know that he'd been working for the state later on, either."

"You must remember him talking about his trip to the Museum of the Palmach," said Rebecca, "when for the first time he met the man who had received the recruits on the other side of the Suez Canal?

Although they were quite elderly men by the time they met, they both broke down and cried. I think the way he tells that says a lot about his motivation and the love of Israel that he's been carrying with him all these years."

"Sure I do," said David. "But you know how it is; unless you know the whole story, it's hard to really understand."

"Well," said Richard, nodding towards the window. "Do you realise that we have been talking all night? Look; you can see the sunrise."

Rebecca and David turned towards the window. Richard was right. The sun was beginning to rise over the cityscape of London. They had been so engrossed in hearing their grandfather's stories, they had not been aware of the hours passing.

"I think we understand him a little better now," said Rebecca. "And while there's still time, we need to get together for the best family holiday ever, with Granny and Grandad—and his amulet—in Israel. Perhaps then we can hear some more stories, straight from the source!"

11986372R00222

Printed in Great Britain
by Amazon